MARCH INTO THE ENDLESS MOUNTAINS

The Beginnings of War on the Western
Frontier of America

The Preface Year 1778 - 79

*Have a good read as through
this portal you enter
the past*

*Ray Ward
Aug 24, 2010*

By

Colonel Ray Ward

By the Seneca named Ha-gah-heh
He-who-shows-the-Way
(The Path Finder)

Weldon Publications, Inc.

Published by

Weldon Publications
432 Pennsylvania Avenue
Waverly, New York 14892
Phone 607-565-2477

ISBN 978-0-9724175-1-8

First Edition

Cataloging-in-publication data is available from the Library of Congress. All rights reserved.

Printed in the United States of America.

Acknowledgments

I wish to acknowledge my debt and declare my gratitude to Dan Levin, fellow author and Journalism Professor. Without his sustaining confidence this work might not have been completed.

Would that I could turn the clock back, my late wife and constant helper Beatrice also to share the satisfaction of giving to posterity this book long in preparation. It is my belief she knows.

Too, I would be remiss were I not to express my appreciation to Virginia Ward my constant companion in this endeavor. I am indebted to several very special persons, one who is of my war-time generation, fellow publisher Frank Resseguie whose expertise always has been as a parachute at times most needed. Too, always at call, Ted Savas has proven himself to be a great counselor in publication preparation and a proven friend. Lastly noted is the invaluable assistance of David Acorn who at times had to surmount pain, yet constantly was helpful in this long and taxing process. Others in the team have satisfaction their efforts have contributed to the advancement of this work.

This book serves as a memorial to Seneca Chief Everett Parker, my always friend 'Two Arrows', who bound me to him by adoption in ceremonies on the banks of the Susquehanna in Pennsylvania. He gave me a new name and more, gave of his wisdom.

'Ha-gah-heh'

He-who-shows-the-way

Commentary

When the tomahawk was first upraised in the Spring of 1778 on the Western Frontier of Pennsylvania this story begins ... but first we must visit ahead to the winter of 1778 - 79 when a British warship by longboat brought a passenger ashore in New York Harbor, a double spy, a man who had served General Sir William Howe more faithfully than his other master General George Washington. Well known and respected in Philadelphia, his name was Samuel Wallis.

Ray Ward

Table of Contents

March into the Endless Mountains

APPENDIX

PREFACE

From the decay of Potter's Field, today disguised as a pleasant park in central Philadelphia, rises the image of Samuel Wallis once a man of substance in that City. A double spy during the American Revolution, he almost changed the course of history.

In the words of Thucydides, regarded as the greatest historian of antiquity, who lived some 400 years before Christ, to whom I refer my reader, "I shall be content if (there are) those (to) pronounce my history useful who desire a view of events as they did really happen, and as they are likely to occur in accordance with human nature, (thus) to repeat themselves - if not exactly the same, yet very similar."

A contemporary of Samuel Wallis, the respected English historical writer James Burgh in his *Political Disquisitions,* published in 1774, this date coinciding with the convening of the First Continental Congress, wrote about the problems attending the reign of King George III and the coming storm. He stated, "History is an inexhaustible mine out of which political knowledge is to be brought up." Burgh was referring to the guidance of the past in evaluating the present thirst for liberty and the strictures of an authoritarian government. His was a Whig's philosophy. Samuel Wallis, by the push of events was inclined toward being a Tory. Wallis would hide his evolving role as a spy, carrying his secret to his grave until trunk loads of documents came to light in the century just completed. These partially cast light on this influential and most secretive man. In my choosing to write a reconstructed history I am able to achieve continuity where gaps exist in textual knowledge, and to recreate logical thoughts and conversations pertinent to advancing the sweeping plot, itself historically correct. In small measure this book seeks to revive interest in our Revolutionary War period better to chart our future, and also to entertain the casual reader by breathing life into the several characters. By so doing one gives today's viewer a relationship to that distant generation. This is the age of electronic entertainment and truncated examination of knowledge, with much of value, inclusive of sensitivity as felt by the various participants, lost in the process. At once this author also seeks to satisfy the student historian by imprinting within these pages certain events both known and little known, if at all, about the warfare that split Americans and the Indians into divided factions within their own cultures. It is for the reader to align himself, if he can, with Wallis or with the young militia Lieutenant Leviticus Brady, a passionate patriot. The story of Samuel Wallis, told in a palatable manner, awaits the turn of this page. One must remember, Virginia's far borders embraced Kentucky, while New York's and Pennsylvania's only reached the Susquehanna River, this river to become the bloody frontier during the last part of the 18th Century.

R.W.

AMERICAN FORCES

Colonel Samuel Hunter - Commander, Fort Augusta

Colonel Zebulon Butler - Commander, Forts Wilkes-Barre and Forty Fort, formerly commanded 2nd Connecticut Regiment with the Continental Army

Lt. Colonel Nat Dennison - Commander 24th Connecticut Militia

Captain John Franklin - Company Commander, 7th Connecticut Militia

Captain Simon Spalding - Independent Company of Volunteers (Free Company) 7th Connecticut Militia

Captain Thomas Boyd - Company commander, Morgan's Rifles

Lieutenant Levi Brady - Free Company, 7th Connecticut Militia, formerly Morgan's Rifles

Sergeant Tim Murphy - Famed sharpshooter, formerly with Morgan's Rifles

Corporal Samuel French - Man without a past

Free Company volunteers - Sergeant Thomas Baldwin, Peter Pence, John Scudder, Bradford Hotchkiss, Isaac Shaffer, The Wandells, Peter Grove, Hugh Swords

Sergeant Major Asa Greenacre - Forty Fort Garrison

Rachael Greenacre (wife)

Dr. Ebenezer Menema - Surgeon

Abby Menema (daughter)

Reverand Samuel Kirkland - Army Chaplain

Robert Menniger - Overseer, Wallis's properties, and Militia Captain, Fort Muncy

Captain Andrew Walker - Military Engineer

Lieutenant William King - Officer at Fort Muncy

Captain Hawkins Boone - Militia Fort Commander

Dan Lebo - Indian fighter, influential citizen

Richard Covenhoven – Courier

Colonel Charles Armand - Commander Armand's Cavalry Legion

Mr. Africa - Black attendant, Wallis mansion, Philadelphia

Captain Lighthorse Carberry - Formerly First City Troop Philadelphia

Colonel Thomas Hartley - Commander 1778 raid into Seneca territory

Hartley Expedition Officers - Captains Stoddard, Foster, Murrow,
    Lieutenant Sweeney

Colonel William Butler - Commander 4th Pennsylvania Line. Led
    1778 sally destroying Tory and Indian rallying places on the
    upper Susquehanna River

Colonel John Gibson - Virginia 13th Regiment Commander at Fort
    Laurens toward the Ohio

Western Delaware Leaders - Sachem White Eyes (colonel), War
    Chief Killbuck, and Chief Warrior Captain Pipe

Hanyerry - Oneida Indian guide

Luke Harbinson - Captive of/ trusted by Seneca

Colonel Goose Van Schaick - Commander First New York Regiment
    and 1779 attack on Onondaga Nation

Lieutenant Frederick Wormwood - Courier, Northern Department

General Lachlan McIntosh - Commander Fort Pitt

Aides to General George Washington - General Edward Hand,
    Captain Alexander Hamilton

British - Tory - Indian Forces

FORT NIAGARA

Colonel Marion Bolton - Commanding-Officer

Colonel Daniel Claus - Superintendent, Indian Affairs

Captain Ian McDonald - In charge advance scouting party

Major John Butler - Commander, Butler's Rangers

Lieutenant Barent Frey - Butler's-Rangers

Captain Simon Girty - Renegade American deserter known as
'Butcher' Girty

Sergeant Pointdexter - Senior enlisted man, Fort Niagara

Corporal Webber - Ordinance supervisor

INDIAN FORCES

Joseph Brant - Mohawk Chief and-Supreme Leader of the
Confederacy

Hiakatoo - War Chief of the Seneca

Little Beard - Second War Chief

Cornplanter - Prominent Seneca Chief

Blacksnake - Seneca War Party Leader

Bald Eagle - Delaware Chief of the Minsi Tribe

Hopkins - Sheshequin Chief

Captain Sunfish - Escaped black slave, commissioned and serving as
a British spy

Tisot - Former Seneca leader during the 1763 uprising organized by
Chief Pontiac of the Ottawa

Handsome Lake - Future Seneca statesman

Seneca Braves - Little Bones, Dry Elk, Wamp, Panther, Greatshot, Large Talker, Naked Bear, Pudding Dry, Cut Nose Johnson

WOMAN OF NOTE

Esther Montour - French-Indian Queen of the Seneca

THE TORIES

Samuel Wallis - Affluent Philadelphia merchant

Joseph Stansbury - Shop owner, Philadelphia

'Death's Head' Cundiff - Former slave auctioneer

Thomas Stevens - Former New Jersey tax collector

Lt. Colonel Robert Hooper - Quartermaster, Continental Army

Roxbury - Ne'er-do-well

Dr. Reverend John O'Dell - Courier

Samuel Burling - New York banker

'Margy' - Mysterious stranger

THE SIX NATIONS OF THE CONFEDERACY

By the French known as the Iroquois

THE OLDER BROTHERS

Mohawk

Eastern Door Keepers

Seneca

Western Door Keepers

Onondaga

Council Fire Keepers

THE YOUNGER BROTHERS

Oneida

Cayuga

Tuscarora

During the American Revolution the Oneida participated on the side of the Americans while the Mohawk and Seneca gave their loyalty to the King. Supposedly neutral were the Onondaga and Cayuga, but suspect of joining war parties against the Americans. To a lesser degree this may have been true of the Tuscarora, without vote in the League.

In the Forest of the Seneca

The fleeting deer from wood is gone,

The hunter, with his bow string drawn,

Alike has vanished in the shade.

And yet I wonder, has he made

Some timeless journey to stand now

Within the wood 'neath pine tree bough,

Unseen by me as he takes aim

To bring to earth the startled game.

Or is it I, in shadows come

Unto the world where he is from?

~RW~

Chapter I

THE WINTER OF 1778-79

The glimmer of canvas on the horizon grew into a three-masted frigate spouting waves off its bow. It hove to, in a swirl of foam, shielding a longboat, which scudded away from its side.

The wind was in the northwest, and the wind and waves all but swamped the longboat carrying Samuel Wallis ashore. Gazing uncomfortably back at the British ship-o'-war which had dropped him at the mouth of Hell Gate, he wished damnation upon its captain. If the channel was dangerous, with shortened sail and with easing of sheets, the sixty-gun frigate could have slowly beat into the harbor instead of standing and lowering a longboat for his passage. Gray skies, quickening waves, and the suggestion of snow in the darkening sky made it a rough haul toward shore. It was a poor goodbye, thought Wallis, as the naval company bent over their oars and pulled for the water of the harbor. Once by the Head of Hell Gate, they came down the roadstead. British transports of the line, swinging at anchor in the frosty sea, their masts like a forest of trees, lay at port and starboard. "An insult!" exclaimed Wallis to himself, deprived of pompous arrival. With a king's document, so to speak, in his pocket, and the winning of the war dependent upon this paper, here he was coming ashore, half-drowned, denied the respect and safety of a dry landing. He sputtered as a wave nearly took him from his seat. An inch of water in his boots, drenched, he shook his fist at the far-off frigate. He had traveled a distance, at peril of life and reputation, to deliver this paper, and much thanks for it from that Whig of a captain there on the deck, no doubt enjoying his discomforts through a spyglass. Bobbing toward shore, Wallis calculated his voyage had been - from point of departure Philadelphia to point of disembarkation New York - some 170 miles by water, or one good day's sail and one poor day's sail, by reckoning of time.

As the light waned and the snow began in earnest he gained the wharf, not unhappy to leave the somewhat worried crew who were to find their own way back across the waters. He stood a moment, uncertain in his direction, then resolutely wended through the maze of goods and war-like supplies piled on the docks. Face buried in his coat against the snow, he passed the British occupied barracks on Dock Street near Coventies Market, these early in the war used by the Continentals under Major General Richard Lee in his attempt to defend the City. Too, after Washington's retreat from Long Island, American prisoners of war from the failed Quebec assault, Morgan's Riflemen among them, were brought here in British bottoms, to be paroled. The lights of the barracks behind him, he groped along the pitch-dark street wishing he had a lantern. One person in the City of New York he must find, Burling, the banker. By chance coming upon a public house, confused and weary from the cold, he hesitated. Here was warmth. In the bitter wind the sign suspended over the entrance creaked on its icy chains. The sound decided him. He pushed on the door and almost tumbled down a short stairway.

Inside he drew off his greatcoat and toasted his hands at a merry fire. There was scarcely anybody in the place. "Rum!" he said to the stocking-capped proprietor, a man with a hook for an arm. He knew, by the mould on the mug and the dust on the table, he was not in the best of quarters. One look at the mug and he called for an unopened bottle. The man with the hook watched him drink to the bottom. Well, anyplace to warm one's bones. It was bad rum. Thereafter he emptied his boots of sea water and laid his stockings before the fire to dry. Barefoot, Wallis struck a light to his seegar, and puffed in silence. Then, as he put on his stockings, he met the gaze of the man. Wallis dug into his pocket and drew forth a coin. He dropped it on the table. "You," he said. The man inclined his head. "I am stranger to the road," exclaimed Wallis, "and I have lost my way. Direct me to the Royal Exchange. I am seeking a Mr. Samuel Burling and am told he is there."

"The Royal Exchange? 'T is closed at this hour. But I can show you where Mr. Burling lives; 't is a mansion, sir."

"I will be obliged to you for directions."

"'T is a cold night to miss the turns of the road, your honor. A man of quality you seek, and such you must be. I'll send a lad with you. Boy! Quick with your bones. This gentleman wants Mr. Burling's - the big house close by the Exchange. Mind, light his feet with a lantern."

The one-armed man gave Wallis a crooked smile. "And, sir, if you be thinking kindly ...." Wallis fished forth a second coin. "You are a goodly soul, sir. Strike me, but I've a fondness for you, and will offer you my friendly advice. When you go from here, walk briskly, your pistol handy. There's more'n one man in the East River tonight with head bashed in, pockets emptied for price of a drink." As Wallis opened the door to go, he remembered the warning. Two sailors who were embraced in each other's arms as if they were lovers, with rum-veiled eyes leered at him. They followed a few steps until Wallis, fetching about, flashed the lantern, disclosing the pistol in his hand.

After considerable walking, with often twists of the road, Wallis ultimately found himself in a genteel neighborhood. Large Dutch-like houses loomed at elbows. The urchin pointed at the silhouette of a very fine structure. Wallis flipped a coin, and the lad took to heels. Alone, he walked to the door and politely rapped. He rapped again. "The Devil to hear!" Wallis cried, at no answer. He banged with both fists and bawled, "Wake the dead!" A servant opened. "Where have you been?" asked Wallis, in evil humor. "Mr. Burling, is he at home? I have business with him."

"If 't is business, sir," said the fellow, equally out of temper, "go to his office tomorrow. He keeps hours." The servant was about to slam the door.

With a sweep of his arm Wallis pushed him aside and stepped forward. In the warm room, Wallis glowered at the surprised servant who, with wits recovered, had seized an iron weight from the desk, a formidable object. "Tell Mr. Burling," calmly said Wallis, brushing snow from his garments," that Mr. Samuel Wallis of Philadelphia is here. He will know the name."

"Indeed," said a voice from above.

Wallis glanced up.

"So you are Samuel Wallis!" A large florid-face man was descending the stairs. "The very famous Samuel Wallis."

"You flatter me. Yes,'t is I, and the worse for wear."

"I did not expect you up from Philadelphia."

3

"The journey just happened - you might say 'accidentally.'" Wallis looked toward the servant who, lifting up Wallis's wet greatcoat, prudently retreated, closing the double doors.

"What brings you?" Burling seemed worried.

Wallis produced a map from his pocket. "This." The document, encased in a wooden, sealed tube, crackled as it was unfolded. At a glance Burling perceived it related to the wilds of the Indian Country, the uncivilized lands west of New York and north and west of Pennsylvania. "This is for the eyes of Governor General Frederick Haldimand at Quebec. I had to bring it myself. Cundiff, poor fellow, my usual courier, is dead; and my second man, Stevens, who next I depend upon, was to have taken this off my hands at Cantwell's Bridge, but he failed in his rendezvous. Knowing its importance, I took the prearranged passage and came all the way. Guard this well. Others have had their blood spilled because of this cursed map. I know not what courtesy of fate has befallen the tardy Stevens, but I suppose he, too, now has a cold bed and solid pillow. Leastways the map is safe in English hands, yours."

"Why mine?" asked Burling, annoyed at the responsibility and queasy about the dire mishaps befallen those in its connection.

"Why you?" phrased Wallis, with lifted eyebrow. "You, because you be as deep in His Majesty's business as I."

Burling, the banker, looked uncomfortably at the map. He had the distinct impression Wallis wanted money. This seemingly was confirmed by Wallis's next remark.

"It was worth my life to be caught with this paper."

Burling gingerly touched it. "Because I have sent sums by Dr. O'Dell to you in Philadelphia to finance your spy ring does not imply I am to 'evaluate' this document for its worth. It will go up to Haldimand, who may judge it. By next pouch, by my personal rider." To Burling's surprise this satisfied Wallis who he had misread. He should have known Wallis, a wealthy man, had larger purposes to be served than a payment. "Enlighten me," said Burling, "what is so confoundedly important about this map?"

Wallis, amazed at Burling's naiveté, mastered a tart tongue, then spoke with affected civility. "Washington's plan is to send an army through the uncharted Indian woods to attack the British lake forts of Niagara and Detroit next summer. It foretells the army's proposed route. Applied properly, from this knowledge we could prepare an ambush and destroy them in the manner Braddock's men were defeated nearly a quarter century ago by the French. Such success could end the rebellion in the colonies! That's what it means. The fate of the war, or in least the outcome of next summer's campaign suspends in our response."

In anticlimax Wallis sneezed. Burling rang for drinks. Sipping from his goblet, Wallis continued, "In times past when as yet I was an indifferent spectator to the movement of the armies, when this expedition to the frontier was first discussed --"

Chapter II

THE SUMMER OF 1778

(In Retrospect)

The two riders paused on the wooded hillside as a shift in the wind brought them the disturbing smell of smoke. Silently they inched forward to a gap in the undergrowth. It was plain as the scowl on the lieutenant's face that he was looking at a scene of death in the clearing below. From his vantage point high on the hill, this impressively built, recently furloughed Continental Army officer, with a sweep of his eye had the details. "Damn!" he said in a deep low voice, his sunburned hands gripping the reins. "The bastards!"

A hundred yards below, in the clearing at the foot of the hill stood a farmhouse. A low tree-covered ridge bordered the field. Clouds of smoke rolled from the dwelling's open windows and doorway as the fire began to catch. The lieutenant scanned the nearby woods for signs of Seneca or Delaware warriors. Then he made up his mind, seeing the two corpses and a hawk circling above. Whoever had been there had gone. The deerskin clad lieutenant turned to his companion, a wiry, angular face man with complexion darkened by the sun. "Tim, let's go down."

Sergeant Tim Murphy also had been studying the woods and the sounds of the birds. All seemed normal. He, too, concluded the wilderness was wholly theirs. He nodded.

They worked down the ridge, rifles at ready. Strewn about were articles of clothing. The war party had been helping themselves to whatever they fancied. The two corpses were those of the butchered settler and his wife. Drawn by the tacky blood of the dead, large black flies had settled in the open mouth of the man and onto the remaining hair of the woman, her head stripped of its scalp. The nearest body was that of the farmer whose eyes stared vacantly at the sky. It produced in the Lieutenant a start. Levi Brady recognized an acquaintance of the past. For men who had marched with the Revolution, who had fought at Saratoga and participated in every battle and skirmish since '75, it might be thought they would be inured to the calamities of war. Murphy, swearing, commenced digging a pit with a pickax, the same with which the settler had defended his life.

By their behavior and dress the pair were not to be mistaken for 60-day militiamen; nor by their rifles did they resemble musket-carrying Continental Line soldiers. These were riflemen, sharpshooters who recently had served under Colonel Dan Morgan in his Rifle Corps. By every measure they were seasoned veterans. Lieutenant Levi Brady and Sergeant Tim Murphy were but a week gone from the Valley Forge encampment, detached for new duty at Forty Fort northerly up the Susquehanna. At headquarters Moore's Hall, they saluted General Washington, and were given orders to assist a Captain Simon Spalding in raising an 'aggressive' militia company in defense of the northernmost river settlements. These far flung communities were plagued by increasing Indian violence. Leaving the stone house they departed camp on May 21st, the day following the action at Barren Hill. The Hill was located between the Camp and Philadelphia, a place where the Lieutenant and Sergeant, serving with Colonel Morgan's Rifles, had been in a swirling encounter critical to the survival of the Continentals advancing toward Philadelphia. They were almost bagged by the British. Pausing in deepening the hole, wiping the sweat from his face, Murphy grumbled, "Spell me. Grave digging's not my best talent."

The Lieutenant replied, "Murph, be glad your alive. Think, we could have been put under at Barren Hill." Brady, handed the pickax, took a swing, his thoughts on their narrow escape. "What with three British Generals about to surround us, and they nearly did, I'm not complaining." He began to dig furiously.

Washington had sent twelve hundred troops and a battery of five cannon under leadership of twenty one year old Major General Marie Jean Paul Roch Yves Gilbert Motier, the Marquis de Lafayette, to reconnoiter the British withdrawal from Philadelphia. The Marquis had proceeded to a point half way toward the City. This place, appropriately called Barren Hill, actually was skirted about by woods and boasted a church and a few dwellings. Commanding British General Henry

Clinton, advised by a spy of the American movement, likewise marched toward Barren Hill, deploying to encircle the Americans. Here Lafayette's command found itself about to be boxed in by three converging British divisions. Adding to their confusion a body of British Dragoons in their red coats were mistaken for an expected Pennsylvania cavalry troop wearing scarlet uniforms. Brady, dispatched toward the approaching horsemen, post haste galloped back shouting "British Light Cavalry!" Immediately Lafayette ordered small parties of riflemen to scatter along the fringe of woods with instruction to show their presence to the British infantry as if the American Army itself was concealed within the timber and about to attack. Two of the British columns halted, forming up to resist the mythical attack. It gave Lafayette precious minutes to escape. As the Americans retired there was a brief intermingling of sides where Brady and Murphy were, with the much advanced British Dragoons quickly to retreat, but not before the rear guard of Oneida Indians had become involved, giving the Continental Army time to reach Matson's Ford and recross the river, the Indians the last to get over. But all this was of the past.

As the two frontiersmen continued in their task of burial, Murphy, before throwing the first scoop of dirt onto the settlers, draped a cloth over their staring eyes and bloody heads. An hour later, taut lip, the two riflemen rode into Muncy, furthermost community on the Susquehanna, tethering their horses in front of Baldwin's Tavern. It was a hot day, a day to drink one's self into imbecility. Honed lean by constant military service, in tattered garments they scarcely resembled the two young men gone from this valley three long war years ago. In a dark corner, seated over their drinks, they went almost unnoticed; and for good reason; a more spectacular event was occurring.

The road into Muncy from the south was dusty. At the hilltop the carriage halted, poised for its descent into the settlement. The diagonal rays of the afternoon sun kindled the hollow, with one beam twinkling like a jeweled lance upon the distant town bell. The only movement in the valley, engulfed in summer's heat, was of the comings and goings to and from Baldwin's Tavern. With clatters and creaks the carriage sped into the settlement, its wheels striking and slowing to the tune of the flying shale. Atop the coach a hard-muscled, blue-shirted driver, about thirty five years of age, urged the horses forward with a long, flicking whip and cursed while he wiped his temples with a quarter-rolled sleeve. "Beasts of slothfulness, misbegotten copulation!" he shouted in English flavored with French accent. His language was as profuse as his perspiration until, remembering his manners, the driver lowered his voice at the settlement. Abreast of the village meeting place, as was the courtesy of the day he flung a packet of eastern newspapers onto the ground. A gentleman in a broad hat retrieved them and waved affably, then headed for the tavern.

Watching the carriage were the gamblers and drinkers who issued from the interior of Thomas Baldwin's. They gazed with envy and respect at the wealthy Wallis as he passed. Only Levi Brady and Tim Murphy remained indoors, in the shadows, each in his own thoughts. Disregarding the novelty, the two continued to drink from their glasses. As the carriage made its noisy progress into the town, Tim Murphy, deferential to none, particularly not to Samuel Wallis, lifted his goblet and, to the thunder of the wheels, smashed it against the wall. For as much or little reason, likewise did Levi.

The carriage rolled onward. The row of houses dwindled into scattered homesteads. Outlying the town, in the shade of an apple grove stood a neat stone house. From a window facing the road, Robert Menniger - man of excellent parlors and chambers - saw the carriage rumbling northward. He followed the carriage with his eye until the woods enveloped it. "Great Jehovah or the Devil, he has come!" The thin, tall man grimaced, then stooped to open an ancient floor safe from which he extracted a thick day book generously entitled 'Properties and Holdings of Samuel Wallis.'

As the town disappeared, Wallis, reclining on flowered silk, sniffed a scented linen. His impeccable dress and his demeanor was that of a person of importance, of authority, eliciting respect. Yet, he could be amiable, down to earth toward those of lesser station. At this precise moment he was savoring his return to Muncy. He shifted his weight for the pleasure of sighting the spur in the forest which would mark the end of his journey. The carriage bounced at the forks. Ahead, on a half-hill half-knoll, by the West Branch of the Susquehanna, close to a large island in the center of that tributary, lay the manorial citadel he had built in the wilderness. Had times been normal he would have disposed of his business to enjoy in retirement the beautiful summers on the frontier. Alas, two of the greatest idiots God put on earth, a Sam Adams and a Tom Paine, had primed the muskets of the minutemen. War had come to the United Colonies and had spread to the Indians, dormant since the French and Indian War. In the woods one is either friend or foe when met. Retirement would have to wait. You can't sell a coastwise shipping business, give it away when British ships plug the harbors, and your own vessels have been requisitioned as privateers by Philadelphia's Committee on Safety. His land jobbing business, too, was at standstill, with no buyers for property with a fine crop of Indians.

Wallis leaned forward to catch the first view of the limestone front of his house standing within a circle of pines and magnificent elms; swatches of sunlight and shadow dappled the lawn and building. Through the trees be glimpsed this thick-walled, secluded dwelling that commanded the knoll. Moated at the rear by the West Branch, it bore the aspect of a feudal stronghold. With the shutters closed the residence displayed its unmistakable vacancy. Its lawn smacked of neglect, dead grass and the last fall of leaves carpeting the space within the circular drive. As though acknowledging the owner's arrival a huff of wind sprang up, bowing the pine and elm branches and swaying the leaves in a dry, skeletal rattle. Elsewhere in the tree-tops, a skinny woodpecker rasped furiously. His tiny eminence contested the domain. Samuel Wallis, Quaker after a fashion, merchant, and God to some, alighted from his carriage.

Sam Wallis by complexion was neither light nor dark; physically he was neither lean nor fat. He was average in height. Not a remarkable man, if he had any distinctive feature it was his propensity toward baldness. With the exception of one large cluster of dark curls, the forward zone was naked. In some respects his physical mediocrity marked him apart. The regularity of his face, being coupled with an impenetrable disposition, suggested massive depths beyond most men. This reserve was often mistaken for haughtiness and had influenced his manner in that very way, although to know him was to uncover a genial soul. He wore his wealth as a shield, affecting finest quality ruffles, shiny knee breeches, and red garters, apparel scorned by true Quakers. An ignorant observer easily could hate Samuel Wallis.

Slowly he descended from the vehicle to the ground. It may have been the solitude, or the release from the journey's fatigue, or the beauty of the place itself, or the pine cones crunching under foot, or the silly antics of the woodpecker, or conjunction of all, that accounted for his affectionate clap of his retainer's shoulder. "First, Mr. French, we had both piss. Then you had best be off to Thomas Baldwin's for supplies, if we sup tonight."

"Oui."

"And fetch a bag of my salt."

"As you direct, Monsieur. With accelerity!" He paused, "Or is it with alacrity?" This brought a momentary smile to Wallis's face.

"First, a hand in the house." Wallis approached the door, twisted the long brass key in the lock, and stepped over the marble threshold. Inside was dampness and chill. A vault-like odor smote his nostrils. The twilight, dust, and spiders were too much. He sneezed. "Mr. French! The windows. Let's have the day!" The Frenchman, answering to a name obviously fabricated, parted the velvet window drapes, coughing as he did so, and threw the catch on the shutters. A breeze swept through the casement and the sudden light revealed choicest furniture.

Samuel Wallis had transported Philadelphia's luxury to the Frontier. In this extraordinary house were gilt ornamented mirrors, cabriolets, black walnut tables, appletree bookcases set with glass doors, bluebottom Ramshead chairs, and a Web and Trotter masterpiece of a desk. The abundance of the furniture, to say nothing of the craftsmanship, was amazing. A grandfather clock, near the spiraled stairs leading to the low ceiling bed chamber, and a map diagramming Pennsylvania and Connecticut claims where they overlapped along the Susquehanna, finished off a room designed for no less than a prince of land jobbers. Everything was for his utility, or for his instruction. A wooden hand, which held a book, surmounted the stairway's newel post. This may have represented the hand of Providence clasping the book of Augury.

With recourse to an English pocket piece, Wallis wound and set the clock. Twice the clock's cumbersome mechanism struck its vibrant bell, to which the smaller key wound personal time piece tinkled a response. Opening a cabinet the merchant selected a pipe and tin of tobacco. He tamped the bowl, and eased himself into a chair. Idly he computed the stand of timber on the island. It should be cut for market or at least thinned. Bald Eagle with his English rifle could do a lot of sniping, concealed in that arbor. He almost jumped when his servant banged open another shutter.

With the windows attended, the Frenchman proceeded in the direction of the kitchen where he ripped an almanac from the wall. His expression never changed as he worked. Going outside with an iron bar, he pried the stone lid off the well. This accomplished, he unhitched the horses, saddled one, and started for Baldwin's Tavern and Trading Post - the while Wallis not stirring from his chair. The clock struck the half hour.

Sounds reached into the room as someone approached on horseback. The hoof-beats ceased at the door. There was a rustle of grass, the squeak of a porch board. Wallis relit his pipe, not turning. "Mr. Menniger."

"Sir," said the overseer, "welcome home. How did you escape Philadelphia, with the British cordons blocking all roads?"

"A stout driver can blaspheme any trooper out of his path. I believe my carriage was fancied for Howe's. Or should I say Henry Clinton's, Sir William having sailed for England this fortnight. Leastways my driver and I were bold. They took us to be on high Tory business. In fact, sir, I was accorded a guard of honor and safe conduct through the lines by a much impressed major of artillery."

Menniger chuckled, "Always your way, Mr. Wallis." He brushed his handkerchief over the dusty chair bottom.

"Don't sit yet. In the mahogany case is the Jamaica, and the goblets." Menniger poured, Wallis proposing the toast. "To your services, Mr. Menniger. May the character of your report on the situation at Muncy be as pleasing as is the quality of this rum." Wallis knew full well what would be Menniger's response.

Menniger presented a wry face and regarded his glass as if it contained venom. "The situation at Muncy? You have a wondrous humor. There is no situation. There is chaos."

"So I understand from your letters. I've come on the frontier ahead of time to see for myself. I apologize for not sending notice. But my alarm prompted my quickness."

"I did not exaggerate." Menniger extended his arm, pointing through the window. "In their paint out there," he indicating the darkish woods "are the Seneca. And I will add, so too are Bald Eagle's Delawares. They are not the peaceful people you remember."

"That is a pity, Bald Eagle and his people, as well as the Seneca and Mohawks are caught in a war not their own. And so can be said of ourselves who are dragged into it just as certain as if we were caught in the vortex of a foundering ship. Just think, by change of a single vote Congress could have come to accord with England. One Whig radical caused the defeat of House Speaker Joseph Galloway's proposition which would have brought reasonable men together. All are now bitter enemies. Galloway defined a middle ground, the colonies to regulate their own commerce and Congress to have a veto on harmful Parliamentary bills. Menniger, just one vote has brought ruin, death, suffering upon us. What nonsense, what a tragedy!"

While master and overseer continued their conversation, the Frenchman jogged along the road through the forest and fields. This was his second summer as Wallis's driver.

When he arrived at Baldwin's log building the place appeared deserted despite a collection of carts and saddle horses hitched to the rail. He heard an almost inaudible mumble-mumble. As he approached, the door open to the warm day, snatches of words were decipherable, 'Franklin at Paris' - 'Alliance' - 'Twelve warships and four frigates, with 4,000 troops, under the Comte d'Estaing.' The Frenchman sidled into the room. Thomas Baldwin, a red face slightly portly man, hairless even as to eyebrows, was quoting from one of the bundled gazettes French had flung to the ground. "I guessed as much!" chortled Baldwin, looking up from the paper, spitting tobacco juice into a pan. "Ben Franklin's made a treaty with France. A fleet sails from Toulon. There'll be French soldiers on the frontier afore long." Baldwin lapsed into conjecture. "I can already picture d'Estaing landing them Frog-lads and Lafayette marching their battle columns down Muncy Hill!"

"Et vous verrez sa que! So one could wish!" blurted French.

"Holy Jonafish! One's come already!" Baldwin shot from his seat and viewing the newcomer exclaimed, "Sam Wallis's Frog from Philadelphia! Boys, now we'll have the news. Have a drink on the house, my friend, and settle the parch in your throat. Has the French Navy arrived with an army, and when do they join us on the frontier to knock the hell out of our common enemy?"

The Frenchman, troubled by their enthusiasm, dampened their ardor. "Come to these God-forsaken woods, monsieur? Why should troops entre these wilds when by plaisant sail they may disembark at the portails of Quebec, and snap! Canada is libere! At one stroke, victorie! Taking Canada will cripple the British. Apres that, perhaps, they will chastise savages."

His answer elicited a groan. "But the frontier - Muncy."

"You must have fortitude," said the driver.

"Fortitude?" Baldwin growled. "It's put headstones in our cemetery."

The Frenchman reconsidered his answer. "Maybe," he improvised, "the Western Department will be made stronger. From Augusta a companie? Oui, so! On my journey over the Pocono, Monsieur Wallis he say to me, 'Stop the carriage!' and I stop while he have conversation with Prefect Colonel Hunter. Maybe the Commandant will dispatch us soldiers. Maybe -- "

From the rear of the tavern a voice thundered, "Maybe! Maybe!" French perceived a man imposing in stature, with red hair prematurely flecked gray, who was dressed in deerskin, a knife and pistol in his belt, and a rifle at his side. It was Brady.

"And you, Monsieur, who are you?"

Murphy chose to answer for Levi. "His name is Brady, Lieutenant Levi Brady of the Seventh Connecticut Militia Company, a free company out of Forty Fort Township, over the east hills."

"Sir," spoke Brady, leaning on his rifle, "and to all you gentlemen," he added, his eyes traveling from face to face, noting sullen looks from several at mention of the Connecticut connection, "I know you view a Connecticut officer much as a reptile, but be done with this! Tom Baldwin, don't you recognize in me your friend, much skinnier, much worn, unshaven and dirty, three years gone serving with Morgan's Rifles? By General Washington's orders I appear before you. I speak for your interests as well as the Forty Fort men. Rest your hate. It's a fact the charters and grants of Pennsylvania and Connecticut are in conflict, claims overlapping when you cite the authorities of old parliaments and dead kings. Our vestibule war should be forgotten, and our border skirmishes with each other snuffed out. We face common peril."

Heads began to nod, voices calling, "Hear Brady out!"

Brady continued. "The soldiers of Connecticut have given me, a Pennsylvanian, a commission in their regiment and an offer to fight side by side with you. The flag we shall fight under shall not be Connecticut's nor Pennsylvania's, but of the new Nation. We will be as one, known as an Independent Company, the Free Company! Neither we at Muncy nor those at Forty Fort can fight the Indian alone. Alone, we and those at the fort will fail and all will die. The scalps from our heads and of our families will hang from Indian belts, will be in their hair bags. Not an hour ago we came upon a farmhouse catching fire. We just missed a raiding party of Indians, Seneca I would say. We buried David Henry, his wife, and the charred body of a baby we pulled from the flames."

In the tavern there was crackling silence.

Brady pressed hard. "Sirs, the decision is: will you go on building forts against Connecticut; will you go on dragging cannon over the mountains to point down their throats, ignoring the Indians whose war parties grow more bold? Their tomahawks are raised. Each victory brings more of them out. Do nothing and by winter they'll drink rum from your skulls."

"Make your point, Levi," Thomas Baldwin stated.

"I already have. Security lies in forming a joint militia ready to challenge any war party. That's best done by joining together in numbers and tracking their raiding parties back to their nests, giving them no sanctuary. Gentlemen, Sergeant Tim Murphy and I can tell you it was our long rifles that kept us alive these past three years, and not any foreign power." The reputation of the famous rifleman was known far and wide. But Murphy, too, though from Muncy, hadn't been recognized, much weathered as he was.

Murphy jerked his head at the gazette. "Them who sets their security by printer's marks would do better to read their defense in the marks and notches on their rifles." It brought a murmur of approval.

Levi resumed his effort at recruitment. "As for French soldiers in our Army, yes we've some officers, but Colonel Armand's Legion of French Volunteers is mostly Hessian deserters, and mixed mess of everybody else, rowdies all. It's French in name only. Aside from those

French officers on Washington's staff, you're dreaming of French shadows. Sure the French are helping us; we have the Boy General Lafayette, and I give him three cheers. But what's he accomplished? What says the Gazette?"

Baldwin thumbed the packet of papers. "It says Barren Hill was a victory and gives credit to Major General Lafayette."

"If you want confirmation on that, I haven't decided how much of a victory it was, seeing as the British flying troop came at us and we under Lafayette at them, both so quick neither expected the other. Their horses were on top of our allied Indians, and our Indians were mixed into their cavalry, and muskets going off in the air. Then all at once the King's Light Corps gave an infernal yell, right wheeling for life, while our brave Oneida having guarded our retreat, whooping in justifiable congratulations, posthaste forded the river behind us as the British fled. It was go-for-home for everybody; one minute two armies, and the next a barren hill."

Murphy wryly remarked, "We were advancing from Valley Forge to spy on and maybe harass Clinton at Philadelphia. He nearly ketched us with his entire army. We 'quick marched' to safety. Maybe it was a victory 'cause all parties came and went in good health."

Not a glass clinked. Baldwin tore the gazette into shreds. "The reading, hoping, and praying society is adjourned. It's time we do something. Brady's argument makes sense to me, so I'm offering myself as first to sign for duty with the Free Company."

Baldwin's remark brought to his feet a man who, until now, had been glaring in silence. "I'll not kiss the ass of any Connecticut bastard, and that goes for these two."

"Hold my jacket," drawled Murphy to Levi.

Baldwin clamped his arms around the troublemaker. "Michael Avery, don't fight Murphy! He'll best you, knife, fist, or gun."

"Hell! I'll take him on all three ways."

"Then compose your soul," advised Baldwin. "Murphy picked off General Simon Fraser at Stillwater, for want of whom the British put up the white flag at Saratoga. On Arnold's expedition to Quebec he went up the ladder with Morgan and put the knife to ten grenadiers in ten seconds. It's no disgrace to refuse the fight. Do you want him to be the last person you remember on this earth? Shut your face and sit." Grumbling, the malcontent obeyed.

"For the record," said Murphy, "I can't exactly recall you being here on the frontier when the Lieutenant and I left Muncy to go off to fight in Captain Lowden's Company. If it's anything to you, it was Pennsylvanians, the Lieutenant for one and me for another, who in the Virginia-formed Morgan's Rifles did our share of the fighting, and we dare any man to call us to account for that. If now we fight in a Yankee company it's for all of us. General Washington's furloughing men from the line regiments to raise militia companies on the frontier, which we're doing. Don't be so damned independent that you hurry the death of your own self and family because you refuse Connecticut cooperation."

"We'll get our help from Augusta," the troublemaker retorted.

"Are troops to be had from there?" asked Levi, and then answered his own question. "Damn well not! Muncy is too far upriver. It is the furthest north settlement on the Pennsylvania frontier. Southeast of here, Forty Fort's in the same bind, too far west from Connecticut."

"Aye," agreed Peter Pence, a man of great girth and prodigious strength, who answered to the name of Dutchy. "We've no choice but worst ones, death or a tuck-tail retreat from the land. Rifle talk is what the celebrated Seneca understand. You've got my gun, too, Lieutenant Brady, if it's a fighting company!"

"'T won't be a garrison guard, fat and lazy," snapped Levi. "Captain Simon Spalding leads us. We will serve along the Susquehanna. The Captain intends to carry the war to the Seneca villages. Captain Spalding wants men who will break path through the enemy forest, who can load and fire in sixty seconds and split the mark at eighty rods. Murphy'll be training you in that."

The Frenchman was thinking, thinking hard as the Lieutenant continued. "And mind you, if you were born for bed and roof, and chimney smoke, stay home. The campfire, the woods, and the west side of the wind will be your lot. The man whose feet aren't crippled by the damp will be lucky." Sam French, with a penchant to live life to its fullest, was sorely tempted.

Avery at that moment spoke into the Frenchman's ear. "Listen if you will, Froggie. I've had enough of his blather! There's Connecticut treachery in him. He'd march us out to join the Yankees with them likely waiting for us in ambush. I know it. Just as I know in my bones he had more to do with this morning's deaths than --"

The Frenchman, rising, smashed a fist against Avery's mouth.

"Monsieur Lieutenant! I have soldiered for France. I will soldier with you. And, Monsieur Baldwin, this poor fellow on the floor with the broken jaw, let him pick up his own teeth."

Chapter III

IN TWO DIRECTIONS

The evening had settled into the room. Using an aladdin, Wallis was lighting the candles. Menniger sat at the drop leaf table, ledgers and account books pushed aside, staring at the candlelight caught within the depths of the polished surface. Menniger vacantly watched the flames sprout as Wallis lit the wall tapers, these bringing a suffused glow to the great hall. They heard the Frenchman come into the kitchen. Wallis called, "What kept you?"

In a matter-of-fact voice French replied, "I have listed myself as a coureur de bois in the Free Companie."

"Free Company? What madness is that?"

"A liberté society, rangers of the woods."

"And whose fatal scheme is this?" The question was directed to Menniger, as if he might be involved. Menniger shrugged.

"Monsieur. There is a man, Lieutenant Bradee, who forms the compagnie which goes from here to meet its captain at Forty Fort."

Wallis wagged his forefinger at Menniger. "Ware! 'T is the prodigal son of Captain Brady. Trouble follows the son. He's tried trapping, school teaching and surveying, with little to show except a reputation for brawling. The father may be a hero spent and hollow from wounds, retired among us, but this son, he's a study. Didn't he join

Morgan's Rifles in '75?" French retreated to his duties. Wallis banged the table. "Damn! If the Indians are not down on us already, they will be if Levi Brady loiters here. Let him begone with the men he recruits." He raised his voice, summoning French from the kitchen. "Well, French, when do you leave?"

"Tomorrow."

"That soon! All right, bring our supper and we'll talk later."

"This Frenchman," inquired Menniger, "he being your driver, man-at-arms, and body servant, why do you let him go? What charity is there in releasing him from his indenture?"

"I have no tooth on him. He is not indentured by contract. I did not pay his passage. And if I had, what good would it do me? Some men you cannot bind by contract. They are indentured only to Adventure. You may have a piece of paper to which they put their mark, but what does it mean? They are gone, sooner, later, inevitably. It is a foolish master who does not recognize his limits. What attracted me to the man has lost him to me. As our local Indians would say of his coming and going, 'The Grand Hoop is complete.'

"'T is strange, and yet 't is not strange that in the two years he's been with me I have not learned his true name, concealed for some reason. He has a name of nothing. On a whim, or as a kind of joke, or for the convenience of it, French I have called him, and he has flattered me by taking my name, Samuel. I met him at the Indian Queen in Philadelphia where he was a yard boy of sorts, scuffling for the sulkies and carriages! I liked him. The rest of his history is conjecture."

Menniger added, "Around here, as tongues have it, fancy talk says he mixed swords in France, killed his man and to escape their tribunal skipped off to sea."

"One could imagine anything, I guess, but I do know he has a badly scarred back. He was flogged. I suspect aboard ship, presumably the one which brought him to the Capes and which he deserted, he to find me at low ebb of his fortune. I liked him at once, probably because his self confidence bespeaks he'll cut a mark in this world. I hired him despite my belief he's not for the routines of ordinary service. His obedience is to Adventure. It is the reason he is under the spell of Brady and why I cannot stop him. He buys with his soul the magically named 'Free Company.'" Wallis paused, whispering "Quiet! Our person!"

French set two basins of soup on the table, this followed by a platter of steaming deer meat. The merchant and the overseer, napkins as big as saddle blankets tucked beneath their chins, commenced their supper. Wallis blew on his hot spoon, but Menniger, more hasty with his, whistled from a scalded tongue and danced in his chair. Having disposed of soup and meat, and refreshed by wine, Wallis leaned his chair on its hind legs. "Mr. Menniger, from the stock we have been breeding, would you favor me with a horse of swift gait, broken to saddle, and steady running under fire?"

"There are several. The best is the Maryland roan sired of --"

"Have the horse ready for morning." Wallis stepped to the wall rack and unpegged a rifle, a prize gun with beautiful bird's-eye maple stock. He beckoned French. "I've no complaint that you go. Nevertheless your notice is as short as your impulse. Mr. French, name your grievance."

"Why, none, monsieur!" exclaimed French, startled. The life you have given me c'est magnifique, mais ce n'est pas la guerre. I prefer to fix a baionnette to a musket, rather than knife to pot beef. Avec regrets, monsieur, I depart from you."

"Spoken like a gentleman," Menniger broke in. "Tell us, who are you, really?"

French hung his head. "Only recently I have had flashes of memories, no more than that, of wines on a long table, of men in uniforms of whom I was one. Perhaps it is why I prefer to sleep in bivouac, and not soft bed. More of myself I do not know, except this recent sudden remembrance. But I do remember awakening with a grand monarque of a headache aboard a Portuguese ship, with ropes bound around my hands and feet, in more ways than one bound for America. Before that awakening moment, however, who I am or was conceals itself in an impenetrable fog. N'importe, I am here."

Wallis cleared his throat. "When you leave, Mr. French, I pray you will carry away more than my name. There will be a packet on this table, of monies due you, and an extra to see you comfortable in the

Service. The rifle in my hand, and the horse at Menniger's stable, are yours."

"For these, merci," said French, "yet I cannot accept."

"Nonsense," Wallis added curtly. "Until tomorrow you will perform your duties. Clear the dishes, Mr. French."

"Oui!"

"And cease this 'oui'. You're an American now."

"Oui!" French retreated, filled with appreciation.

Wallis paced his spacious hall, hands dug under his waistcoat. "Confound this war!"

Menniger stared at him, wishing to open his mouth, yet hesitating to act like a bumpkin. Menniger respected Wallis's perception of events and, in light of rumors the British had made reconciliation offers, burned to know if there was any promise of peace in it, late though the date. "What's the story? Congress has a proposal from Lord North? Is there substance to that?"

"Substance, yes. Possibility, no. 'T will not happen. Franklin, who is world respected, floated a balloon seeking reconciliation in '74 when he was in England, there arguing for 'kissing and making up', his own words. Parliament cursed the man. They would have no part of colonial independency in matters of taxation. Franklin's sensible position, his credibility and character were destroyed when upon a visit to the House of Lords Lord Sandwich reviled him in chambers."

"What then is there to Lord North's present proposal?"

"Well, let me just say this, General Washington when he received a copy of North's letter and of the Conciliatory bill while he was at Valley Forge camp, had these publicly burned by the common hangman. So much for prospects of peace." Wallis drew breath, then resumed his pacing. "Confound! Confound! Confound! War is ruining tradesmen on both sides of the ocean. Can one sell sawn timber, horses or pig iron to the Caribbean sugar islands and Spanish colonies along the Gulf? Can I return with sugar and molasses, though there's 14 distillers in

Philadelphia going out of business for want of these? No! My fleet rots in port. What is there left, land speculation? Ha! With the frontier on the boil, who buys what the Indian may overrun tomorrow? One can be land rich and money poor. Even the acres under cultivation, you report, go without harvesting because the men are afraid. You'll wake, Mr. Menniger, one dry morning and find five hundred acres up in smoke after the Indians visit our fields with torches. My tobacco should be cut and loaded, and by now punted down-river for curing; my hay bundled. Menniger, you're the overseer. You know methods to get this done. You're quick enough with your salary."

"And as quick to repeat we need regular troops, in garrison here, to protect the harvesters," shot back the overseer.

"Double ha-ha. I've importuned Congress and failed. You'd think they'd oblige me. Who if not myself provided cattle to their troops starving at Valley Forge? The poor skeletons in their extreme were roasting shoes they had stripped off their dead companions. Not only were farm barns bare of cattle, with the herds long gone into the gullet of the British Army quartered at Philadelphia, but the outlying farmers spurned those 'Resolution of Congress' notes offered by the forage parties of the Commissary General. So, by persuasion, I offered Dutch guilders, sending out my own purveyors with these, and then sold the beef to the Commissary. For each dollar owed me, because the Continental dollar isn't worth its weight in rags, I took 300 Continental notes, a wagon load, knowing I had a way of recouping my investment plus be able to offset the discount rate at which the Amsterdam bankers bought these from me. It was my gesture of good will. For the Dutch 't was more than an act of charity. They had a dog in the fight. It was to their purpose to support the Americans. Too, their risk was small. Prompting the Dutch in their currency swap was the Franco-American Treaty of Commerce and Alliance signed three months past in Paris. The Dutch foresaw, as I did, the French treasury would rescue the Americans from their financial mess, the dollar now to have an anchor. Two things preserved the soldiers, my effort in providing beef, I could not bear their starvation, and the earlier than usual run of shad up the Schuylkill, enough fish netted to be salted and stored, a miraculous manifestation."

"What about the Commonwealth for troops?"

"I've made a pest of myself. General Thomas Mifflin argued my case before the Legislature, he himself involved in frontier speculation.

But he may have been the wrong man. While he is the leader of the 'Free' or Fighting Quaker faction pledged to the Continental cause, Mifflin has lost importance within the State Legislature and Congress because of his part in the cabal to displace Washington as commander in chief, Washington maligned as a weak general. Led by that Irish braggart Major General Thomas Conway, they tried to replace the Virginian with Horatio Gates."

"Aside from Mifflin, who else have you approached?"

"Let's reverse your question. Who haven't I? Colonel Samuel Hunter at Augusta, I visited him yesterday. No results. He's a cautious man, though likable. Last week I visited General Edward Hand in Philadelphia. While not speaking for Lachlin McIntosh, the General appointed to fill Hand's post in the Western Department after Hand received his star, Hand discouraged me from seeking help from there. He stated the Pennsylvania garrisons were stretched thin. Forts Pitt and Augusta suffer one year enlistment problems. 'One day you have troops, the next you can't command your walls,' he as much as said. Help us? Yes, were the commanders of the western forts given more levies."

Menniger grimaced. "Small comfort. I've heard as you said about these forts. Instead of receiving reinforcements, more militia companies are to be siphoned toward the depleted Continental line, to replace the winter losses; the Army is about vanished. The stream of muskets flows from us, not to us, Mr. Wallis."

Wallis meditated on this. "I've as much suspected this, but I tried anyway. And I've meditated on our position. What difference does it make that Muncy is deserving of protection more than other settlements, being northernmost on the far reaching Susquehanna; or that it is nearest the enemy, quickest to feel the downstream thrusts from the Seneca? The truth is Muncy must, like all other communities on the frontier's edge, shift for itself. That thought is inescapable."

"That is no answer," stated Menniger. "The problem remains, how can we stiffen the will of the harvester when he knows the Indian who came twice in April will return?"

"What are our numbers, Menniger, those of our people able to bear arms?"

"I'd say ninety. There's two thousand Seneca floating in the Woods."

"I dispute that. I think the figure describes the total warriors in the Confederacy."

"Even if you cut it in half, the Seneca outnumber us eleven for every one of us, men and boys. If they sent one third of a thousand, we'd sink under three hundred hatchets."

"Whatever," said Wallis, "we can fight them off provided we have walls for protection. They don't make war in large parties. They hit, they run, they build their nerve by small actions rapidly done, ambush rather than onslaught. Muster your farmers, Menniger, and you shall have a fort."

Menniger shook his head. "I would have submitted a plan for one myself, were it practical. A fort and a militia may be a comfort, I grant you, but what value is there in such a crib? It may deceive the people to stay, yes, but the hostilities will escalate. You know that. Larger numbers will be coming down against us. Momentarily the Indian attacks are small and sporadic. But once they become Tory led with the British Greens participating, we'll be in it for bad, in line for British planned large scale expeditions, not just sorties. War parties! And how shall we fare against this, Mr. Wallis? How fare the scabbies when the piss in the horse-trough runs high?"

"You employ a scientific argument." Wallis paced from window to fireplace.

As Wallis paced back and forth, thinking, Menniger added, "A friendly Seneca, who has just been up to Fort Niagara, tells me the loyalists, who are enlisted in the Green Rangers under Major John Butler, have grown in numbers. Mr. Wallis, you've had the ears of the important men in Congress, forewarning them of our growing peril, as stated in my letters. Yet you say there is no promise of relief."

"Correct. Certainly not timely to our needs. I pleaded with Robert Morris who holds the purse strings, and he does not view the frontier as a priority. As to sentiment in Congress, they say 'At soonest this August.' Even then, it's not to be a war with the Seneca, but with the Mohawk near Albany."

"God's sake! Why the Mohawk?"

"They are the yeast in the loaf of dissension. Their brothers, the Seneca, as is the opinion at Philadelphia, will lose courage if Mohawk villages are put to the torch."

"Mercy on us if an expedition lays fire against the Mohawk villages. The Longhouse is a hornets nest; disturb one part and all will swarm, Mohawk and Seneca. The comb must be burned the wall around or we are lost!"

"Not so fast, Menniger. I am not half done in finding a way to save Muncy. If you have inquired for protection as I have, and in defect of these find yourself alone, then you would seek further."

"Where further?" asked Menniger, mystified.

"Having failed in one camp, I am now obliged to negotiate in another. Mr. Menniger, I shall solicit the Royal Green Rangers!"

Dumfounded, Menniger's jaw flew open. "You will pronounce yourself a Tory?"

"Not exactly. I propose we remain as we are perceived, each as good a Whig as ever sat upon a pot, men opposed to government from afar. At the same instant we will negotiate with the King's military in behalf of our own preservation, they to pass around Muncy, we to be safe from harm."

"What!" declared Menniger, shocked. "Do you realize such an arrangement compromises our honor, places us in the position of becoming ears and eyes, yes, spies for the Crown!"

"Mr. Menniger! The expression is vulgar. Let me use a more charitable word. It is a business arrangement. We have a propertied interest which gives us posture and privilege of a sort. It serves our interest to protect ourselves from harm from any quarter. Would you not agree?"

"Of course."

"Then let me use the Latin expression 'virtus in medio'. There is virtue in the middle ground. Whichever faction prospers in this war, we shall prosper with it."

Menniger shielded his eyes with the palm of his hand, thinking aloud, "'T would be sensible - the middle position." Then, to Wallace he said, "Sir, you are with Patrick Henry in your eloquence. You have given to our problem fresh thought. Yet, how would you manage the miracle of arriving with a whole skin at Fort Niagara? First you must pass through the Seneca Country above us. You will be dead meat if detected. They will put you in their kettle."

"I disagree. The Indian Country may be safely entered. Nor is the Indian as barbaric as you paint him, 't is an expression, this 'kettle' thing. He has feelings like us and a full range of emotions, sometimes taxed to extreme. Met properly, he can be Amity personified. I speak from first hand observation."

"What's this?" said Menniger, ears perking. "First hand?"

"Menniger, about four years before Pontiac's Rebellion I traveled to the furthest villages of the Seneca."

"You explored the country of the most savage people ever put on the face of this earth?"

"This lump of wax has. In my youth I had a love for danger. I toured the western reaches of the Longhouse, my companion a young Mohawk of Christian upbringing. We traveled lands to this day uncharted. My friend of yesteryear, now in his maturity, is today the supreme chief of the Mohawk, therefore of the Confederacy. He is no other than the feared and respected Joseph Brant."

"God!" Menniger was awed, astonished Wallis these years known to him had concealed this colorful and amazing past.

The proprietor added, "l will not say Brant holds great affection for me, but together we shared pleasant times and 't is a bond between us. Aside from Brant, among the Seneca I have other friends. Not the leastways among those who once valued me is Esther Montour the French-1ndian woman who is viewed as a 'queen' by her people. Legendary to you, she is a flesh and blood person, the very memory of her arousing my passion. Do not smile, you cold dog. It was my fortune, or curse, to have known this fascinating woman. All these years she has been in the recess of my mind. Enough, I digress. Yes, if by way of Esther Montour or Joseph Brant I can send word to Fort Niagara that we, here, intend no harmful act against their interests --"

Menniger interrupted, "You presume Brant will be unchanged toward you. Time makes men strangers. And as for romantic feelings toward the Montour woman, you may be in for a disappointment. That which you seek to recapture is best left a memory. Further, how will you beat your way north to meet these people, with death in the form of war parties filing down every path, and war canoes on the Susquehanna? The journey seems an impossibility. And look at your age. You undertake a task for a younger man, you to tire traveling that distance, as you must, despite the vigor that you have."

"Menniger, to answer you, I can still straddle a horse. I will get there. Boldness, sir, has its own merits. I shall approach by the ceremonial route, traveling the path to the guarded 'southern door', this located at the confluence of the Teaoga with the Susquehanna. I shall not take to the forest and sneak at the guard at that location as would an enemy, nor steal toward their fires. Their forward outpost of spies shall see me on the great meadow, the Sheshequin plains, and see me fording the Teaoga. One who so openly approaches their sanctuary will in effect be under a flag of truce. And, if I should be met by war parties, I speak their language."

"And, once to have met with your friends of the past, what would you parley for neutrality, your ancient friendship? These friendships may be as dead as is General William Johnson and his world." Menniger alluded to the Crown Superintendent who, until his death on the eve of the American Revolution, had held to the policy his Indian charges should remain out of the growing confrontation among colonials.

"No, I have something else in my bag of tricks. I will appeal to lust, or should we say thirst of the British for information as to the goings on in Philadelphia, and along the Susquehanna. My access to knowledge is my coin. Cooperation for cooperation."

Menniger reviewed the whole of it. Were Wallis to be killed, or to be successful, he Menniger profited. Free lands Wallis had promised him, but that was a 'some day' type promise. However, should calamity overtake the merchant, there was a forged document in his safe, a codicil to Wallis's 1768 will, naming him the beneficiary of a plat of rich bottom land, a modest enough self reward for his loyalty. Bolstered by this thought, Menniger stood in agreement, the trip should be made, but first there was the business of a fort. There was reason, now, for its construction, if but to calm immediate fears.

All evening Menniger the proselyte and his master, Wallis, sat or paced, the grand plan evolving. Wallis, referring to the liquor cabinet, celebrated their progress. "We need to replenish our fervor with Madeira!" He poured the rich amber wine and lifted his glass in toast. They had sketched their fortification, but were yet to calculate in detail the height of the walls, the firing platforms, the size of the moat to be dug, and trees to be chopped to enable the men on the walls to have clear fields of fire. They were at this until the candles guttered out.

Wallis with a suppressed yawn saw Menniger to the door. It was extremely foggy, the mist rolling in from the nearby stream. Caught in the rip-tide of his master's intellect, Menniger sleepy as he was, parted company from him with reluctance, hardly able to contain his now genuine excitement. To him Wallis's words were, "Sleep late. In the afternoon we shall plant the pegs." Wallis, in the doorway, listened to the last of the muffled hoofbeats.

Scarcely had the morning advanced and the sun begun its course, when the Frenchman, who had tossed all night in anticipation of the new life, was aroused by the squabble of sparrows. He cast his window shutters open, blinked, gargled, spat, brewed a cup of tea, relaxed, relieved himself, and afterwards with steaming tea urn and a bowl of hot cakes, and a box of razors and basin of hot water, with towel, lather and soap, marched upstairs to the snoring proprietor. He placed these on a side board, the urn foremost where its fumes would dispel Wallis's slumbers. Wallis turned, groaned, and would not waken, whereupon Samuel French, hesitating, retreated to the staircase. From there he gazed with affection at the man who had been his employer. As yet the large hall and main parlor beyond, scene of the night's efforts, refused the pallid morning. He struck fire to the kindling. On the table, which was littered with crumpled sheets of paper, he found twenty gold coins, a rifle, a shot pouch, and two horns of powder. Scooping up the coins and dropping these into a tight little bag at his neck, he exclaimed, "My soul of mud, âme de boue, I shall miss this man, if it is only to clean after him." Gathering up the superbly crafted gun, he briefly admired it. For careless inspiration he stuck a quill pen in his cap, proudly viewed himself in the glass and, laughing with the image, to the random fellow whispered, "Yankee Doodle!" With flintlock under arm, blanket and the two horns of powder slung across his shoulders, he strode down the road. He glanced at Menniger's pasture. The horse was nowhere to be seen, Menniger fast asleep. "Cour bleu, one can walk."

At Baldwin's Lieutenant Levi Brady waited impatiently for the coterie of recruits to assemble. Baldwin was holding the hand of his wife, reassuring her by his bald-face lie it was a short enlistment for only sixty days. First to arrive was Peter 'Dutchy' Pence, the portly Hollander who, for all his ponderous frame, moved with grace. Pence was wearing armament that staggered description. At the sight Levi choked. He carried one yager rifle, two pistols, eighty rounds of ammunition, a small sack of charge powder, a rusty ax, two stab knives, an iron tomahawk, and a war club. To a rope hitched to his waist in supplement to his leather belt, he had attached a pair of high top moccasins, a clay jug, clay pipe, bullet mould and bar of lead, and a large cured ham. Were there more to carry, he would have.

There were eleven recruits. One was a trapper, Bradford Hotchkiss, with a sharp chin and black beady eyes; another was an itinerant peddler, Isaac Shaffer, a short man with a round face, poorly dressed, who sported a fowling piece of skeptical value. Then there were six farmers, two appearing to be twins, a father and a son, the Wandells. Of the four remaining farmers, two were lads barely of age. The two older men, Peter Grove and John Scudder, who had faces lined with the hardships of life, deported themselves as the former soldiers they were, having served in the French and Indian wars. The contingent was rounded out with French, Pence and Baldwin. A small crowd of relatives and friends had gathered to see them off. Baldwin at the last moment presented each volunteer with a flask from his storehouse, these filled with whisky. Not all had horses. Some were to ride double. When all was in readiness Brady leaned forward in his saddle, with a grin whispering to Murphy, "At Quebec, how many grenadiers was it?"

"Oh, shut your mouth!"

Restlessness went from rider to horse, each man eager to be on his way. They made their good-bys. Sergeant Tim Murphy glanced the group over, counting. In all, they were thirteen. Some he recognized had previous service. In spite of bad luck connected with the number,

Murphy knew it would not be superstition that determined their fate. It would be the prowess they demonstrated, and the Providence of God Himself that would deliver them, once they were joined in battle. Lieutenant Brady was mounted in the saddle. "Ready?" he asked of Sergeant Murphy, who nodded. "Then God bless us," the Lieutenant stated, upon which Murphy shouted, "For - ward!"

With a lift of hooves the body was in motion, along with several outriders who would bring back the mounts needed at home. Thomas Baldwin sighted his gun and fired at the town bell which protested with a leaden clang. It was a keen snap for a man on horseback, and roused a cheer. Trees slipped, the ground reared, and walls of rock towered on either side; they rode the mountains. In the Frenchman's imagination he galloped to the sound of bugles. A mad lyric of the *Continentals,* 'Yankee Doodle' bubbled to his lips, all in the contingent adding their voices, they in unison singing "Yankee Doodle - Yankee Doodle dandy" as they ascended the hill, entered the woods and followed the road leading toward Forty Fort. Thus began, in joviality, the adventurous journey of thirteen American frontiersmen of the Free Company who were about to write themselves into history.

For Lieutenant Levi Brady, defender of liberty, and for turncoat patriot Samuel Wallis, while their respective paths were about to diverge, a curious twist of fate, never the cleverest pen to forespell, would bind them forever together in the annals of the Frontier.

Chapter IV

JOURNEY TO TEAOGA

It started with Wallis and Menniger in the yard. Menniger would pace a distance from the house, then he would stop, setting a peg into the ground, and then repeat his performance. Already a series of pegs, connected by twine, three-quarters surrounded the estate. Wallis had a gold-headed cane in his hand. He backed to a window, sighted with his cane, indicating a gracious elm. "That, with the brush, will go. A pity it must." Toward mid-afternoon a detail of settlers armed with axes obediently felled the doomed trees, while a second detail, faced with the task of digging the moat outlined by the pegs, threw up prodigious quantities of dirt. A fire blazed in through the underbrush. There was no respite.

By sundown of the fifth day a substantial abatis, made by cutting, sharpening and planting pine and elm logs on the inner edge of the trench, lent the house the atmosphere of a fort. A wall of upright logs enclosed the structure. Windows of the mansion were barred, gun apertures carved, a covered watershed built from the house to the well. When all was ready, waters from the West Branch River were diverted into the moat. By torch light Wallis's precious salt supply, heretofore kept at Baldwin's, was transferred to the armored house, along with slabs of ham, tubs of beef, and war supplies of powder, lead and muskets.

During this process Wallis confided, "I have taken steps to see you are appointed a militia captain." Menniger had expected some such recognition. "But," added Wallis, "be aware of the politics of your position. Colonel Hunter has delegated to Colonel Hepburn the responsibility for the safety of the settlers. Hepburn, well meaning though he may be, will do nothing. I fear Hunter, cautious man that he is, and Hepburn without real power have little to offer the settlers except to abandon their homes, these to be burnt and their crops destroyed by the gathered war parties. You must look to yourself, if to survive, and to have starch enough to preserve your authority. Be alert. Rotate your militiamen. Part of them always should be on duty within the fort."

"Sir," Menniger responded, "may I add one more dimension to our preparation. Your lands are extensive, your settlers scattered, with some homes at great distance. 'T would be simple to turn one of the outlying farmhouses into an armored redoubt, true less defensible than Muncy, yet functional. It would be meaningful to settlers nearest it."

"Excellent idea. Do it. Strengthen the doors and block the windows, carve apertures, and garrison the place by recruiting those close by. Call it Fort Menniger, if you wish."

"You know, Mr. Wallis," waxed Menniger, savoring his new role, "I am carried away by your enthusiasm. It may be, now that my pessimism, a cobweb to my thinking, has been brushed away, I find myself believing, by our formidable preparations, we can prevail in a major attack."

"All this," reflected Wallis, "these stresses placed on the frontier, were forecast by Franklin 30 years ago. Prompted by rumor five pirate ships were about to make war on the City of Philadelphia, he procured cannon to confront seaward peril. But he also perceived a less immediate danger from inland attacks to come upon the City. At that time, when we were colonial subjects, and at sword points with France, he envisioned the French, with the Indians to join them, would strike at the British settlements along the Susquehanna. In that manner, by the back door the Good Doctor expected the French to approach the City. He formed an 'Association' of armed citizens to reduce Philadelphia's vulnerability. For like reason, not ten years thereafter we erected Fort Augusta, to forestall the French. Now we confront a reverse alliance, the French belly to belly with us in this struggle with the British. In self-preservation, Menniger, nations and individuals behave of a pattern, no foe unworthy of friendship when necessity requires it. Such is the politic of war."

Again Menniger, overwhelmed by the sweep of Wallis's mind, by the persuasiveness of a man respected for his precise logic, nodded agreement. He could not have imagined himself wearing two hats as a captain of a fort defending against British-Indian attack while resident manager for an owner about to treat with the very people he was commissioned to repulse. This was a topsy-turvy world. For the present he rested his thoughts, devoting himself to the challenge ahead, the fort to be.

To further the ambitious defense, a letter had been dispatched via the courier Richard Covenhoven, from Wallis to Captain Spalding. It described all being done. He congratulated the old soldier upon his formation of a free company, and pledged cooperation in matters of mutual concern. Reassuringly polite, Wallis pointed out that a fort at Muncy was a reply to the common foe, and not a threat to Forty Fort, the Connecticut stronghold. Equally well mannered, Spalding praised the builders for their foresight and made suggestions one of which they immediately enacted. A spirited alarm was installed, a melancholy-sounding affair. Even a cannon was begun, two barrel makers commissioned to bore a log, gird it with iron hoops, and mount it on a swivel. A town militia had its first duties thrust upon it when guard tours were established to patrol the road and to stand as lookouts on the surrounding hills. This preparation invoked memories among the old settlers who recalled how, years earlier, the Delaware had swept down from the hills and almost bested the pioneer settlers in a sharp, bloody clash.

The elders could name twenty men who would be applauding in Paradise Wallis's wise preparation.

In the space of a week the house had become a fort; moreover, the mantle of disaster which had clung about Muncy had dissolved in the atmosphere of change. Men cheerfully shouldered the military burden. Talk of a retreat to eastern and southern towns below the Poconos died.

Robert Menniger, but an hour from the tailor's, resplendent in the uniform of a Northumberland captain, surveyed the frontier citadel. Hearing a call from Wallis, who had arranged the commission through the Committee on Safety at Philadelphia, conscious of his impressive appearance, Menniger strolled into the house. The courier Covenhoven had killed a horse riding to and from Colonel Hunter at Fort Augusta to pick up the commission which had been forwarded to Hunter for endorsement. In the scullery, now converted to a headquarters, Captain Menniger and his sponsor conferred. Menniger reveled in his new authority. "Assuming that the nasty bell is clanging," Wallis began, "what's your move on such short notice?"

"In event of a threat, I have advised the settlers they should fall back toward our fort. The garrison will send out a cordon of militiamen to straddle the road, to cover the settlers' retreat. The militiamen who are outside, in turn will be under observation from sharpshooters on the roof, with a cavalry ready to sally forth."

"Continue."

"When the families have reached our palisades the militia on the road will make a slow, defensive withdrawal."

"If they are flanked?"

"Small chance! On the sides of the road, in the deep grass, I'll have stakes similar to the impalements bordering our moat. And I am about to send down to Colonel Hunter at Augusta for three-prong irons, barbs, crowfeet, which I shall sow in the small grass, and beyond a pace. These pointed jacks will skewer a moccasin as neat as a hook catches trout in yonder creek."

"Charge these iron to my account. Remind Hunter that, on the credit side, he owes me for salt," said Wallis.

The decisive hour was at hand. Having eased the fears of his people by building a center of resistance Wallis prepared for his journey into the Indian Country. The torpid afternoon had succumbed to a sultry evening. The late day tour of inspection completed, guards posted, Menniger drew off his boots and flung his sword upon the kitchen table, meanwhile watching Wallis. To fill the silence he observed, "Sir, you do not lack for courage."

Wallis had discarded his silks for leather jerkin and trousers, and had laced up a soft durable pair of Indian slippers. It was the raiment of a frontier traveler. Oddly Wallis, Menniger perceived, in some ways was changed, had a new personality heretofore hidden which fitted him for the role of frontiersman. He was reaching into his past, no longer the reserved, cogitative and calculating man to whom Menniger was accustomed. For one, there was excitement in his eye, and his complexion seemed more ruddy against the rich browns of his garb. Here was a different Samuel Wallis with whom one could readily identify. The awkward moment of departure at hand, Wallis hesitated, then confessed, 'Ridiculous as this may sound, I feel I am about to meet my former self, time in its winding to roll in reverse. But, to be pragmatic, have you taken care of the final details of our plan?"

"Yes, word is common that you are south-bound to-Fort Augusta for talk with the military commander, then on to Philadelphia."

"And Favel, she is saddled?"

"In the yard this moment."

"Menniger," said Wallis, inhaling, "keep vigilant. It is early June. With allowances, at worst I'll be home before this month is done, or a fortnight with any luck. Do not despair, even were my absence protracted. Fear not for me. I am an indestructible man. Have faith. Our plan is achievable."

"Take care." They shook hands.

Wallis stepped into the yet starless evening, adjusted the girth of his saddle, fitted his foot into the stirrup, swung himself up, and with a look to the wind-swept sky, dug his knees into the animal. With hat cocked low he journeyed into the descending night.

He rode at a moderate gait, reining periodically to listen down the road for any noise beyond or behind. The only challenges to his presence were those of posted sentries, but these were in the form of good luck wishes, they given advance notice he would be on the road. To corroborate Menniger's lie, he headed south over Muncy's hills in the direction of Fort Augusta and the southern settlements. Three miles from the town, well beyond observation, he jack-knifed off course and skirted a stand of aspen, to double back and arrive northwest of Menniger's furthest sentinels above Muncy. From there he would break course toward the Indian Land. Without path or moon, from field to narrowly spaced timber, from timber to brush-choked upland, from brush to timber he picked his way. Duly he intersected the road that ascended northerly out of the valley. From there he peered down.

On the floor of the valley nestled his fortified house, as a twinkle of lights in the gloom. High on the hillside the black of night pressed in upon him. As if by rehearsal the moon opened a path, fitfully casting its beam of silver onto a patch of the ground before him. However, the main forest was a sea of darkness.

The wagon tracks, felt rather than seen, degenerated into a footpath. This, too, expired in unbroken woods. Somehow he had got off on a spur of the Indian path, this spur a dead end, and he would have to stumblefoot about until striking one of the north-south Seneca paths in the vicinity. There were three, as he remembered. Almost at his elbow a moose, huge by its sound, was frightened and plunged by him, crashing and bounding, seeking forest depths. Wallis pushed on, lost, making use of what bit of light there was. The appearing-disappearing moon transformed the black hills into Cimmerian monsters. In descending from one of these, he nearly missed his footing. He was to escape this once. He was not as fortunate on the second mishap. Crossing a flinty outcrop, while blindly inching down its steps, leading his horse by the reins, the embankment crumbled, and he tumbled into a blackwater swamp where he sprawled, half drowned. He struggled erect, cursing the marsh; he could not see - he could not find his horse! He was about to cry out when, suddenly, the hot tongue of Favel licked his muddy face. Laboriously he regained the saddle and reached firm land.

The moon broke from envelopment and floated clear of the clouds, shooting silvery arrows across the blue-black heavens and into the receding cumulus! The pale light illumined a hitherto unsuspected path, upon which Wallis set his horse. By luck, his provisions having been lost in the swamp, an opossum died beneath Favel's hooves. Wallis circled, dismounted, slung the carcass over the pommel, and rode on to discover an escarpment sheltering a tiny rivulet. Tethering Favel, he wiggled into a bush, relying on the sun to rouse him. At dayspring, bathing his face and hands in the tiny stream, in the protection of the ridge he then kindled twigs, then cased and rashed the opossum, ate what he would, then saddled Favel and resumed the journey. Serving him were the skills of his youth.

Wallis crossed broad, empty meadows, so luxuriant that the grasses by their start promised heights to engulf a mid-summer rider. This Indian meadow, on which no trees grew, had been farmed by the Indians until the soil was exhausted, then the land burnt over, the villagers migrating to nearby fallow lands. Too, the changing river laid claim to bordering trees. One broad valley merged into another. Often, when it seemed inevitable he would have to climb, the valley, turning with the river, would divulge a natural channel into the next and more northern valley.

This chain of valleys held like an avenue for the traveler. To his right and left, touching down upon him, the mountains rolled ever onward with their impenetrable fastness of woods. He knew himself to be deep in terrain frequented by the Indian. Entering one of the linking valleys, less for reason than from premonition he stood in his stirrups. Was it a tremble of wind in the bush; or had he blundered on a watch of the Seneca? Again there was a perception of persons in hiding as he came between a stand of pines and creek. He felt their eyes, narrowed and speculative. Once through the pass and into a broad meadow where the copper-skinned fellows could not follow, he breathed more freely. From time to time he stopped and looked to the rear. The plain continued empty. This, and the genial sun, restored his humor.

On this day his thoughts dwelt on Esther who, though briefly met so long ago, had left him with memories he could never quite erase. Her beauty, their shared passion, the voluptuousness of that relationship flooded his senses as he rode northward. Theirs had been an immediate love of such intensity and overwhelming depth that the flame of their mutual ardor was all consuming. Each came to the other in privileged ways. As he half closed his eyes while resting in the shade of a large, handsome buckeye tree, erotic memories returned, these associated with their intimacies.

It was while traveling with Brant that he had met the Montours when they lived more southerly. Brant knew the value of visiting Andrew, her uncle, a much respected translator between the Seneca and the British, and a friend to Sir William Johnson. Brant was grooming himself for the important role he would play in the Confederacy. For Wallis, it was a visit of another kind, of wildest satisfaction, of passions unbridled, of a marriage proposal half offered and half refused.

During the intervening years, at Philadelphia he prospered, indulging himself in buying frontier lands and building a lovely home in Muncy. He had wondered about Esther, but saw no purpose in intruding upon her life. Now, suddenly, there was a reason.

On the third day of his journey he happened upon the remains of a home, a blackened, half consumed structure. The door hung from one hinge; the part of the roof that had not been burnt had fallen in. In the meadow were four graves, newly turned, with rough crosses. On the chance that the maker of these crosses might be in the vicinity, he lifted his voice. "Hello!" he called. 'Hello!' faintly sounded his echo, springing off the mountain wall; whereupon from the house came a wild, unearthly yell. A creature of rags and filth, a living atrocity, pushed aside the door and hobbled into the daylight. The eyes of the man were vacant of expression. Wallis repressed a shudder, slipped his rifle from its banding, rested it upon a crook of his arm and centered the muzzle to cover the caricature. The man's head along the crown had a raw welt. Mud had been pressed into the region. An Indian's knife, in the hands of an unskilled 'soft knife', had severed the temple muscles, loosening the skin of his forehead. The sight prompted Wallis's impromptu exclamation. Fascinated, unbelievingly attracted by the grotesque madman, wondering what might be done for him, he debated the sport and justice of a bullet. He hesitated. It was obvious this poor creature, his wounds festering from the butchery, was beyond assistance. Wallis questioned him, "Lazarus," for Lazarus he was, "will you not be dead?" He indicated the graves. "Ah, Lazarus, you have lain among them, and the stink is in you, and the light of the sun is absent in your eyes. In vain the Lord has raised you. May God take you under, as a matter of mercy." Wallis's pronouncement could be construed as a sermon of sorts. Lazarus's sudden hysterical chuckle caused Favel to rear up and neigh. The astonished madman paused, and then, after a sullen moment, with a peculiar grimace given to those who are advanced to the very end of reason, he leaped at the rider. "God spare you!" cried Wallis, as he tripped his gun. Whether the intent of Wallis was spoiled by a split second deflection in aim caused by the humanism in him, sparing the tragic figure, or more likely this poor devil was saved by Wallis's rifle being jostled, whatever the reason, God may have had a say in it. The discharge blasted a nearby sapling. The hideous man, stunned, stood unharmed. Nauseated, Wallis cantered away. He had almost killed a man as an act of kindness. It troubled him for thinking to do it as much as for not. Calmed by the beauty of the region, he put the scene behind him.

He followed the winding Lycoming, then came over to a smaller stream which flowed easterly. He camped early, short of Sugar Creek's junction with the Susquehanna, a place he knew from times before, and slept fitfully. The next day, fatigued, he did not break camp until late, not raising the Susquehanna until well past two. Even so, he stopped at its shore, watered Favel, and splashed his feet in the cool current. Outwardly he had not a care in the world. But the incident yet disturbed him, more for its disclosure of a weakness within himself, namely an inability to judge what course of action best should have been taken. In his character indecision had never before shown itself. He let the matter rest, to himself thinking, fate itself is the ultimate determinant, or said differently, it was God's Will.

During his travel Wallis's thoughts reverted to his secret interactions with General Sir William Howe who had commanded British land forces. The General had just been relieved by Henry Clinton, and was now in sail for England. Wallis knew the consequences of Clinton's hasty preparation to abandon the City. Prominent Tory friends would seek asylum aboard Clinton's ships. All would be in haste, everyone aware the French fleet under Admiral Compte d'Estaing was plowing the waves to bottle off British evacuation by sea. Thousands would flee inland. Clinton's escape would be a narrow one, French sails almost to the capes of Delaware. Wallis sourly meditated, 'Just look at things now. A world turned upside down. Damn England for picking Howe to lead this war. They knew when he held a seat in Parliament he opposed its repressive policy toward America. And yet in '76, I was certain the rebellion would be crushed, backwoodsmen and farmers facing a trained army landed in New York City. By courier and in cipher I provided General Howe with the doings of Congress. And by a simple scheme I supplied Howe with flour enough for his entire army, and at a cheaper price than were it transported from England, for his Hessian bakers to make bread.' Because of the extreme shortage, Wallis's offer was not to be refused, a favor indeed what with flour unavailable to New York's populace at large. Local prices were astronomical. For Wallis, even if he bought at premium from mills in Jersey and Pennsylvania, the market price the flour could command if shipped out of Delaware River made the risk worth the taking, provided he took care to insulate himself through layers of intermediaries from being discovered. He sent agents up the Delaware to bargain with gristmill owners, many of Tory disposition, these mills located on the Jersey side as well as Pennsylvania. His agents bought everything in the bins, this price including drayage to Wallis's schooner laying-to on the river. Only his ship's captain was in on the scheme for a share of the profits, no others to know this newly loaded cargo was bound for the British Army. His was not the first nor last sailing ship to put to sea for profit through trade, howbeit the laws. Sailing downstream in darkness and once at sea, in the early morning light his captain made rendezvous with a waiting British ship of the line, this interception counterfeiting a seizure of the vessel. The warship assured safe delivery of the 'captured' cargo. Any privateer which might venture their way would speed elsewhere, no match for a broadside. By this trick Wallis circumvented the illicit trading laws. Reimbursed for the value of the seized ship, and with a tidy price for the flour, his captain rewarded, his crew released no wiser, the world was all well at that juncture. 'Now' thought Wallis, coming to the reality of the moment, 'how times have changed. The General is on the high seas bound for England and to be censored by Parliament for dragging the war, while my friend Joseph Galloway, formerly of the Congress, source of my clandestine tidbits sent Howe during the time he was in New York, has fled, he too gone to England. And my unfortunate courier to Howe, caught on other matters, has been exalted by a rope. In one respect, with the man's lips forever sealed and Galloway beyond reach, my past is safe. It is best left at that.'

He mused about Howe's playmate, the voluptuous Elizabeth Loring who had so pleasured the General. A quatrain from a ballad came to mind. It alluded to Howe's dalliances with her in lieu of conducting the war. The blonde blue-eyed Mrs. Joshua Loring, a beautiful Bostonian, had accompanied the tall, full bodied, gracious Howe to New York and then to Philadelphia. Her brute husband, in compensation was appointed Commissioner of Prisoners, he to finger the monies of that position while Howe fingered the obligingly positioned Elizabeth. To himself Wallis hummed:

"Sir Willian, he as snug as flea
Lay all this time a-snoring;
Nor dreamed of harm, as he lay warm
In bed with Mrs. Loring."

Wallis refocused on reality. From another perspective, that of his immediate problem, he chastised himself. 'Why had I not earlier heeded Menniger's forewarnings about Muncy? Why did I allow myself to be distracted? A word to Howe might have brought about the relief to Muncy I now seek, making this trip needless. Again, why should I expect Howe to be my benefactor, the General too busy a-bed? As rascals say of his indolent military record in America, he is Washington's best general. Yet, I owed it to myself to have asked, this my own failure; he by a pen stroke could have cast an invisible blanket of protection around Muncy. One does not always think correctly.' Having reproached himself, he concentrated on the present. He must keep sharp; he would soon be at the Teaoga junction with the Susquehanna. Despite nature's peacefulness, danger could be anywhere, everywhere, increasing with every mile of travel. It induced an edginess.

He paralleled the Susquehanna, its flats covered by a tapestry of red top spikelet grass. Riding north with the river, he had its burbling companionship. There were secondary diversions, the snap of a fish come to the surface, the skip of a pebble dislodged by Favel's hoof, and the inconsequential movements of a rattler, dry and sinuous, which poured into the brush. A dithering black squirrel, suicidally confused, fled at his approach and pancaked into the water.

As often happened in this season, the veil of evening was late but sudden in descending; he hurried his horse. He was in the final valley, a valley of encampment where charrings in the earth, ring-shaped marks of ancient cook fires, spoke of settlements fallen into oblivion. Too, as he carefully picked his way along the western shore of the wide Susquehanna River, he could see in the dusk about fifty Indian cabins clustered on the flats, canoes pulled up on the embankment. He passed unchallenged. In part this was because the dark shades of night had slid down from the mountains into the valley, obscuring his presence. This well could be Esther's town, but he dared not inquire. He must press on. Soon he would meet the Seneca chiefs, the gatekeepers, or if unlucky the watchers in the wood. Death could come easily, with a twitch of a finger.

Although the Susquehanna, which he followed, continued due North, his progress along its western embankment was blocked by an arm of water flowing easterly into the Susquehanna, the mouth of which was not fordable. This was the Teaoga. Within the Y formed by its junction with the Susquehanna lay that point of land where an eternal guard kept watch. That point, also called by the Indian word for point, Teaoga, was a curiosity noted in every traveler's journal. Embraced by the two arms of water, at times of flood this peninsula became virtually an island, itself shrunken by high rushing waters. North of the junction the two rivers again turned toward each other, in false junction. In shape this formation of land was much like an arrowhead, the fork of the rivers forming the tip, and the indentations being its notches, in all when seen from cliffs above likened to a menacing arrow pointed south in forewarning to travelers. The indented neck acted as a land passage from river to river, a canoe-carry over which parties of immemorial adventure had repaired. Lately the Seneca and the Mohawk, in coming to each other's aid and to shorten the trip, used this portage, inverting their barks so as to straddle their shoulders, then walking the scant 550 feet to gain the next river. Those going downstream either river and wishing to go upstream the other, saved three miles of paddling.

Teaoga likewise was a crossway of paths. By foot or canoe invariably a traveler came to Teaoga. Here the great east-west path dipped through the valley. Here all traffic from the south entered the Forbidden Path which, as the largest path through the Longhouse, led generally in the direction of Fort Niagara. Here, whosoever wished to be admitted into the Seneca dominion would find himself accosted by the customary guard of distinguished sachems, judges and defenders by honored appointment, keepers-of-the-Gate. Wallis plunged Favel into the current of the Teaoga, making his approach toward a campfire burning midway on the peninsula. He touched the far shore, dismounted, and led his horse into the firelight.

He confronted a circle of silence. Coppery men, besmeared with ocher, vermilion; white lead and soot, breasts glorified by hieroglyphics of war, appraised him. One, by his ornamentation was a Delaware who, on seeing him, gave a start and then kicked a smoldering stick into the flames. Plainly, there was hate. Unable to contain his anger, the man bounded erect, paced from his side of the fire and stopped in front of Wallis. The warrior, glistening from grease and sunflower oil, towered a full head over Wallis. It was the merchant's turn for surprise. Bald Eagle! The scourge of Muncy Valley, the Delaware chief of the Minsi tribe, while holding no place in this council, was here! There would be little reason and much emotion in the coming deliberations. Bald Eagle's hatred, Wallis knew, stemmed from a land sale. The Delaware, defeated by the Seneca, had been resettled on Seneca land where their victors could be watchful of a former enemy. The very land, now to become their home, thereafter had been whittled away, whites entering the valley of the Minsi. The late Shickellamy, a person of consequence serving as the Six Nations ambassador, in 1736 by a treaty with the proprietory governor and provincial council in Philadelphia had negotiated away the Minsi occupied lands, making his bean mark to achieve a lasting peace. The ceded land then was parceled and large tracts sold to speculators, Wallis one. The presence of Bald Eagle would be an obstacle deflecting him from the purpose of his visit.

Wallis sensed he must cut the man to size. Employing their language, he lost no time flinging a taunt at the warrior. "Behold, the Seneca have given weapons into the hands of a woman. A Minsi sits at the council of those who have defeated him. Well may the other nations in the Confederacy wonder at the confusion in the lodges of the Seneca."

Ignoring the enraged Minsi, he saluted the assembled Seneca, "Brothers! Is the sun ashamed? Where is the hospitality of the Seneca? Have all the Elder Brothers nodded off to sleep, that a visitor is welcomed by rudeness? Where is a friend? Surely have I come as an ambassador with open hands and heart. Why, then, am I affronted by the leader of a conquered nation, the Delaware chief of the Minsi Tribe? Who gives Bald Eagle the right to insult me?

I came here to root up the tall weeds grown over your path to my house, that you may not stumble or be further oppressed in your travels. I am here to extract the thorns from your feet. I take away the sand and the gravel from your toes, and the bruises made by briars, all of which have made your last journey unpleasant. Henceforth in my house shall you be welcome. In your house may I be the same. I open the path between us. Even unto Bald Eagle I will extend my words."

Bald Eagle's lips had compressed. Studying every meaning in Wallis's face, he cried, "Judge if he has a double tongue! Be wary of this honio, this father of treachery. Do not be persuaded. The mountain of affection which he describes is but a nothing of words. It is not in his heart. This honio would stroke your heads with a knife."

Those who listened knew the source of the quarrel. It was the relinquishment of lands to Onas, William Penn, in exchange for eternal peace. They disregarded Bald Eagle's further tirade. Like a great roaring fire he needed containment.

A gesture from one of the seated sachems followed by shouts of disapproval for his bad manners silenced Bald Eagle. He retook his seat. The sachems knew it could well be an obligation, and as well be to their advantage to protect from harm those seeking to live in friendship. Wallis, they knew, was not as the Connecticut men who had earned their eternal enmity, who seized land and killed. He had bought fairly. The sachems waited for Wallis to continue.

Wallis began slowly. "Brothers!" he exclaimed. His voice boomed through the night and the fire seemed to flicker. "Brothers," he repeated, "I am pierced by the grief that prompts hatred. Rightfully has Bald Eagle broken glass into my eyes. He would make me feel the pain of his dead warriors. He is chafed in his heart and is sore in his mind. Yet, we all know the beginnings of this quarrel, and no good purpose is served by dwelling on the reasons when now is the time we all should be brothers. Let us not discard the long hope for peace. Were I covetous of more than the lands fairly purchased, covetous of your green grass and deep water, well might you close your ears against me. But this is not so, for then I would not dare to appear among you; and I say to Bald Eagle, 'O neighboring Delaware, I would take the ax from your skull; I would restore the breath of your kinsmen, were that possible.' I am not a man of war-like humor. I am a Quaker as was Onas. Stay your hatchets. Hear me. Then, if it be your decision, and I am adjudged an enemy, you may bring your ax and put me away all my days."

"Orenda! said one. "We would be each and all diminished, not to listen to a man of peace."

"Orenda!" seconded another, much impressed.

"Orenda!" grudgingly admitted Bald Eagle, admiring the fearless reply. "There is merit in what has been said."

An Indian who wore a cap of cowhorns produced a calumet and a pouch of tobacco, and made place for Wallis.

A horseman, a diminutive brave, forded the river. He pulled short of the circle and bounded into the light and to the kettle. Hair stiffened with beeswax, ill-favored features marked by small pox, he had covered his defects by emblazoning a white stripe down his left cheek. He ladled for a gobbet of meat, in the steam and ruddy glare resembling a devil-spirit. "This honio," he spat, pointing with his fatty fingers and using broken English, "him crazy oki. Little Bones hide in grass, in o-win-o-kah. Want him scalp. Paleface go like he no care. So me no scalp. Then me make ambush in kah-hah-go-na. where the pine grow by the water, between the two meadows. Little Bones say this time me send honio to oyadedionndiade. Me put him out like candle. Me raise tomahawk for big knock. Bah! Him come at me same as yeo hot for gakno wehaat. Him want to give away scalp. Him eats wiggling things. So - me no scalp. No know why no scalp" Little Bones concluded with an invective. There had been repressed laughter at Little Bones's reference to Wallis's coming at him much like a woman hot for a roll in the leaves.

Wallis puffed from the effigy pipe, the bowl a miniature angry face, twin to Little Bones. To the Great Spirit, as prescribed, he launched clouds of tobacco, much as he had done as a young man when he participated in Mohawk and Seneca ceremonials traveling with Joseph Brant. He handed back the pipe to the doorkeeper. "Isega onentgayei?" queried the man who wore the cap of cowhorns as he presented the pipe to the sky and to the fire. "Render us a sign!" A green log, propitiously, popped and sizzled, the heat striking into it.

"Ata!" cried one whose breast bore the emblem of a pine tree chief, "A speaker from the fire; the manito's reply."

The others wagged their shaven skulls. "Niio! A sign!"

The pine tree chief, who held the respect and affection of the others, then made a speech, a forty minute dissertation favorable to Wallis, which his auditors applauded with cries of 'Ho ho!' "We must consider," he concluded, "the circumstance which gives us life or death decision over this man. We have one foot on his neck because he has placed himself in a posture of humility. He did not come against us, but to us. Therefore he is his own recommendation. Let us not interrupt his good purpose."

Wallis then did the unexpected, pleasing to all and to the Delaware in particular. He produced a black blanket. "Older Brothers, Keepers of the Gate, this I spread, no blood of your dead warriors to remain on your garments, that your seats shall not be bloody. I cover their graves." Wallis didn't know the gesture had timely meaning, a war party now returning from Muncy.

Also in the lap of The Eagle he laid a silver buckle. "This I put on the shoe of the chief who 'was' my enemy that when next he comes toward my house it may be as a sign of my devotion." To each chief Wallis presented a cheap bracelet, "So you shall be reminded of my eternal clasp." Finally, putting his rifle into the hands of Bald Eagle, he said, "And I give you my rifle that you may pour sand into its mouth, as henceforth I shall go unarmed." Unhesitatingly Bald Eagle returned it. Wallis now prepared to press the issue of Muncy.

"Brothers, I am a Quaker. I am not warlike. I seek advice. There is one among you who I remember as your Councilor, who has foretold the long hope of your nation. I see nothing good for the Indian in the argument which has put white brothers into opposite camps. Brothers, I would talk with Cornplanter."

At Cornplanter's name Little Bones plucked a tomahawk from his, belt. Unknown to Wallis, the young warriors anxious for glory had renounced Cornplanter. His name, to some, was anathema; of his policy, moderation, they being contemptuous. Instead, as replacement the dark star of the cruel Hiakatoo was in the ascendancy. Passionately Little Bones screamed, "The Planter is a chief who has outlived his virility."

If the Planter had friends at this council, their silence indicated fear of Hiakatoo. The Seneca chiefs looked furtively away. Only Bald Eagle, a Minsi, seemed offended by the caustic tongued Little Bones. The Delaware chief was no friend of Hiakatoo, who once had called him a leader of a pretentious nation that could not be trusted, ever! Little Bones was denied more time to strut back and forth praising Hiakatoo by damning Cornplanter, for at that moment The Eagle in one leap fastened the fellow under his arm and dangled him much as one would a puppet. "Masters of this gate; is this a Seneca or a little bird, a noisy little bird? Were I Hiakatoo, who twists the necks of birds when he can find no other living thing to destroy, I would show you how fragile a spine may be." He flung Little Bones from him. "Go, sing your song on a far tree." Little Bones, deflated, gathered himself up and melted into the night.

Rid of the spy for Hiakatoo, the Elders gave Wallis welcome. The Pine Tree chief, in behalf of all, stated, "Brave Traveler, we accept your gifts; we welcome an alliance that would open a path through Muncy. Yet, with war voted against the settlements, and that war the decision of the Confederacy itself, only an authority higher than all of us can grant to Muncy the relief from war, which you ask. That is Joseph Brant of the Mohawks." The Pine Tree chief continued, "You are in favor with the Great Spirit, for Chief Joseph is a visitor in the Seneca Country, and this instant is at Chemung." Chemung was a village just a few miles upriver from Teaoga. "It would be best you go immediately there," the chief stated. "But I must warn you. The Mohawk visits with persons that can do you harm. One of these is Tisot, enfeebled by age, whose mind retires into the shadows. He believes he is a prophet for Pontiac, though Pontiac is many winters dead and the quarrel of that day forgotten. There you will find a second person who once was friendly to all, but because this war has claimed by death a son, is now bitter and may be revengeful toward whites. I speak of the powerful French-Indian queen known as Es-ter, queen of the village you passed just below here on the flats. She, too, visits Chemung this evening."

"Esther!" repeated Wallis. And then he chuckled, "Ata! May all my enemies be as Esther." His heart quickened at thought of her.

"It is not wise to go by yourself," advised the chief. "The United People brandish the hatchet. The woods conceal warriors." Clapping his hands, he summoned one of the warriors who had come in from scouting. "Dry Elk shall guide your footsteps."

At this Dry Elk, a broad shouldered brave, belched, wrapped a shabby blanket over the sharp ribs of a horse, tied a rope under its belly and knotted-another piece around his own. With a belch noisier than its predecessor, he draped himself on the wheezy animal which, after kicks of encouragement, testily trotted into the gloom. After him came Wallis, both men following the silvery Teaoga.

Chapter V

ESTHER

A quarter moon hung in the lisping water. Imperceptibly the country altered. Ruin and wreckage revealed where there had been migrant villages. An unkemptness marked the area. Trees were canted into the river, each become a sort of dam to catch the debris floating downstream. This wretched congestion was surpassed further inland by the profuse disarray of toppled trunks, oak, ash, spruce, hemlock, birch and magnolia, in crisscross heaps, swath upon swath. At one place, so vast was the destruction, wood piled on wood, that one could swear that giants plucking trees for war clubs had battled here. Again the country altered, the slender light of the moon encompassed by the heavy overhead of foliage. Darkness oozed from the earth. It was a resilient honeycomb of moss, absorbing all sound. They traveled thus, disembodied, earth and selves merged. Night and the forest had enveloped them.

Wallis sensed Dry Elk, more than he saw him. Twisting with the path, they traveled several miles north, then westerly with their only light that which was returned from the Teaoga. Abruptly Dry Elk jerked upright. He was swearing, belching, and rubbing his head where a low branch had bumped him. "O-en-kah! 'Goddam' as you say; tree take scalp!" Wallis, laughing, got down, led his horse past the hazard, and was about to remount when persons with bodies that smelled of grease pressed in upon him. Dry Elk, in quick exchange, identified himself to the security guards, these warriors then melting away.

Leaving the woods they struck extensive flats, cantering down a path through hundreds of acres of corn. Indeed this was a granary.

49

"Chemung," announced Dry Elk, gesturing at cheerful lights spread along the elbow of the river. By moonlight and fires Wallis counted thirty neat structures, framed and carpentered. The largest, unlike the others, was a typical Indian lodge, a thing of bark and skins with rounded roof and a slit at the apex to let out the smoke. In the center of the town, it was an anomaly among the European style buildings. Here Dry Elk halted. With a farewell eructation he wheeled his horse and padded off through the rows of cabins. 'Dry Belch' thought Wallis, coining a more appropriate name.

Wallis was alone, alone but for the dogs in the street and the voices behind the walls. A mongrel curled its lips, growling, hesitating between attack and retreat, when a woman's voice spoke out, whereupon the dog fled. The bearskin flap of the lodge lifted. In shock, unprepared for the sight, Wallis was unable to speak. In the entrance stood the yet beautiful Esther Montour so fondly remembered from his youth! God, she was a vision. She peered into the darkness. Stepping into the yellow triangle cast from the door, he swept his hat from his head, choked with emotion. Esther, half believing it was truly him, likewise remained wordless, then almost with a question, she softly spoke, "Samuel - Sam, is it really you?" He still could not gain his voice, advancing further into the light. Tremulously, she touched him. "You are real." And with this, tears of joy in his eyes, he swept her into his arms, the two embracing, entwined unashamedly. Momentarily all else ceased to matter, neither the passers on the street nor those within the lodge. Then, containing herself, but squeezing his hand, she dropped her voice to forewarn him, "Let us talk later, when we are alone. Come in. There is someone inside you know."

As he was about to enter, he whispered "I still love you. Have in the past, do so now, and will always."

She responded, "You are a fool, Sam, but that makes two of us." Then she masked her feelings, these to be beyond scrutiny.

Inside were two smokeyheads sitting cross-legged, their features wreathed in pipe eddies. Above the chieftains leered a collection of falsefaces. Mementos of battle and of ceremonial torture were hung from the wall. Axes, war clubs, knives, and an array of fiendish instruments suggested this lodge to be less a dwelling than a heathen museum of horrors. The younger of the chiefs, in the prime of his life, a commanding, personable man, extended his hand. "Giawiayia! Wallis!"

"Brant?" Wallis replied uncertainly, then repeated, "Joseph Brant! Devil if it isn't!" The youthful Joseph Brant that he had known was still traceable in the chieftain before him. The Mohawk was heavier than when he was emissary for Sir William Johnson and had ridden with Wallis from Johnson Castle to the Genesse. Brant wore little, a white breechcloth trimmed with a belt of purple wampum, and elkskin moccasins adorned with porcupine quills. At Teaoga Wallis had seen chiefs, their faces and breasts made into sunbursts of color and design. In contrast the War General of all, Brant, wore no manifestation of rank. The one ornament he affected was a gold finger ring, massively plain. In his eyes - with their moody expression and the brow perpetually furrowed - Wallis discovered the scholar friend of long ago.

"Yes," said Brant in cultured English. "A life time has passed since my leaving Moore's Charity School. It was a learning time as were the months that followed when you and I gained from each other, this being Sir William's intent."

"He was building bridges between our two cultures," Wallis remarked. Then he added, "That is why I am here, to rebuild that which has fallen apart. My people in Muncy believe the warriors of the Longhouse are on the 'high path', the 'warrior's path' rather than the smoother path of peace, and carry a red belt intending to bring harm to our valley. And it is happening as I speak. I come to plead for your hatchets to be sheathed. I extend a white belt of friendship between our peoples; in our standing together here, providence has meant for us to renew our personal good will."

Having said this, Wallis looked in the direction of Esther, overtaken by her beauty, with the light from the fire pit producing a sheen accenting her raven hair. There was a depth of expression in her eyes reflecting the suppressed passion they both felt. In her maturity she had not lost the delightful round of hip and the firmness of breasts of her youth. If anything she had grown to be more womanly. Her physique was enhanced by the stately bearing associated with her responsibility as a chieftain or queen among her people. The French-Indian woman, so near, prompted his involuntary sigh.

He awaited Brant's response to his overture for peace. But neither Brant, nor Wallis, nor Esther for that matter, were to carry the conversation further.

From his corner in the dwelling, the other smoker, an ancient warrior, a venerable whose sharp tongue compensated for smoke - dimmed vision, tottered toward Wallis. His face was parchment, his fingers talons of bone. This was Tisot, known to Wallis by repute, whose hatred for whites was proverbial. Here was a man with a pulse that beat to the drums of yesteryear. Tisot the implacable, careless to reality and confusing Brant with the dead Pontiac, was aghast that the Mohawk chieftain should be pleasant toward a white man. He asked in a high pitched voice, "Why is this one admitted to the councils of the Seneca? Is the door unguarded? Have the watchers fallen asleep, this paleface to have come unbidden from the night? Or have we here a dream-person, a ghost-walker? Brother, this is no friend; this is no real man; this is a skin, the jaw and flesh of a corpse which the steam-demon has dug up. The Death Giver has sent him to us. Dispatch this Devil-One with your knife, cut this sack that its evil may fly off into the darkness, or your strength shall go to the ground." His vitriol delivered, the grandfather warrior seated himself upon a fur and fanned himself.

Wallis was at loss. Brant remained impassive.

Esther, Wallis perceived, was embarrassed, and was groping for words. She spoke slowly to Tisot, knowing him far better than most; this from her often visits to this village which was nearby hers. She reprimanded him as she would a child. "Who speaks? Is it Seoewatha the tormentor that such evil blows from your mouth? Why is the peacemaker spat upon? Tisot, why do you dwell in another life-time? Come you forward from the past. Today the white men are not all our enemies. Some are friends. Have respect, Old Man!"

Tisot, still confused, would not put Pontiac back into his grave. With one last effort he cried, "Kill! The Ottawa orders it. War to the knife!" This said, Tisot seemed to slump in upon himself, and by degrees the madness left him. Fumbling in the residue of his disorder, plaintively Tisot called out, "How - but how shall I reason with Pontiac if we let this one go?" Then, flustered, he admitted "Ai-ee, Pontiac is dead. I have been brooding over dead fires. I dream with my pride." The old and withered chief, for an instant, drew himself erect and beat upon his chest, "Yet, I have lived! As ten men I have lived. I have boiled French and English heads in my kettle. I have warred with the Cats, Hurons, Neutrals and Carantouani." Then, with a crafty look much like a man about to make a bargain to his own advantage, he added, "And I have witnessed peace. Is there a peace-maker in my lodge? Come, why do we

52

not take the white wing from the wall and with it sweep the house clean, that there be no speck to fall into his eye, that his vision may be open? Be seated and honored, visitor, for we shall welcome you as a grandson. If my throat grows dry from greeting you, it is because it needs to be sweetened. Have you the 'milk' that comes in the kegs from Ny-ag-ara? Ai-ee, my grandson from the great English Fort, have you brought me my keg?" He licked his lips anticipating the whisky.

"Grandfather," Wallis told him, responding in the native tongue, "I came not from the North."

"Do not prolong your jest. There are many kegs kept in the North. Where is my gift?"

"I have no gift. I have journeyed from the south, from my home in Muncy. There are no kegs in the South."

"Eh?" stupidly said the old one.

"I came from Muncy," Wallis reiterated.

"Minsi? The Minsi-land? Otzinaschon! "Tisot's disappointment turned to wrath. "Otzinaschon is our land; you have stolen the land!" Seizing and shaking a rattle, he reproached Brant, "I have desired you not to let the palefaces build in that valley, in the land set aside for the Minsi. Burn his dwelling to the ground. If he has put up a strong house he will make bad use of it. Of certain he has violated our country, has usurped what is not his."

"Not true!" Wallis ejaculated. "The land was sold by the Confederacy to Onas, who then resold it."

Tisot feigned deafness. "You did not buy - you stole!"

"Bah!" said Wallis in English, then reverted to the old man's tongue. "How can you accuse me? You yourself have eaten and drunk of the price."

"You stole! - You stole!"

"The price has passed through your guts," patiently Wallis replied.

"Hey-a-a-hey! Gifts, trifles for which you would say the land is yours. My fathers sleep in that earth. None may buy it. The Longhouse, like the sky, is not to be divided."

Wallis gestured for Esther's interference. "Grandfather," she responded, "are you in pain? Has a bean become stuck in your ear? Does it deafen you to reason? Must I repeat after our guest, the land was sold to him? It is his."

"Land cannot be sold. The Great Spirit gave it to our fathers. Say what you will, Yeo, your guest shall roast and I will pick his bones. Tomorrow I will listen to the howls of the white dog." Chewing on his lips, he lay back unable to continue. His features had become livid.

Brant sought to shift the conversation, to question Wallis. "Foster Brother, it is reported you did not give our warriors space to rest their heels when last they passed through your valley."

"They came with guns under their blankets, meaning to make war. My people only defended themselves. Does not my appearance here prove my wish for friendship?"

"Why, then did you not announce yourself earlier, when came the others who are loyal to the King, and of whom some have joined together, to be known as Butler's Rangers?"

Esther took up Wallis's defense, the liquid quality of her Seneca speech being womanly soft. "Joseph, as for Sam's not coming when came others, what matters it? So he is late, but he is here! Are men a field of standing corn to nod their heads all together? If the war is not his, is it to be put upon him? Is he a stranger that you treat him with suspicion? Is he to hear himself reviled by Tisot and doubted by Brant? Let Tisot strangle with indignation; his is the prejudice of another generation. But you, Joseph, why have you put aside that which I cannot, that Sir William looked upon both of you as his sons? Remember, he is your brother, Joseph, and should not be faulted for seeking peace."

Brant shifted uneasily, then with a half laugh reacted. "Woman, you have a tomahawk for a tongue. Say on."

"Joseph, there may be a reason why Sam is slow to have set foot toward us. Perhaps he left his heart here and did not wish to come back for it. "

For a moment there was absolute silence. Then Wallis flashed her a look that bespoke of his deeper feelings. As for Brant, her eloquence persuaded him. He nodded his head, sensitive to the bond between the two. It was a suspected but new revelation.

Tisot, grunting, reentered the conversation. Typical of the older generation, he made his point by a parable. "Hear this! I have reflected on this newcomer. He presents himself as a brother to the Great Chief Joseph. Yet Joseph, oh mighty Theandeaga, I forewarn you! He is evil." Tisot fumbled for a belt, a masterpiece of beadwork from which he prompted his memory. "There is an early story of our forefathers. In the dawn of life they tell how big animals spewed from holes in the earth, animals with big horns upon their heads. They would rush upon our people, killing all, if not with their horns, by trampling upon them. And if not by these ways, by cunning. It is told how Neeonwaachi, a chief first in renown, was informed of an animal in the woods. Having armed himself well, and having painted his face, he entered upon the path only to meet in the depth of the woods a friend reported to have been killed by the beast. Overjoyed to find this friend alive, Neeonwaachi sat with him and partook of a gourd of honey, the while being informed by his friend, 'Neeonwaachi, did you not hear? The beast is destroyed, so sit with me awhile, and do not hurry.' Truly the warrior chief was glad. He sat and visited with his friend long into the evening. At last when he came to rise, he found the sweet honey made him sluggish. He could not lift himself. Then did horror possess him and beads of sweat stand on his brow, and his eyes disbelieve what he saw, for his friend was the animal disguised in man-shape! Then did the animal throw off its false skin and stab the sagamore with its tusk. Theandeaga, I tell you this because the paleface is that kind of thing; his sweet words delay you, and will enervate you and draw your strength to the ground. Go, Theandeaga! Go from here before you are no more. Do not refuse my wisdom, 0 Mohawk."

Brant cracked a walnut and picked at the meat. What could he say in response to this garrulous fool? Throwing the broken shell to the floor, conversation impossible, he rose, nodded to all, then stamped into the night seeking the log house where he was quartered. They heard a dog ki-yi as he kicked it from his path. Brant had vented his frustration. Wallis opened his mouth, then clamped it shut, feeling Tisot had effectively destroyed the purpose of his mission. All was lost. Equally disquieted, furious at Tisot, Esther hissed in his face, "Who, Wrinkled Face, are you to twice offend a guest? Why do you make an insult of the hospitality of the Seneca? And who are you, standing on one leg in the past, to show disrespect for Theandeaga, the Mohawk Chief, to drive him from this house with your childish fables? Remove yourself from my sight, Old Man," the woman chieftain warned, "or I shall put you in the darkness wherein your mind dwells." She snatched up an axe as if to brain him, and struck a support post with such vehemence that chips flew and the skin-and-bark lodge shuddered.

The wizened grandfather glared from almost sightless orbs. "The Demon sits in your mouth," he muttered. As if Esther and Wallis did not exist, he groped toward the fire. With unsteady hands he poured himself a cup of fish broth, sipped it, then tottered to the farthest end of the structure where he enclosed himself in a trade blanket and fell to snoring.

"Come," said Esther. "We shall go to my cabin." Wallis followed.

CHAPTER VI

THE VOLUNTEERS

The departure of the volunteers from Muncy had been, to a degree, buoyant. Their waysore arrival at Forty Fort was in contrast. Shoulders slumped, they halted in the center of the town, being met there by Captain Spalding. "We have had Indian trouble upon the road," reported Levi. "One of my men, Hotchkiss, needs medical attention." The wounded man, listing in the saddle, blood caked to his shirt, a bullet in his side, was eased to the ground. Brought into Captain Spalding's home, laid on the kitchen table, the former trapper awaited the surgeon, biting his lips in pain. Dr. Ebenezer Menema was sent for. In the meanwhile, the Captain heard Levi's account.

Levi gestured, "It was an ambush, neat put, never a gun barrel nor a face to be seen until we had dismounted to water our horses."

"There was one man, sir," added Tim Murphy, "who was a wonder for size, seven foot if an inch. He seemed to be running the show, leastways till I slightly nicked him."

Spalding's eyebrows shot up. "Hiakatoo!"

"A-Who?" asked Levi.

"Hi-yak-atoo," repeated the veteran captain, rapping off the name in clipped sections, like bullets. "He's a chief from the west newly come to power. A giant. He's seldom turned in a struggle. Having survived, you may brag of it."

"The Lord saved us." It was Baldwin speaking. "Yes, sir, the Lord and the Lieutenant and the Sergeant's shooting. If the Lieutenant hadn't ordered us to catch saddle and rush the laurel where they was hid, and if Sergeant Murphy at gallop hadn't done a piece of fancy shooting, putting a notch into that heathen, they would have had fair sport with us, my scalp to be in somebody's hair bag."

Spalding reserved his opinion until after Levi's contingent had dispersed to their quarters in several homes. "Mr. Brady," he said, clearing his throat. "In what fool's paradise were you, not to have reconnoitered your advance? Where were your flanks and point? Sir, you lay claim to having had a commission with Morgan. Was it in barracks that you commanded?" As Levi's face reddened, Captain Spalding laid into him again. "That you had a level-headed group, who obeyed your command to catch saddle and charge, rather than succumb to the fatal instinct to scatter, reflects to their glory, not to yours. I dare say, had you given them a formula for their protection, had you posted scouts, such men would have smelled your Indians. Further, sir, it wasn't the charge that broke Hiakatoo - he'd stand you and cut you to the ground - irrespective of a flesh wound. You probably fatally scored on one of his subalterns. Rather than have you gain his lines and bring dishonor to the corpse, Hiakatoo left off fighting to pack his cadaver to the rear. In battle Hiakatoo will accord his enemy an advantage, in this instance a precious reprieve, to preserve a departed brother from having his scalp whacked off."

Levi, fortunately for his temper, was distracted from the lecture. He saw a better subject deserving of his attention. She stood in the doorway. She was petite, five foot, with all the right things properly placed.

Over his Captain's shoulder he could see she was bursting with contained laughter. He wanted to laugh, too, but maintained his stiff posture. As he more closely examined her, he took notice how she put her hand to her corn-silk hair as if to adjust a comb, perhaps more to point up her bosom, or to bring attention to the milky complexion of her lifted arm, this suggestive of the womanly concealments awaiting the pleasure of discovery. Captain Spalding's words were interrupted by the appearance of Dr. Menema from the kitchen, where he extracted the bullet and treated the wound. "Your man," he said, as he unrolled his sleeves, "will live, but he is very tired. Move him to a bed, and fetch me at once if he is feverish, though the cure now lies in nature. Now, sirs, I too am tired. Lieutenant Brady, I have agreed to your being quartered at my home. It is the first house beyond here, down the path. Come, sir."

While the doctor packed his surgical case, Levi escaped outside. He was disappointed. His enchantress had flown. He sauntered along the path, more to catch the air than with expectation of finding her, of mind to question the doctor as to her identity. As he came abreast a lilac bush someone stepped from around the heavy shrub. At once his cutting knife flew to hand, his overplayed nerves imagining an Indian. "Oh Mr. Brady!" The voice was feminine. It was she.

"You spoke in time." He sheathed his knife.

"Now I am safe, or am I?" she flirted.

"Would you want to be?" opportunely he replied. Dr. Menema opened Spalding's door and stood on the porch scanning the path. "Hist!" Levi whispered. "Shall I see you again?"

For reply she laughed.

"Please."

"Abby?" called Dr. Menema, descending from the porch, adjusting his coat, then finding her with Levi just up the path. "Well, my dear," he said, "I gather you and the Lieutenant have introduced yourselves." Confronted by a terrible thought, Levi gazed at her, then back toward Menema, a man about forty, thinking, 'What an ass, I. She's Mrs. Menema.' Then, in further admiration of her charms, he repeated to himself with twist of meaning, 'What an ass.' He sighed. Twice today he almost had been entrapped.

To add to his consternation and utter confusion, he heard Dr. Menema suggest, "Lieutenant, you and Abby walk on ahead. I've forgotten my surgeon's apron."

'A curious family,' Levi thought. 'Assuredly the Doctor must know his wife would turn her hip into another's bed. Does he invite me into his home, I to be a lamb come goat? Or is he resigned to himself being a cuckold?' Abby, not to be put off, locked her arm into his, she smitten by this handsome, tall officer. If a moment ago it would have delighted him, sending wild thoughts through his head, now he was miserable. And when, in a secluded stretch, she paused and gravitated her body against his, in a brazen invitation, her breasts burning holes through his jacket, in his dismay he cried out, "Ambushed!"

Startled, Abby looked about, saw nothing of danger, then with widened eye commented reproachfully, "You misled me with your words, Lieutenant. My response was to what I thought was a mutual attraction."

Stepping back from her, he stated, "I would not offend Dr. Menema."

"Offend Dr. Menema? And what about me?" Thereafter they walked in silence, she miffed, he trying to reason how she could be so forward and damn it, so married. And yes, so beautiful and so wantonly available.

The Menema home was a hospital. Bookshelves bulged with materia medica. Potions of all sorts existed in crockery pots. Flagons contained somber fluids and biles. On the floor were larger sealed jars holding kidneys, a brain and sundry organs, all immersed in liquid. When Menema waved him toward the table with its bottle of port and slab of cold ham, the small carving knife the Doctor wielded reminded Levi of the knife used on Hotchkiss. Perhaps it was. The ham and trapper Hotchkiss somehow became inextricably one. Appetite lost, he narrowed his interest down to drinking. "You put everything to double purpose," he remarked, observing Menema dip his seegar into a bleeding bowl.

"The Menema family is that way, practical," said the good Doctor with a brief smile. "In life sometimes one uses whatever is nearest to respond to a need that must be met."

"You are a philosopher," Levi mumbled, not sure where in hell the Doctor was leading.

"Pragmatist is a more pointed word. I have an observation I wish to share with you. I recognize you are a venturesome man. Because I know my Abby, frankly, in all candor and absolute openness I say to you be careful."

Levi jumped to his feet. "Are you accusing me of playing Romeo to your wife?"

Abby looked thunderstruck. Menema lowered his seegar, then began to shake with laughter. "My wife? Abby, my wife? Dear sir, Abby is my child, my youngest and oldest, my whole family. I but say, if you have an itch, an affection for Abby, and I detect she too is so afflicted, to each of you I say just take caution."

Levi summoned courage to voice his embarrassment. "To both of you I apologize, to you Doctor, and to your most attractive daughter, to you Abby, if you will forgive me."

"Then make sure you keep in mind my candor. See that you bundle, not bungle. Seegar, Lieutenant?"

Thereafter the evening passed pleasantly.

As the Doctor had promised, Levi and Abby found themselves abed, divided by a wooden rail. "Hell," said Levi, frustrated. "Hell," echoed Abby. He tore out the rail, she immediately in his arms, her hand reaching for his throbbing manhood, he moving his fingers to her nipples, these standing erect in all their glory. It would be a night of little sleep and much discovery. In the next room the Doctor snored, careless to the world.

Chapter VII

THE MILITIA AT
FORTY FORT

To understand the people at Forty Fort Township a dweller in Boston, or in Philadelphia, or any seaboard city had but to consult a map. The six thousand were a people diluted in a vast area, dependent upon forts such as Wilkes-Barre to the south, Forty Fort midway up the valley, and Fort Jenkins, a pompous designation for a farmhouse at the head of the valley. A fourth fort downstream from Jenkins was also a farmhouse, one of substantial size and garrisoned by the large Wintermute family. The Wintermute structure however was considered a menace. The Wintermutes courted none, spoke seldom, and shared only a geographical proximity; they were viewed with suspicion as were the Amalekites and Midianites in the land of Israel during the days of Gideon. They never showed their faces at a Connecticut funeral or wedding; and their language was guttural German. His Satanic Majesty in England was of German blood. The hired soldiers imported by the boatload to America were Westphalians and Hessians. Unseen and uninvited at council the disassociated Wintermutes kept to themselves. Augmenting these forts were the blockhouses, rude but effective rallying points. Other than Wilkes-Barre the nearest post, Forty Fort was almost cut off by inhospitable terrain. Relief, at best in small numbers, could come to Wyoming Valley only after extreme hardship through swamp and forest. Such was the tenuous lifeline of a community virtually deprived of assistance. The settlers likened their valley to an island within a rising flood of Iroquois hate.

Forty Fort, entrenched in its own stubbornness, defied the war chiefs. Despite its untenable position, Forty Fort held forth relying upon one paramount attribute. In the valley's citizenry were numerous ex-soldiers of merit, officers formerly with the British North American Army, and younger officers wounded and furloughed home from service with General Washington. These, while they scarcely could discharge their strenuous profession afield, were able to advise and train their fellows to resist aggression. If Forty Fort had lent its youngest and best to the main war, there were many among the very young and the old who could drill and did. One in three of the elders had served ably in the Indian wars.

For a decade the Connecticut men had known the bugle and the clatter of cavalry and men streaming to the high mountains to repel poaching Pennsylvanians. Having settled these rich tracts under a King Charles charter, to have their claims disputed by Pennsylvanians with authority from a succeeding English ruler, they had resisted this encroachment until the Rebellion. And then they ceased shooting at the Pennamites to level their flintlocks in a second direction, at the common foe, personified by Hiakatoo whose hordes, rising like hornets, were in deadly swarm. Forty Fort Valley knew war and how to cope with it. It was logical that Forty Fort sponsored the Free Company. It was also logical that bipartisan Captain Spalding, whose friendly disposition toward the Pennamites antedated the colonial misunderstanding, was nominated as company commander.

It was natural for Wallis, also facing difficulty from the Indian, to correspond with the Captain on this common matter prior to his secret journey to Teaoga. In a letter to Wallis the Captain noted his men were 'at your service', his company designed to be an aggressive body to go in pursuit of raiding war parties. In this exchange Wallis mentioned that his former man of all purposes, Samuel French, was coming to the Company. He trusted the Captain would recognize the man's worth. In due process, French was appointed a corporal. The honor, if a gesture of politics, was not misapplied.

A little authority is as a yeast for a man's character, puffing up the good or the bad. In French it created a fine soldier. In Timothy Murphy, when Levi hinted to the famous marksman he was being considered for a commission, it inspired agitation. Tim, setting his cap at belligerent cock, marched up to Spalding, saluted the Captain, and swore, "Sir, I will bolt to the enemy afore I would be published on the company roster as an ensign. I am a sharpshooter and proud of it, but not an officer. Any fool can line up a passel of men and snap at them as they march." If Spalding meant to elevate Murphy after that, it would have been with the toe of his boot.

On a dusty bit of earth fenced around, Spalding called out the names of the motley collection of recruits from which so much was to be expected. The lanky and the rotund looked at each other, as they answered the roll. So this was the company. "For sure," muttered Grove to Baldwin, studying his twenty companions, "if we don't find action soon, we'll get it squabbling among ourselves, some of us having practiced our aim shooting at one another in the past, this company being Pennamite and Wild Yankee cross-mix."

"Anytime you're ready," growled a lanky Connecticut recruit, itching to start the argument up.

"Silence!" shouted Lieutenant Brady.

"How'd this Connecticut place come to be called 'Farty' Fort?" the feisty peddler Shaffer asked of the lanky fellow, deliberately mangling the pronunciation. This almost touched off a free for all. It would have happened but for the intervention of massive 'Dutchy' Pence who interposed his bulk.

A more amiable man, Jim Plouser, a schoolmaster prior to being wounded soldiering, and now recuperated, explained, "The name's from the original 40 Connecticut proprietors, granted township shares by the Susquehanna Company. They built this fort to fend off Pennsylvania counter claims." He pointed to the double walled enclosure of planted, sharpened logs. "The barracks roofs are carpentered to the walls and serve as platforms from which to take aim."

In sight of the fort the Free Company was to practice military drill, sharing exercises which Colonel Zebulon Butler imposed upon the regular garrison. Apart but in the loose grip of Colonel Nat Dennison was the 24th Connecticut Militia. Butler, who commanded the 2nd Connecticut Regiment Continental Army, had been furloughed home to ready the valley for war. Altogether he had eight companies, these though, sprinkled with veterans. Of these the Free Company enjoyed a peculiar status; it was neither free nor a company. It was skeletal in numbers. With the passing days the cadre was augmented by a series of transfers, Butler providing Spalding with the select marksmen he needed for adventuring up the Susquehanna. Spalding also got rid of his troublemakers.

In uniform and weaponry there were marked distinctions between the Independent Company and Butler's militia. The militia wore blue or brown coats usually trimmed in red and was equipped with small bore muskets capable of hitting a target at 80 yards, 100 the best. Beyond that one might as well shoot at the moon. Several were stamped with the date of 1717 vintage, these with wooden ramrods. Spalding's Independents had been issued the coveted Pennsylvania Rifle, which could drop a man at 150 yards. Its one disadvantage was its lack of mounts for affixing a bayonet, but this was offset by issuance of iron hatchets and long knives to the Rifle Company. Their uniform was the same as Morgan's Riflemen, that of the frontiersman, a leather frock or hunting coat, and high top Indian leggings. In an exhibition well attended, Murphy demonstrated his sharpshooter's skill which had taken down a British general and two aids at Saratoga.

The company, honed to readiness, wondered why its marching order was not issued. Butler advised Spalding, "The Seneca are spying on us from the woods, maybe in some numbers. They're up on the ridge. It would be unhealthy to sally out, watched as we are. Later, yes, when their eyes have left the mountain tops."

Spalding passed this on to Levi. "You know, Lieutenant, in view of our thinness, it's unhealthy to go now. The fort's being watched. Later. Our best weapons are stealth and audacity both in departure and in future engagement. As a company we're rather light for head butting with a heavy war party."

"We're really a forlorn hope," Levi commented, mentioning the term describing a body posted to duty beyond a main force. "Too big to avoid detection, too little to do battle."

Spalding added, "With differences. The forlorn hope is sent out to make the enemy show itself, and it has an army behind it. We'll have no army behind us. Our purpose is to fall upon the Seneca with surprise, then skeedaddle as fast as we can. That's the hand we have. Our thinness works for our mobility."

Butler used the delay to inflict more discipline. Plouser explained his insistence on drill. "In January '77 the Colonel saw General

Hugh Mercer's brigade take its stand at Stony Brook Bridge, but two miles from Princeton, and then, for want of steady response to his commands, fall in disarray and crumple before Mawhood's British bayonets. The British regulars came on, moving as one man. The General went down, gunbutted, stabbed many times, expiring as General Washington intervened and personally rallied the troops. Butler holds the bitter thought our victory at Princeton should have been less costly. This past winter at Valley Forge he watched Prussian General Baron von Steuben give the troops firmness of response by practicing them at marching, so drill your asses off, boys, and don't bitch."

Thus, the air of Forty Fort was rent with cries, "Slope Arms! By fours, quick march! Come along there, quick march!" Butler harried them until they wheezed. The Free Company was learning, painfully, its capacity for endurance. When they buckled from exhaustion, he wheeled them twice around the broad meadow. If a man complained, he had a sure-fire cure; he would run with a bayonet behind the offender, and woe if the man faltered. None did.

Under friendly trees by the banks of the Susquehanna the women of this valley tended their knitting and breast-fed their babies while their menfolk, viewed from a field's length, to the faint cries of the officers gave flawless, effortless response. At closer surveillance all was dust and ragged turning. Weary of drill, Tim Murphy could think only bad thoughts, that his trusted friend, the Lieutenant, had fouled him up royal. As an army marksman he had enjoyed more freedom than this life offered. So, why was he here? Talked into it. Corporal French, too, had doubts about this constant marching. He had discovered Yankee Doodle could have fallen arches. As for Sergeant Baldwin, despite his recent promotion, he, also, had reservations. His face a mass of sweat, twenty pounds lost, he pondered the limits of patriotism and of his personal endurance. "The Company will go for the hills and home," he grated to the Lieutenant, "if this Jack A of a colonel doesn't let up. Sir, we came for a shooting war. When do we get it?"

"Careful," hissed Levi, having spied the Colonel hoving round the company.

"Captain Spalding," shouted Butler, "get your men toward the trees and dismiss them. Storm's coming."

Bad weather was forecast in the black clouds to the east. As the companies pivoted one upon the other, the women, clucking to their children, took the little ones toward the wagons. They were women of one stamp, a patient, chore-burdened lot whose only holiday consisted of being away from home these few hours. Their presence here was dictated by their vulnerability, were they to remain unprotected at home, those furthest out more likely to be visited by marauding Indians. These devoted women, each a sermon of fidelity and obedience, each a bringer of endless children into the world, each with torso thickened and spread, while they were friendly among themselves, studiously avoided one woman, Rachael, wife of Asa Greenacre, a farmer. Unlike them, unlike these women with care-worn and sometimes angular features, Rachael possessed all the attributes, if ever theirs, that inspired their jealousy, their hatred, and offended their Puritan ethic. If, in certain respects, one made a comparison between Abby and Rachael, both with great beauty though of different type, the comparison ended there. Abby was unmarried. Abby was for one man. Abby was not a competitor.

Rachael by her very sensuous body language, hip swing and bursting jiggling breasts, was a hussy. She posed a threat. Women hated her instantly, and for reason. Rachael was a creature to disorder all men's senses, to make bachelors sigh and married men to compare their own catches, suffering heartburn while at it. She was an effect rather than a description. To fashion words, her hair was chestnut, her eyes full of suppressed fire, her lips generously formed and amenable. To those few whose refuge was piety, this figure of voluptuousness represented temptation as only Satan bestowed. But the Parson, in agonizing distress himself, reasoned, he ever windy with his words, 'The Lord is never a one to bedevil mankind. No, she is not a temptress but a perfect creation of the Almighty, a mold given to angels from heaven.' Then the preacher, his own lechery surfacing, added, 'So why should we complain? Let us look to beauty as we must, as God's reminder of that which is good.' Whatsoever his logic, to those who dared pass a greeting to her, her low pitched acknowledgment was pulse stirring. Yet, she meant nothing by it. She was not as she appeared to be; regardless, the blame was upon her.

For Asa Greenacre it was a late marriage, for Rachael an early one. To hear tongues wag, it had been a parent's wish to settle a daughter more quickly than she could gravitate into sin that had influenced the speedy union. There were times Asa wished he was still a bachelor. Prior to his marriage he had demonstrated an inventive nature which somehow had ceased. In chemistry he had excelled, perfecting a mixture which, when cloth was saturated with it, discouraged the rain from wetting one's bones. Reasoning his discovery might be a tonic against the sweats by acting as an internal waterproofing, he had swallowed part of a cupful, and for ten days lay at death's door, in vain the hopeful undertaker waiting. Asa's trip downstream and his bringing back a bride had arisen out of his desire to procreate a son. After two years, there being no issue, the pleasures involved having worn away, he had taken to coupling with a jug rather than with Rachael, giving her blame for his impotence. "I have bought a dry cow," he had been heard to say when in his cups.

And he had had other setbacks, dabbling as he did in the chemistries of leaves and grasses. This would-be botanist had attempted to cross the elixirs of the four leaf clover, both as to its mystical exudence of good luck, and as to its appearances, these somehow to be grafted into the leaves of the poison ivy, masking the devil's curse within the proposed hybrid. He was motivated to plant this nefarious and illogical anomaly of nature, were he to be able to create it, in somebody else's lawn, after dark of course. The owner of that lawn, an Irishman toward whom he had an intestinal dislike, he expected would pluck the clover for its luck. Instead of befouling his victim, Asa infected himself navel to crotch, he a marvel of discontent, scratching at his nether parts as he drilled.

At the home of Sergeant-Major Asa Greenacre, of the 6th Company, Corporal French was quartered. The two men, much alike in general build, in their moods were opposites, Sam French vitally happy, Asa hard-drinking, dejected. On militia afternoons the Frenchman and Greenacre by horse drawn cart rode to and from the drill ground. Invariably Rachael would drive. Dismissed early because of the brewing storm, the two men clambered into the cart. the threat of rain increasing as the trio approached the farmhouse. Dark clouds had arched the sky, accumulating in such density that one could expect a disgorge of water immediately. A lightning flash and rumble lent urgency. "'Twill be a sea come down upon us," predicted Asa, not far from the truth, backing the cart into its shed and unhitching the horse to manage its own comfort against the lee wall. Rachael had gone ahead into the house, escaping the torrential downpour that burst upon them. The two men ran for the house, as if on a bullet swept field. A blinding bolt exploded among the apple trees, hitting the nearest. "Saint Benedict Labre!" howled the Frenchman, knees buckling. Asa, ashen, stood weaving. A second bolt, scarcely more removed, brought order to their senses. Legs strengthened by fear, they hurtled into the house, Rachael laughing at their bedraggled looks. 'By the Saints!' French thought, infected by her throaty laugh, 'Here is a woman!' It was a laughter by gesture, the storm cannonading the house, walls of water falling. A cataract spouted off the eaves above the open door. Rachael turned to shut it.

At that precise instant the unexpected occurred. Virtually, as her hand reached to close the door, through the wall of water floundered a man. Spilling the storm from his cape, muddying the floor with his boots, he stamped into the room.

Mouths agape, Asa and the Frenchman watched him untie his cape and hang its dripping mass on a peg near the fire. He then removed his hat with the green and white feathers denoting he was an aide-de-camp to the Commander-in-Chief. He stood close to the warmth of the hearth. Asa and French forgot their own dripping state. The man's handsome, forceful face broke into wrinkles of good humor. "Madam, sirs," he shouted, his voice pitched above the cannonade, "I think the Susquehanna, if not the ocean itself, has moved its course. My escort is back along the road lost under a breastwork of water; my horse no doubt miles ahead, having thrown me and bolted with the lightning." He said no more, waiting for the noise to subside.

Wondering why the man wore no rank, Asa buttoned his half-undid shirt with the chevrons. "Bound for Forty Fort, Sir?"

"Sergeant-Major, by the looks of the weather, no; by my intentions, yes! I was enroute to Colonel Zebulon Butler."

"Sir, when the storm breaks off I'll carry you to him."

Asa surmised the officer bore marching orders for the militia, all militia answerable to Congress. Why else was this stranger here? In this opinion he was strengthened upon hearing the visitor's name to be Kirkland, he the famous Pastor Kirkland. Kirkland had been a missionary among the Oneida and now was serving as military chaplain in the Continental Army. Perhaps Kirkland had come to the frontier to assist in organizing a campaign against the Seneca.

The storm abating, it now a steady rain, Kirkland showed impatience to be about his business. While Asa and the Dominie hitched up the mare, afoot Sam French slogged in an opposite direction to rouse out Captain James Bidlack and others. Kirkland wished to convene a board of war in the council room of Forty Fort. French agreed to start the process of notification.

They were quick to assemble, all highly elated, their visitor perhaps bringing news that an expedition soon would be mounted. Those present, from the most junior ensign to Colonel Zebulon Butler, were therefore astounded when the tidings proved otherwise. Each had been prepared to hear orders for action against the Indians; instead, they were being drafted for duty in the Continental Line! A quarter of their number would be leaving.

Stunned to silence, they suddenly broke into a babble of protest. It would be a fatal error, a senseless decision. They were needed here, not on the Hudson! The Indian would be certain to push in on the valley, as one captain asserted, once its protective companies were reduced. The reality of these orders shook every man. "Preposterous!" cried a dozen by their expressions. "Unthinkable!" they argued. They were not regulars to be ordered up, but volunteers for home guard. Some had already served in the regular army. They complained that although Congress had the right to seek State levies, enough was enough! That right had been previously well exercised, the valley having met two drafts, their quota fulfilled in the preceding two years. It behooved Spalding to indicate there were, currently, two hundred men from Forty Fort on duty in the Continental Army. "To strip off more would be to leave our families naked of defense," he stated.

"We've been bled enough," seconded Captain John Franklin. "The Indians will be here as soon as the companies march out." So argued the captains and lieutenants while Butler kept a sympathetic silence.

"Sir!" cried Levi, addressing Pastor Kirkland. "I am prompted to remind you, sir, of the number of us who have already had service in the Continental Line. I, for one, more than once have had British bayonets at my throat. I am no slacker; I was with General Morgan from the day he recruited his Corps. I was in Boston, sir; I was at Paoli, and I curse that day; I held the ladder for Arnold when he climbed the walls of Quebec; and I was out of my head nineteen days with ague at Crown Point, with never a stitch to cover me, and my body buried in sand, and the rain pelting down. I was, sir, also at Saratoga and Stillwater. And I cannot remember my countless skirmishes in meeting up with patrols of the enemy. Sir, today I see my duty here! I am under personal orders from

General Washington, having been sent to this western border to bolster its defense. A critical time has come to the frontier." As Levi spoke, the officers listened intently. He continued. "You say the war is to be won on the coast. For the settler such victory would be meaningless, with his home burnt, his family and friends slaughtered. I am told by my own Captain that in two years, if we count the companies you request, this valley will have furnished by volunteer and by draft seven companies to the Continental Line! I do not say we object to service in the Army, but I do declare those absent - were they here - would give us a comfort we do not now enjoy. To take more of us would be fatal. And it would be foolish inasmuch as this valley is the link by which the chain of smaller frontier forts suspends, Antes, Horn, and so on. I beg, you, sir, search elsewhere for your reinforcements! And if you find anyplace with men to spare, send us some quick-time. We're all stripped." The officers, even Butler, cheered.

Beet-red, Washington's emissary exclaimed, "Impassioned speeches aside, by the authority of the Continental Congress the Commander in Chief's order stands. Colonel Butler, two companies will march!" The grumbling was loud. Kirkland, leaning sideways, whispered something to Butler. Whatever it was, the Colonel seemed pleased. Then, puzzled as he heard more, he finally nodded in agreement.

Butler got to his feet. "Gentlemen, after I select the two companies, their respective commanders will be informed. You are dismissed. Lieutenant Brady, please remain." With stony faces the officers filed out, convinced Levi was to be tongue lashed if not stripped of his commission. In a voice that carried to the last of the departing officers, Bulter said, "Lieutenant, as of this moment you are relieved of duty with Captain Spalding's Company."

Unflinchingly Levi's eyes settled on the real author of this order, Kirkland. "If this is a board of court-martial, Sir, I would like to hear the bill of particulars."

"Hold up! This is not a court-martial, in no way, sir, but it will be if you do not bridle your tongue. Reverend Kirkland was patient enough to hear you to your last word. Be patient yourself, he to be heard. You may just like it, hot head!"

"Lieutenant, I came to this valley with two purposes, one you know, and the other being the discovery of a man such as you, your name suggested to me by no less than General Washington. I have a secret to impart. It fits my purpose that others view you in disgrace, relieved of duty and to be stripped of rank. When you leave this room you must give that impression, none of which, of course, is true. You are still a lieutenant acting under direct orders from the General. Listen carefully, Lieutenant, for you are about to be charged with a task which might well lead to the winding down of this frontier war. Its success or failure hinges on a man of your cut. It requires a man of your temperament, and conviction in oneself. Too, knowledge of the frontier, which you have, as well as mastery of the tongue of the Senaca. To it we must add luck and fortitude in the presence of utmost danger, and this last you have demonstrated many times. Mind, you may lose your life. But risk is not new to you. There is only this comfort, our young nation ever will be grateful. And you will have my prayers. Sir, will you volunteer for a business that, dangerous though it be, could save lives and achieve peace?"

"Yes, Sir!" Levi responded without hesitation.

"This is what must be done. You know I served as pastor among the Indians. An Oneida tribesman, bound by loyalty to me, with ears that hear much, gave me insight to British strategy. Colonel Bolton at Fort Niagara is pushing the Indians to broaden the war. He wants the tribes to combine into a large war party, something except in Pontiac's time, they have never before done, and to strike south. If Bolton convinces the independent minded Indians, those who are wavering, to take up the hatchet, were that to be, then no force of ours would be able to resist them, had we eight companies or twice eight companies to guard this valley. Indeed the two companies for which you argued so eloquently would not stave off the calamity. I have talked with General Washington and he agrees our best way to halt the Indian is at his own council fire. By the grace of providence we have a friend at that council fire, a chief who could split the Seneca Nation in twain."

"And who might that be?" Levi asked.

"Patience, Lieutenant. First, let me say were the Seneca to remain divided on this war we would be cutting their potential to do damage. Since they are the most numerous of the several tribes, outweighing by far the Mohawk, the success in keeping them divided would be a telling blow against their ability to make war. In essence the key to circumventing Bolton's strategy lies in keeping the Seneca off the war path. While we have the Oneida on our side, as the Seneca say in comparison with themselves, in number the Oneida are 'cat's meat'. You are to seek out the one Seneca leader who can help. The chieftain of whom I speak, if he is to win the minds of his brethren, must be given assurances meaningful to the Seneca Council when he addresses its members. Otherwise he will not speak in our behalf. The General wishes to offer each Indian Nation a seat in the American Congress, they to be properly represented in matters to come before our new government. You will deliver that message. The chief is Cornplanter, once visitor to your father's home. Reportedly he is at Chemung on the Teaoga River. But Chemung harbors many who have hatred toward us. Hiakatoo and Little Beard who stand to gain power by this war, have posted spies around him and these braves will cut down any man, red or white, suspect of being in sympathy with peace. Carry this white belt. Tell the mighty Planter if he shall place his hand upon it so shall our great General, we to be joined so long as the sun and the moon, eternally present, give light. Tell him we shall give the Seneca as many presents as do the English, and more."

"Sir, one question. If war cannot be averted, then what?"

"For that reason you must note every path, stream and village that you encounter. Familiarize yourself with the geography of these lake and river dwellers. We may need your knowledge if we are to invade their territory. We have in consideration such a plan, premature at this point, and not for you to know."

"Sir, I've one request." Kirkland nodded to Levi to continue. "You've heard of Tim Murphy, known throughout the Continental Army for his sharp shooting. He's here in my company. By taking him with me I would enhance my possibility for survival."

"'Sure Shot' Murphy, the man who took down General Fraser depriving Burgoyne of his best general? Who hasn't heard of him? Done. Tell Murphy nothing until you are well on your way."

"I also have another suggestion, Reverend. Not to excite the curiosity of Tory spies in this valley, such as the Wintermutes, we'll slip away while their eyes are bent toward the two companies you have ordered to march. And if there is a post of Indians on the hills, they will be jabbering over the spectacle of two full companies assembling and marching south."

"Well planned," said Kirkland, shaking Levi's hand. It was Kirkland who saluted Levi. "Good luck, Lieutenant. Bring your scalp back."

"Thank you, Sir. I shall. The attachment to it is of long standing." They smiled and parted on this bit of humor.

As Levi walked along the darkened path leading to the Menema house, with a pang he realized that the golden-hair girl who he was beginning to find so necessary at evening time, Abby, would be hard to renounce. This, more than the dangers ahead, occupied his mind. The thought of death was remote. A man lives on chance and expects danger, and the Divine Hand interposes sometimes, if one prays deep enough. And if not, why worry? Fate will have the say, not worry which changes nothing. It was Abby that troubled him. How would she react to his story of court-martial and disgrace? Abby had been the only woman whose body he had possessed. It would be a difficult parting under any circumstance; and in the face of the opinion she would have of him, formed by his lie, that parting would be particularly onerous.

When he entered the Menema house he knew instantly she had learned his company would march. He sought words, weaving the lie as he must, which would explain his absence from his company. He began bluntly. He had offended a superior officer, refusing to march to the war in the East. He was dismissed, his commission revoked, and he had been given orders to be gone about his private business. As Levi finished, he saw by her hostile, bitter eyes that he had told his story well. Too well. He had hoped she would have shown faith in him. Yet, how could she express anything but contempt. She knew nothing about the fact he had been in more battles than any man in Connecticut Valley. On the eve of battle, afraid to march with his company! She viewed him as a coward. Saddened, Levi let it rest at that.

Night had come down off the mountains. Brightly the constellations, much like necklaces in the washed sky, were to be seen through the open door of the Greenacre house. From the porch French had incomparable view of the heaven and of the darkened valley with its lighted homes. Pipe in mouth, he kept thinking of Asa gone into the town, and of Rachael whose occasional footfalls he could hear within the kitchen. From the direction of the Susquehanna the frogs were setting up a mighty cadence, their blended songs an overtone to the slap of the river. A beam of the moon lay along the peaceful, empty road. This was the road toward the meeting house, the road which Asa had taken hours ago. Were he Asa he would not be overly long this night, or any night when such a one as Rachael waited at home. He visualized the sensual agitation which she, by her all consuming wantonness, might well produce were he the wedded one. He imagined her hair upon his cheek, his fingers toying with her delicate ear, passing from there to her buttoned dress. In frustration he quenched his pipe, shook his head to dispel the image, and sucked at the cool night air. 'I am not her husband,' he reminded himself with some degree of guilt. She was to be regarded, not coveted. At that moment Rachael stepped onto the porch. He sensed she was there before he he heard or saw her.

"Mr. French." Her voice was tremulous.

"Oui?"

"I am told you have but recently come to America. It must have been an experience to cross the great Atlantic."

"Oui. The experience, as you call it, was not so much of plaisir. The ocean, she has taught me to love the land."

"Why did you come?"

He thought on that, then answered, "I do not know. My mind tells me nothing. It is as silent of thought as are the dead, without knowledge. My past, like theirs, no longer endures."

"Nevertheless, your life is full of meaning, is it not, by this change in your circumstance?"

"Mais certainement."

"You, then, can understand what I say when I speak about my life, my empty meaningless life. By wedding ceremony, and only by that can I be considered Asa's wife. We are nothing to each other, never, never even in the bed."

Startled, French asked, "Why confide this to me? I am no priest? I can give you no advice."

"I want more than advice. Give me of your comfort. I am as everybody else, needing to give love and be loved. I sense there is a current that runs as deep in you as in me. What infidelity would be in it when love never was in my marriage, were we to indulge that passion? Asa sleeps in a room apart. Nothing goes on between us. Sam, be with me tonight. Give me a moment of happiness. None exists in the life I live. Sam, I need a memory to which to cling. I need you. I need you now."

Sam floundered for words. "Can you not see," he protested, "I am human and you torture me. What will it really mean? Tomorrow nothing changes. You are a married woman."

Thinking of Kirkland and the rumor awash in the community that the militia would be given marching orders, she replied, "Tomorrow you may not be here. Give of yourself to me. Make tonight into something magical, beautiful." She wrapped her arms around him.

He closed his eyes and pushed her away. "Non!" Repelled, she turned and ran indoors.

Try as he did, he could not apply logic to this rejection. He couldn't quite determine why he, of French blood, an admirer of all women, and especially those as gorgeous as was Rachael, had been so idiotic as to refuse an affair. Was it because she was a married woman and he respected her husband? Maybe yes; maybe no. What then? Baffled, he blamed his monastic conduct on the drinking water. 'Dieu. I have what we say, messed it up, not to have crawled into a warm bed.'

He reentered the Greenacre house, mounted the stairs and went into his bedroom where he began to collect his few belongings, a razor, rifle, blanket and changes of clothing. His position in the house was untenable. Preparatory to going he settled himself on the bed, thinking, drumming his knuckles backhandedly on the side rail. He should write some explanation to Asa about his abrupt departure, lest it be misconstrued. He paced the room, inviting a calm solution. He would go to Forty Fort where Murphy and Baldwin had set up a bivouac, they preferring this over a private dwelling. He would say he grew tired of the farm. Even so, Asa might infer something. In final judgment he decided to stay as if nothing happened, which was the truth.

While thus debating, a vague sound somewhere on the road brought him to the window. In the moonlight he saw Asa, head on breast, arms dangling, being borne toward the house by his horse. Horrified, French watched Asa lurch as the horse halted, and saw him stagger for the porch, there crashing to the floor. 'Indians!' French thought. He bounded into the hall and raced for the steps, meeting Rachael. At a glance they saw that Asa, in falling, had clutched at a railing, pulling it with him. And, with one whiff of the stench of him, both French and Rachael knew he was drunk. This was confirmed by a bloated, smothered hiccup. "Leggo!" bellowed Asa, coming to life, thrashing at the Frenchman who, ignoring Asa's incoherent yells, hoisted him to his shoulder and trudged up the steps. Abruptly Asa babbled some sense, "March - march - march," he reiterated, appending one phrase, "march on Sunday." His head touched the pillow.

"Sunday?" French shook the man. "Asa!" A gurgle issued from the pillow. "Asa! We march?" The snore had majesty.

"March on Sunday," Rachael repeated. Absently a towel dropped from her limp hand and as absently Sam recovered it for her, thinking that the grand adventure promised by Lieutenant Brady was here! At last! A journey into the woods, a march of immortals. Jerked back to reality, aghast he saw Rachael on her knees, clasping his legs, weeping profusely. This was madness. The woman loved him! "Please," she pleaded.

The thief that had taken her pride absconded with his resolve. Raising her gently, he guided her into his chamber. Disrobing, pulling aside the quilt, she positioned a pillow beneath her buttocks, then with her hands assisted him as he penetrated her.

There is a process by which news travels before the bearer. Levi made that discovery when, from his men rather than from Captain Spalding, he learned that they would march on Sunday. Stories were in circulation, the more incredible the more believed, as to the purpose of their march. "'T is an assault upon Fort Niagara," one man said, supplying further detail which he fabricated as he spoke. "We're to join regiments from Pitt and Augusta. Why, I expect we may go into Canada!" And there were those who swore to another version. "We'll be meeting up with the Oneida who are on their way toward us, we to fetch up with them, we together to go for the throat of the Seneca villages on the shores of the lakes and rivers north of here." So spoke the optimists.

In offset of their enthusiasm, a report of far less comfort flew from mouth to mouth. It concerned a statement of a drunken but supposedly friendly Indian living nearby the fort whose besotted boast had been that 'the woods would return over the fields of Forty Fort.' Based on this utterance by the Cayugan, much was built. It was predicted the militia were being readied to blunt an offing Indian thrust, that the ex-missionary Kirkland had received intelligence hostile forces were about to come down on Forty Fort, and the two companies placed on alert would be deployed in the woods to ambush them.

Along with this circulation of nonsense, any man going into the valley, if he so much as saw a bush quiver, or a tree bough tremble, and fancied the swaying to be Indian-made, at once a wide publication was sent out on it. If by hearsay a large party was sighted southwest of Forty Fort toward Muncy, an equally large party was sighted both elsewhere and everywhere. At each quarter of the compass Indians were moving inward toward Forty Fort. From Wednesday through Friday the community was in painful suspense. By Saturday, with Kirkland closeted with Colonel Butler, and officers entering and leaving wearing the gravest of expressions, with not a word to be had from these, the public - in its anxiety - was ready to accept the worst. On Saturday Spalding's Company was formally alerted. In quick succession Captain Franklin's received marching orders.

The Day had come. Butler had commanded the company captains that *all* troops, those to march and those to stay, were to muster. The townspeople who gathered to see their militia depart, found themselves barred from the church, its capacity taxed by the soldiers from the two departing companies and their families. As the Sunday morning bell tolled the appointed hour, outside the portals Colonel Zebulon Butler chewed on his lower lip.

Two frontier companies were about to be lost from his command. He scanned the faces of the women who arrived with their menfolk, and saw their own worries reflected in their strained eyes. War's torch was burning. As the men appeared with their families, each in his homespun, before entering they placed their guns against the sidewall of the House of God. In the pulpit, stern in his Continental blue, stood the pastor, Reverend Kirkland.

With the fading reverberations of the bell, this followed by a hush from the seated, the words of the soldier-chaplain rang through the stone room, rang with clarity to those beyond the open doors. "To every man who has love for Country, who has public virtue and bowels for posterity, there comes a moment for prayer. We shall bow our heads. 0 Lord, in Thee is our courage and strength. We ask you to spread your protective hand over our heads, and to bring your wrath upon those who would destroy us, who have shown no mercy, who have spoiled our fields, burned our homes, thieved our cattle, taken into imprisonment our families and friends, some for inhuman torture."

Kirkland cleared his throat and reached for a glass of water. "Our text is from the first book of Samuel. 'Now the Philistines gathered together their armies to battle - and Saul and the men of Israel were gathered together, and pitched by the valley of Elah. And the Philistines stood on a mountain on the one side, and Israel stood on a mountain on the other side: and there was a valley between them. And there went out a champion out of the camp of the Philistines, Goliath, of Gath, whose height was six cubits and a span - and he stood and cried unto the armies of Israel 'Choose you a man, and let him come down to me. If he will be able to fight me, and to kill me, then will we be your servants.' And David heard and said to Saul: 'Thy servant will go and fight with this Philistine.'"

Kirkland's eyes slowly swept his audience. "Men of Forty Fort, the war that broods on the frontier has raised a new Goliath, Hiakatoo, a foe merciless and unpitying. His hatchet gleams over our land. Yet, our faith shall be a weapon to stifle his proud cry and bring our foe unto dust. Before this shall come to pass, however, it may be we ourselves shall suffer affliction. God may wish to test our resolve. It is befitting we continue in our prayers, for there shall come a time His great strength shall be ours, and He shall then surely smite down Hiakatoo. This said, it is not easy to say more. But I must.

"Two of your companies, Captain Franklin's and Captain Spalding's, within the hour shall be on the road, answering General Washington's call, bound for battles first to be won. The Nation's fate rests in defeating the British Army, victory there to spell the ultimate collapse of those Indian forces arrayed against us. The Indians draw their weapons from British stores and take counsel at British Forts Niagara and Detroit. Their audacity is British encouraged, Defeating the King's army will enable us to free men and arms, to raise up an expedition to come onto the frontier and route out those who terrorize us by their hostilities." It was the best face Kirkland could put upon this reduction in force at this critical time.

"Amen!" he concluded, choked not by his eloquence but by the bald truth. Taking away these men took away everything, life, hope. The tattered scream of the defenseless settler, the scalp halloo of the Indian was a reality.

Stepping up to the pulpit, clearing his throat to cover his personal despondency, Colonel Butler announced, "All companies, whether marching or staying, will assemble on the road facing in direction of departure. In the lead will be the two designated companies, Spalding's and Franklin's, which, on my command, will move out." A soldier pumped the organ, conjuring forth pontifical chords. As the church emptied, the music flowed sonorously, reaching to the men shuffling into ranks. Then the hymn quickened, the organist now playing the tune in quarter time beat. The same notes came flying forth as the celebrated marching song, 'Yankee Doodle.'

Farewells interrupted by the cry, 'Fall in!', the men of Spalding's Free Company and Franklin's Volunteers, without waiting for the next command, shouldered rifles and muskets. They were ready. Butler, from the flank, snapped his final command. "F-o-r-w-a-r-d March!" A drummer boy in Spalding's contingent, his son, a lad of eleven years, beat the cadence. Down the rutted way, by their very own farms marched the incalculables, the drum taps growing weaker, then lost entirely. A wind from nowhere blew in the faces of the lingerers.

Chapter VIII

THE OPENED DOOR

Esther opened the door to the log cabin, explaining to Wallis while lighting a wall lamp, "This was Catherine's, my sister's home. She moved with two hundred of our people to the foot of Seneca Lake, a pretty place with pasture for their cows and horses. It offers security, if security is anywhere to be had. She, as I, have the same wish you have for your people, they to be spared the bloodshed of this growing war."

As Esther spoke she lit a second oil lamp, setting this on the round table, this supplementing the soft glow from the wall. The cabin consisted of three rooms. The room they occupied was sparsely furnished, equipped with several chairs, a table, a wooden bench along the length of one wall, a shelf of books, a pair of snow shoes serving as ornamentation over the bench, and the pelt of a black bear covering the floor in part. The floorboards were painted red. He had a glimpse of the bedroom. It had a bed on legs and a red, black and white coverlet with beautiful Indian design. Inconsistent with the simple furnishings, Esther brought out Wedgwood cream-colored porcelain plates and cups, 'queen's ware' the popular name, decorated in cameo relief with blue tinted lions. She carefully arranged these on the table along with two settings of sterling silverware and beverage glasses of purity, which bespoke quality, then went about preparing a small frepast.

Watching her, Wallis remarked, "You manage to retain the ways of your mother, lovely French Margaret. Her home, where you once welcomed me, was simply but decoratively arranged as is this. You inherited from her the remarkable beauty of that Algonquin bride of long ago who your great-grandfather had married. I say to myself what an honor it is to be in the presence of a stately, eye-compelling Montour woman. I feel the magic which overwhelmed him."

Esther placed on the table a bowl of rabbit stew, mushrooms, and a dish of strawberries. "Sam, you are blind. You flatter a woman worn by the cares I have for my people, I am now more than forty years in age, with what few years I may yet enjoy clouded by uncertainties. Life has become hard, Sam, very hard. I have lost my husband Egohan, killed during a hunting trip. I have had my son snatched by death in recent battle. Must there always be killing? I fled to Teaoga to escape the English-French war. I fear this new war may force me to flee again. You imagine me as I was, carefree, and not as I am, of French descent but hating the French; and torn between my loyalty to the Crown and belief in Cornplanter's wisdom this war is not one in which the Indian should take part." She shook her head. "Tell me why there must be so much anguish! Why is it that Cornplanter's voice for moderation, and my prayers as a mother have gone unanswered. Are we wrong?"

"No," said Wallis. He reached across the table, grasping her hand. "Sir William anguished as do you over the coming of this war. He foresaw what today we know. It has divided the indivisible Longhouse."

She responded, "I fear the future. I am powerless to alter our young men's death-love for glory. I sicken at this madness, at this need to kill. My great-grandfather's son Louis, brother to my grandmother Isabelle died at the hands of brutal men by order of the French Governor of Canada.

"Why?" asked Wallis.

"Money. It's a quick story. He, too, had been an officer in the French Army until wounded in a minor skirmish. Further service impossible, he resigned his commission to regain his health in the home of the parents of the woman who he married. To support his new bride and growing family, he took up trapping. He became too successful."

"I don't understand."

"The Huron consigned to him their pelts, which he sold to the King's buying office in Montreal. But a trapper by the name of Joncaire was close to Governor Vaudreuil. They had a 'special arrangement'; the prices charged the government for pelts was inflated to hide the

Governor's share. My granduncle's furs were priced below Joncaire's. He prospered at their expense.

"Vaudreuil issued a royal decree giving Joncaire exclusive rights to trade with the Huron, this shutting out all competition. Their hatred was further inflamed when he traveled west 800 miles, striking up with the Ottawa, he selling their furs not to the French government, but to the English at Albany. For this, trading with the enemy of the French, he was named a traitor and Joncaire came with 50 soldiers, shooting him before the eyes of his family, leaving his bloody corpse on the cabin floor. The Governor stated were he not to have been killed, he would have personally hung him at the end of a ship's yardarm in Montreal."

There was a long silence following this terrible history. "So that's why your family fled Canada, and your Uncle Andrew became a negotiator, in behalf of the English, convincing the Seneca to side with the English rather than the French during the unrest twenty years ago."

"Yes. And as far back as 1754 when Washington was a colonel in the colonial militia he traveled with the Colonel toward the Ohio, as a friend and interpreter. Washington intended to win over the western tribes and construct a fort at the forks. But the French, nearly a thousand, aided by 300 canoes of Ottawas and Chippewas arrived first. They built Fort Duquesne, now Fort Pitt. Then, the next year Uncle Andrew, as you said, kept the larger part of the Seneca from joining the French following the French victory over Braddock in 1755. The French were planning a sizable river fort at Shamokin and were urging the Seneca to drive the British colonials from their settlements along the Susquehanna. Had the majority of the Seneca not been influenced by Uncle Andrew's persuasion, the Susquehanna would have been dominated by the French. The tragedy is the English, the people who were our friends and neighbors, who we had sought to protect, began to think all Seneca were bad because a few had taken up the hatchet. No longer safe in our cabins where we had lived in friendship many years, my sister Catherine and I, advised by our Uncle, fled with 500 of our kinsmen up the Susquehanna. That, Sam, is why you saw me no more after that star-filled summer night of long ago. While my passion was as a fire that could not be quenched, I knew we must never see each other again. My world was falling apart."

"My dear Esther," stated Wallis, "I too must confess, often my thoughts have been about you, about us, about that beautiful beginning, which was only to be that and no more. The years could never erase you. Time has made me a man of means, with fine homes, one at the mouth of the Susquehanna, one in Philadelphia, and one on the frontier at Muncy."

"I have heard, but kept my distance."

"Though I am married, I live as a bachelor. I have had the urge to come toward you, but this, reluctantly, had to be abandoned as impractical. For the most, I live alone in Philadelphia, my frontier house seldom visited. Life has been barren of the joys a man knows when a woman is in his arms, held closely, held lovingly, each exploring and caressing the other."

"So it was with us," Esther said softly.'

"So can it be, this night," Wallis added.

To which she replied, "So shall it be," as she snuffed out one light and carried the other into the chamber where she would turn back the coverlet. Slipping from their garments, they joined their bodies, he finding her firm but copious breasts, gently touching their areola, tracing his finger around each, then with care kneading her nipples these taut and fully protruded. Her hand reached down, first to his buttocks, then cupped his swelling member, her fingers contracting, moving expertly. She shifted her lips downward, bringing him to further excitement as she squeezed his scrotum. Exclaiming in his pleasure, changing position, he mounted her, reaching for and finding entry, she the while inhaling sharply as he plunged into the mystery and pliancy that was waiting. She pulled wide his buttocks with each stroke. Once in the dark night she stifled a cry. They slept well thereafter.

Morning's bright light beat against Wallis's closed eyes. He awakened, the couch deserted, to hear singing outside. It was Esther. He found her preparing a cook fire at the outdoor hearth. Esther had tidings to alarm him. "The Rangers came in at daybreak," she said, alluding to a Tory-led war party, her voice dry of enthusiasm. "They've been toward your woods and encountered a sore welcome. Were you known to be here they'd do for you quick."

"Then help me be away. I have overstayed on the venture that Brant would solve the woes of Muncy. That hope has vanished. Brant half believes himself to be what Tisot thinks he is, a reincarnated

Pontiac. Besides, with Green Rangers in this village, I will be lucky to escape, to leave this place with a whole skin. There are only those here who would harm me."

"Wrong - wrong, Sam. Brant will help you. I have talked to him this morning. Joseph is not beyond sympathy. Yet he must hide his feelings from Tisot. Were Tisot aware of his regard for you, as Joseph himself just told me, there would be repercussions throughout the whole Longhouse. While Brant has great power as the leader of the Confederacy, he cannot offend Tisot who hates your every breath. Tisot is too influential. Brant's leadership depends on his ability to manage extremes, to keep war leaders such as Hiakatoo and Little Beard from getting out of hand. Brant wishes to unite the war parties under his leadership. Even Cornplanter who is here in this village has agreed to soften his opposition to this war, if but to retain Brant in power rather than let others of more violent nature displace him. Last night was not the time, nor was Tisot's lodge the place to discuss Muncy. Nor is today any better. Your problem only complicates an already complex situation. All is in ferment. With Tisot about, with the Rangers angry, with war chiefs stirring against one another, vying for power, his plate is full. Yet, for all these distractions, Joseph will help you as he considers Muncy imperative to his military plans. He knows if you silence your guns in that valley, or turn them away when he passes, he has an uncontested pathway to Fort Augusta. But he needs proof you are one with us before he would trust himself before you."

"Willingly!" said Wallis. "Any proof he desires!"

"Giawaya! Hasanowane Theandeaga!" she whispered, warningly, Brant appearing from around the corner of the house. The chieftain presented three wriggling shad. These Esther crimped and seared over an open fire.

"I bear you news, Joseph," Wallis spoke slowly, employing the tongue of the Longhouse people. "In Philadelphia I heard of a plan to bring battle against the Mohawk villages."

If Wallis expected consternation, there was none. "You know this?" Brant weighed this news for its dangers.

"It will be soon."

"If the information is true, then I must lie back from supporting the Seneca in their attacks against the Pennsylvania settlements, and instead redouble my campaign to reduce the American forts and communities in the central Mohawk Valley."

"The information is true. I swear."

"Then it becomes of importance to Colonels Bolton and Claus. It affects the use of the Indians this summer as a united force. I must visit Colonel Bolton at Fort Niagara. Too, it is he who must endorse any change in attitude toward Muncy. It is viewed as a thorn to be removed from our path. I alone cannot sanction protective treatment." Brant had grasped, in Wallis's forewarning, the challenge to his leadership should he take his Mohawks out of the unity of Mohawk-Seneca forces. This arrangement which accorded him dominance over all warriors, just as Tory Major Butler had command of all the Rangers, was imperiled. Brant wrestled with an imponderable. He would weaken his position as Supreme War Leader by withdrawing his Mohawks. Yet If he disregarded Wallis's warning, and led them south and away from their villages, were disaster to fall upon the Mohawk communities during their absence the consequences would be too terrible to contemplate. Either way, he had a problem.

"You will speak for me at Niagara?"

"My friend, this time as before we shall travel together. Eat meanwhile. I'll get the horses." Brant turned away.

Esther was agitated. "What's wrong?" asked Wallis.

"There's a matter needing mention, something which occurred all of twenty years ago soon after the time you visited me in my mother's home."

"Incident?" said Wallis, puzzled by the word, trying to recall whatever happened, other than the beautiful time spent with her, that long ago summer of 1755.

Esther flushed, then she indirectly led into the subject. "'T was after the winter had passed, when flies were learning to hum, when things growing were beginning to enlarge, the bean within the pod --"

"Esther!" he exclaimed, half comprehending.

"Then was I opened up, and did have a daughter."

"Holy God!" he wiped his forehead. "Why didn't you send me a message? Shouldn't I have been informed?"

"It would have provoked your return. With it you would have requested I leave the Seneca for the society of your choice."

"Twenty wordless years! more, twenty two! Everything about this is preposterous. I, father of a girl-child, no, a young woman, a soft-as-squash! Tell me, would she be married?" He paused, drew breath, and then with after-thought declared, "Yea Gods of minnows, I may have Seneca grandchildren!" He pointed at two babies by the cabin who were sunning on their backs, kicking their feet. "Are these mine? No, don't tell me; I am unnerved enough. I shall come back this way from Niagara. If it has waited these many years it can wait a couple more weeks." Flabbergasted, he could not bring his wits together, even to ask for his daughter's name, Brant reappearing.

Brant, astride a speckled mare, his saddle an Indian blanket, rode up leading Wallis's animal. Mounting, he made no attempt to conceal his affection for the mother of his child. With premonition that the journey ahead might entail a roundabout and delayed return, he remarked, "I shall come back to find you here or at Teaoga. Whatever has taken us apart, this daughter shall bring us together." He bent, lifted and kissed her, and set her down, then struck his horse.

As Esther's cabin was in the center of the village, their movement attracted notice. Wallis, being recognized, produced startled and angry cries. It was well he was in the company of Brant. Families were beginning their morning fires. Seated unobserved was the fearsome Seneca Hiakatoo. Brant and Wallis guided their horses, careful to avoid children playing near the kettles. Typical of village life, as numerous as were the children, so were the dogs, these expectantly waiting by the kettles. A dog, a wife, and a daughter were the three necessaries of the lowliest warrior, the first for hunting, *the* second for lifting his pack, and the last for perpetuating the clan. In taking leave of this scene Brant studied the sky, frowning. "It will rain," he said. "The beaver is eating a hole in the heaven." Wind-driven and dark-tinged clouds were rising on the horizon.

Brant chose to climb the steeps bordering Chemung, entering a region differing from the adjoining countryside. They seemed to be crossing a celestial hunting ground. Both fell silent, succumbing to the lavish splashes of flowers, colorful, variegated, beautiful, overwhelmingly profuse, that bordered the river. They gave themselves momentarily to admiration, inasmuch as the threat of rain was yet held aloft, though approaching by the sound of distant thunder. On the nearby piney, rolling hills grew white brackets of flowery dogwood, attaining heights of forty feet. The wild honey suckle, the rosy xalia - by the Dutch called pinxter - spread a pattern within the wood-cranies, and at times by mischance a random, rare swamp laurel appeared as companion to the more easily found leatherleaf. The travelers passed a galaxy of Indian pipes, smoked black by the season before, nodding their heads. Inasmuch as the terrain over which Brant and Wallis traveled was irregular, the changes of the land as well as the flowers accorded them new and pleasant vistas. If the trailing arbutus favored sandy, rocky soil, the wild rosemary preferred the swamps, while bounteous indiscriminate huckleberry drew nourishment in places high, low, wet or dry. In this paradise the "Amen!" of one flower succeeded that of its neighbor. Starflowers, scarlet pimpernels and wild vined black swallow warts lined the downhill slopes while the blue phlox and the moss pinks fastened upon the stream embankments. Everywhere were paw-paws, snowberries, blue bells, and black Indian currents.

As clouds covered the sun, the travelers hurried. The neighboring hill disappeared, blotted gray as the rain-beats multiplied, obscuring everything. The storm was upon them. Brant, forging through a thicket on the hillside, led him to a dark orifice somewhat concealed by a large boulder, into which they could turn their horses. Inside, the war chief struck fire to dried bramble, illuminating primitive diagrams which he ascribed to the extinct Susquehannocks, a race of giants, each a Hiakatoo. These were the only people the haughty Confederacy had dreaded, and they suddenly vanished on the verge of victory. "This was an arrowmaker's cave," Brant explained as Wallis's eyes detected imperfect flints scattered about the cavern floor. Tying together several twigs and dipping these into the fire, and employing the fagot as a torch, Brant paced toward the deep, undefined extremity of their shelter. "His bones are here. Tisot told me of this. The shelter has become my lodge whenever I travel the Seneca Country and wish solitude." The Mohawk reached down. "This one who looks upon eternity," he said, handling the skull, "is thought to have been a henneyo, a chief wizard. He had poisons which made the merest scratch from his arrows fatal."

"I remember," said Wallis, "Sir William telling me they were decimated in one generation, having no resistance to smallpox and the venereal diseases."

Brant attended the fire, heaping sticks upon its sinking flame. "My friend, let us be concerned with the present. This shall be our shelter till morning." From his leather pouch he unpacked colloped venison, then shared his flask, bringing forth two small cups.

Wallis proposed a salute. "The King's health!" The words rang hollow in the rocky crypt.

"Skano!" approved Brant.

"Tell me, Joseph, what prompted you to encourage your people to take up the hatchet, when Sir William always claimed the Indian should stay out of the quarrels of white men? Before all others, you have convinced the Mohawk and the Seneca otherwise."

"All as you say is not true," the Chieftain replied. "At first I thought as you and he, that neutrality was possible, but then the war of the thirteen fires was thrust upon me. Hiakatoo, a new leader among the Seneca, was as a wind upon a spark. He blew upon the red hot coal cast onto our blanket. He appealed to the younger braves who desired fame and honors that peace cannot bring. Hiakatoo was a bad bird croaking in the ears. When the younger Seneca, the braves and soft knives, took up the war hatchet we Mohawk held secret council. We considered our position. We were but four hundred in warrior strength. The Seneca were upward of two thousand. We could not gamble cutting ourselves off from them. We recognized Hiakatoo's growing strength. My power as supreme war chief would have been weakened if not lost if we did not keep our nations together. Eating our words backward we threw down a black belt. 'Eniaaiehuk; so be it!' we shouted, entering the war."

"Did not your trip two summers ago to England, about which I have heard, play a part in your decision?"

"True. I was reminded by King George of our long allegiance. I told the Great English Father our lands were being eaten up by the plows of the Americans and that we, the Mohawk, reasoned that only the British could give us security. I added my long journey's purpose was to brighten the covenant chain forged together by my Father and his father

89

before him who visited the King's forefathers. The King was pleased with my words."

Brant described his sea voyage from England. He with Sir Guy Johnson in July 1776 were aboard a ship that was in the first of several waves of vessels, transports and warships 500 in total, that were bringing 40,000 soldiers and sailors to the shores of the rebellious colonies. "I watched them disembark more than 100 regiments of Highlanders, Grenadiers, Hessians. Too, I was permitted to participate in driving the Americans from Long Island, going with a force of 15,000 commanded by General Cornwallis which on August 22nd crossed the narrows from Staten Island to assemble at Gravesend Bay, Long Island. We advanced to Flatbush where the Continentals five days later put up a rear guard action under Lord Stirling. With 200 Maryland troops Sterling made five counterattacks, they sacrificing themselves to enable others to draw off and join General Washington at Brooklyn Heights." Brant concluded by painting the picture of Sterling surrendering his sword to Hessian General Philipp von Heister who now could be in a gracious mood. In contrast, because of Von Heister's orders, the rear guard almost to the last man had been overwhelmed by numbers and slaughtered by his bayonet-wielding Hessians.

"Seeing all this reaffirmed my allegiance to the Crown. Too, my birth obligation demanded I preserve the Confederacy from division, some for, while some were against the war. I then proposed to General Howe that I risk crossing the American lines to rally the Indians. But Howe had no desire to employ native warriors. He would not write an order recognizing me as their leader. General Clinton then took Sir Guy aside, observing that Sir Guy as Indian Commissioner could give me a verbal order to cross the lines and assume command. At first Major Butler of the Rangers viewed me a threat to his leadership, he with the backing of Hiakatoo denying my authority, there being no written document. Cornplanter with less love for Hiakatoo than for me, cast his weight on my side. Since then Butler has come to trust me. Hiakatoo contains his hatred."

Wallis meditated on this reply, convinced the Chieftain had bound the Mohawk with the Seneca for yet another purpose. This war to be won, then Brant would attempt to achieve a portion of Pontiac's old dream, that of extending the Longhouse westward to the setting sun, to encompass the many peoples of distant nations. The views of the former colonies, now the United States, were not compatible, nor to give strength to this vision of one powerful native leader. Wallis knew it. Brant, too. Inwardly Wallis sickened, thinking of the blood to flow. In the same instant noting Brant's keen observation, he forced a laugh. "The weather and the conversation compliment." He stirred the fire against the creeping dampness, the enlarging flame magnifying Brant's and his shadows on the wall. He reflected, 'What good will come of it? 'T is bottomless.' Being drowsy, each wrapped himself in his blanket and stretched by the fire.

The storm ended just before daybreak. At dawn they resumed their travels. The irregularities of the country engrossed them, their path wending and twisting where it followed a stream, and at other places flying as an arrow through broken woods and fields. From time immemorial, generations had traveled this path, known as the 'high path'. In general it traversed the heights that overlooked the canyon-like valleys. Sometimes the path degenerated, offering the traveler a series of connected rocky ledges which jutted several feet out from the lip of the almost continuous gorge. These were look-out platforms employed over the centuries, being as a convenience for war parties, enabling them to scout the depths of the land beneath, ahead and behind. On the highest part of this airy passage way they halted to welcome the sun. Its rays touched to green the long ridge of continuous mountains, these seemingly endless in their splendor.

The heights they traveled began to melt downward, with the gorge at last falling away and the terrain flattening into a broad valley. Here, from the previous night's storm, they encountered fallen trees. On one of these had been blazed crude figures, the tree a totem which proclaimed the tribe and clan and tenant to which this preserve had been allotted. Brant shot a muskrat and skinned and roasted it. They loped along replenished when - abruptly - they happened onto a bark lodge. To its occupant Brant surrendered the pelt. "It was necessary to sustain life," he informed the Cayugan on whose lands they had trespassed and of whose game they had partaken. A poor man, a mountaineer who tilled his ground with the shoulder blade of an elk, he extended to them the full of his hospitality. This simple soul offered 'tune-hah-kee' corn, beans and pumpkins. They ate of this lest he be offended, though they knew well that he was hard come by the food. His land was stony; his health and age were hobbles. Until the man had crammed Brant's leather sack with dried meats, berries and nuts, he would not let them go. "Niawe," said Brant, thanking him.

In the days to follow Wallis was to see a less serene fellow traveler. At times Brant was deep in reflection, thinking through the problems confronting his leadership. On other occasions he was moody and withdrawn. With each day of their journey, by degree he shifted from being the urbane, civilized person Wallis long ago knew, to being an introspective, sometimes frightening individual. He painted his face, roughed his breast and cheeks, and when Wallis spoke to him in English Brant retorted in native tongue. He set himself, by these means, apart from Wallis who, in turn, became less and less inclined to carry on a conversation. They were two men on the same path together, yet separately proceeding. Wallis was thankful to lag behind rather than be at Brant's heels, or worse be before him in the deep shade of the forest. This unknown side of Brant disturbed him. In one particularly dark and ugly bower Brant half-turned while drawing his knife and chopping at some annoying briars. He waited with unsheathed blade as Wallis drew near. Wallis gave Brant a cold stare, whereupon Brant reseated the knife. 'Unintentional?' thought Wallis. A man might reflect whether or not evil was contemplated.

Wallis contained his apprehension until evening when they camped. As they spread their blankets, he asked of Brant, "With whom do I make camp this day, with Joseph my friend of many years, and former companion, with Joseph my brother by adoption, or is it with the great and fearsome sachem and War Chief of the Mohawk and allied Seneca?"

For a moment Brant reflected, then with a smile warming his face, stated, "It is Joseph, Sam." He spoke in English. "You have become unfamiliar with my ways, 0 friend."

"You never had these ways, as I remember you," blurted Wallis.

"My apology. Perhaps it is the heavy burden placed upon me. I am faced with a distasteful choice in the news you bring. The strategy of the British, as you will soon learn at Niagara, is to concentrate all our strength in a strong blow, this then to be followed by others against the settlements in Pennsylvania. It is I who has urged the many war chiefs to unite as one. Now you bring information which can turn me against my preachment. I may have to withdraw my warriors from this united effort to protect our own threatened villages by taking the war, first, to the American settlements nearest ours, such as Cherry Valley. If I withdraw from the united plan, Hiakatoo and Little Beard gain more power."

Wallis in turn apologized for his mistrust.

Wallis used the moment, while their faces were reddened from the glow of the burning log, to bridge the silence which had become awkward. "While we are joined in purpose, Joseph, I must confess I too have had a difficult choice. This is a war for me that is two wars in one. It is a war over the conduct of trade, and superimposed on this is the doctrine found in the Declaration, sentiments not apart from mine, idealistic yet perhaps attainable. But, as is the soul to the human body, the Declaration of Independence creates a cause above self interest for which men will give their lives. And yet when you come to the core of the argument that brought about this war, we must remember that wealthy men in Parliament, who were not about to give up their powers to tax colonial trade, were confronting wealthy men in the colonies who with equal vigor opposed their regulators. In consequence, within our own American colonies the drift was toward war. Then, there are men like myself, not wishing to choose sides. For me it was patently evident instability would overtake us, even to proceed against my remote community on the West Branch. I wanted no war. I want not its insecurity. I desire peace at this stage in my life. I am a Quaker opposed to war. That is why I am here, why perhaps in my fragile insecurity I have made much out of nothing, in the flash of your knife as I did just now, and for which I apologize."

Darkness settled upon the woods about them as they drifted into sleep.

The forest game seemed to have been eavesdropping. A buck, transfixed by the campers' fire, gazed at them, eyes green phosphorus. From nowhere a magnificent blackbird, as jet as the night, with scarlet epaulets burning on its shoulders, swooped to their heels, and with a caw fled into the darkness.

Early in the morning of the fifteenth day they wended through nature-strewn gardens of large-flowered white and red wake-robins, and purple trilliums. The pretty blue-eyed grass supported a braid of white moccasins, and the timber as it deepened altered from lighter woods to oak mixed with pine. At first, imperceptibly, then distinctly Wallis heard a muttering and rumbling as of a wind rushing out of a vault in the earth, or of waters tumbling over the end of time. It was the orderly abandon of vast streams dropping into the bowels of the earth, a great castaway of water. It was Niagara. "Stupendous!" shouted Wallis, come upon its brink. Here they tarried, exhausting their senses in the compelling sight at their feet. Just above the cataract's spray an eagle wheeled in indifferent flight.

"See!" cried Brant, barely heard above the noise, pointing at the piratical bird, "The giver of luck. You shall prosper, Sam, in your task." More than the words, Wallis read Brant's lips. When they had moved back from the perilous edge, Brant undid the roll of cloth he had been carrying, spreading a British uniform, complete to the sword, on the grass. The cloth was of finest quality, in brilliant dyes of green and scarlet trimmed with golden epaulets. These he donned. In five minutes his metamorphosis was accomplished. A stern captain replaced the Indian. Thus arrayed, with starchy English to fit his characterization, in the phraseology drummed into him by Reverend Wheelock and Sir William Johnson, he remarked, "Now, sir, God's help you may need. We enter into the presence of Colonel Marion Bolton who commands the Western Department. Bolton answers only to the Almighty. Pray that he is in good humor. Yet, do not misread him or be offended by his threatening way. For all of this, beneath that appearance there is fairness. This said, I also forewarn you, while he may heap upon your plate whatsoever you may ask of him, be ready to pay the piper; the dinner will cost you as much as you are prepared to give, and more. He already knows you have put up fortifications. This will not lend well. He will have suspicions. You have to win his confidence. In your favor is your arrival in my company. Come, Sam, the fort is not too distant."

Unknown to Wallis, on the heels of his and Brant's coming to the Fort, Hiakatoo too had reached its walls, he as leader of the Seneca to be briefed on detailed plans for use of his warriors. He and Brant, and Wallis for that matter, were aware of the rising importance of the Indians in the eyes of the British.

CHAPTER IX

TWO SCOUTS ON A SPY

Tim Murphy was worried. Levi was neither communicative nor confidential. With his secretiveness he was as silent as the forest. Tim did not wish to believe what might be the reason for it. From public gossip he knew Levi had quarreled openly with their orders to march, and it was said Levi had been dismissed from all duties, So tongues wagged. As for his own personal fortunes, Murphy reflected, since this was rarely apart from Levi's, he accepted his friend's disgrace as his own. Whatsoever the cause, he reasoned, their natural next move would be to hole up, trapper style, and stay to hell away from the war. At least until the wounds of censure had healed. Then they could rejoin the regular forces. Meanwhile there were places where a pair of sharpshooters could lose themselves and if to be bothered by a stray redskin, woe to him for his mistake. One thing, though, didn't fit. The direction of their travels had turned toward the Seneca Country. Why? Even the most resolute deer-slayer or trapper would take wide berth of those lands. Could Levi have shifted loyalties? Preposterous, yet for an angry man possible.

Their course brought them from a wooded slope onto a pleasant meadow where Levi halted, confronting the unbroken forest before them. "These woods," ventured Murphy, "are full of native barbers, and pissed off Tory rangers. As for you, you are a close mouth son of a bitch about your mind. I pray it isn't to connive as a turncoat with them as are Green Rangers. If it is, I stop here!" Levi, who was studying the woods, glanced at Tim, their eyes meeting. The seriousness of Tim, his set jaw, his quizzical stare caused Levi to smile, and when Tim saw the smile, he began to chuckle, then burst into laughter. So did Levi. "My God," confessed Murphy, "for a pace you had me sober scared. I thought we were deserters to our sworn enemy. What are we on, a spy?"

"You've split the mark," said Levi. "Dead on."

"A spy, eh?" chortled Murphy, delighted with the prospect of a quick sally along the fringe of the forest. "Wherefore?"

Levi dodged the question. "Soon you'll see." Tim shrugged, and swore under his breath. Though Tim burned with curiosity, Levi couldn't tell him they were to seek out Cornplanter. Not yet.

"If you can't tell me anything, if you've been sworn to secrecy," hazarded Tim, "at least give me an unofficial idea. Your opinion."

"Are lieutenants supposed to have opinions?"

"Most janurally they do. I gather you're still a lieutenant, Sir!"

"Our spy is up the Susquehanna to its forks with the Teaoga, and beyond to the Tory-Indian village of Chemung."

Tim threw his hat on the ground. "I quit. That's asking for it." He gazed somberly at Levi. "Look me in the eye. Be you gaming me?"

"I said Chemung. We're going to probe right into their bowels."

"You could say it's us, not them, that's getting the up-the-ass treatment. There's too many Indians 'tween here and there. How're we going to make it in, let be make it back out?" He filled his water jug from a rill straggling through the meadow, talking to himself.

"Here's our answer," Levi remarked. He bent and with his knife harvested a plant, in profusion. It was bloodroot, commonly called Indian Paint, used by the natives to color their skin. With a chop of his blade, blood red fluid poured from the root system. "See," he said, holding up a reddened hand. Without ado Levi produced a razor. "First get rid of your head of hair, sparing your crest for a scalp-lock. Then smear everywhere, including you-know-what so the squaws will cuddle with you as one of their own. Head to crotch, butt to toes paint yourself."

They fell busy building a thin fire, shaving themselves and smearing their bodies with the cherry-like stain. With the tip of a charred hickory stick Levi traced clan designs upon Murphy's breast. Each, Tim and Levi, painted three black stripes across his cheeks, which was a signification of war. Tim, sitting cross-legged, ripped and stabbed at his discarded shirt, employing a pine sliver and strip of gut to fashion and sew together a wrap around garment, front to rear to cover one's nakedness. He flung a breechcloth at Levi, then - from Levi's discarded clothing completed another for himself. He watched Levi bend and inspect his image in the water. "Marry," swore the militia officer, taken with his own reflection. "A savage!"

Tim scanned the monster his friend had become. "Likely, waking tomorrow morning, I'll brain you by impulse," he said, gathering his powder horn, patch and shot pouch, and his gunsmith tools. Tim was ready to move ahead.

"Hold up a moment!" Levi pointed at Tim's gun, the famed piece that had established his reputation. "'No Indian ever carried a double trigger over-and-under two barrel rifle."

Reluctantly Tim hid gun, file, vise, screw plates, bellows, and powder horns in the bush. "Now that you've got me practically naked, except for my knife, do I kill 'em with dirty looks?" He questioned Levi's judgment since the Lieutenant kept his own rifle. "That's no Niagara trade musket."

"Mine could have been taken off a dead man. Its for extreme danger."

"The whole damn trip's extreme danger," Tim retorted. Then he muttered, "Me, hero of the Continental Army, deadeye of deadeyes, the celebrated 'Murphy the sharpshooter', me without a gun, with only a knife, and he keeps the gun, not me. Disgusting. Makes sense if you're an officer, which I'm not, thank goodness."

Levi brushed aside the comment. "It's knife or nothing, more'n likely, if killing's got to be done. We're to avoid detection. We're spying, not ambushing."

Wryly referring to an expression of Continental troops under Major General William Alexander, claimant to a Scottish earldom and the title Lord Stirling, Murphy responded, "Well, as the Jerseymen would say, we've the 'Lord' on our side." Levi started toward the north end of the field.

Disgruntled, Tim trudged after him. Levi seemed to have a well thought route in mind. They crossed the meadow, passed through the bushes, and entered the forest. Tim, by now resigned to the circumstance, was whistling a nonsensical air when he abruptly stopped in mid-tune. "I say, what happens to our bodies when it rains?" Levi was mum. Tim again pestered, "How do we expect to find Chemung?"

"By following our noses northward," testily answered Levi, astounded that Tim should make a problem of it. "I told you, we'll follow the Susquehanna, dumb head."

"Sir! With no disrespect, one of us is for sure an ignorant dumb head. 'Follow the Susquehanna!' The shores are watched, and besides there's a pow-wow full of smoky-heads that sit on the portage at Teaoga, pleased to hook their axes into such soft heads as we."

Levi responded, "The country from here to Standing Stone is fairly much deserted, unless bad luck crosses us with a floating war party. You forget, Colonel Nat Dennison's 24th Connecticut went almost to Sheshequin, burning all the Indian villages south of that place. We can travel that far using the river, then step back into the woods, camping, and going at night until we reach the Teaoga River. At its mouth with the Susquehanna, we'll be turning west, following the south side of the Teaoga, skirting wide the smoky-heads at the junction. We will parallel the Teaoga until we come to its biggest settlement, Chemung Town."

Having described their course to Tim, he reviewed their signals and precautions. "From this instant, no talking. Keep behind me by about 125 or 150 feet. And keep that interval! If you hear a shot, freeze; don't come on 'cause if it's trouble I'll soon be going by you as fast as I can go, and I'll want the fastest man - you - behind me to decoy them off my heels. Don't fight; just take a different compass, and shake them. At nightfall, since they'll pursue until dark, you can halt, then double back over the ground you have just run. We'll rendezvous on the north star, Hoot to raise me. If we miss, go back to our last encampment and stay there one or two days. If one of us doesn't show, the survivor should break off the spy."

Sarcastically Tim responded, "Thanks for telling me, 'Don't fight.' Fight? That's a funny word. With you going by me, and maybe with twenty heathen on your tail, and me with a knife only, I'll be passing you. You got the gun."

"Ignore the man," tartly stated Levi to nobody, then to Murphy. "Personally, I think a search for either by the other would only endanger the searcher, rescue all but hopeless. I'll loiter two days, unless the country is hot with braves, and then I'll make tracks."

He paused while Tim repeated the instructions with modification "Right. I'll loiter one. That's it, sense tells me."

"Push off, Tim, and sharp."

Their route kept them within reach of the wide Susquehanna. It was a pleasant beginning, the sun vigorous, but a cooling breeze tempered the day's heat. Nor did their journey bring them to laborious ascents. They elected the flats which bordered the river rather than the mountains close to hand. At times they stopped to rest and look about. Once Levi scrambled to a high peak, assuring himself that the winding path ahead did not harbor any enemy. Disencumbered, light footed, they made spectacular progress. Later they would travel slowly, and even at night, often up and down mountains, testing the twigs underfoot lest some piece give off a snap. However, at the onset, this worry was needless.

As the hours and miles moved behind them, their caution increased. They approached and reconnoitered the abandoned Vanderlip farm toward dusk. Set in a hollow above the river, it was an ideal shelter. They encamped and had the cheerful experience of being roused in the night by a snake which sought the warmth of Murphy's body. They ate snake in the morning. Levi chided Murphy, "Is this the way to treat a creature which loved your body last night?"

"Go stick your head up you know what," growled Murphy, munching away.

By late afternoon of the third day they reached an old site of the Wysochin Indians, a place of wild grapes. Here the pair encamped upon a semicircular cap of land, a delta created by two shallow streams. They bivouacked in tall weeds and among ancient burial mounds. Erosion had dislodged sections of the delta, exposing a thigh bone and set of ribs. "At least he won't hurt us," said Murphy wryly. "Come to think of it, 'tween the snakes and the dead, I'm beginning to admire your judgment. You know how to pick campsites." Nearby the dead had had their village.

There had been a wooden palisade about it. Though this defense was long rotted and gone, it had left signs of its location. Where birds had perched on top of the palisade, the seeds that had dropped from their beaks had created a tall growth of pines in a well-spaced line. Near these pines Levi and Tim ate the last of their journey cake and jerk before bedding for the night. They marked a flat pebble and flipped it for first watch, Levi losing. Levi had calculated as had the long-gone villagers, that anyone approaching would not come through the surrounding streams, but over dry land, the palisade built to close off the village on that side. As Tim settled himself he clawed at a rock under his shoulder, discovering in the moonlight he held a skull. He heaved it toward the trees where Levi had taken stand. "Here's company," called Tim, turning on his side. He was soon awakened by Levi.

"Stop talking in your sleep. You'll wake the dead."

"Damn! I was dreaming of buckwheat slapjacks flowing with butter and honey."

"And a dish of chocolate, I'll bet," stated the irate Levi.

On the following evening just as the darkened shape of a bordering mountain range was disappearing within the greater darkness, they toiled up a high ridge, a sickle moon at their shoulder, and looked down upon the Susquehanna River valley. They had been traveling north, avoiding the river itself, their course along the heights east of the river. Levi and Tim stared. There, at their feet, breaking into the Susquehanna was a sizable arm of water which could be only one river, the Teaoga! It was a black stream issuing from a dank forest. Forward, and to their right, midway up the peninsula and near the carrying path that crossed just north of the junction of the rivers, a fire burned. The dull red glow forewarned danger.

"If we could surprise them at their guard post ...." suggested Tim, eyeing the point of land between the Y of the rivers. Murphy wormed his way along the canted trunk of a tree outwardly bent from the cliff-like mountain edge, from that aerial perch better to survey the country below.

Obligingly, the fitful moon's light brought into relief the floor of the valley. He hung suspended over the river, hundreds of feet beneath him. He cocked an ear, listening, then slid back, remarking to Levi in a low pitched voice, "The air is so clear you can kind of hear them talking, though I dare say it is more'n three miles 'tween them and us."

"Can we get down to the river?" asked Levi, examining the drop as best he could from the rim of the mountain ledge.

"Oh, it's not as steep as it appears," ventured Tim. Confidently, he illustrated by deed, going off the edge. Levi could see him, in the moonlight, slipping and sliding, clutching at a tuft of grass here, a protruding rock or small boulder there, pausing midway down to raise an arm and beckon Levi to come on, which he did, he using the butt of his rifle as a brake to his rapid descent. He reached bottom amid a shower of pebbles dislodged by his moccasins, the stones crackling down the mountainside like gunfire. At the river's edge, chalky face, they froze, listening. Sure enough, there was a splash upstream and a canoe put out from the far shore.

"Into the river," whispered Levi, hiding his rifle within a bush. They clung to a dislodged half submerged tree trunk, one end of which was washed onto a sandbar in the Susquehanna while the other was wedged into the embankment. With their eyes parallel to the tree, their feet barely touching the river bottom, their arms wrapped beneath the log, they barely held their balance against the current. The Indian patrol approached, then turned, satisfied the disturbance had origin in natural causes. Chattering from the river's temperature, the two climbed back on land, removed and drained their high top moccasins, hung them at their necks by the laces, and prepared for the long, chilling swim to the western shore. The rifle Levi had concealed he now recovered. As for his shot and priming powder horns, these having been slung around his neck, each now contained a soggy, useless black glob. Rifle in hand, he re-entered the Susquehanna. Numbed by its cold and the mill-tail velocity they were hard put at mid-river, saving themselves by flopping onto a tiny island and resting before braving the last half. Again they were in the stream, fighting the drag of the current.

They crawled ashore, lying on the western embankment, too weak to do anything but blow, cognizant of the perils their heavy breathing could bring. Somehow the white belt had been swept away.

Having drifted downstream in their swim from the east to the west side of the river, they had landed on a meadow, the upper part of which undoubtedly was used for the grazing of cattle of the Indian villagers just to the south. They were on Queen Esther's flats. Murphy had proof it was a cow pasture. "Ung-gah-wah," he hissed in disgust, using a Seneca graphic expression, he having stuck his naked foot into a copious cow dropping. Other than this mishap, for the immediate they concluded their troubles were over. Murphy cleansed his foot in the river, his distaste obvious by the grimace on his face. They scudded into the woods along the western shore, not sure of the distance to Chemung - town, and if within reach while the moon still hung. They continued past the junction of the Teaoga, then followed this stream's southwest shore from its mouth and as it bent toward its western origins. Lest to make a sound, gingerly they stepped over fallen limbs here and there. Across the river loomed in mysterious darkness an isolated shape which, by the again reappearing moon, was disclosed as a small hill in a curious location, on a flat plain. It had the semblance of a palisade around its brow. As the moon disappeared, again all to be in blackness, more by water sound than sight they paralleled the river until, with the gray of dawn sifting through the dark, they stepped back from the shore, going inland. A tumble of trees matted over with weeds attracted Tim's notice. Beneath this they buried themselves. They would rest here.

Close to mid-morning Tim issued forth on all fours to find birds chirping, and the woods alive with sunshine. Rousing Levi who had spread his powder on a rock to dry, Tim thereafter probed the timber for small game and stumbled upon a godsend, a hunter's cache of fresh venison left on a pole. On second consideration - he had seen men die from eating meat spoiled by the enemy. He let it be and again went in quest of game.

If there was game, it kept well hidden. And when an opportunity finally came, there was nothing he could do about it. A buck, head down, circled the scout. Had he a gun, and were there no fear for noise, that buck would have been his. He could almost taste it. It was a hunter's ultimate frustration. They would have to suffice themselves with unpalatable snails and several roots which Tim plucked. At night they crept forth with scarcely an afterthought about leaving their 'charming' burrow which they dubbed 'Starvation Lodge'. From atop a hill they saw in the river-valley a series of evenly sided lights. These were made by square windows. "Chemung!" said Tim.

"The end of the path," said Levi, and added, "I hope."

"Now can you tell me the why of it, why we're here?"

"I've come to meet Cornplanter."

"Stop pulling my leg," said Tim, viewing his friend with disbelief. "Why would we want to be making a social call on him?"

"General Washington thinks Cornplanter is the key to convincing a sizable number of Seneca to stay neutral, not to join the war-lovers. This would split the Seneca."

"If our own skulls don't get split, instead."

"Murphy, you're a worry head. Cut it out. You'll outlive us all. However, were we to fail in our purpose, we are charged with a second task. We are to return with knowledge about this uncharted country. I gather that one of these times we may be coming this way with an army behind us, to squash this Tory-infested town and all the Indian villages from which war is conducted."

Tim sharpened a stick. "Afore famine overtakes me, and afore you chew on my ear further, as you are doing, either we go fishing or I'll chew on you for real. There's fish in that river, and this wooden poker is going to spear me a big, fat, luscious perch or salmon."

"Wait," said Levi, laying his hand on Tim's shoulder. "Every move we make in this neck of the woods can invite disaster. If we fish, it'll be further upstream away from here. We'll use the darkness to push westerly. I can hold my hunger and so can you. Tomorrow we'll fish and feed ourselves, after we lay to for some rest. And then we'll return at dark to make our first try at reaching Cornplanter."

"By tomorrow morning, I'll be too weak from starvation. Levi, you do a lousy job feeding your troops. You remind me of Morristown and Valley Forge, only here, instead of a hut floor, when nature moves us, we've got the whole woods to piss into. And how in hell are you going to find Cornplanter?"

"The place is full of green rangers, some painted like Indians. I'll pass as a newly joined Tory."

They moved down the far side of the hill. Two hours later they reached level, dry, and open land where, within the nearby woods, they made camp. At sunrise Levi, with a spear similar to the one Tim had fashioned, and with little thought setting aside his knife and rifle, headed toward the river. He left Murphy to assemble twigs and sticks for a cautious fire. At the water's edge Levi scanned the depths, spear poised. A splendid bass wiggled toward him. Food!

No, danger! He whirled at a sound from behind and confronted four barbaric creatures, each more frightful than the next, painted for war. One was Blacksnake. Blacksnake warily scrutinized Levi who by appearances, hair shorn, painted and decorated, and far removed from his usual haunts, was saved from being recognized. It was fortunate. Levi in physique favored his father. The elder Brady and Blacksnake were violent foes.

"What kind of creature is this?" the warrior chief asked, puzzled. He wiped his hand across Levi's chin. The stubble and the root stain were conclusive. "Seize him," grunted the Seneca. "This no Mingo; this white-skin dog. Where I see you before?"

"Chemung," lied Levi, designating the favorite Tory rendezvous. Levi knew it was not uncommon for whites to dress as Indians and participate in war parties.

"You at Chemung? Not so." At signal the Panther pinned Levi's arms, twisting them back to where Levi thought they would snap; the while Greatshot grabbed his scalp lock, tilting his head. Levi saw only blue sky. In this painful position he was viewed by the imaginative Blacksnake.

"Hear" said their spokesman, "what he has told us, and judge for yourselves if a wind of deceit blows in our ears. Let us unravel the mystery of this man, and by what better way than to pin his bowel to a tree and walk him around until he has unraveled himself?" They bound his arms with leather thongs.

"My cousins!"` croaked Levi. "Before you debouch me of my guts, know that I am a ranger, not a spy, and the great wrong you do me shall reflect against your reputation."

Blacksnake hissed, "What is your name?"

"Secord," said Levi, naming a Tory, and then wishing he had palmed himself off as a less known person.

"Secord? Not true! I am Secord's friend. I trade pelts to Secord. Secord and I drink firewater."

With a touch of pure inspiration the captive elaborated and amended, "He is my father, yes." 'What the hell,' reckoned Levi. 'I have nothing to lose, my life as much as lost already.'

"Well," said Blacksnake, taken with humor, "I will bring you to your 'father' that he may caress you, and should he be slow to fondle you, we shall comfort you in our own way. Then we shall cut you like meat into small pieces; then shall you wish backward that you died here."

He was spread-eagled on the ground, 'staked', limbs tied to saplings. As casually as they had decided his reprieve his welfare was ignored. The Panther collected brush for cooking their meal, flashed a gun igniting an ant heap of powder, the flame from which in turn caught the brush afire. Meanwhile Wamp trimmed four sticks, each with a crotch and pointed end, poking these sticks into the earth, the crotches of each pair to support a crossbar, with sheets of bark laid upon this frame. In all, a platform was constructed whereon the fish netted by Greatshot were soon brought to a delicious brown. The warriors squatted in idle conversation as they ate. For a joke they threw the fish heads at Levi.

They pulled him to his feet, rebound his arms, and brought their canoe from concealment. Toward noon they again came ashore, the Panther needing to urinate. They lit another fire, cooked and ate some deer meat, throwing a chunk at Levi's feet. By falling to his knees, he picked it up with bound hands and fed himself. From the direction of their journey, downstream, he knew the town soon reached was Chemung. In one of the cabins they bound him to an upright post after chasing off a score of women and children armed with switches. Then occurred an unexplainable act of kindness. The local sachem ordered that his ropes should be untied and he given food. More amazing the man who brought him the bowl of soup and meat was a white man, a rebel! "Luke - Luke Harbinson!" exclaimed Levi.

"Aye," said the Muncy man, at loss to identify Levi.

"It's I, Luke, Levi Brady."

Luke looked hard and long. "I wouldn't have known you," he said at last, his voice devoid of enthusiasm.

"When did they catch you?"

"Two years ago, after you left for the wars."

"What's my chance of escaping from here?"

"None. There's a guard outside your door."

"You could give him sweet dreams with a big rock."

"I could, he trusts me. But I won't."

"To hell with sentiment. Do it. Let's go."

"You don't understand. I could walk away any time. I don't want to. They treat me well. They trust me; they let me go for salt all the way to the Cayuga country. I like this life, hunting, fishing, no worries. If I go back with you, it's a struggle to live, and I must take off my cap to those who think themselves my betters, like Mr. Samuel Wallis. Among the Indians I am no more or less a man than the next fellow. You'd do well were you offered the chance to accept this way of life."

"Luke, you're mad."

"Yes, from where you view things."

"At least," said Levi, resigned, "leave me a knife."

"No."

"'Mercy of God, leave me your knife." Luke was backing through the door, shaking his head. "God help you, Luke," called Levi to the man who knew not his own degradation. Toward Levi, in an alike pity, Luke responded, shaking his head. Alone, Levi wondered what made a man accept slavery. Harbinson was never a spiritless fellow, but he was now.

In the morning his captors, abandoning their canoe, started overland. During succeeding days, with his being sometimes fed, often not, and what with the torments of travel, the trip was telling on his strength. He wished that his fate would be made known, the uncertainty preying on him. There was one hope. Blacksnake's party was going north, with the war chief apparently having forgotten his threat to confront him with Secord. They traversed land sparsely sown with evergreens. Reaching a lake of great length, his captors talked of whisky and Canandaigua, central Seneca village lying 40 miles up the lake and along its northern shore. They gestured at him as they talked. He heard them say they would be traveling along an 'easy shore.' They might, just might hand him over to the Tories for whisky. This was confirmed the more they talked and looked at him. The journey occupied a full thirty six hours. They arrived before Canandaigua on the next day, near sunset. Within two miles of its palisade, they heard a drum beating in the town and they accelerated their pace.

Blacksnake and his warriors approached Canandaigua, whooping they had a prisoner, at which the women formed a gantlet of welcome, screeching, "Come, let us caress this one!" Coppery children, 'soft metals', switches ready, lacerated his legs as he was led into the community. "We shall boil you in a pot," taunted a young squaw who, under different circumstances, would be worth a caress herself. A sharp stick bloodied his thigh. He was spat on and reviled. "Gakaweehat!" cried another, ready with a pan of live coals. "You will dance in flames." They reviled him, dug their nails in his flesh. Dogs yapped, tearing at his calves. Pinching, probing, gouging him, beating his back and legs with their sticks, they pushed him down the human avenue, its terminus a scaffold. He imagined ashes and bones beneath the platform. Blacksnake screamed invectives at the women, sensing he would have no prisoner to trade, this spectacle to continue. As rapidly as they had beset Levi, they desisted and scattered, their fun over.

This minor incident detracted not one iota from the main show. In process was a great and grand performance at the center of the village, where all was paint, feathers, and uproar. Buffalo drums thumping, tortoise shells rattling, and voices chanting in cadence, two hundred braves stamped and circled around a pole, the base of which was splashed a sticky crimson. They hacked at this wooden symbol, whooping and boasting. For a moment Levi thought he was to be the replacement for the post. But Blacksnake pushed him past the circle and into a doorway. At first he could not see the room into which he had been thrust. Blinded by the smoke, and by the change from light to dark, he accustomed his eyes, and saw he stood in the center of a council quarters.

A fire licked up from a pit in the dirt floor of the Indian lodge. Seated along the walls were, he had time to count them, fourteen war chiefs and six whites, these last in green uniforms and round caps of the British-American Green Ranger Corps. With what remnant of dignity he could muster, Levi endured the scrutiny of a Tory sporting major's epaulets. "Who's this with glory all faded and English skin peeping through?" inquired the Major. Since Blacksnake was unable to answer him, the Major redirected his question to Levi. "Sir, who are you?"

Levi did not respond.

"Come, my question, your name? Are you ashamed of it, or don't you have one. Your name or your scalp."

"That's no inducement; the first will fetch the latter."

The rejoinder elicited a smile. "I like your impudence, sir. Lieutenant Frey, shuck this nameless one's bonds."

Levi was grateful. "Sir, I dare not reveal myself, except within the walls of Niagara."

"Blacksnake," said the Major, "I give you a thunderstick and a blanket in trade. The captive is mine."

Blacksnake, if delighted at prospect of a new gun, nevertheless pressed his fortune, smacking his lips. "And firewater."

"No rum. One horn of powder, but no rum, my dear monster.

The ranger officer, a muscular, medium built man, had charisma. Brady felt it. The Major regarded his purchase who stood all but naked before him. "You, my nameless friend, are more in need of the blanket than Blacksnake. Why, sir, even your breechcloth is in tatters. Now, Rebel, you are a British prisoner, specifically mine. I am Major John Butler. Pray, sir, announce yourself." There was kindness in his voice, compassion in his eyes.

"Major," replied Levi, drawing himself erect, "I am a lieutenant of the 7th Militia, Forty Fort, Connecticut Valley. I was caught scouting the frontier."

"You could hang for it; you were out of uniform."

"That's absurd. In our army as yours, officers buy their own uniforms. It wouldn't be sporting to hang a man for lacking funds to properly clothe himself."

The Major leaned back, slapped his knee, and roared with laughter. "Well put, you consummate liar, though there well may be a thread of truth in the tale. All right, Mr. Pauper, confound your bones, just who in the hell are you? Lieutenant who?"

"The name is Brady."

As if a keg of gun powder with sputtering fuse had been tossed into the lodge, haughty chieftains flew from their seats. The name Brady was long in their hatred, the father an old Indian fighter, the son in his footsteps. "Give him back," spat Blacksnake, now realizing who his prisoner was. "He must die!" He remembered Dipped Tobacco for one, who he suspected had fallen before Levi's gun when, early in '75, they prowled the woods of Muncy. "I will cut off his fingers with clam shells and fasten a collar of red hot tomahawks around his neck, then shall I see how brave is this one." He appealed to Major Butler, "Oh, my English cousin, turn my palm right side up, that I may grasp him again. Give him to me to fondle."

"None of that!" admonished Butler, waving aside Blacksnake's brandished knife. "You have traded. Go caress your presents."

"Great Person, you would not harbor a snake under your shirt, would you? Give me this reptile who has crawled to your bosom. He is yet alive with venom and must be milked of poison. Give him back!"

Wrathfully Butler clenched his fist. "Offending one, are you a child that you are so unruly? You have my praise. I have given you presents. You are the envy of all with your English gun, horn of powder and blanket. Go fondle your new possessions and do not molest my ears, as would a bad bird, by your screeching."

At signal, Lieutenant Barent Frey hustled Levi past the glowering chiefs, removing him to a hut near the woods, leaving him with a ranger guard. He was given his first decent meal, the first in seemingly forever. Worn and near collapse, wracked by the fatigue in his body, Levi tried to sleep, but it was not to be.

He was alerted by surreptitious sounds at the rear of the hut. Levi seized a gourd, prepared to hurl it, waiting while the intruder finished his slicing a passage through the fabric. Levi considered the danger. If the man meant him harm, the fellow would have waited until his intended victim had time to fall asleep. A small stone was tossed through the slit. Then appeared a hand followed by an arm, and finally the visitor stood in the dim light. He was tall, dignified, and spoke in a voice so soft Levi strained to catch his words. His language was English. The man was a Seneca of importance. "My son, I once was welcomed in your father's house. I am ashamed few make you welcome here."

Levi's pulse quickened. "Cornplanter?"

The orator put his finger to his lips. "Speak low. I am discredited at the Council and more prisoner than you. Nevertheless I am a man none dare to destroy, not even Hiakatoo who kills for pleasure. There are yet two hundred Seneca braves who view me as their leader. Let us be brief. I have been waiting for a messenger with words of importance from your General, but from the quickness of events waiting far too long, if I sense their purpose. Yet words from an honorable heart, words sent by a messenger who risks death to bring them are worth my ear, though late coming. What says the Tall Hunter?"

"The war between the people of the Longhouse and the people of the United States is at its beginning and should not be permitted to grow. So says my General. He has put his hand upon a white belt, peace to be eternal between your *nation* and ours. My General feels you may stop this war, knowing the evil it brings"

"I wish as you that this could be done, but the once small fire has by now spread quickly and cannot be easily put out. War has been declared. The vote has been taken. In the taking of that vote I made a pact with War Chief Joseph Brant that I would no longer oppose the war because, in so doing I would undermine his leadership as war chief above all, and then Hiakatoo would seize power. What more does the Tall Hunter wish me to know?"

"The General wishes you to convene a council, that he may offer each of the several Indian Nations a seat in our Congress, your nations to have representation in all matters brought before that body. This is the message I bring."

Disappointment crept over Cornplanter's face. "My son, there is only parch in my throat from preaching peace to unreasonable men. Measures stronger than words or promises are needed. I must tell the Tall Hunter this is not the time for a white belt. It would be better to show your cannon, to make a great display of your troops. Then I will speak out and propose we come to terms lest your troops destroy us."

"Troops?" answered Levi, equally disappointed. "We have not the strength this summer. I would exceed my authority were I to say more."

Cornplanter prepared to depart. "I will send your General word of our meeting. One of my trusted braves who has lived near Fort Augusta will carry my word to Colonel Hunter. As for your fate, Levi Brady, sleep without fear. In the morning you will go north to Nia-gar-ah. Rest, for you must be away by dawn." With this, the Chieftain made his departure. Levi now knew nothing stood in the way of the terrible bloodshed about to inundate the settlements. His General's offer had come late, by far too late.

Chapter X

FORT NIAGARA

Before clearing the woods and coming upon the scene at the end of the military highway, Wallis knew that Fort Niagara lay just ahead. A bugle's silvery notes sounded through the virgin forest. The two halted at sight of the British Union Jack rising from the center of the impregnable army installation. Distance lent Niagara the aspects of a toy fortress, its portcullis, causeways, battlements all miniature. At close survey, it was no toy. Banks of cannon, protruding from high walls and watch towers, dominated the land about the fort. It commanded the eye by its immensity, and promised a hard fight with its sweep of the fields of approach. And it as well controlled the river traffic to its west, as ships put in from Lake Ontario. To its north lay that infinite expanse, or so seemed the Blue Ontario, this great lake constantly trimming its waves at the abutment of the fort. As they neared this military bastion, Wallis discerned a man-swallowing moat running the length of the west wall, which they were approaching. At the far side of this they waited, facing an entry tunnel which passed through solid brick, this concealed by the lifted underside of a drawbridge. An officer at the watchtower gave orders for lowering the bridge. Operated by a winch in the hand of guardsmen, the cross-bridge came into position on creaky chains. A crisp grenadier officer saluted Brant.

They traversed a broad, grassy compound with intersecting walks, one of these leading to the headquarters building by the lake. In the middle of the quadrangle soldiers busied themselves at polishing an artillery piece while captives, stripped to the waist, fed a crude oven, readying hot shot for challenging an unrecognized ship lying-in toward the fort. Niagara, disciplined, was no lazy obstacle. Sickly Colonel

Marion Bolton injected his own body-wracked fever into his minions. Thus the constant pacing of the ramparts, the presence of soldiers in the tunnel of ever-ready guns, the prompt vigilance everywhere.

Brant, striding before Wallis, acknowledged the greeting of a kinsman, Cut Nose Johnson, who referred him to a disabled soldier sunning on the west wall. The convalescent, a Lieutenant Dochester, had led a party that had been mauled by enemy fire last April in the vicinity of Fort Pitt. Dochester had witnessed the death of a warrior of whom Brant had been fond. The Lieutenant was anxious to relate the details to the Mohawk Chief, since betrayal by unknown persons was the cause. The conversation afforded Wallis time to look about. He was struck by the number of warriors at hand. For the main part these were kept outside the fort, admitted in limited parties through the well guarded entrance known as the Indian Gate. The British were skittish about too many inside the walls. Wallis wondered why such numbers were gathered here. Brant, his conversation finished, started toward the Headquarters Building. Wallis scurried toe on heel behind. A brass-capped Hessian presented arms, letting them pass.

Coming from the bright outdoors into the gloomy headquarters building, Wallis's eyes probed for details. The hall in which he found himself he remembered from his youth when it was more ornamental than busy. It functioned as a waiting room for the various departments. Those persons yet to have their appointments, and those who moved hurriedly off on their special businesses painted a scene overly animated and ill-fitting with his memory of the leisurely fort that was. He concluded by the activity that some great blow was soon to fall upon the rebels. This scene of commotion was lent a picturesque character by those in military garb. In contrast to the soldiers in scarlet uniforms, the wearers of which were King's and Eighth Regiment officers, was the forest green garb worn by the loyalists, drab and unmilitary by their plainness. These volunteers moved about, ill at ease in these environs where gaudy uniforms and click of heel, and pivot to an inward drum was ordained. Indians in war hieroglyphics and feathered headdress lent their presence to this colorful river of humanity.

A wooden face sentry guarded the Colonel's doorway. As Brant and Wallis entered a man in deerskin came out. With tardy surprise Wallis realized he had brushed elbows with an old acquaintance, the unsavory Simon Girty, Butcher Girty, White Savage Girty. When Edward Hand was colonel in command of Fort Pitt Girty had held a militia captaincy. He had turned his coat in spectacular fashion. On the eve of his desertion he tried to set off the fort's magazine and blow his erstwhile comrades into Kingdom Come. Fortunately for the garrison, the train of powder was detected. Worse than this, after his aborted fare-the-well he had embarked upon a campaign exquisitely his own, making his name anathema; he had leagued himself with the foremost whites and Indians in bestiality, catching and roasting men, women and children. His pig eyes, survivors related, glistened when at his signal his followers would spread-eagle a woman on the ground, hitch up her legs as though at a delivery, and then thrust a red-hot gun barrel into her. This agony not enough, if she pleaded for a merciful death, or she fainted, he would order her revived and placed on a couch of fire, he and his followers howling like so many wolves as her cries and struggles increased until the tortured creature twitched her last. "Bah!" involuntarily said Wallis, with a glance behind, and then hastened into the room. The Mohawk bade him wait, as he spoke to an adjutant on duty. Brant disappeared through a second door. Conscious of the observant captain, Wallis surveyed the banners, weapons, and portraits in the anteroom. The waiting was overly long. He fidgeted, stared into space, ignored the adjutant captain who, tiring of watching Wallis, nodded in his chair, half asleep. Wallis walked to a table map, pinpointed with flags where the Crown held sway and where militia, British militia, loitered in the forest. He was amazed to see clusters of symbols around Unadilla and Chemung. He could understand Chemung, a Tory hangout; he had seen the rangers come in. But he did not like what he saw at Unadilla. Twin forces spelled trouble on the fringe of the Longhouse, trouble possibly concentrating against Muncy. Time was on short wick.

A bell roused the captain. Looking into the room beyond, beckoning to Wallis, he announced, "Mr. Wallis, sir!" Samuel Wallis advanced, jaw set. With the Boltons of this world he knew how to act. Be timid and the martinet would be thin on concession. Wallis knew he must out-Amherst him, lord it to him, be peremptory. Yet he must appeal in other ways, in usefulness. The room he entered was painfully bare, a monk's cell. It had four chairs and a desk.

Bolton, scarcely an impressive man, was of small stature with an owlish face, a product of Eton. 'Why,' thought Wallis, 'he is no different from a dozen I know. I'll have him in the palm at quick rate.' Wallis was to find his opinion premature and erroneous, the Colonel as brittle as regimental law, as inflexible as the Code of Punishment. In addition to Brant, Bolton had another visitor. A big man, this latter guest was all sword, the blade suspended by his baldric as broad as two fists knuckled together. As he paced the austere room, brow knitted, the tip of his toe and the point of his scabbard did not move in unison. It was a wonder that the pendulums of foot and sword, at moments at cross-purposes did not come to mischief. Daniel Claus, the German son-in-law to the late Sir William, loved food, this obvious by his girth. It also prevented him from seeing his sword, slung a bit too low, was perilously close to banging into several stacked muskets.

Brant, with a sweep of his arm, introduced those present. "Colonel Bolton, Colonel Claus, this is Samuel Wallis who comes in friendship."

The grim countenance of Wallis caused Claus to throw up his hand and chortle in his heavily Germanic accent, "Ha! By God, Bolton, look at his face. He trusts you! Ha! Ha-ha!" At that moment his sword tangled with the stand of muskets, this freakish accident sending him sprawling. With guttural oaths he picked himself up, glowering at the gale of laughter from Bolton, even taciturn Brant. It broke the tension.

"Please be seated, everybody," said Bolton. "You, Claus, ere you join Dochester in Cripples' Corner." Canada's Superintendent of Indian Affairs promptly dropped into a chair. Bolton nodded at Wallis, "You are a man about whom Brant speaks highly. I had thought to see a younger person making so arduous a trip. You are of importance in Philadelphia, I'm told, being an individual of some sense and posture there. And knowledgeable on frontier matters, too, by your acquaintances. Now that we are met, in your own words, sir, repeat what you have already told Brant."

"I learn there is to be, if not already, deployment of the New York Line. The First under Colonel Goose Van Schaick is to be positioned west of Albany in the Schoharie Valley and Colonel William Butler of the Continental 4th Pennsylvania line will join him there at Fort Defiance, as will a detachment of Morgan's Rifles. Butler is one hell of a fighter. Last August, as you Brant too well know, he with Arnold, both fresh from victory at Stillwater, stopped St. Clair and you from taking Fort Schuyler, almost in your pocket. The bad news doesn't stop with that deployment. Colonel Philip Van Cortland's Second New York Regiment is to serve as a reinforcement to Colonel Peter Gansevoort's Third New York at Schuyler."

"We heard about Fort Schuyler being reinforced, but thought the deployment defensive. Of news is Butler's presence with the Riflemen at Defiance. This places a different cast upon events."

"'T is not garrison duty they go to, although 't is made to appear so. These troops are to march, upon their commander's nod, to burn the Mohawk, Onondaga, Seneca and Tuscarora villages. There's talk of a party to be sent up the Susquehanna, the numbers unclear, even the fact in itself an uncertainty, they to intervene with the line of march of those coming down from western New York, all together forming a sizable body."

Bolton dryly commented, "If this scheme has as its purpose the taking of Niagara, our hospitality will be as was Quebec's. Any American trying my walls will find death or captivity."

"I merely say one can surmise an attack upon Niagara. The boldness of the move, its rapidity, and the plan to destroy the villages along the Susquehanna invites that further thought. It could be not so ambitious. If only to scatter Brant's warriors, it would deny you their services. As I have implied, Colonel, this can be a precursor raid forewarning of a greater force yet to come."

"From what source springs these powers of augury?"

"Several; largely from your counterpart Colonel Hunter at Augusta. When I asked for troops to guard Muncy, instead he told me of attacks to be launched up and down the river."

"And when is this to happen?"

"We are almost upon the date. This August, if not sooner."

"Interesting," stated Bolton, drumming his knuckles on the desk. "However, the rebels talk a better war than they fight."

"It may well become your nightmare. Can you afford the consequence if I am right, and you ignore me?"

"Well put! But I see you have come here petitioning for my protection indicating you yourself have little faith in the Rebel cause and plan."

"Yes, and no. My best protection lies in cooperating with the King's forces, the war to spare me. I offer my services, you to be informed whatsoever I hear, in exchange for your friendship."

There was an awkward silence, broken only by Bolton's renewed knuckle drumming. Then he responded, "And you could as well sell our secrets to the rebels. You are an ambidexter, a knave, Sir." After which he startled his visitor, further adding, "While I am a crude, distrusting bastard who once was a gentleman. Ours should be a famous relationship. Tell me about yourself, what can you do for me? What are your connections? What level of access do you have to those who make war against the King? Who besides Colonel Hunter do you know?"

"First, I am a merchant of some standing in Philadelphia. I also am a Quaker, professed politically neutral; yet there are those who assume me to be a deep and close-mouthed rebel. Within the compass of my acquaintance are prominent men of Congress and the Continental Army. The aforementioned possess knowledge which could be at your disposal. Am I too astute, Colonel Bolton?"

"You could particularize."

"There is scarcely an officer in the Western Department who I do not know. " From an inner pocket he extracted a sheaf of diagrams. "As proof of my wide management, here are sketches of the forts on the north and west branches of the Susquehanna, the armored farm house of John Brady near Muncy, the forts Freeland, Freehold, Boone, Swartz, Ogden, Forty Fort, Wintermute, Jenkins, Wheeler, McClure, Antis, Horn, Reid, and Bosley's Mills. There you have it, the forts above Augusta, the obstacles between you and the Blue Mountains, their numbers and quality of soldiers, irregulars or militia. And, Sirs, my opinion how these forts will be affected by Washington's draft of the militia."

Bolton pounded the desk, spilling ink and sand. "You propose denouncement of your friends, neighbors, and commercial associates! Could you not as capably treat us given the chance?"

The merchant calmly refuted Bolton's rebuke. "My friends include those loyal to the King; they took the rebel loyalty oath to preserve their estates from confiscation and themselves from imprisonment. If among my associates are arch rebels, this is dictated by my circumstance. You reproach me for being in their company when my position in Philadelphia, now with the British gone and Congress returning, has benefits which would accrue to you and the loyalist cause. I ask of you no reward. I ask but one thing, that you avoid my lands in your conduct of war. I have given you a foretaste of my importance. In exchange I want John Butler's Tories and Indians to respect Muncy, making wide berth around the settlement. Call it request, or condition, that is the trade."

"Wallis, what you ask seems simple, yet works to our disadvantage, unhinging our battle line as it flows southerly. Sir, I gather that you are a perspective man, if only by the information *you* supply us, its timeliness suggesting you foreknow our plans. The taking of Augusta, straddle as it does the Susquehanna, is imperative. More-so now that Burgoyne's surrender at Saratoga shifts upon us the attempt to cut the rebellious states apart. This we can do by advancing down-river to where it empties into the Cheasapeake Bay. The prelude to all is the removal of Forty Fort as an obstacle preparatory to taking Fort Augusta --"

Claus interjected, "Were we to slide by you, with view to forcing Colonel Hunter to yield up Augusta, you would become a large pocket of armed men on our flank as we advanced, and a threat to our rear once we passed you in our going downstream. Can we afford that risk? Can we trust you? Mr. Wallis, we must consider the matter at length."

Colonel Bolton looked at Wallis, saying, "Sir, if you will, I beg your indulgence in the outer room."

With Wallis excused Bolton debated the request. "He is," ventured Claus, "a deucedly clever fellow. Why does he give us information? We know, as he does, were his conditions met Muncy would be an ideal location for rebels to assemble undisturbed and unspied upon, we lulled into believing it disarmed. Those forces could come against us."

Bolton turned toward the Mohawk. "What say you, Brant? You brought him here."

"The men of Muncy are not as quiet as you would think. They have not sat still these past few weeks. They have plucked up trees and made a fort with stout walls. With much grief to themselves any who would attack the place would find it difficult to scale the walls, much more knock in the heads of the defenders. And yet, I see no real danger from this force. The garrison is purely defensive. They are not in great numbers. Though Muncy rattles with a drum, you cannot fault Wallis for these preparations. I know the man. Personally he boils no kettle. He is a Quaker. As he says, he has a weakness, his attachment for his valley where he keeps a fine home. He loves his valley as most men love a maiden in the spring."

Colonel Bolton finally made up his mind. "He can be useful, but first I must test his loyalty." Wallis was recalled, finding Bolton engrossed in the material. "Mr. Wallis," purred the Commandant, "this is an instructive collection. You amaze me with the detail." He smiled disarmingly. "You can appreciate my eagerness to be working with you. But first I must be in comfort that you will do us no harm. From time to time we may seek information from you which in itself will give inkling *as* to our future moves. We must feel confident you will neither communicate unintentionally nor under strain what you know of us. Colonel Claus, how shall we test Mr. Wallis's adeptness at keeping a secret?"

"Easily, Sir. Tell him our next border operation."

"No!" sharply said Wallis. "I will not have the responsibility. Were it to go awry I would be blamed."

Bolton's voice became icy. "In this instance, Mr. Wallis, it is unlikely we would fail. Claus, I defer to you."

"In a few days," stated Claus, "three hundred Seneca and two hundred rangers embark on the Susquehanna waterway. Their destination is Forty Fort. Once and forever we are determined to squash this obstacle. By the disaster to be visited upon Forty Fort's garrison we shall influence the depopulation and abandonment of the Valley. Hiakatoo leads our Indian allies."

"You could not do worse," distastefully opined Wallis. "He's a cruel and inhumane man likely to subject the population to the extremes of terror and to unspeakable torture if to fall into his power. The effect you wish to produce could be counter to your interests. A less sanguinary leader might avoid the retribution such a blow would assure." At this point Wallis's eyes rested on Brant as if to nominate his friend for that leadership.

Bolton was sensitive to Wallis's unspoken choice. "Hiakatoo's selection is inevitable after the news you bring. Chief Brant and his Mohawks are needed in New York." Bolton paused, considering his next comment. "Hiakatoo accurately reflects our determination to remove all obstacles to our future advances. Fully grasp our plan. Despite your plea, this is a war of utter destruction. The purpose of the Americans is the same, to burn rival communities. Yes, I know your apprehension about Indians and their sometimes outrages. But Colonial Secretary Lord George Germain authorized their use." Bolton looked at Brant while speaking. He was exonerating himself.

To himself Wallis meditated, 'That's why Brant went to England to visit the King. It was to urge employment of the Indians, this to further his quest for power and leadership.'

Bolton continued, with a death-knell finality in his voice, "We shall sweep Forty Fort Valley with a sickle, turning the Susquehanna into a river of blood, and throwing the heads of the fort's defenders, like so many pumpkins, into its waters. So be it. War is war, a rotten business. There shall be an undoing of the hand of man. Some shall call it unmitigated horror, some war's necessity. By which name will you call it, Mr. Wallis?" Wallis said nothing.

Bolton, who perceived the stunned look of their visitor, picked up the refrain. "We are going to release you for your journey homeward, knowing you are as of now in a contract with us. You are also in the Procrustean couch. You may forewarn the Connecticut settlers. Should you do this many may be spared the mischance of war. Families will fly south. However, if you truly cast your lot with us, you must withhold the news. By doing nothing to advert this catastrophe 't will be on your conscience until the day you die. In fairness to you we by coming in such numbers, whatever be your decision, cannot materially be defeated. With or without surprise Forty Fort falls. Your choice, sir, is the saving of lives versus absolute silence. If you cannot tolerate our secret, then you are not our ally, and one day we shall honor Muncy with a similar call. It you remain silent, you justify our confidence."

"One last observation," interjected Claus. "You should restrain your own militia from any activity if, by arrival of survivors, your men are motivated to fly to the rescue. Their interference will only add to the slaughtered. No sizable garrison is near enough to Forty Fort to affect our forces, save Augusta. Should you alarm Augusta, I dare say Hunter will not venture forth"

Wallis acted as a fish hooked and brought to air. Fear jabbed his mind. Voice reduced to a strangled whisper he cried, "You've made of me a Simon Girty!" He covered his eyes. Truthful had been Brant's forewarning, that the price of the dinner would cost him as much as he was prepared to give, and more.

Bolton shuffled a group of papers. "By the way, Wallis, here's a report Brant kept from you. Seneca and Green Rangers raided your neighborhood and drove the settlers back to your stone house and fort. In the future, not to raise suspicions, we shall repeat minor sorties, feinting at you. It would not do to ignore you, questions to be asked why you enjoy fortune's smile." The Colonel reached for his braided hat. "We are in readiness for your homeward trip, once you have freshened yourself. Your transportation has been arranged. In exchange, we thank you for the good horse you provide us."

Where the river Niagara had junction with the choppy Ontario, at the base of the fort Wallis stood waiting while Colonel Bolton explained to a loyalist captain who was overseeing a war party of Indians preparing to launch a canoe, that a last minute passenger would be taken aboard. The captain and the several Seneca were an advance reconnoitering party. They were bound for Forty Fort, their mission of great import by the wealth of rank among the Indians. From the conversation Wallis concluded they were to arrange with the Tory family, the Wintermutes whose armored farm house commanded the northern end of Connecticut Valley, a token capitulation. Further, they were to receive from the Wintermutes assurance that some provisions would be available to feed the force that would descend from Niagara and Unadilla. and encamp on the Wintermute farm before going into battle. Wallis looked in disbelief, finding himself in the company of a man, Hopkins, a Christian Indian. This Sheshequin chief was an often visitor to Muncy. These were strange times. "How-do," said Hopkins, smiling through a row of broken teeth. In a way, the lower reaches of the Susquehanna was Hopkins theater of action. There was another, a cruel featured fellow who strutted the pebbly beach, to whom Hopkins was deferential. This was Little Beard, a powerful sachem of meager intellect whose adulation of Hiakatoo, supreme Seneca War Chief, had made him a shadow and aide-de-camp to that monster. Where Little Beard appeared, in close order was to be found the six and a half foot giant Hiakatoo. Hiakatoo at that very moment came up the shore and joined the group. He was wearing a multi-feathered war bonnet, his gargantuan frame daubed with body paint. Nominally the royalist captain was to be in charge; yet this was titular, Hiakatoo their avowed leader. Chief Hopkins, obviously a nonentity, nevertheless had something to say as to the plan of the voyage. In this one respect all were obedient to him. Using the beach as his slate, he sketched their route. For Captain McDonald's and Wallis's benefit Hopkins employed tolerable English. "Here we make portage; in this next place the current will be swift and resist us; again we shall make portage, a long walk to this lake. From lake we go on the river, on which we can glide to Wyalusing."

McDonald appraised the plan, mindful of his passenger's destination. "We can disembark you here, a bit of a walk to Muncy. We'll give you a talisman against harm." McDonald handed Wallis a small stick with a black dot. "This will protect you, and proclaim you as one to be spared, should you meet with any of our parties." He turned from Wallis to Hopkins. "Once we have landed our passenger, we continue on the Susquehanna to Wintermutes." Hopkins nodded. Two canoes were being dispatched. The route would carry them west, then south to the narrows of the Genesee River, east-southeast overland to Chemung, southeast via the Teaoga to the Susquehanna, then southerly following the great loop westerly. On the Susquehanna, above Wyoming Valley's northernmost outpost, Jenkins Fort, the two canoes would separate, the chiefs to make their way to the Wintermute Farm, there to prepare the attack on Forty Fort. The second canoe, Wallis meanwhile to be transferred to it, would await darkness, then its paddlers would strive to reach Augusta before dawn. In the darkness dipping their paddles vertically, they would slide noiselessly by this fortress at the junction of the West Branch with the Susquehanna. Somewhere beyond this they would deliver Wallis as near to Muncy as they would dare go. Once they discharged their passenger, they would pull to shore and hide their canoe, waiting nightfall to venture once more past Fort Augusta. Or, if a hue and cry were to come from the fort, they would abandon their canoe and rove about as a small war party. From the place where he would be landed Wallis would walk due north to Muncy. This was the plan.

Bolton watched them cast off. Standing, lifting his hat in salute to the Colonel as the canoe separated from the land, Wallis called across the water, "You may depend on me, Colonel."

"B'damned," bellowed the Colonel, "and sit!" Wallis shrugged and obeyed. They were away into the river. Bronzed arms steadily, rhythmically propelled the craft. The fort and its cannon slipped into the past. Dreamy, peaceful shores, laden with blossoms, encompassed them.

Wallis had been tempted to speak of his association with Howe, then thought silence far better. What purpose would it serve? None. Conscious of Hiakatoo's stare, he stared back. The distaste was mutual. The War Chief had overseen the braining of Fort Freeland's wounded defenders last year. Once that fort had been surrendered and the British had taken away those able to walk, leaving the helpless behind, they were systematically slaughtered, their pleas for mercy ignored.

Chapter XI

THE FURTHER MISFORTUNES OF BRADY

At 2 A.M. Levi was awakened by the whispers of Lieutenant Frey. "Shake your legs, Mr. Brady; your security hinges on our speedy departure. One of Hiakatoo's subordinates arrives is this town. A nasty fellow I'd rather you not meet. If you are not gone by sunup he will see you a corpse." Frey hustled through the sleeping settlement, at the edge of the forest meeting three Indians who were to accompany them. "They believe you are a ranger," breathed Frey. Levi mounted one of the horses, these being poor cast-off nags.

"Where to?" Levi asked.

"Niagara."

Levi looked askance. "If you believe these horses will get us there, you are mistaken."

"Oh, these," chuckled Frey. "We change mounts up the path. Scratching Feather stole five good ones from Forty Fort a fortnight ago. They are in pasture at the next settlement." Thereafter Frey fell silent. The morning was half-formed in the sky when the Ranger officer exclaimed, "See ahead! It's Indoi."

Indoi, totaling 15 houses, was deserted; its men, women and children, save Scratching Feather's squaw, were at Canandaigua. Indoi being a regular Tory way stop, the squaw had been provided sundries for

124

the convenience of loyalist visitors. She presented her guests with apples fried in bear's grease, and dried fish wrapped in a baked crust made from corn meal. Scratching Feather wryly suggested his woman should go with the party on the trip, to cook and tend their fires, to which Frey raised objection. "Gakoga, gluttonous beast, would you bring a woman because you cannot sleep unaccompanied?" Whereupon the Indian candidly insisted they delay until he had copulated with her. He was adamant on this head, only thereafter would he get the horses. Frey fumed inwardly. The other Indians, who had gorged themselves to the limits of digestion, staggered from the house and hid on the far side of a fire-pile where they fell asleep. Soon, though, discovered by their snores, they had the pleasure of being kicked awake. "Get Scratching Feather!" howled Frey, dinning out their protests. "Must I wait for a fornicating fool? Must I grow old waiting, slothful ones?" To Frey's credit, his command of the native tongue, and his scowls motivated them. The pair strolled from the hamlet in the direction Scratching Feather had taken. Scratching Feather and the two braves reappeared.

"You want me?" inquired Scratching Feather, innocently.

"I want you in Hell. Where are the horses?"

"I now go get horses," said Scratching Feather, and retraced his way, the others shuffling behind him. Indifferent to the heat, Frey paced back and forth, disgusted. He chafed; the afternoon was half-gone. Levi squatted in the shade, sifting dirt through his fingers. Suddenly Frey stiffened, folded his hands over his stomach, face ashen, and pitched to the ground.

Levi scrambled erect. "What is it?"

Frey gasped. "My guts!" Pain trenched his face.

Lifting up the pain wracked Britisher, Levi carried him to the hut. "You damned jackass!" Frey managed to enjoin, "I can't stop you; go on; run for it! Run!"

Levi hesitated, then set him down and sprinted across the field, leaping into the woods. He struck a path that ran parallel to a stream, continuing until he found a tree cast over the water, a natural bridge on which he crossed. Taking his course from the sun, he veered south, encountering a main path, large and well beaten, going in a southerly direction. Chancing it, he jogged along, ears attuned, ready to fly into the bushes at moment's danger.

He had been 40 minutes free when a tug at his stomach drained his cheeks. With a cry, he doubled over, vomiting. Vaguely he knew he must hide himself. In terrible agony, he attempted to crawl on forearms and knees. In this he partially succeeded. He must have lain unconscious for a long while. The sky - when he opened his eyes - had darkened from blue to a rich purple, with shiny jewels appearing overhead. He had no pain, only a dull nausea; but when he tried to sit up, he could not, being helpless. He could do nothing but listen to sounds. What he heard was ominous.

The first warrior down the path reined his horse and jumped to the ground, and in the same blur of motion trained his musket on the body. Behind him seven braves - likewise slipping from their horses - split their party right and left, beating the bushes for signs of ambush. These seven converged beyond the crumpled form and, by signal, indicated the underbrush was free of concealed rifles. They had feared the supposed Indian corpse had been placed there as bait. Thereupon the chief of the small party examined the man on the ground. "Ata!" exclaimed the warrior chief, noting that the man yet breathed. "He lives." With widened eye the warrior perceived Levi's red complexion to be a matter of artificial coloring. "Truly," he further exclaimed, "this person wears flesh not his own. We shall soon be enlightened about him, for he wakens." Levi, who had deemed it prudent to feign unconsciousness, opened his eyes. 'Lucky!' he thought; the warrior examining him was Mohawk! "Are you ill - are you hurt?" asked the chieftain. Levi gestured at his stomach. In English the Indian asked, "Poisoned meat?" Levi nodded dumbly.

The curiosity of the Mohawk was slow to express itself. Abiding by the weakened condition of this white man, the Mohawk stooped, lifted the prostrate militiaman, and carried him to a tree where, using his own blanket, he wrapped him against his chills. Mercy from a cougar! "Make camp," ordered the chief. "A new fire."

The group of warriors, Levi soon discovered, was strangely composed. The five nearest him were Mohawk while the three seated to an aside were Seneca. These two groups had come together, by chance, on their journey. One of the Seneca, Large Talker, avidly argued with his companions, with constant glances at the bogus red man. At this juncture Levi, weak and ill, dozed off.

Levi woke to find the campers stretched in slumber, the fire reduced to a dull glow. Something had wakened him, something indefinable. On the far side of the fire a warrior who had been addressed as Naked Bear was also awake, studying the woods. 'Hoot, toot, hoot-a-loot' came a cry within the forest. If this mournful sound, the nocturnal monologue of an owl, had excited the suspicion of the Indian guard, it also had set Levi's heart pounding. Murphy's signal! Naked Bear nudged Pudding Dry. The two Seneca scattered the fire and slipped into the dark, pausing only to crawl from Indian to Indian, waking all. Soon the pair materialized and, after hurried whispers, their Mohawk leader apportioned watchers to scan the darkness, English muskets on their laps, senses probing the patterns and shapes of the forest. Whether the hoots and loots had originated with owl or man, the sounds failed to recur.

Dawn began with a gray glimpse in the night, then an abrupt fading of the darkness, the fireball sun climbing over the treetops, melting the lowest blankets of clinging fog. The sun lanced its rays onto the clearing where they had their campsite, flashing upon their gun barrels. Huge spiders, one might imagine, had spun the many cobwebs of dew woven onto the grass and into the bushes. These nebulous gossamers evaporated as the sun quick-marched through and around the trees. The travelers stood up, yawning and chattering. They renewed their masks of ocher, retouched the faded sections of their designs, and then ate a frugal breakfast of dried corn. A lively and vehement discussion of last night's alarm occupied them. By daylight they searched the woods; if there was any conclusion, it was that whatever had created the noise had departed on wings, leaving no footprints. Large Talker alone dissented. "Be not deceived," adjured the Seneca; "the owl flew off on two legs. He will return. Where one owl hooted last night, many may hoot tonight."

"My nephew," responded the Mohawk leader, employing the salutation, which designates an inferior, "are we to tremble at a noise?"

"Take heed, Mohawk! Kill this man and go quickly from this place."

The Mohawk's temper flared. "You who are Seneca would kill for the sake of killing. How can you say he is an enemy? How do you know?"

Exasperated, Large Talker declared, "Does it matter? Somewhere, some place I've seen him. I feel danger has come among us. There is an itch in the ceremonial slits at the nape of my neck."

"But," persisted the Mohawk, "can you prove what you feel?"

"Quickly," replied Large Talker. "I will persuade him to confess himself." He lifted a burning stick from the smoldering fire and advanced upon the Lieutenant. The Seneca had not advanced five feet when the Mohawk sprang from his seat on a log, and stood between Levi and his would-be tormentor. The Mohawk's eyes glittered. Large Talker hesitated. With wounded pride the Seneca dropped the brand and returned to his kinsmen.

Levi, convinced he would be murdered, struggled to his feet. With his shoulders against an oak, he broke into dialect, the language of the Seneca. "Attend!" he voiced, to Large Talker's amazement. "I see that you are perplexed as to who I may be. I will answer your doubts. It is true that Large Talker remembers me, for I am the adopted son of the Turtle, who lives in the west toward Detroit, and who came to war against the Seneca before the war of the 13 fires put all true men together and made them as brothers. And it may be true you have seen me more recently, for often I come and go from Niagara to Detroit as an ambassador and Courier of Depester, the General at Fort Detroit. It is from my many travels that I have learned your language, which differs from the tongue spoken in the west. My cousins, I have spoken." Indeed Levi had spoken, perhaps the biggest lie ever concocted on the frontier. It was contrived out of absolute nonsense, inspired by and cooked up from his desperation. It worked!

The Mohawk, whether or not he believed the yarn, which he did not, was delighted to further torment Large Talker who gaped at the white man. "My nephew who eats dogs," the Mohawk chided the Seneca, "open your ears to your own language. Surely this man speaks the tongue well. He has traveled your bad roads. No wonder he is crippled. Well you may regret insulting the adopted son of the Turtle, the ambassador of Depester. I will apologize for your humor and beg this worthy person to view your mistake as that of a child limited in judgment." The Mohawk had alluded to the 8th King's Regiment co-commander at Fort Detroit. If Large Talker had any stomach for coming to blows, he was dissuaded. Five flashing hatchets and knives against his three made him an unhappy believer. The question of Levi's status settled, the Mohawk offered him a place by his side. Thereafter, in Mohawk pride and in Seneca sullenest the cavalcade resumed its journey through the woods.

Levi realized his lie had secured a respite, not a cure, his position remaining most fragile. Biding the recovery of his strength, he set his plans for a nighttime adieu to his eight companions. To serve this end, and bolstered by his belief Murphy was somewhere in the rear, he the maker of the owl-like sounds, at the next encampment when the supper fire had settled into ash and the braves had drifted off to sleep, except for one watcher, Levi feigned slumber. He was waiting for a shadow to steal from the woods, Murphy a shadow with a knife, woe the warrior on guard. At false dawn, Levi's hopes having thinned, he himself drowsed off.

On this day's journey he nodded and yawned, which excited Pudding Dry. "Observe," he harangued, "our visitor sleeps by day. Why do his eyes close more than those of Naked Bear whom has kept watch one part of the night, and those of Handsome Lake who has sat until sun-up? Has the Longknife been planning to pound out the brains of our sentinel, should either have fallen into dreams?"

When evening again arrived Levi found his position of bivouac changed. He no longer slept aside. The Mohawk chief wisely listened to the clamor of the Seneca. Levi, from that night on, slept at the center of their bivouac between two braves. If he but twisted, they would waken and lift on elbows, then scrutinize him and the forest before returning to their slumber. Furthermore, with a change of heart, the chief thought it advisable on the third night to fasten his hands to bent saplings. Time meant nothing to the Indians. They halted when and if their fancy directed. One morning, in fact, they did not break camp at all, Pudding Dry having dreamed that they should stay off the path. His dream spirit had gone ahead, returning with the message that a heavy tree would fall on their heads were they to proceed. That morning the sky clouded over and a storm lashed at the forest; the boom of thunder and toppling of trees was prodigious, one hemlock narrowly missing their campsite. The next afternoon they wasted visiting the graves of ancestors, shooting a buck, feasting and narrating stories of their own bravery, each tale more preposterous than the previous.

On the succeeding day they rode single file down a path that widened into a portage road, this guarded by a small stockade, Fort Schlosser, along the Niagara River. This was a transfer point for goods come by water, with an improved road to Fort Niagara, 50 miles distance. A subaltern, inured to sights of savages laden with scalps and occasional prisoners, tapped his pipe on the heel of his hand as he stood on the fire-step. A god glancing from the heights, he encountered the eyes of Levi. 'At last!' thought the American, 'a civilized person, an Englishman, safety!' This prospect was immediately dashed by the officer's stony stare, his attention invoked by the novelty of Levi's paint faded face, differing from the usual pale and drawn countenances of hapless settlers. Out of curiosity the subaltern ordered the gate opened.

As soon as the gate was unbarred, the Seneca Indians were into the redoubt, they expressing difference with the Mohawk, stating this man was their captive, solely theirs, clamoring for rum, 'walking stick'. They wanted the rum for themselves. At once the Mohawk, hearing this piece of treachery, protested that the Seneca were interlopers and had misrepresented the facts about the white man, who was no captive but a Tory officer of sorts, being an ambassador from Depester. Further, they stated, they had rescued the ambassador from 500 rebels who would have hung him by his testicles had not they, the brave Mohawk, appeared and chased off his would-be tormentors. In proportion to their bragging, and the counter-insults between Seneca and Mohawk, the subaltern's temper waxed. His sergeant, who preconceived the wish of his commander, led out a platoon, the full garrison of this isolated post, and managed at bayonet point to clear the compound. The Indians and their prisoner were pushed through the portals and the gates were slammed in their faces. "Plenty 'walking stick' - Niagara, you damned idiots!" shouted the subaltern, glad to be rid of the brawling lot. The devil he would give them rum. Once intoxicated, they would knock his flimsy structure to pieces. "No medicine this place!" he reiterated as they continued their cries, threatening to besiege and sack the 'pile of kindling'. The officer resolved upon a stratagem. He cupped his hands to his mouth and managed to out yell them, saying, "Why, Brethren, do you tarry? I have heard that many hundreds of American troops have crossed the Mohawk River, and are out to burn Mohawk homes." The British subaltern was embellishing on a tale told him by a passing captain from Niagara: that the Mohawks which had been at Fort Niagara had disappeared, having rushed off in reaction to a rumor of a rebel thrust at their Nation. The subaltern's distortion had a pronounced effect. The Mohawks, instantly stilling, conferred in hushed voices, and then whooping, eyes afire dashed for their horses and their homes. The peril to Mohawk homes was of no concern to the Seneca. With the prisoner now entirely in their grasp, they renewed their exertions to be readmitted to the fort. The subaltern, confronted with the alternatives of either shooting at allies otherwise to surely cast his walls down, or of acceding to their demands, ordered one small keg to be delivered outside. The sergeant was almost ahead of him in fetching the keg. "Now, go away," the officer admonished, "and do not so much as look over your shoulder or, by your unholy souls, I shall make you sorry!" A shot lent incentive, imparting to his words furthers comprehension. The Seneca scampered off, dragging keg and prisoner. What they did not know was that the sergeant, anticipating the subaltern's order, had pulled the stopper from the keg, emptied some of the rum, and then had his men pee down the bung hole, replenishing the contents.

When the stockade was out of sight, they encamped, roped the Lieutenant to a tree, and cracked the top of the cask with their musket butts. At first swallow they looked at one another strangely, but continued to drink, though somewhat unhappy with the salty taste of the rum. But they drank it until they were in a stupor. Naked Bear lurched toward the tree to which Levi was tied, fumbled for his cock and pissed on tree and prisoner as well, inadvertently distributing the refiltered contents of the keg, thus captor and captive sharing the donation given by the British. The small war party slept late into the following morning.

It was during this day's travel, Levi trotting ignominiously behind Large Talker's horse, a rope stretching to his fetters, that he came close to losing his life. When he stumbled it fitted Large Talker's humor to swipe at him with the flat of his tomahawk, which dropped a red-sparkling cascade across Levi's right eye. It was a glancing blow, enough to break the skin of his forehead, near blinding him with the blood, leaving him with a terrible headache. Though the day's journey was a short one, their encamping came none too soon. His pain kept him awake most the night. Some words from Levi mitigated their cruelty. "If I die," he argued, "my one scalp brings you but one blanket at the trading post. Can three Seneca divide one blanket? Keep me alive and at Fort Niagara I bring you a big keg of firewater, trade muskets and powder. This you may divide." After this, they fed him, and traveled at a less rapid pace whenever he swayed at the end of the rope. Even so, despite the reduced pace, he fell, choking blackness engulfing him, he to be dragged several feet before their judgment persuaded them to stop. Since they were almost to the fort, after reviving him they tied him to the neck of Naked Bear's horse, continuing.

A King's sentry spotted the visitors from his tower and called the sallyport, whereupon four guardsmen lowered the traverse. Answering for the prisoner who was momentarily recovered in senses, an ensign shucked his bonds. "If he walks it's a miracle," observed the officer, receipting for Levi's custody. Levi, his hands gripping a protruding brick in the wall of the tunnel, swayed on his feet. The officer signaled two soldiers to convey the captive by elbows. Levi, too far gone to note where he was being conducted, appreciated only the graduation from sunlight to darkness as he came into the shadow of some sort of building. He dimly heard the rattle of a key and the hollow magnification of the boots of his escorts as they crossed a brick walkway. The sounds, the guardsmen's boots, were amplified by the echoes which bounced off the nearby walls. They had entered a vault-like structure in which, unceremoniously, he was left. A door clanged and a bolt thudded behind him. With the inertness of a sack of potatoes he keeled over, dropping where they placed him, in Fort Niagara's prisoners' cell. The occupants, eight in number, cagily gathered around him.

"Is he dead?" asked a large man in shabby dress, putting a thumb to Levi's head and peering into his glassy eye. "By God, if it isn't a corpse they've brought us!"

"Maybe he's our supper," guffawed a second man, "seeing as pork and beef is mighty scarce for prisoners of the King."

"Be thankful that they haven't stretched your neck as yet, you damned rebel," said the first speaker, a rebel himself. "Give here with the cure and curse." He alluded to a bottle of rum. The self appointed leader of this scarecrow crew was a hawk-nosed fellow who sported raiments that scarcely held together over his torso. So frayed were his garments that there were patches on patches. These were discards, their origins unknown, his original uniform fancied by his Indian captors. This collection of patches could have once been a continental uniform, a tory's green garb, a frontiersman's buckskin, and in probability consisted of all these, one to look at the multicolors. "The rum!" demanded the big man, feeling Levi's chest.

"It's wasted," argued a squat inmate with toad-bump skin. "'T will lay in a dead man's throat, a dying man's at best."

"Shut your mouth and fetch it!"

"Yes, sir!" agreed the fellow, digging into the straw of their common bed. Levi had an awareness of being swung onto this ramp which slanted from the wall, and of the fiery liquid passing down his gullet."

"Thanks," he said, weakly, and was asleep the same moment.

Moments later, it seemed, a musket butt was prodding his ribs. "To your feet!" commanded a guttural voice. The light in the narrow window had gone, as well as the occupants of the room. He focused on a Hessian, then a second figure standing behind the first. Both were outlined by a lantern held by a third party. "To your feet - snell! Qu-hick-ly!" repeated the Hessian. Instinctively Levi's hand contracted around the musket, shoving the muzzle end into the redcoat's ribs. The soldier screamed, his weapon falling from his grasp.

The second figure, a lieutenant of grenadiers, chuckled involuntarily. "Damn, 't is a fair return!" The officer, a Welshman with a merry face, motioned Levi to stand. Tired, aching, but alive, he was thankful for his resiliency, the product of a life of strenuous adventure. Prisoner and gaolers, the klop of the Hessian boots the only sound, marched from the stockade and onto the quadrangle. "Interrogation," enlightened the officer, surrendering his prisoner to a sergeant posted at the door into the military headquarters building. Along the length of its gloomy hall this guardsman escorted him. The silence of this veteran soldier and of the almost empty hall was oppressive. Levi wanted to whistle just to hear a human sound. The deathly quiet abruptly was shattered as a cannon let go outside. Whatever the purpose of the shot, this a signal to a ship at sea or evening gun regularly fired, the sergeant was indifferent. "In here," he said, conducting Levi to an inner room, then vanishing with a click of his heels. Levi, alone, fixed his finger to his battered eye. The lid was tender. With his good eye he made a circuit of the room, swiveling his neck. The room was bare except for a desk and several chairs. Believing himself unobserved he was about to examine a paper on the surface of the desk when, from behind, he heard a voice, its tone arresting.

"Well, Brady," said the voice. Colonel Bolton stepped around his prisoner. "Be seated." This was a command and as well a realization by

Bolton of Brady's condition. Levi surmised Lieutenant Frey had passed word about their encounter. For Levi it was obvious this was the famous Colonel Bolton. The Colonel wasted no time, minced no words. "We hang spies," he said, dryly. Levi had confronted this accusation before.

"Spy, Colonel? If paint and a shaven crown say I am a spy, and as such am to be hung, you would do well to keep my execution secret. Down country your blue-eyed 'Indians' have been captured. Raising one set of toes raises others."

The Colonel brushed aside Levi's point. "Why aren't you with your company?"

"You tell me - sir."

Bolton crimsoned. "Since you will not confess your purpose here, does your recalcitrance measure its importance?"

"I am flattered."

"You admit not being with your company; therefore, you came not as a soldier; you came as a spy. You shall hang."

"I admit nothing. Whether or not you wish to believe me, 1 declare only to my being a prisoner, never a spy, taken while on an independent scout seeking my personal vengeance for murder of a friend whose hair was lifted by Seneca."

"Bosh, pure bull shit! Brady, you are a militia lieutenant. Supposedly your Company was to have arrived at Coryll's Ferry on the Delaware, marching by way of Stroud's to Easton with orders to join Washington. Now, answer up! Is the Free Company at the Ferry, or is it somewhere in our woods as were you? And how many more companies are there with it?"

"Colonel, I have a profound respect for your ability to gather facts. I will leave it there. If you think you have a crop of Continentals on the prowl, that well may be the case. Think as you please."

"I think you a spy and fit to hang."

"And I make you answerable to the rules of belligerents. I am a prisoner, in your custody until exchanged, whether this be soon or not until the war's end which may too soon for your comfort."

"Damn you, Brady. If you will not answer my questions, I will not be answerable for your fate. First, you were brought here not as a prisoner taken by the British. Just to the contrary, you came as a captive of the Indians who would barter you for trinkets. I'll not have you. It's no swap. My duties as commandant do not embrace compulsory exchanges."

"I have been brought under the British Flag, and am entitled to its protection."

"You demand protection of the very flag you would tear down? A pox on you! Am I to treat with the Indians for every blockhead? It's not my concern if they take you and play lacrosse with your head. As sure as death, they'll pack you off to Canandaigua for ritual, and I shan't interfere."

"Is this a threat?"

"It's my decision, in the event you do not confess your business and throw yourself upon my clemency. I leave you to settle your own disposition. Certainly, in the hands of the Indians you will not fare as well as you would here. It would be a pity to reduce a man by charring his elbows, as they often do, and gouging his flesh with hot irons, or broiling him slowly 'til he begs for a merciful clout on the skull. And I've heard it said that the Indians, in their delicate humor, will bite off a finger, then thrust it into a tobacco pipe, and offer it to the victim to smoke."

Levi's lips opened. Then he thought better. If Bolton feared Americans were moving in the woods, not only would the interrogation continue, but also it would be of service to the frontier to bluff the Colonel into retracting his war parties, collecting them back into and about Fort Niagara, bastion of British power. Brady thought that Bolton had ample precedence upon which to found his fears. Had not surprise blows caught the British off guard at Princeton, Trenton and Fort Ticonderoga? Levi pretended being goaded into a rash rebuttal. "Colonel, it is you and not I who should be fearful." He bit his lip as if regretting his statement.

"A-ha!" said Bolton. "Sergeant Pointdexter!"

The nearby Sergeant snapped his heels, and purred "Sir-r!"

"Who's got the detail at the hot-shot oven?"

"Webber - Corporal Webber, sir."

"Take this fool to Webber. Break him lifting ordnance shot. When he's ready to collapse, quick time him to me."

As Levi was led away Colonel Claus sauntered in. "Pray, who's that?"

"A Connecticut Militia lieutenant. A fellow named Brady. Caught at our doorstep, too."

"No!"

Bolton stared out the window, fingers drumming on the desk. "First we get Wallis from Muncy, and now this one from Forty Fort. The pot boils." Claus inquired, "Have they wind of our plan to attack down the Susquehanna in force, Wallis to come running up to sue for peace, and now this one snooping?"

Bolton thought further. "No, not as far as Wallis. He was shrewd and timely with his guess as to the drift of events."

"And Brady?"

"There's the puzzle. He was on a spy. But for what purpose? To reconnoiter us for an army yet to be assembled? Or are the rebels aware of our plans? Are they setting up an ambush to catch us along the way?"

Claus dismissed the notion of a large force anywhere close at hand, his Indians to know this, were that so. "Further," stated Claus, "it is beyond credibility!"

The Commandant of the Western Department made his decision. "Claus, we must prevent any force, small or large, from assembling to entrap us. Speed up by a day or two your preparations for the attack on Forty Fort. These are my orders to you. All Seneca and what Mohawks you have are to go post haste to Unadilla, there to join Butler with his Rangers. Once Butler has put together his force, he is to press on without delay. Tell him he is to 'help' the rebels celebrate their 4th of July Independence Day, timing his attack no later than that date."

Having settled this final detail, the two colonels opened a bottle of brandy. As it happened, the cannoneers chose that moment to commence a nighttime practice. At the first salvo of guns the brandy from Claus's brim-filled glass splashed Bolton in the face as he reached to fill his glass. The sputtering, half blinded commander, yelling for a pitcher of water, dashed from his quarters vowing eternal damnation upon his gunnery captains. Bolton had forgotten he himself had ordered the night artillery display to impress the natives whose canoes were anchored at the foot of the fort.

The artillery dueled with mythical ships at sea. The noise was appalling every time a gun breech was touchholed into action. Guns danced in their mounts from the force of their recoil. If Bolton had intended to impress the Seneca by this display of British might, he succeeded too well. The stalwart savages - even the most loyal - were they first-time visitors to the fort, reacted violently. Terrified by the 'thunder trees', they stayed only because their war chiefs went from canoe to canoe calming the occupants. The chieftains cursed the stupid English.

Chapter XII

IN HEADLONG FLIGHT

Levi had been detailed to the hotshot oven, an oven in the sense that an iron grate was supported over a pile of burning wood. Upon this grate rested cannon balls like so many loaves of bread, with the flames licking up and around them. Located near the west wall, these red hot projectiles by ladles were passed upward to the gunners who dispatched them on their short, hissing arcs through the dark, to plunk into the river that had its mouth on the lake. Lake and riverside of the fort thus were as watery plains over which no enemy could approach without meeting up with terrible consequence. Levi found himself in the company of the hawk-nosed, raggedly dressed man. The man, watching for his opportunity, whispered when Corporal Webber looked elsewhere, "Greetings, friend. Did you get to Cornplanter?"

Astounded, Levi, bending his head towards the fellow, asked, "How do you know this?"

"Pist! I'll explain later." The man busied himself and at the next chance added, "I'm Carberry of the Light Horse, First City Cavalry, Philadelphia." Again the corporal strutted by, eyeing the pair. Carberry resumed, "Are you alive enough to break for freedom? You looked like hell, yesterday, mostly dead."

"That was yesterday. What's your plan?"

Both fell silent. Webber stared at them, then walked on. Carberry continued. "Can you get us through the forest, take us down the North-South Path?"

"I came up it, half-conscious; I guess I can - if need be."

"Good man!" He briefly showed the handle of a knife concealed among his rags. "Webber's habits are fatal. He always sparks his pipe in the corner of the wall next to the hotshot oven, away from the breeze off the lake. He's taking out his tobacco now! You're to grab for his musket. I'll do the rest."

"Then?"

"Along the wall - I'm dog, you're the tail - and up to the parapet, then jump for the beach; any canoe will do." The corporal had turned into the shadows as the guns on the wall ceased their exercise. A cup of light glowed, then died and the smell of tobacco drifted into their faces. With a leap Carberry was upon Webber, twirling the big trooper with ease, clamping a hand over his mouth and bracing a knee against his back. "If you shout," hissed Carberry, extending his knife and substituting the point of it for his knee, "you get a billet in hell." The corporal strangled an oath. The pair trussed him with his own belts and gagged him, stuffing his mouth with a remnant of Carberry's shirt. Carberry peered around the side of the oven, noting that the other prisoners, ignorant of the proceedings, were leaning against the oven's forward wall. Carberry darted forth, Levi on his heels. Two of the prisoners, unbidden, followed, pounding along some distance behind. "Damn!" grunted Carberry. The footfalls slowed and stopped, their makers lost in the dark. As though Carberry had counted the yard to the last stride, and had been over the stretch in a thousand rehearsals, he halted abruptly, stuck his hand out, and caught and brought to a standstill the onrushing Levi. In the pitch black Carberry guided him up several steps and onto a parapet. They felt past a battery of silent guns.

Inches in front of them a mistaken and friendly guardsman chided, "Blast you, Walter; don't you creep at me that way." In reply Carberry lunged at the sound, missed, and cracked his own head on an abutment. Levi, clubbing Webber's musket, swung it in a circle. There was a noise like a pumpkin being shattered, and a groan.

"Carberry? Lighthorse?" called Levi, wondering who he had hit.

"Underneath," came back the muffled voice. "Haul off; he's an ox of a man."

Levi gave a violent shove which released the Philadelphian, who again took command. Carberry mounted a narrow ledge. "Jump!" His voice was authoritative, assuring. He and Levi jumped into the black awfulness. Carberry struck the beach and bounced erect. Levi, for a spirited instant believing his bobcat of a friend had led him off a hundred-foot precipice, involuntarily stiffened; he crashed onto the pebbly strand. A pair of hands jerked him erect. "Death if we're slow!" Off they went down the beach. They could see the dark contours of slumbering braves huddled on the shore, some of whom stirred and sat up. One sleeper involuntarily being trod upon, shouted. They sprinted for the nearest canoe, the beach becoming alive. "Here!" exclaimed Carberry. Levi climbed into the birch-bark hull. A bewildered, half awakened occupant sat up on his couch of robes, and was baptized head-over-heels, flung from the canoe and into the water.

By then the beach was moving with startled Indians. And, inside the fort, the escape had been detected; a drum was beating. At a cry from the wall, "There, out there!" torches converged on the parapet; the indecisive light painted the upper battlement. A quick-witted soldier hurled a smoking brand onto the spit, illumining part of the Indian fleet. A Hessian lifted his tar-saturated brand. Someone with authority shouted, "Bring rockets!"

Levi, weighing wind and distance, with his one good eye aimed at the Hessian disclosed in his own torch light, and snapped a shot. The torch fell. 'T was a lucky shot, muskets poor weapons beyond the range of 100 yards. The next minute His Majesty's Regulars sent a volley whistling 12 feet overhead. This provoked further yowls from the confused Indians. "The Devil! Thunder! Hanisseono, Hino!" Believing the fort had changed hands, the red men fired at the guards on the wall. In the pandemonium the canoe slid into deep water.

The Seneca were convinced that an American Army had surprised Fort Niagara and a horde of longknives was about to pour down. The pair churned their paddles and fled the site. A flotilla of canoes filled with angry Indians, directed by the vociferation of the half drowned Indian, began in pursuit. Ahead of this company of warriors, chiefs, and squaws, the fugitives drove onward into the concealing expanse of the Ontario. Now, like a huge fan the armada spread itself behind them. Were conditions less dangerous, the two Americans might have paused to laugh at the spectacle of swearing, cursing red men and the night's mischief. What had begun in stealth had ended in bell-clapper idiocy.

But it was not the moment for laughter; Carberry and Levi with frantic energy continued to ply their paddles. After twenty minutes of scudding through the waves Carberry looked about and saw the horizon was clear. Only at one far point a dark splotch was to be seen. There a mid-lake council was progressing, the harangues of a chief wafted to their ears as that dignitary, shouting out, attempted to restore his affrighted peoples' senses, they having fled every which way.

"Nice shot," gasped Carberry. "I say, there, nice.... Brady!" Alarmed, he looked toward the stern and at the slumped figure. He crawled to his limp companion. "Damn, sound asleep!"

Easing easterly, Carberry slanted inshore at dawn. He buried the craft in the reeds between two sycamores canted into the water. He laid branches across the parallel tree trunks, in effect creating a lattice while Levi slumbered on. Next, Carberry dove into the cold lake. Though his teeth chattered, he breasted the current affixing more sticks, some extending downward into the water. On this mesh of branches he strewed mud, old grass, and leaves, and packed in prickly briar to hide chinks in the surface. The fabrication viewed from afar resembled a beaver dam. Satisfied, Carberry crawled into the canoe tucked within this contrived screen, and established himself, musket ready, near a slot in the framework. Through this opening he could survey the lake. In this way he kept watch over his exhausted friend.

Chapter XIII

TWO FOR THE ROAD

Levi woke to an unreal world. It had been night and it was now day; it had been open water and now the canoe nested against an embankment; he had been in the company of a fellow named Carberry, and now there was no one about. He lay alone in the bottom of a canoe concealed by a cover of bramble and sticks. Gingerly Levi wormed his way out of the cocoon-shaped structure and stood groggily on the embankment. His eye, puffed from Large Talker's blow, was measurably better. His body ached from fatigue and the bottom of his stomach rumbled from hunger. Carberry's disappearance was solved when the Philadelphian appeared from among the trees. He seemed the worse for wear, scratches on arms and legs. Several of these were more like punctures, claw marks needing makeshift dressing, a mud poultice if nothing else. Carberry must have been one of those rare fellows oblivious to pain. Over one arm was draped a cougar's skin. It was plain he, being mostly naked, intended to fashion this into a fur apron to restore his dignity. "Welcome back to life," said Carberry.

"How long did I sleep?" Levi asked, squinting at the sun.

"Well, it was nigh midnight when we took leave of the brotherhood of red men, and it's near tea-time for Bolton and Company. You've sawed wood for a period more than half around the clock. Also, you've missed the best-damned cougar fight. At one point I was about to bet on the cougar."

"Invite me to your next performance," dryly commented Levi, shaking his head. Carberry was crazy, jumping off walls in the dark,

142

leading a parade of canoes with unhappy paddlers, and now this! Apprehensive about their pursuers, Levi scanned the lake.

Carberry gestured victoriously, spreading his hands in wide-open symbolism. "Poor souls, they've lost us completely, not knowing how far we paddled before putting inshore. They had too much shoreline to examine." Actually Carberry had spent about four hours if not more on the lake, by guess covering between 25 to 30 miles following the south shore in its easterly direction. "A mixed party of Tories and Indians searched past this spot just past daylight," he said, "working well beyond us. About two hours ago, in sore disposition, they made their glum return. We sure added to their calluses." Then he asked, "Be you hungry?"

Levi crinkled his nose. "Smells great!" he exclaimed, spotting the thin fire and wisp of smoke. "Wild cat's better'n the fish heads thrown me afore now."

A more strange sight in the woods there could not be. After gorging themselves on cougar and a few berries, Levi reddened his skin with several handfuls. Carberry amazed Levi. Reversing the pelt, inadequately scraped, he sliced it into various size pieces, including a large rectangular section. Then, with the fur surface to be placed nearest his body, he created a breechcloth for the lower part of his torso. Along the upper edge he belted the garment by introducing a long strip threaded through short slashes. His shoes, beyond repair, he replaced by turning two smaller pieces into moccasins. He cut thin slices for laces.

For Levi, it was astonishing to find a Philadelphian with mastery of these frontier skills. "Let's introduce ourselves," he proposed, watching Carberry at work. "How do you call yourself by?"

"Well," said Carberry, "you already spoke my name. While I was stuck under our much damaged friend Corporal Webber, without your realizing it you used a name pinned on me by my friends, it being 'Light-horse.' I am captain of a light horse troop recruited in Philadelphia, known as the 'Silk Stocking' Troop."

"As for my own," Levi responded, "my father had a passion for the Bible, and opening it to the Third Book of Moses, he chose Leviticus. A hell of a name for a kid. It chews in my mouth like uncooked porridge. I prefer 'Levi'. Yes, I too do, as you, hold a commission. I fought under

Morgan in his Rifle Corps until I returned to my frontier home to help raise a militia company. This leads to the question as to how you came to know about my attempt to reach Cornplanter?"

"I will answer your question, but first an unspoken one. How does a man like me know about survival in the woods when my commission associates me with The First City Cavalry?"

"You call it the 'Silk Stocking' troop?"

"I did. The troop's membership is made up of city dandies, not rough cut lads. I was not of their ilk. Don't ask me how I became involved. They needed to be 'properly officered', so I was whisked away from a Pennsylvania cavalry troop of light Horse, to be transferred to Philadelphia. I'm a misfit. I'm a 'feather up your ass', go for hell at a gallop type, not a Sunday soldier good at prancing a horse, looking nobler than thou and a hero by virtue of my brass buttons and lavishly gold-trimmed uniform. But by God was I wrong about those brave fellows. They were tested at Princeton and found not wanting in courage. Mainly, though, our duties were dispatch riding, scouting about, and to relieve this monotony sometimes in our country travels grabbing up a stray enemy soldier startled by our abrupt appearance. So, I left. Does that answer your unasked question, how did I learn to paddle a canoe, engineer its camouflage, and to best a cougar? My friend, like you, I've been raised on the frontier. I was fed up to my throat with dispatch duty. Then luck fell into my hands. I was ordered to report to General Washington. He was worried the Indians, the Mohawk and the Seneca would join the British and bring war to New York and Pennsylvania settlements. Washington needed a rider to go to Cherry Valley carrying a special dispatch. I was told to whom the message was to be delivered. Save me, good Lord, from dispatch riding."

"And how did that bring you to Niagara and you to learn who I was and my purpose?'

"Let me finish. In the last week of May at Cherry Valley I delivered the dispatch to Lieutenant Frederick Wormwood who was expecting me. The dispatch was intended for Cornplanter. Then this Wormwood fellow surprised me. I was to go with him. He advised me two separate attempts were to be made to locate the Chief. You were described, but not by name. Someone in the chain of command presumed I knew how to find Cornplanter, which I didn't. By Wormwood I was told was he might be at Onondaga, to attend a conference there, a sort of shot in the dark suggestion. Wormwood knew less than I how to find him. I've never been in the Onondaga Country. Then Wormwood passed along instructions I alone was to read the message for Cornplanter contained in the wooden sealed tube. That I did. Then I shoved this tube back beneath my jacket. We were two idiots. We could quicker find water with a peach tree branch than Cornplanter.

"We followed a wagon road leading out of Cherry Valley and, as we were passing an outcropping of rocks a few miles from the settlement, a half-dozen painted warriors rose from concealment calling on us to halt. Instead, we spurred our horses to a gallop, the Indians firing at our backs. I don't know how I missed being hit. One ball passed near my ear and another tore my sleeve but never touched me. I was later to learn Wormwood had a ball pass through his back and exit his chest, he attempting to draw his sword as he fell. A warrior rushed up and buried his tomahawk in his forehead. As for myself, as soon as trees and rocks screened me from view I jerked the damn tube from my jacket and flung it into the woods, and not too soon. As I rounded a curve some whites and about 50 Indians stood on the path. I surrendered. So, when you arrived at Fort Niagara, by your timeliness I knew why you were there and suspected that our purposes had come to naught."

"What is your reason for wanting to go south, risking recapture, rather than continuing to the lands of the Oneida? There we can be safe."

"Because. The Seneca are gathering at the Fort. All is buzz. There is a major blow coming, and everything points to an attack down the Susquehanna. The talk is Wyoming Valley, Forty Fort, so I overheard."

"My God! You confirm what the settlements on the Susquehanna most dread. For sure, we have no time to waste. The best of our militia have just gone from Forty Fort to serve with the Continental Line! They were marching off as I left. Oh my God, Forty Fort is undefended! We must get there before the war party. We've got to organize a falling-back fight of the militia to give the women and children time to flee. And we have to seek help from Colonel Hunter, at Augusta, if there's time to support the militia in their withdrawal. We need - God - we need horses. Human legs won't get us anywhere. Our best bet is to reverse direction, abandon our canoe here, then cross overland so as to be south of Fort Niagara, and to come astraddle the well traveled portage road connecting

Niagara and Schlosser. We'll find horses on that road, forelaying their riders."

Carberry's head was crammed with facts gleaned from Oneida guides. "Devil's Hole is the place to form our ambush. By a narrow pass the roadway skirts a chasm, and where the road to some degree climbs there are embankments hard by where, concealed from view, we can set our trap. Whosoever happens along elects either meek surrender or a fatal plummet to the bottom of the abyss. There's no retreating. A handful could defy a regiment with ease at Devil's Hole. I cannot lead you to it, but the road is close upon the Great Falls. Do you remember being brought by such?"

"I recall nothing of the last 50 miles. If it passes by the Great Falls, we'll find it. Let's go."

They struck overland. Their travels lay through deep, unbroken forest. The further they penetrated, the denser became the pines, leaving them in a kind of twilight. Through this gloomy, trackless stretch Levi led Carberry. Just as Carberry began to have his doubts in Levi's ability to get them out of these woods, the forest abruptly ended. Again the sun flashed in their eyes. However, instead of timber, they now confronted brush amazingly thick and higher than their heads.

They could not see whether this wall of brush ended a short distance ahead or continued indefinitely. They tried making a passage by cutting, slashing, wiggling, and crawling. Exhausted, having discovered a stream, they bathed their faces and feet. It was apparent they were being defeated. "If we go with the brook," ventured Levi, "it'd be easier and faster. It courses easterly, and just might intersect our path. Better'n fighting brambles anyway." They sloshed upstream. The noise of their movement along this watery passway was the only sound, save the one grunt of a bear and the harsh cry of a kingfisher. The silence, otherwise, was that of a world depopulated. Their advance was short-lived - the stream failed in a swamp. Despairing, they pushed on by continuing along the swamp's border.

There was logic behind their plan. The Hole had been employed to advantage by Pontiac's followers 15 years earlier. Both Levi and Carberry had been acquainted with the tale. Farmer's Brother, a Seneca sachem, had recognized the value of the Hole. With a few warriors he had waylaid an outnumbering convoy of 80 British soldiers and teamsters bringing supplies to Niagara. The teamsters and guard of soldiers, but for one, were annihilated. They had been pushed into the chasm, tumbling and screaming. Levi and Carberry sought to find the spot for less sinister purpose, horse conscription. In the waning light, baffled, they conceded themselves lost. They knew they must encamp and await daylight before stumbling forward. This troubled them, they aware this delay could spell doom for Forty Fort. "Two more minutes of light," estimated Levi as he parted a thicket, looking for a place to camp. He and Carberry stepped through the bush, and gazed at each other, thunder-struck! They had intercepted the elusive road. A moment ago they would have sworn it was anywhere, but not on earth. Here it was, at their toes! They knew it to be the main path by its hard, wide surface. At once, with this piece of fortune, they perceived the ideal place for their concealment. From the wall bordering the rising road protruded a rocky knob, somewhat flattened on its upper surface, whereon they could squat unseen. To reach it they first had to climb to the plateau overlooking the rock, then let themselves down upon it. The road immediately beneath the outcropping passed in such a way as to favor plucking from the saddle whoever ventured by. Scarcely had they settled themselves when the moon splashed her yellow illumination onto the clearing.

Strapped to Carberry's waist was a pouch taken from the canoe, the pouch containing the former owner's cache of dried strips of beef, commonly called jerk. They divided this, and also ate berries from a nearby bush and some edible roots they dug up.

Off to the right the eerie howls of a timber wolf, a half-bark and mournful complaint so like an Indian's signal, amused their fears. They listened, then breathed easily, deciding 't was only the animal. Then a new peril presented itself. Above their heads, from the terrace by which they had let themselves down onto the rock, they heard the sharp crack of a dry stick. Outlined by the moon, over them loomed a giant shape, that of a black bear. At last it wandered off. "Listen!" said Carberry, moments later, breathing into Levi's ear. At length eleven Mohawks leading two mules crossed the glade. For twenty minutes thereafter the highway remained empty, when six more warriors, in paint and heavily armed, passed beneath them.

"So," whispered Levi, "the Cayuga pretend to be neutral, yet come from Niagara."

In the second hour, the forest meanwhile best described as 'lawful quiet', Carberry slid from their rock and started across the glade for a drink at a rivulet some one hundred feet away. Like a shot, he was back, climbing to the plateau, letting himself down onto the rock. He pinched Levi's arm. "What?" asked Levi, who could hear nothing.

"Mum!"

Levi, too, detected the thup-thup, thup-thup, and gathered himself in a crouch. Whosoever were coming, they could not be many by the sounds. At last, gracefully two horsemen swept into the long bore of the hollow. Conveniently a cloud blotted the moon and glen. Levi and Carberry had a brief glimpse of their quarry. The lead man was a British officer, his epaulettes and buttons presenting a brave show in these remote quarters. His fellow traveler wore a monk's cowl and robes. " 'T is an evil hour for the Church," whispered Levi, and launched himself at the hooded figure. Carberry, a split second ahead, flung his arms around the officer, and sent him bowling from his seat. The Britisher's foot catching in the stirrup, he was dragged, leg twisted and broken, head bounding over the ground until Carberry managed to seize at the bridle and bring the frightened horse to a stop. The Britisher screamed in pain and, by way of gratitude, damned Carberry. The foul explosion was too much. Carberry's blow silenced him. Levi, too, had a problem on his hands, but of different sort. He beckoned to Carberry.

As Carberry walked in his direction he urged Levi, "Hurry, Get Holy Orders out of his robe. Put it on."

"His robe - you mean *her* robe. 'T is a sister, but not of the Church."

Carberry examined her. "I've seen this wench. She's a whore. This past fortnight she was landed at Fort Niagara from a sloop of the Royal Navy, an unusual event, she certainly special baggage, whether deliberately landed or thrown off the ship. Whichever, no matter. I dare say the purpose of her visit was cockloft rumping with ranking personalities. She'd stroll about, as much as advertising herself by the invite and sway of her hips." Levi looked for life signs. "Well?" said Carberry.

"She breathes."

"And we shall not if we tarry longer."

"Would you abandon her to wild animals?"

"Damn, Brady, you are inconsistent. She's mutton. Let the mutton loving British who are in constant travel on this road take care of her. We have greater responsibilities."

Refocused on reality, Levi agreed. "You're right. There's women at Forty Fort, one who is special to me, in grave danger and who may suffer a worse fate." They divested the officer of his jacket, boots and pantaloons. These Carberry donned. He kept the officer's traveling kit and sword but tossed Levi the rifle, this a work of accuracy and beauty, this type firearm a rarity among British officers. Levi had proven himself the sharpshooter by his shot during their escape. Carberry adjusted his stirrups. Levi, to maintain the character of an Indian, heaved his saddle into the night. The fallen officer let out a deep groan.

"Time to depart," stated Carberry, his voice precise, he conscious of their immediate danger and responsibility as couriers of warning. The two mounted. They galloped down the road risking head-on collision with any persons coming north. Carberry was calculating that his uniform and Levi's Indian disguise would get them by small groups. If such were to be met, they would hurry through them, shouting imperiously for the path to be cleared. A larger party, however, would insist on friendly parley and news, and that would fetch the hatchets down on their heads. One factor they counted upon was that few, more likely these to be stragglers, would be coming north and apt to confront them head on; every Indian in the woods in these parts was at Niagara and about to start south, or had already started south. Although danger lay in overrunning the advance elements, speed - they also knew - was essential. It helped insulate them from being overtaken by war parties somewhere on the move behind them.

At about 3 A.M. they rested their horses. They themselves, too, needed rest, fatigued by the long, trying day. But they didn't wish sleep, preferring to save that for daylight when they intended to depart from the intersecting paths and squirrel away deep in the trees. There, having sufficiently distanced themselves from the fort, in relative security they could catch their sleep. Once refreshed enough to resume travel, their plan would be to start in late daylight, reducing detection, and then continue under the protective cover of the following night. By this schedule they concluded they would minimize discovery.

To make small talk, Carberry asked of Levi, "Is your wife at Forty Fort?"

"Wife!" Levi echoed. What a notion. I've been too occupied dodging bullets, bayonets and scalp knives to have a wife. What makes you think I'm married?"

"As we were grabbing the horses, you made a comment about someone special at Forty Fort."

"Oh. That part is true. At Forty Fort I recently met a woman, the daughter of a doctor, who is just about the most beautiful person I have ever seen. Small, but built! She's a golden hair vision of perfection. Tantalizing, curvaceous. I melt thinking about her."

"And?" asked Carberry.

"She won't have me, in fact detests me. She thinks I am a coward, a deserter from the Army. That's the story that was spread about me to conceal my abrupt and secret departure. My orders like yours, to find Cornplanter, could not be told anyone. If I survive this war and come home with a full skin, I'll marry her in a minute if, when she learns the truth, she changes her opinion about me. But sometimes a wrong image is just like a bad spot on an apple; it spoils one's appetite, and the enjoyment is gone. Anyway, I had a magic moment with Abby."

They regained their horses. They rode until dawn's brush strokes were in the sky, when they discovered the dull red embers of a very recent cook fire, this located at the intersection of two paths. Examining the matted grass, they calculated a party of eighteen warriors had bivouacked here, there being seventeen depressions, where men had slept, with the final tally allowing for the one sentinel. "It looks like they've just left this place," Levi observed. "Had we come on a few minutes earlier, we would have had a big problem on our hands." The frontiersmen elected to take the branch path, which also led south. They soon saw signs, too, on this less beaten course, but the moccasin marks were old and covered by pine needles. They made one more halt, this time at the ruins of a hunter's lodge. Here they ate the provender found in the British officer's saddle bag, a cheese, some hard crusted bread, and a cured ham, and to their delight a flask of refined whiskey. They were kings! From the officer's traveling kit Levi extracted a brush, razor, and soap. He shaved and freshened his paint, then handed the razor to Carberry. Carberry rid himself of his prison beard. At this place they chose to encamp, taking turns at watch while the other slept, they waiting for late afternoon to resume their journey.

In this manner, with each day bringing peril, but with their luck phenomenal, the two Continental soldiers managed to shorten the distance to Forty Fort. They flew on, trees slipping by, strange paths opening, and at times they found the sun had turned itself around, their direction changed by the path of choice, they misled by their ignorance. They could not avoid delays. Intersecting passages confused them, and their steps had to be retraced. Once they burst by encamped warriors of the Cayuga tribe who scattered, not to be trod down. Carberry's red jacket was their talisman. And the Seneca oath, which Levi shouted as they went by, left the children of the forest to gape and scratch their heads, wondering what madness and rudeness was this.

They wasted two days, one by misdirection from an old hunter, and one hiding from pursuers the hunter had dispatched after them. But luck continued with them. Unmolested, virtually unchallenged they swept brazenly, boldly forward, pushed on by desperation. The precious two days they had lost, and the time spent backtracking off false paths made them wonder if the main war-force had reached Forty Fort ahead of them. From a hilltop overlooking the Valley they could look down on the most northern of the small forts, Jenkins Fort. Between the fort and the mountain from which they looked down, meandering south, was the Susquehanna, flowing toward the larger fortifications of Forty Fort and Wilkes-Barre. With shock they observed Indians in and about Jenkins Fort. Its occupation had not been contested!

"Smoke!" bitterly ejaculated Levi, the source being another upper armored farmhouse. Putting the tree-covered green wall of the mountains behind them and roweling their horses, they plunged into the Susquehanna, gaining the far shore south. They were beyond the view of of any hostiles in Jenkins Fort. As they galloped south, distant but distinct musket fire grew in volume. They entered the town of Forty Fort.

Those not fled were packing. The women, at glimpse of Carberry in his British uniform and the painted rider at his heels, dropped their bundles screaming that the vanguard had penetrated the town. Some fled into the fields. Belatedly, Carberry ripped off his cross-belts and bright jacket, while Levi yelled his own identity, this happening as a shot whistled between them. Fortunately their combined shouts produced some sense. James Scanlon, the crippled militiaman from Muncy who had fired at them, hobbled onto the street, perspiring and apologizing as much for his bad marksmanship as his mistaken act. It was a ludicrous bit of conversation in the midst of calamity. "Yes," he related, "the forts of Wintermute and Jenkins were surrendered in the morning." He described the unfolding sequence, how the Indians, Tories, and British regulars had split into several parties, these overrunning the isolated farms, "They are on a pre-organized plan, with help from within."

Elsewhere, Colonel Zebulon Butler, upon hearing that Major John Butler of the Tories had captured the outposts at the head of the valley, had decided to march with his men to join Lieutenant Colonel Nat Dennison at the Forty Fort redoubt. There, midway between town and the enemy, with a barrel of whisky as their table and its contents to fortify their spirits, the colonels held counsel. They determined to engage the foe, march out from the fort, rather than see the country despoiled and people murdered throughout the valley.

While the invalid Scanlin had been talking with Levi and Carberry, Sergeant-Major Asa Greenacre galloped down the street. He stopped in a cloud of dust at Colonel Butler's home, flew indoors, and issued with a stack of records. Recognizing Levi with a nod, he mounted and grimaced, "Can't fight a war without paper!" And before Levi could speak, he blazed by, the shine of battle in his eyes as he rode toward the shaping Armageddon.

The faint rifle-fire and musketry, sporadic at first, was assuming broad proportions. Levi commented grimly, "The Battle of the Butlers is begun!"

"'T is a pathetic fact, our men don't know what odds they face," said Carberry.

Hatless, Dr. Menema came running down the road, only to stop short. Mistaking Levi for a painted warrior, but seeing no leveled gun, he hesitated, then came forward a step. He narrowed his eyes. "Levi! Alive! Tim Murphy told me you were captured; that you and he were on a secret scout; but he swore me to silence, to tell no one, not even Abby. Well, you're back, and just in time; there's going to be a battle, and I should have been with the troops an hour ago." He set down his bag of instruments. "Confounded child birth! While I'm delivering Ann Wells, her fool husband, at news of the enemy, delivers me of my horse. Off he goes clippity-clop, not knowing whether he has daughter or son, in a cramp for Forty Fort. 'S a wonder he wasn't faced backward. And here am I, my feet slow servants, left to walk. In the words of Richard, 'My kingdom for a horse!' Levi, give me the use of yours. I'm needed on the battlefield."

"Up with you, Doctor, and hold tight. As for your surgeon's tools, there'll be few wounded for you to mend. The Indians are too many. 'T is not a battle that's shaping, but a slaughter."

"If it comes to that, I can wield a sword as deftly as I can handle a forceps."

The Doctor having mounted behind Levi, the trio were about to ride forth when a company of New Salem soldiers overtook them. The major of this company, informed of conditions, at once proposed the whole party take stand in the village and organize a retreat of the women and children. "We'll act as a delaying party, or rear guard." In the next breath the New Salem major abandoned his logic. "Oh, hell; no matter what good we might do, it'll be said we were afraid to join the battle. Lads, we've come to fight and shall. However you, Lieutenant Brady, in your masquerade as an Indian very likely could be taken for what you appear to be, and invite being shot by our own militia. Therefore you're elected to remain here and organize the retreat!"

"Like hell! The devil I will!"

"The devil you won't. That's an order."

"But --" expostulated Levi.

"Lieutenant, no 'buts.' Get off your horse." He leveled his weapon.

"Please do it, pleaded Dr. Menema. "Abby's among those women. Save her! Obey the major."

"Do your duty," roared the major, "or I'll shoot!" Levi came down. With a grin the major blew him a kiss. In vexation Levi clenched his teeth and watched the party disappear around the curve of the wooded road. Menema, vaulting onto the horse, put it to use.

The Menema house close by, Levi strode to the door. "Abby!" he called. She appeared in the doorway, a musket pointed at him. Her beauty flooded his senses anew, but there was a pallor of fear and terror in her eyes. "Abby, it's me, Levi. I came to help, to save the women and children."

"A lie! You're painted. You're with the Tories, another blue eyed Indian. You've come to take me into captivity, or worse. Before you shall, I will kill you, you turncoat!"

"I love you," he simply said, adding, "believe in me. It is true I was ordered to leave my company, to go on a spy up-country from which I am returned. That order came from General Washington. He chose to give me his confidence, but It was not mine to share." She lowered the musket, gravitating into his arms as he explained the reasons behind the urgency all should flee. "Go, find everyone you can, fetch them into the street. Tell them they are dead if they so much as delay an instant, the Indians coming this hour. There shall be no holding of the foe at our battle line."

Levi wished he had 10 voices, 20 arms, and as many sets of legs. Aided by Scanlon, Levi put those first arrived into the boats and on makeshift rafts, dispatching these down the river. Others late-come he gathered together, preparatory for a trek up South Mountain and toward southern safety. Again he found Abby, and then was diverted away. "Be off!" he admonished a woman who had seized him by his arm, begging him to find her son, a lad who had marched out with the troops. "Your boy today is a man! He, along with every one of us, is in God's Hand." Again, he could not find Abby. "Join the group! Catch up!" he kept calling to stragglers. The women expressed every degree of emotion, some inarticulate in their fear, several so shaken they had difficulty holding to their feet, others in transports of rage and wanting weapons that they might follow after their husbands, while the majority, by taking comfort in their faith, were able to inspire all. Some 70 women formed up in the procession, with that number to bedoubled, were the children to be counted. Two men attached themselves to the group, one enfeebled by age and one by dysentery. Scanlon calmly sat on a porch step, gun propped on his knees, watching Levi shepherd the dolorous train to the foot of South Hill. From a distance Levi saw the militiaman priming his gun. Levi, an infant under each arm, once more catching sight of Abby, motioned her to come to the head of the column. He noted, as she silently walked besides him, that she seemed at the edge of her strength. The group rested on the crest of the hill, by common accord looking back and down, each with an eye to home and to the battleground beyond. Tiny figures already raced from house to house; in quick succession a dozen, then two, then three dozen columns of smoke rose skyward. The town was dying.

The exodus from Forty Fort brought the refugees into vast woods where trees grew so thickly that a traveler, facing to any quarter, could not see 20 feet. Many tremendous trees lay fallen, each like a grand galleon under a sea of moss. These blocked and taxed the overwrought women. In their distress they tripped or became entangled in the cancerous, snake-like roots that covered the floor of this portion of the darksome forest, this adding to their anguish. Then they came upon moist, watery soil, mucky and foot catching. This swamp, for this it was, was as a grave. Sometimes a woman would fall into the fetid water, from which she would pull herself out, if she did, the slimes clinging to her hair, face, and arms. Those who began to lag called for the party to wait. But such was the urgency that Levi, who reckoned on pursuit, had to keep the column moving.

His responsibility demanded he not imperil these women and children by delaying their flight toward safety. It meant abandonment of the weak, with this causing him the worst of suffering, he to be numb to their pleas and prayers. If, at the onset of this flight the strength of the hardy had supported the weak, now the fugitives had come to the place where mutual aid was impossible, so close were the woods and so strenuous the journey. And in the minds of all were the war painted Indians, more dreadful than the wilderness. Levi, burdened as he was by two children, when he saw Abby step off the route and seat herself upon a mouldering trunk, made a step toward her. "Up Abby," he exhorted, knowing well his imploration was ineffectual. She shook her head. Gently he bent, and pressed her lips. In turn, she touched one of the babies, and smiled.

All through the woods, through the Great Swamp, small and large parties floundered. A Mr. William Searles, wounded in a previous skirmish and unable to participate in the battle, fetched 12 women and children across the mountains. The panic spread as the trickle of survivors arrived at various blockhouses. Settlers near the small forts of

155

Antes, Horn and Reid added themselves to the refugee contingent. Convoys of fugitives invested the Susquehanna waterway and its roaring branches. As a stone, when cast into a pond, sets off wide ripples, fear spread, to every farm the refugees passed. People were in the river paddling hog troughs, trusting themselves to rafts of dried sticks hastily thatched together. A flood of skiffs poled by women and young boys passed downstream, these sometimes protected by men who marched in single file along each bank of the river.

Elsewhere in the woods a drama of military disobedience was unfolding. Captain Spalding, senior officer of the two Forty Fort companies enroute to Coryll's Ferry, had marched his men at snail's pace from the valley and toward distant Easton. Kirkland's pious explanation notwithstanding, the men of these two companies marched with increasing bitterness. Each step away was a step of betrayal of their families. If Spalding had cared to order a quick-march toward Easton, which he did not, there would have been mutiny. The ranks were in ugly mood. Captain Spalding, Captain Franklin, and every man down to the drummer boy knew the season favored Indian attack. The Indians would be coming to Forty Fort. In consequence they dallied from encampment to encampment making late starts and early halts. True, they were somewhat delayed by incessant rains and, their provisions being short, they were chronically pausing to hunt. The proverbial snail could have come in first, they so slow that when they reached Stroud's Fort in the Poconos they were fully two weeks overdue. At Stroud's Fort their smoldering unrest was fanned into flame by a transient Continental officer on furlough and on his way home to Wilkes-Barre. He looked at the two companies, recognized who they were, and beat his head, damning the stupidity of military orders. The captain had argued his case before a battalion commander for a furlough, this based on words of an Oneida Indian that a British-Indian move in force would be coming down the Susquehanna if not already rushing upon the settlements. This he told Franklin and Spalding. It was enough! Instantly the volunteers under Franklin executed a right about wheel, following the glorified wagon road back toward Forty Fort Valley. Spalding's men chose a more direct way, they would cross-cut the mountains. Captain Spalding did not need to drive his men unmercifully. They did that to themselves. They snatched whortleberries from the bushes, munching as they marched. Where the impenetrable laurel resisted their effort, with frantic sweeps of their knives they hacked passageways, mindless of the briars which slashed their faces and lacerated their arms. To make time, on occasion they made blind drops from heights into depths camouflaged by greenery. At last they struck the path which led through the Great Dismal and into Forty Fort Valley.

They had come abreast of a tall magnolia when a sobbing group of women burst from the nearby swamps, falling into their arms. "Brady!" exclaimed Spalding, recognizing in this 'Indian' his adjutant. Then he asked, knowing beforehand the answer, "Forty Fort fallen?" His next question, as to the fate of Mrs. Spalding, was on his lips when this grizzled soldier, his heart leaping up, perceived his wife coming from the swamp. "Lord, I thank Thee!" he said softly, aware of the grief about him. The pandemonium, some of joy, mostly of weeping, was deafening. "Mum, ladies!" shouted Spalding. "Will you have Hiakatoo upon us?"

Levi was able to be heard and attempted to render the Captain a coherent account. "The Seneca are pouring down the Susquehanna. At this hour they have their victory. No power north of the Poconos can chastise them."

Corporal French, who had asked from woman to woman, "What of the Greenacres; did somebody see the Greenacres?" came at last to Levi. Wordlessly Levi jerked his thumb in the direction of Forty Fort. "Mon Ami," begged the Frenchman, "Rachael, non, she is alive?"

"Corporal, if she survives, you would not be able to search for her now. The place is in possession of the enemy." The Frenchman took out his knife and began stabbing at a tree trunk.

Forty Fort was lost. Under the protective Free Company rifles the survivors slowly were brought from this melancholy place, not knowing but reasonably sure they were widows, their children orphans.

When Levi and Carberry had first come upon the scene of Jenkins Fort freshly surrendered, in that time frame Colonel Zebulon Butler was informed of enemy activity at the northern head of the valley. He ordered his militia to stand alert at the several blockhouses. Then, with his second order, he directed all able-bodied males to bring their weapons, shot powder and ammunition with them, and come into the fort. He sorely needed as many men and boys as he could find to augment his weak numbers. He had a report a Tory-led party of Indians was loitering near Fort Wintermute. With anger he learned they were being fed by the Wintermute family. For some time the Wintermutes were suspected by their neighbors for their Tory leanings. In responding to the Colonel's muster, Sergeant Major Asa Greenacre, before departing from home, expressed foreboding as to the future, advising Rachael. "Woman," he said, "should you hear musketry give it a proper respect; go at once for the hills. Hide yourself. It may happen we shall have second best in this brewing trouble, with the Indians thereafter free to plunder and rape. If you are spared and I am among the fallen, do your duty as my wife. See to my Christian burial." He would not let Rachael try to dismiss his gloom. "During the French-Indian War I viewed the scattered remains of Braddock's command, caught up in violent death and left to molder in the woods. 'T is my horror to be like them." With this morbid adieu, and a wave of his hand as he mounted, he turned away, riding toward whatever the future held.

Alone, Rachael tried to pass the hours of waiting by involving herself with a multitude of household tasks. Dreading the stillness about her, and seeing how the shade lay among the great oaks and elms, she went outdoors. On the cool grass where the shadows lay she kept watch of the sun-beaten road. Scarcely had she seated herself when she heard the clatter of hoofs. As she jumped up to view the rider her heart came to her throat. The man, arresting his panting horse, cried, "Fly! Fly for your life! Get to Forty Fort if you can!" And then he was off, a cloud of dust spilling along the road to show that he and his message had been real. For a moment a feeling of sick horror possessed her. Though Asa had given her guidance, to go toward the hills, the fort was much nearer and this messenger probably had more knowledge, were he sent by Colonel Butler. But of this she was unsure. Deciding to follow the latest instruction, she set out upon the road. To reach Forty Fort she must cross over country about to be, if not already, infested by murderous red men. She had not proceeded more than a quarter mile when, perceiving smoke and flames from a burning farm ahead, and thinking the bloodthirsty foe would be making their way along this very road, she started into the flanking timber. Within the woods her fears did not leave her, the gloom and the unexplainable noises feeding her imagination. The sounds of her own movements were magnified to her senses as if these were sounds made not by herself, but by a stalker. Frightened by a sudden rise of birds, Rachael concealed herself under a thick bush. In this posture, trembling, she lay until dark when again she began her slow journey. She soon realized little progress could be gained because of the roughness of the way. Exhausted, near fainting, she fell asleep.

At length, dawn breaking, wearily she arose, her bones aching from the damp, and continued slowly in the direction of the fort. She regretted not listening to her husband. With furtive glances Rachael scanned the woods on all sides expecting every tangle of thicket to hold a painted Indian. So real were the horrible faces produced in her imagination that she fell down, unable to contain her terror, trembling and moaning for mercy. The sound of gunfire roused her. Recalling the advice of Asa, Rachael turned inland away from the river, and toward the far mountains. To venture across a considerable open space, which accorded no protection, she fastened a garb of twigs and leaves, arranging these about her person in such manner that at slightest provocation she could sink down, becoming as it were a piece of shrubbery. In this guise she safely crossed the valley meadowland and gained a high embankment.

With a gasp Rachael saw the details below, and why every Indian had been absent from her path. Colonel Zebulon Butler, flinging wide the gates of Forty Fort, had brought his command onto the plains north of the fort. Apparently thinking the enemy inferior to his own numbers, now that he was bolstered by additional muskets, and not wishing to be bottled inside while the valley was wasted by an unchecked foe, he had marched out to smash the enemy in the field. A pitiless sun bathed the broad meadow. Like so many small groups of ants the Forty Fort companies toiled northward on the river flat, on their right the south flowing river, and on their left a border of scrub oak which concealed a marsh. Ahead, and obviously the place which interested them, at the far end of this meadow was a log fence fortified by the presence of Tories. From behind this the foe were directing a fire. By this show of arms, noisy but ineffective, Zebulon Butler was completely beguiled, convinced the number he confronted was overstated. It would be easy, he thought, to overwhelm the force at the breastwork. Rachael could see the militia as they advanced, the sunlight flashing upon their guns. A covert motion in the scrub oak caught her eyes. There, in the woods, flat on their stomachs to escape detection, but now rising, were hundreds of warriors! Unaware of the force on their flank, the troops hastened onward, expecting a swift victory, from the weak show of Tories ahead. Their flank at full exposure, they came on. It was a death trap.

Rachael, rebelling at the certain slaughter, renounced its reality. This was a delusion concocted in her mind. The tiny figures were creatures of a smaller world. Here was a war of lilliputs. Even as the clamors of battle arose to her ears, she hearing the intermingling of shrill voices and thin bulletsounds, these she dismissed as bloodless fancy. The firing quickened, the militia rushing toward the fence. With detached perspective she watched the hidden Indians spring from the woods and assail the flank. Butler's left wing dissolved, crumpling, disappearing in the haze of smoke which obscured the details of slaughter. Now the men at the center started to fall back, cohesion lost. Bewildered, some stood a moment keeping an irregular line, then - wavering - fled. In their flight they scattered dismay to the men comprising the right wing who, seeing the numbers endeavoring to leave the field and the many swept down, began to flee. Those who tried to hide in the marshes were at once entrapped and slaughtered. Others, the men on the right wing, momentarily fared better, jumping into the river and swimming for its far shore. A few made it, but the majority were cut down at the embankment or shot in the water. In heaps the dead and dying lay on the field and along the river bank. Still the reverberations of musketry went on, carrying with it the supplications for mercy. Thereafter the work of the hatchet and scalping knife was methodical.

By degree the firing within the hell-pit died away. Only random shots marked the final extremity of wretches flushed from hiding. Rachael, stupefied, her reason now entirely absconded, hands clapped to her ears, her eyes protruding, kept singing to herself. The song was a nursery rhyme. She sang it continuously, breaking off into sobs as prisoners, among whom she recognized her husband, were led to a rock and placed in a ring around it. One by one they fell before the axe of a vindictive executioner. As the twilight thickened, the victors, having gathered wood from the fence, threw the pitch pine rails at the feet of several hapless captives. Soon, in the night, outlined by the flames of this funeral pyre, she saw writhing bodies and heard horrible screams. At last these were silenced. Silence, an agony itself, settled across everything.

At the flushes of dawn the lifeless valley had different visitors. Rachael, waking late from exhaustive slumber, saw great turkey buzzards wheeling and wheeling overhead. These would settle their wings and descend to the cadavers. Taking up her song Rachael too descended. She had barely reached the ghastly plain when she stumbled over a body. It was face down, the skull split open by a tomahawk, and the scalp wrenched away. At the man's belt was a water flask; in his pocket a piece of cheese. Rachael drained the flask, then gnawed at the cheese. Refreshed, she made her way across the corpse-strewn field. A bird with a gruesome flapping of wings arose from her path, a gobbet in its beak. Everywhere lay the relics of battle, guns, knives, powder horns, articles of clothing, and the more grizzly reminders, bodies in first stages of loathsome putrefaction. Under the July sun all was hastening into decay and decomposition. The sun bloated bodies cast forth their sick-sweet stench. She stepped around a fried corpse with protruding bones, the man having been broiled alive on the logs, and came to the river. Here, within reach from shore, floating in the weeds were the bodies of those who had managed to break from the encircling enemy only to die from a marksman's musket ball. As she walked abreast of the Susquehanna, while passing about 30 dead piled in a festering heap, she heard the piteous appeal of a wounded man, miraculously overlooked. He had been shot through both hips. Rachael stared at him, and then blurted, "I must bury my husband," sliding by him, ignoring his outstretched hand. In another place two wounded men, who for some unexplainable reason were *in* a merry humor, were congratulating each other that they should be alive at all. Perceiving Rachael to be in a state of dementia, they realized that they would get *no* help from her. Ignoring her, they continued with their own affairs. The one whose feet were crippled had shot a buzzard, while his companion having a bloody useless right arm, and the fingers of his left hand mangled, had kicked this buzzard within reach of his friend. By the same method they had collected firewood, he kicking the nearest pieces of wood into a pile which his fallen friend was about to kindle, they intending to prepare a repast. A quarter mile further Rachael reached the rock where she had witnessed the braining of 16 captives. Among them she found Asa. With a discarded hunting knife she attempted to scratch out his grave.

Toiling at this, she did not hear the footsteps behind her. That which was predestined to be was to come suddenly. Seized by her tresses, icy eyes of a Seneca looked down into hers. Rachael with a gesture of indifference answered his scrutiny. Knife uplifted, briefly he fondled the long chestnut locks, twining them around his wrist. Then he pulled her towards him, his face twisted in a hideous smile. It was the smile of a snake, of a reptile about to strike. Quietly she awaited the irrevocable stroke.

Chapter XIV

TROUBLES AT MUNCY

The dark mirror of the water, with its border a frill of reeds, reflected the sky. The city beneath this surface seemed to be affected by the heat above. A sluggish waggle of silver over the pebbly bottom, a fin waking the surface with a shallow ripple, these haphazard aquatic gestures indicated the presence of the creatures feeding, sleeping, lying in this watery depth. Suddenly the sky of this under world was shattered by concussions occurring on its surface, the turbulence of which penetrated downward. The canoe bearing Samuel Wallis, propelled by the powerful strokes of its warrior crew, shot toward shore. With a hasty adieu Wallis hopped from the canoe to the land, missed his footing, and wetted one leg. He scrambled up the water-loosened embankment and from its braid of bushes signaled for the war party to proceed. The Britisher in command nodded to his warriors. Their paddles lapped into the current, drawing them swiftly from sight. Wallis was alone. With his elbow he broke the bushes which fenced the river, to discover himself upon an extensive meadow. Part of this bottom land was under cultivation; a log cabin was hard by. The owner of this house, he had been told, was neither Tory nor rebel, yet was marked for death, having offended several Seneca visitors a few weeks gone by.

Wallis perceived a man hoeing in the field. "Halloo!" the merchant called, cupping his hands, whereupon the unshod farmer dropped to the ground, slid behind a stump, and pointed a musket. Another man appeared at the farmhouse door with a leveled weapon while a third fellow came running from the outhouse, buckling his breeches and juggling a musket, Wallis's call given preference over nature's.

"Stand where you are!" warned the man behind the stump when Wallis had proceeded sufficiently close. "Who be you?"

"A friend."

"A friend? Stick it up your ass. We don't welcome friends, whether of one feather or another, Tory or rebel."

"I see," said Wallis, unperturbed. "You are for yourself. That's a safe politic. Sir, I am Samuel Wallis."

"Samuel Wallis of Muncy?"

"I am he."

"Mischief you are! I'll not credit that."

"In my pocket are papers that say I am."

"Tricks. Likely taken from his corpse. If you be the rich man that you claim to be, why are you afield and afoot; why were you yonder?" He indicated the river.

"I was walking by the shore."

"Tell me a fairy tale. And who was with you in the bushes? Moses in the bulrushes? More likely cut-throats, either villainous Indians or trouble-seekers of another stripe, which?"

"Not a one. Believe me, I was seized and made prisoner by some Tory rangers who, after talking with me, decided to let me go."

The lanky man was all caution. "Isaac," he called to the lad who had come running, "go swish the bushes; search the bank. If there's mischief in the making, this man dies."

"But, Pa," pleaded the lad, hopping from leg to leg, "I'm with corruption."

"Discipline boy, boy, discipline."

The boy loped across the meadow, inspected the shore, and trotted back. "This stranger is as he's said, by his self, Pa. can't see other than his prints, nor any keel mark. Yet his prints begin at the shore. He's been put off by boat. Look, he's got a wet leg!" Father and observant son leveled their guns afresh.

"My captors, who had me in their canoe, decided I've taken no stand against the Tories, never given them harm, so they let me go, putting me ashore. I slipped before gaining the embankment. That's the truth."

"What do you reckon, Pa?" The farmer meditated, then lowered his musket. "Can I go now, Pa? If not, there'll be a mess."

"Tend your bowels, boy." The dutiful son was gone like a shot, groaning as he ran. The father extended a knotty hand to Wallis. "My name's Beery. As you see, I trust no man. Caution's the byword when you live as we do on the banks of the river. You're a lucky man I didn't kill y', and that's because you named yourself for who you are." His eyes were narrowing as he said this. "As you see you're alive. Had I squeezed this gun on you, then thrown you in the water, who's to say who done it. I could easily have killed you. Might've, had you been other than Samuel Wallis. I figure there's money in saving a rich man's life."

Wallis scanned the features of the man. "It might be," he said coldly, "and it might be that you'll not get a penny."

"Maybe you're deader'n you think," responded Beery fingering his musket.

Wallis folded his arms and stared at him. He was about to forewarn the fool of the Seneca intentions, that the man was marked for death, then thought otherwise. He would keep his own counsel. He put on a broad smile. "I see your point." He named a generous figure which satisfied the farmer who was urged 'Take it!' from his nearby sons.

"Also I must have transportation to get me home."

"I can't rightfully spare a horse, but--"

"Sir, I understand you well. Say, fifteen dollars for any horse that will last me to Muncy and, for your courtesy to me, the sum mentioned of thirty dollars, all of this when you come *in good health* to my residence." His offer for the horse was extravagant, ten dollars the going price.

"The amount to insure your good health is payable now, and thirty for the horse, none of it in six-dollar or thirty-dollar 'continentals', good only to wipe your ass. I want hard money."

"I have only a traveler's purse with some Spanish silver. Whatever's in it I'll give you this minute. The balance you can collect when next you come to Muncy."

"All right, I'll take your purse, but don't gull me. The difference owed is secured by your word. The price is as agreed, no less." Wallis surrendered the Spanish silver dollars he had.

Wallis thought to himself, 'Why argue with a dead man, this fool will die from a hatchet sooner than he knows.' He nodded his head, the debt as much as extinguished.

"Bring me the critter. I'm anxious to show Muncy I'm alive."

It was a moment's doing. "Godspeed," said the farmer when the horse was brought forward. Wallis quizzically eyed it. The horse needed carrying more than he.

"What keeps it up?" The horse was skin and bones, and in its dotage. It cocked an ear and cast a baleful look at Wallis with its one good eye, the other gone white. That look implied the creature understood and resented the comment. In better spirits Wallis made his farewell to the farmer. Confronted by the animal's cantankerous temper and its extreme age, for all his wish to hurry, Wallis was obliged to nurse his charge as he plodded toward Muncy.

In approaching Muncy Wallis decided against dropping all pretense at having visited Augusta. He would tell a story of capture and escape, a tale well supported by the recent Indian raid on Muncy, the knowledge of which he had gained from Esther when at Chemung. Not to be fired upon by error, he waited for dawn to brush the hills, then, setting his horse to the descent, with the rising lamp of the sun at his elbow, he rode straight into an outpost. "Thank the Almighty you have returned to us, Mr. Wallis," hoarsely exclaimed the picket, John Harris. He was hollow-eyed and could do with sleep.

"Has there been trouble, Mister Harris?" innocently he asked.

"Trouble! Why we've been in perpetual alarm from the night of your going to Fort Augusta. The Indians were on us, sir. 'T was thunder and lightning from a clear sky. We stood to, with muskets, saving our homes and this fort. But they led off our prime beef and most of our milkers, nobody to stop them. Yet, 't is not our cattle, nor the damage to the fort which grieves us." His voice choking with emotion he added, "There's been massacre at Lycoming Creek."

"No!" said Wallis, genuinely surprised. His Muncy garrison included Lycoming men. He had sold to the Lycoming settlers the tracts upon which they had erected their homes.

"I was on a scout from the fort," continued Harris, "the day it happened. At the Loyalsock Creek I met a wagon crowded with folk from Lycoming. They thought it best to come on into Muncy rather than stay at Lycoming. Both Peter Smith and his Missus, and his six youngsters were in the wagon; also William King's wife and two daughters. Besides Peter Smith there were four men - Campbell, Chambers, Snodgrass and Hammond. I cautioned them not to go on, that it would be folly, 'cause there had been firing in the woods less'n an hour before, and the shots sounded as if from a place near the creek which they must parallel. I told 'em they ought'er get back to Lycoming Stockade. Though I argued it wasn't safe ahead, some of 'em said it was likely a hunter's gun and were for pushing on. So I continued my scouting business, as it was Captain Menniger's orders that we move up the mountain and sit tight looking for stirrings in the woods below. It must have been 20 minutes, no more, after I left them that I heard a burst of musketry, and I ran toward it. Then I thought, best to come away and get help at Muncy. That I did. Lieutenant King, whose family was in the wagon, led out 15 men who followed me back."

Harris paused, swallowed, then further elaborated, "It was late afternoon by time we got to where the Indian path winds through a grove of wild plums. And there they were. Peter Smith's wife was stabbed twice; Hammond was shot 'tween the eyes; Campbell lay on the grass where he had been dropped by the first fire; and in the cart were a boy and a girl, butchered. Snodgrass was stretched out near the wheels of the cart with a knife in his belly. The only one alive, Mrs. King, had crawled to the bank of the Lycoming. We found her with blood from her neck and breast running down into the water. When Lieutenant King tried to lift his wife, he felt her stiffen and die. One man alone, Peter Smith, escaped, and he managed to snatch up his youngest daughter as he fled. I reckon three of his children, along with King's two daughters, and Chambers were taken captive."

Evidence of the Indian raid had not been effaced from Fort Wallis. Every tree in the carriage turnabout bore bullet scars. And the fort itself had suffered damage. Impalings had been hacked and splintered, a breech made through these pointed stakes, and one wall of the palisade half thrown down. Wallis's mansion was pocked with bullet chips; gunpowder stains were at the loopholes. Even the stout front door, after the men retreated inside, had been smashed at, hatchet marks into the woodwork. Here, at his doorstep, the red tide had been halted.

With drawn faces the garrison collected around their foremost citizen. Menniger, rubbing sleep from his eyes and thrusting a pistol into his belt, not perceiving who it was, cried, "What have we; more news of misfortune?" The militiamen parted their circle. "My soul! Mr. Wallis! I thought you for certain taken; Indians buzz these woods like flies. A wonder it is that you slipped through them; more, that you are alive. We had given you up for lost, and ourselves as well until they suddenly drew off."

"I am here by a miracle," said Wallis, keeping up the pretense he had been toward Fort Augusta. "I was caught on my way to Augusta and transported a captive to Teaoga, from which place I made my escape." All ears were attentive as he spoke. "But, 't is not of my own experiences, as it is to yours here, that I wish to speak. You have felt the enemy. Your stout hearts have brought you safely through the worst Hiakatoo's warriors have to offer. Believe me, he will not come so eagerly here again."

A faint cheer greeted his fighting words.

Menniger shouted orders. "Back to your duties, men. Let's be secure by being ready. Where are those replacement timbers?" As the detail erected the final post to mend the broken palisade, he beckoned Wallis. "And you, sir, come within. There's much for saying on either side."

"First your story, then mine," said Wallis, when they were in private."

"Mine is quickly told, for I am impatient as to your success.

"Aye, it has been a gory month. It began when five of our men, hearing Indians were about, left the fort to save Thompson's livestock and personal effects. While rounding up stray horses they stumbled into an ambush. Bob Covenhoven got clear, but two of his brothers were not as fortunate; nor Shoefelt and Thompson. They all died. Then came the attack on the fort, and almost simultaneously with it the massacre of 16 men, women and children coming toward this fort --"

"Harris told me about the massacre," interrupted Wallis.

"Our good luck absconded with you; leastwise, I hope it is returned. As planned, I defended the fort. Sir, it's a testimony that we held. The hellions broke into our outer works, overlapped the shed in which we had cached your salt supply, and might have won the house if they hadn't desisted to lug off the salt. Thereafter they couldn't regain the ground as I put men on the roof, and we kept shooting them down as fast as they jumped into the gap of our wall. This portion of the pallisade required complete replacement. Now, what of you?"

"I saw Bolton, Commandant of Fort Niagara; Claus, Indian Superintendent; and Brant, the Mohawk. I also had conversation with Esther, and with Bald Eagle. And I have had the doubtful honor of taking passage home in a canoe with Hiakatoo, the Seneca."

"Extraordinary!"

"We need fear no more attacks," added Wallis.

"You blow my ears! Say on."

"No attacks other than token stabs, that *none* may wonder how we come by our security."

Menniger shook his head in admiration.

Wallis continued. "It's an old trick. Fort Wintermute in the Connecticut valley enjoys the arrangement."

"The terms are most generous," interjected Menniger.

"I have not done."

"Your pardon--"

"We of Muncy and they of Niagara have agreed that this fort must remain neutral."

"Pshaw! If they trouble us not, we'll do them no harm. Easily kept!"

"Think twice. The agreement forbids our aiding our neighbors."

"Neighbors?" commented Menniger. "We have none, except Sunbury which would sooner be helping us, not we them; and Forty Fort which is equipped to repel formidable attacks; it is unlikely the Indians would try Forty Fort."

Wallis looked long and hard at Menniger before disillusioning him. "We seem to have traded positions. Was it not you who forewarned me of the 'growing peril'? Now it is I who speak as you once did. No fort can resist what's to come. I have been made much wiser by my visit with Colonel Bolton at Fort Niagara. Do not judge the British lion by the tickle of his whiskers, as you just felt. British officers and Tory rangers are to lead all war parties in the future. In great numbers, as we speak, just such a British-Indian force is descending the Susquehanna."

"Forty Fort is to be raided?"

"Raided?" answered Wallis. "The raid you experienced was but a miniature rehearsal of what now comes upon Forty Fort. At this hour along the paths north of us are endless warriors. Forty Fort is to become a coffin."

"Death!" said astounded Menniger. "If Forty Fort falls, the path is open to Fort Augusta. Winning there, they'd be at liberty to strike anywhere along the Blue Mountains. Oh, God!" The Captain was visibly shaken by the enormity of the carnage to be visited on the frontier. It began to sink in, the position Wallis had put upon him as senior officer at Fort Muncy. He was not to respond to pleas for succor. "You have mortgaged our honor! We are left only to pray for those poor souls at Forty Fort--"

"Dear Menniger. Yes, people will die, but not us. And perhaps the frontier war will pass the sooner, there to be decisive victories by one side over the other. We ourselves, I remind you, will survive! Is that not enough?"

"'T is a compact with the Devil," said the broken Captain.

"'T is also a way the British test our loyalty, putting upon us advance knowledge of the magnitude of this blow, and binding us to neutrality for the price of their neutrality toward us."

There was a noise upon the road. From a sentry on the parapet there came a yell. Menniger and Wallis rushed to the door. A rider, his stead flecked with sweat, bucketed into the compound. The man reined his horse perpendicularly, and tumbled from his saddle. He saluted Captain Menniger. "Sir," he gasped, "Colonel Butler's compliments. Forts Durkee and Wintermute are surrendered to a superior force. So has Jenkins Fort. Colonel Butler requests troops of you, and has also sent a courier to Augusta, not sure of the numbers he faces.

"Just where were the savages when you left?" asked Menniger, biting into a seegar.

"Not come to Forty Fort as yet. Colonel Butler states he is going to march out to meet them, otherwise the hellions would have a free hand at torching the homes and killing anyone about. The Colonel says, if by their numbers he is to be bested in the field, his plan then would be to retreat back into the Fort, hoping to hold those walls until reinforcements arrive. He begs your help; by it we may very well turn them."

The soldiers looked at Menniger. Cheeks suffused, eyes meeting those of the messenger, he shot commands. "To saddle! Every man with a horse, to saddle!" Wallis, waving his arms, attempted to speak, but went unheard. One of the militia yanked the bell rope, this producing a dismal clang which alarmed the valley, by so doing bringing in the outlying sentries, and calling out the garrison, and as well advising the scattered population.

The able bodied men, as they appeared at the fort, were told what was expected of those with horses. The volunteers raised a shout of readiness. They were sanguine. "It's a ruse!" cried Wallis, finding voice. "The Seneca purposely feint at Forty Fort. If you go out they will decimate you, after which they will fall upon defenseless Muncy." He strove to save the fragile negotiation he had with Bolton, this brushed aside by his emotional overseer turned captain. Irresolutely they looked from him to Menniger, but Menniger troubled by a caracoling beast, could not or would not resolve their indecision. It took the intercession of the fateful news-carrier from Forty Fort to urge them to action. Everywhere soldiers were mounting, streaming toward the gate, crowding across the narrow bridge that spanned the deep-cut waterway. Wallis made his last attempt. "You idiotic handful! Hotspurs! Come back!" His cries were swept away.

They addressed themselves to the road, flying for Forty Fort, a motley force strung along the forest road, weaving up the mountainside, then down into the valleys, ducking low-slung limbs, clattering over stony stretches only to come upon lush meadowland bordering the dark forest. Had there been any Seneca in the flanking woods it would have been an easy matter to have decimated this mob of riders, scattered and uncoordinated as they were. This realization growing, both Menniger and his aide Lieutenant King, pulling at their horses, slowed the foremost riders until the rear element had sufficiently come on. In column thereafter they rode for Forty Fort.

It was during one of those brief halts to spell their horses that Menniger weighed Wallis's arguments. At the head of the column he had fretted over and reconsidered Wallis's truce with Colonel Bolton, which momentarily he had brushed aside. Unsettled in resolve, cooled in spirit, he flung himself down by the creek bed, bathing his face. The war cries recently heard in and around Muncy, the vision of their makers who almost overwhelmed Fort Muncy, were both implanted in his inward ear and mind's eye, possessing his senses. He tried to shut out the wretched consequences that might overtake his own men, the slaughter into which they might be moving, and the real possibility the enemy, the main battle won, now might in great strength be racing this way on collision course. Caught up in the passion of his men, he mounted, continuing forward. But, in his growing uncertainty he saw Indians at every stretch of the road. No longer a proud commander riding assured of victory, he became a stooped, distraught man, hunched in his saddle, driven by the troops behind him. He was caught in an avalanche of his own making.

Menniger had little time for speculation; the battle, if not lurking in the next bush, was only minutes away. Snapped from his reverie by the clamor of his men, he too detected gunfire.

Again they rushed forward, the battle almost here. The militiamen, striving for the valley beyond, shook their whips in their horses eyes, crowding Menniger. Night had closed round them, a night full of stars and sporadic gunfire. Coming to meet them, down the moonlit path staggered a blood-matted survivor. Menniger brought his detachment to a restless halt, listening as the man blurted, "Turn about! 'T is hell ahead; Forty Fort Valley is lost, her people damned; Sheol!" In his eyes were the horrors of which he spoke. "Beezelbub's sons have smashed our line; town and forts are taken!"

The Muncy men milled in dismay. "We're too late," ventured one.

"No!" cried another, and appealed to Menniger, who briefly questioned the survivor.

"When did you quit the field?" The man could not answer; he was too dazed to think. Menniger rose in his stirrups. "I say," he addressed his men, "'t is a destroying wind. We can do nothing."

This prompted a hail of criticism, mostly from Lieutenant King whose wife had been killed on the Loyalsock. "The New Salem and Connecticut Company out of Wilkes-Barre might have come on after this fellow deserted the field. Together, we can give the enemy second battle."

"What if Salem Company has held back and Forty Fort has capitulated? We'd be alone." Menniger's dispiriting logic dampened the reckless. "Think of your own safety! Providence will spare those on the battlefield who will be saved. Here is a man escaped from Hell, saved not by us, but to save us. Heed what he advises."

"The Captain's right. Let's get out of here." Lifting up the survivor, the squadron wheeled and took the road of retreat.

In the hours since Menniger's departure, Wallis, raging at his Captain's disobedience, silently damning him, had exhausted himself. That idiot Menniger had destroyed the delicate fabric of the agreement woven at Fort Niagara. At last he mastered his runaway emotion. He gazed in the mirror, noting his reddened complexion, sign of his inward stress. 'Anger rests in the bosum of fools,' he told himself, remembering the Ecclesiastes. 'Aye, 't is anger which disorients the mind. I shall not anger; I shall not hate; I shall not fear.' Having lifted himself above vexation, he sat relaxed in a deep seated chair, undisturbed either as to Menniger's action or fate, or as to his own. Muncy and Forty Fort and the peoples thereof were far removed, unreal, detached. However, his philosophy could not ameliorate the hot weather which seemed no cooler despite the sinking sun. Perspiration rolled off his chin. Perspiration glistened on his brow, jaw and cheeks. It was as if a fever padlocked within the chamber of his body had burst through to his countenance. He stuck his finger between his neck and shirt. "Damn my bones," he said. Whereupon, as if the Devil had eavesdropped, he heard the thud of hooves and the creak of leather, and knew it to be Menniger's men.

Once into the fort's confines, the wayworn men tied their lathered beasts at the railing. Their faces were masks of despondency. Listlessly they attended their Captain's shout. "Post guards! Bolt the gates! You there, Scudder, grab cold venison, pick your scouts and deploy into the hills. Fire a gun if you spy anything. Lieutenant King, take a squad to the outlying farms, and warn the families to return to the fort." The blunt commands stirred them into activity. They converted the ground floor, as well as upper floor of the mansion, into barracks space for the anticipated survivors from Forty Fort. The survivor they had brought back with them, his cuts dressed, lay in the kitchen singing psalms. A few more unfortunates arrived that night.

At dawn Captain Carberry, with three Forty Fort riflemen, broke from the woods, having traveled all night. Theirs was the first coherent account. "It was awful. I joined Jim Bidlack's company of 32 men. Only we," he indicated his three companions, "made it out. A *'forlorn hope'* was all yet standing after the initial drumfire, and before long there was less than one out of four still on his feet. We had to scatter. We could offer no resistance. I saw Indians converging on us from every direction, seemingly my fate determined, when in despair I dropped into the long grass. As they searched the grasses, I thought they'd hear my heart throbs. One bastard even stepped on my foot, yet passed me over, thinking me to be a corpse. Not daring to stir, I could hear the shrieks and cries as the butchery proceeded. I could do nothing but peer through the tall grass and watch the dead bodies float downstream. They took Captain Bidlack. I saw him thrown on the burning logs of the fort, and they held him there with hay forks, he skewered and grilled as if a pig, with the sound of him much worse. I was vomiting as I watched."

Wallis, listening, turned ashen. Others had equal reaction.

"The sky was a rolling flame," continued Carberry. "I crept near the town, the center afire, and within those flames I could hear the screams of women." Carberry hid his face with his hands. In a weirdly calm voice he resumed, "The Connecticut troops made their mistake when they sallied from the fort, their sanctuary. With several of the armored farm houses surrendered and afire Colonel Butler must have presumed the Indians satiated, or at least likely to cease their plundering if confronted. Supposing their numbers to be inferior, he pushed forward to engage them. They got us when we reached a place between the river and a marsh, wherein their main force was concealed, they hidden by the tall grasses and the nearby trees. We were cut with a point blank volley; they then smashed in our flank nearest their hiding place, and pressing around our crumpled wing sealed off our retreat. God! It was over in 30 minutes. Those who ran for the river were shot in the water. I chose the marsh grass and survived."

Carberry's three companions corroborated his overall description by the addition of details. "They scattered firebrands everywhere," claimed one, "and threw children alive into the burning houses." And another: "The heads of the slain are on poles by the river." The third man whose family had been killed, wept. He had seen the Indians rush upon his eldest son, with yelps of triumph strip him naked, and had watched them gash and hack his body, scooping his blood in their palms, bathing their faces in it, thus securing for themselves his bravery. More stories were to float in as additional fugitives arrived. If the mind embellishes upon horror, it does not detract from the agonies placed upon those who defended and those they defended.

Wallis, shaken by the slaughter so near, sat in his chair, taking neither food nor sleep, nor offering wisdom or direction. Paralysis invested him. The scope of the catastrophe was apparent. All that day and through the next the refugees, winged by fear, spreading their terrors, arrived. The population of Muncy was becoming infected, many talking about fleeing the frontier, throwing themselves upon the charity of friends, relatives, or seeking temporary refuge within the walls of Fort Augusta. A triumvirate of stubborn men, King, Scudder, and Isaac Walton, sensing a lack of direction from Menniger and Wallis, sought to remedy that deficiency. Swords buckled to their belts, rifles in hand, they petitioned the pale, empty-eyed Wallis. They spoke of a muster, not so much to defend Muncy, but to intercept, aye! Intercept the booty laden Seneca, who would be reduced to six and seven man parties on their separate travels north toward Teaoga. To do something positive would lessen the defeatist attitude. Wallis listened attentively. The pallor left his cheeks.

"We are not lost," said Wallis. "Indeed, we are not lost! Who's a stalwart fellow and swift? Bob Covenhoven? Then let him ride for Augusta."

Seizing quill and paper, Wallis wrote Colonel Hunter, 'Sir: I expected to have heard marching men by now. The Indian is down in this quarter and will next lay waste Muncy, we to be saved only by your interposition. Failing your aid, we shall fall, your position likewise to be weakened should our fort disappear, as has happened to the fortifications in Forty Fort Valley. Come you quick. Whatever is done ... it must be done in the course of today.'

In postscript Wallis petitioned for a token force, to give the West Branch respite from panic. Sealing the message, when Covenhoven was brought before him, he handed it to the man. Covenhoven, with a flash of his eye as much as to say 'No man stops me', mounted and flung his horse across the bridge and onto the road south. Covenhoven gone, Wallis trod the floorboards, dictating, "Circulate notice of a meeting tonight; no, set it for tomorrow. That'll give Hunter time to march up, if he is to come. Tell every man to bring his gun and his *opinion.*"

Wisely Wallis knew panic would undo everything, would be productive of a runaway. Some sort of action was required to reduce public fear. He also knew, were he to further improve his defenses the British might construe such action as a breaking off of neutrality, Muncy then would know carnage similar to that visited upon Forty Fort. Only by a public meeting could he resolve the dilemma of the moment.

The issue contained the destiny of Muncy. The argument was simple, an aye or a nay for staying. Sensing the magnitude of the decision, from distant hamlets the hard-bitten freeholders presented themselves in the Great Hall of the Manor. In the audience were Captain Hawkins Boone and Captain Foster, and sundry officers who sat in grim observation. From the Loyalsock, from Pine River, from farms westerly toward the Sinnemahoney they came. None lacked courage, yet many were determined for flight, while there as many for staying. Somehow Dan Lebo became self elected chairman, Wallis not adverse. Lebo, Wallis felt, was the ideal man for the job. He was an Indian fighter, therefore would be against abandoning the farms; he was a freeholder, with much to lose. Wallis, on the other hand, had the defect of not being a resident, he to be viewed as protective of his vested interest, foremost, and not the life-threatening danger confronted by those in the audience.

A spittoon handy, he directed accurate ejaculations at both the tin bowl and the audience. "Sixteen years ago," Lebo began, "I came to Muncy. It was a wilderness. I had three things: guts, a gun, and a vision. I still have my guts; I still have my gun; and I still have my vision. Back in 1762 there was a sore evil upon this land. Like today, the Indian was against us, there being a difference of opinion as to who owned the land. There was some hard fighting. But, by holding our ground, sticking together, we put the Minsi into panic, instead of ourselves. Today, again, there's Indians in the woods, lots of them, maybe 800 warriors at tops, who have lifted the tomahawk in support of the King. We're talking of running because they took Forty Fort. Why did that happen? Simple. 'Cause Colonel Zeb Butler marched his men into an ambush for want of knowing how many heathen he faced. I'm not saying we should shun the field and sulk inside our fort, nor am I saying we should be rash enough to march out as did Butler, and be massacred."

Wallis was beginning to wonder where Lebo was taking his argument. He whispered to Menniger. "What is he saying?" Menniger shrugged. Wallis added, "We've already seen the strength of the foe. Can he be urging our taking the war beyond our gates?" Lebo's next remark made Wallis wince.

"My belief," Lebo stated, "is we ought to remind the Indian two can play the game. We should burn their nearest nest, Teaoga. We've the men to do it, now that our militia is reinforced by the survivors from Forty Fort. And we have captains to lead us. We've got guts, guns; and we have a vision ... revenge." He turned toward Captain Menniger. "Captain, what say you, will you be for this campaign?" In a way, Lebo was uttering the same idea proposed by Levi Brady, inter-community cooperation. The difference was that the garrison at Forty Fort existed only in the scattered survivors. Even so, the idea of hit and run actions as proposed now, and as once proposed for Spalding's company, was unworkable. It would folly, too, to attack the present forces in superior numbers, even though now broken into large elements in nearby movement. The vision of the past did not justify today's grandiose ambition of Lebo.

Menniger slowly rose to his feet, nodding assurance to Wallis. "Men, I agree we should make a stand. But I cannot advise, much less support a campaign at this moment. The trip to Teaoga is long, and our risk doubles with each mile. Instead, gentlemen, we all know this fort has proven itself defensible.

"Perhaps because of my recent sally from this fort, I know the hazard first hand of going toward an enemy of undetermined strength, and adept at ambush. We have a good fort. I will neither march from it, nor run from it. I like its comfort. It would be to repeat Butler's error, to march out. At the same time we'd be fools to run away when we have already punished those who would do us harm, red man or ranger. They will step around us, having tasted defeat here. I propose that we continue in this valley; we've a damned solid fort."

Menniger's comments touched off a babble of approval and disapproval. The audience was split into several factions, those heatedly championing or denouncing Menniger's plan for defense, those for or against Lebo's suggested campaign, and those who would fly the country, dissatisfied with what they heard. At this juncture a young, blonde fool named Schneider, suddenly remembering milking time, rushed for the door. In his blind haste he collided with the proprietor. Wallis, not alone in his belief, mistook his flight as inspired by fear. The result had a disastrous effect. Talk of defense was drowned in voices calling for retreat. Wallis, ruffled, shouted angrily, "I tell you, if you are to be destroyed, it will be yourselves that do it!" His voice went unheard.

A burly farmer pushed his way toward the exit. "Here, now, neighbors!" bellowed the man as he parted the crowd. "We have our lives only once. The heathen creep nearer! I'm packing and getting! Goodbye!" Men jostled for the door. They were tired of speeches, of living close to death. They would load their families into wagons and fly the country. They would --

There was a noise upon the road. It grew and was upon them, the clank of equipment, the bounce of a cannon being drawn by horses, and the tramp of men marching across the bridge that led to the fort. Now there was the huzzah of excited sentries, they first to glimpse this spectacle, they cheering their heads off. Instantly in the great room every voice was stilled, each person listening, each face plain with disbelief. From the vantage of his position by the door Wallis, open mouthed, watched with gratitude as a double-column of soldiers marched down his roadway and into the fort. Colonel Hunter had more than answered his petition. With a grounding of arms these new arrivals confronted the avalanche of frontiersmen who poured forth from the house waving their caps. "You were never more timely, Captain," exclaimed Wallis, pushing to the front. "I am Samuel Wallis, and this is Captain Menniger, senior militia officer."

"It is to you, sir, then," said the officer, "to whom I am to report my command. He tendered Wallis his orders.

"Ah!" spoke Wallis, displaying the written orders to Menniger, and to Captain Foster. Introducing each, he stated, "Gentlemen, by these credentials we have Captain Andrew Walker among us, by command of Colonels Hartley and Brodhead, and in answer to my petition to Colonel Hunter at Fort Augusta. He is detached as an engineer to improve our defenses. Welcome, Captain!" Turning to address the audience, the much relieved proprietor called for quiet. "Everybody, listen! By letter and by personal visit I solicited Colonel Hunter, commanding at Augusta, and General McIntosh, senior officer of the Western Department. I begged for troops, and at last the troops are here! It changes our fortunes for the better. Yet this does not entitle us to complacency. Only by a close watch of these surrounding hills will you maintain liberty and life. Do not seek battle, but guard against it. Let those among you who stand for authority be as a committee of safety, the regulars under Captain Walker assisting you. It is now plain to the most doubting of you, we are no longer hopelessly situated. Perhaps, as in the Bible, we are pitched in the wilderness of Kadesh. Yet, whosoever keeps his arms and his senses in order will come through these times. If I say to you that I have done certain things for our defense, the proof being this fort and this increment of troops, I shall also promise I shall not rest at that. Rather, I shall be taking leave for a time, returning to Philadelphia, there to present our critical military position to men of high responsibility. I shall rehearse the terrible sacrifice of Forty Fort; I shall tell them of your brave stand here, waiting aid. Be assured every gazette shall stir public demand, knowing we on the frontier are the fence against deeper incursions. More troops shall be sent us. I vouch it. We shall be as we are becoming, a place no enemy can easily take."

They gave him a huzzah. A voice had spoken for Muncy.

And they gave another huzzah, even louder, when the Captain presented Menniger, who unfolded the package, a flag. Colonel Hunter had been thoughtful enough to send up a banner, the UC or United Colonies flag. Yes, with the red and white horizontal stripes of the East India Company, to which had been added in the upper corner nearest the pole a small rectangle, this rectangle being no less than a miniature of the British flag to which the colonies had belonged. Stitched into the design was the lettering 'United Colonies.' It had been flown in 1775 prior to the Declaration of Independence. In some respects it also imitated the British naval flag of red which reproduced the royal design in the upper corner and in similar scale. It would do. Hardly had their cheers subsided when these were renewed, the colors being erected and catching the breeze, to become a living thing. They had a flag!

South of Muncy, on the bend of the Susquehanna, within the walls of Fort Augusta, at the very moment that Wallis at Muncy was rendering his impassioned farewell, Colonel Samuel Hunter was writing a letter that echoed Wallis's words. Hunter, to the State authorities wrote: 'At this date in the towns on the frontiers, a few virtuous Inhabitants and fugitives seem determined to stand, t'is doubtful whether To-morrow's sun shall rise on them, freemen, captives, or in eternity.'

As for Samuel Wallis, himself, he knew not where he stood, he in straddle of two canoes.

Enroute Philadelphia

Having momentarily settled his affairs on the frontier, a strong defense established for Muncy, a runaway prevented, and his secret compact with the British secure, pleased with himself Wallis began his journey back to civilization - Philadelphia. This time, without carriage, his driver French gone, he rode the Maryland roan promised but not taken by French in his departure from Wallis's service. He wondered if French, and that fellow Brady had survived the recent turmoil. It was but a passing thought. He wondered, too, about Esther, her village as insecure as his, the growing war requiring punitive response soon or late, from the Continentals.

Leaving the woods and swamps behind him, Wallis gained the post road from East Town into Philadelphia. Fatigued from his travels, he was riding slowly when he heard cantering hooves rapidly overtaking him. A stranger, dressed in black from head to toes, mounted on a spirited charger, was approaching. 'Evil forbid!' Wallis muttered, his hand clapped to his breast and fingers curled upon the stock of a pistol.

"Good day, sir!" said the stranger, in a tone as deep as his wrappings. The voice left Wallis uneasy, but he seemed to have heard it before.

"Good day to you, my friend," the merchant responded, appraising the sharp eyes just beneath a much too large tricorn which hung down to the man's eyebrows. The rest of the man's face, what little he could see of it, the chin and nose buried in a cloth to keep off the dust, was leprous white. There was no humor in the cadaverous eyes which chilled and which gave any viewer the frightening impression that here, reincarnate, was a skull. The black orbs were deep set and burned into him.

"I note," said the stranger, "your hand is in your coat and a pistol's bulge is thereabouts. Thus you greet a former acquaintance?"

Wallis inspected the man, ransacking his memory. Something stirred, something about the small size of the man. Being uncomfortable in his presence, Wallis wanted to be away from the rider. "This side of death, I have not seen you, nor do I care to further this visit. Away! I crave no company."

Ah, Samuel. Am I an emmet, a mote, a nonentity, to be cut from your conscience? Or has the mark of my disease so changed my face? Many a black trollop danced to my whip and jiggled her breasts when I was auctioneer of slaves at the docks Who, Squire Wallis, procured your household servants at the House of Auctions? And to think of it, pow you high and mighty Quakers renounce slavery. Bread from my mouth. Yes, I see recognition. Tell me, Grand Master, who am I?"

"The imp Cundiff"

"No less. Hell's obedient chevalier. Cundiff, the dark stain, a maggot of wormwood."

"That you are, wraith of hideousness. No wonder you hide your face. How live you; by what misbegotten employment are you supported, you leech upon all that's rotten?"

"Spoken eloquently. I am tool for whatever dastardly purpose man wishes. I murder my betters if there's price for it. Right now, you and I have a common bond. I pry, I peek, I am a King's spy. And so are you." Cundiff relished the disclosure. His voice had dropped to a basso profundo and he clicked his teeth like Death itself. He whipped off a glove, rummaged in a pocket and read from a paper: 'Cundiff ... please to locate the Friend discussed Who is either on the West Branch or in travel to Philadelphia. He may be helpful in further business transactions.'

Wallis snatched the paper, reading further: 'Impart to him those with whom he is to be interactive.' The paper had no signature.

Cundiff grinned and clucked his tongue from behind a web of rotten teeth. "You must fix three names in your mind, with your goings and comings mostly to be with these. One, Robert Hooper."

"Hooper? My close friend!" Wallis registered astonishment. With Hooper, an officer in the Continental Army, he had been for many years associated in the buying, shipping and selling of livestock. Never in their association had Hooper shown the least tinge of Toryism, but to the contrary. A hundred afternoons if not a thousand Wallis had sipped tea with him at the 'Indian Queen.' Hooper, a committed patriot by every measure, his friend of rough language now disclosed as a closet Tory. Ha! What a revelation!

"And the second?" asked Wallis.

"Joseph Stansbury."

The crockery merchant and sometimes poet, was long a confidant of his. While yet in New York, prior to Howe's sailing from there to disembark at Head of Elk where, last August the 25th one year ago, he started his march overland to Philadelphia, Stansbury had been courier for Wallis. He had carried to the British General Wallis's amazing offer to provide flour for the British troops, this an item of scarcity. Stansbury's shop was well known, even Mrs. Washington having visited it to purchase crystal.

The last to be named was 'Stevens.' "Stevens? Which Stevens? Give me his full name."

"That's the whole of it. I can add no more," the imp responded. "You will receive directions from him. This group has been designed to gain what it can about frontier military plans. In the Pennsylvania Council and in the Continental Congress discussions go forward which can be of value to our New York frineds. Once you've settled in, dispatch your man servant to find me. Do you still own the slave I sold you?"

"'Mr. Africa? I emancipated him. Yes, he continues with me."

"When ready send him to the Old Tun Tavern on the waterfront." Without so much as a good-day Cundiff wheeled his horse and cantered away. For Wallis it was not a good day. It rubbed him wrong a nonentity, a stranger to the City was to be 'captain' of this secret enterprise. Why Stevens? Why this unknown when he, Wallis, had the intimate connections and would be doing the work? He surmised Howe before sailing had set up this link.

For Wallis, meeting Cundiff on the road had stirred up old memories. It was true he had abolished keeping slaves after an acquired incident in which his coachman of that time had repeatedly struck a new houseboy with his whip until the slave, rebelling, broke the man's neck and then vanished. This incident led to the hiring of French and had strengthened Wallis's resolve to acquire no more slaves.

The day following Wallis's return he met with his old friend Lieutenant Colonel Robert Hooper, as usual at the Indian Queen. Hooper was sometimes addressed as judge. He amply projected that image, being weighty and impressive in girth. After some fumbling each confessed his part in Stevens' clandestine circle. Recognizing their shared danger, Hooper was prompted to think of the fate befallen a mutual friend, Joseph Galloway. Prominent in Pennsylvania government and a former member of the Continental Congress, Galloway had fallen out with the radicals, disillusioned because reconciliation appeared doomed. When the British Army marched into Philadelphia he became manager of the City during its occupation, only to flee for his life as did thousands when the Army abruptly withdrew following General Howe's recall to England. "We must be very cautious," stated Hooper, "or we shall be as Galloway. During your absence his estate, which is not inconsiderable, and separate from his wife's, was seized. Why, Galloway owned 210 acres, two-thirds of Hogg Island. He was worth in the least 40,000 sterling, and that's not counting his wife's personal fortune. Under Tory-hater Reed the list of foreclosures grows. The Pennsylvania Journal next will be advertising the sale of his property."

Wallis, aware Grace Galloway had stayed on in the City, was shocked at Hooper's next statement.

"And Grace's property, too. She thought because she brought to the marriage an abundent estate, these being in her name, hers would be immune to seizure. They've taken the beautiful residence on Market Street her parents left her. She literally was stripped of all she owned, beggered, sir, everything grabbed. Upon arrival of the American Army, that same day she was visited by Charles Willson Peale, the painter fellow. Acting for the court, to play on words, Peale 'peeled' her naked of her possessions, forcing her from her home. He confiscated everything, even to the broken china and empty bottles, everything down to the chamber pot. She is penniless, living in a room provided by her one true friend, Debbie Morris, her many 'good time' companions giving her a cold reception. Sundays she despairs anew, seeing a hod carrier wearing Joe's clothes pass beneath her window going to church. It reminds her how low she has fallen. It makes her burst into tears. 'T is sad."

"I presuppose her needs are met."

"She suffers from being changed in fortunes, now recipient of charity, wherefore she's been strong willed, independent."

"Then the decent thing to do," said Wallis, "is to search our pockets out of friendship and quietly provide for her, we to claim to her the amounts come from Joe."

"Don't attribute it to Joe. They were argumentative, quarrelsome. Claim instead, the money comes from a benefactor who prefers anonymity. *It* will be the truth." They were agreed.

Chapter XV

EXPEDITION TO TEAOGA

After Wallis's departure from Muncy, small scouts of Indians sulking in the woods, with swift and darkening shouts made sallies at Muncy. At night, up in the forest, the individual and peculiar war cries of Wamp, Blacksnake, The Panther, and Greatshot came to be recognized. If the Niagara colonels had passed word along for the Seneca and the Delaware of the Minsi tribe to tread lightly around Muncy, it was not evident. To the contrary the gadfly tactics of these warriors, who in two's and three's haunted the forest reaches, attested to their loose form of leadership. Several Indians, one of who would be viewed as leader or 'chief', would do their own special thing when they sought fit. In joining larger war parties this independence was subordinated, but not entirely, with the smaller bodies sometimes indulging in unspeakable acts against a vanquished surrendered foe. The larger the party, the more these unruly elements had opportunity to indulge their blood thirst, unmerciful war to the knife the practice. Because of this, there was further disheartening news reaching Wallis at Philadelphia.

As reported in an August 4th newspaper, 'By authentic accounts from the frontiers it appears that on the 28th of July a small fort, called Freeland's fort, about 17 miles from Sunbury, was attacked by about 200 Indians and 100 whites, who called themselves regulars, but are supposed by some to be Tories dressed in red regimentals. They are commanded by one McDonald. There were in the fort about 30 men and 50 women and children. Upon the attack being made, Captain Hawkins Boone, a very brave and gallant officer, with about 30 men, went to the relief of the fort but before he got there the fort had surrendered, and with the neighboring houses was set on fire and burnt. McDonald consented to let the women and children come away, but it is not yet known what has been the fate of the men. Captain Boone advanced to the fort and engaged the enemy but was soon overpowered by numbers, and fell gallantly fighting for his distressed country. Captains Doughtery and Hamilton are also missing, and 18 of the party. Some prisoners who escaped say, Captain Boone's and 11 other scalps were brought into the fort in a handkerchief before they came away ... Fort Muncy is evacuated.' As Wallis read further about the attacks along the Susquehanna, he could not accept all to be true. Not about Muncy. It shocked him. The commitment of Bolton and Claus at Fort Niagara seemed ephemeral. Or had Menniger been persuaded by local fears to abandon his West Branch redoubt. Damn the man, that to be.

Menniger had not abdicated his responsibility. Bolstered by belief his fort would be spared serious assault, any appearance to be token in nature, he nevertheless took thorough precautions. Under his strict injunction the villagers barred doors, latched shutters, and were prepared to fly to the fort upon signal of an alarm. The garrison stood watch clock-around. Too, the detachment of regulars kept close watch in their palisade in the meadow, about 500 feet removed. Thus, an infilading fire could be brought to bear.

Despite remonstrance about ventures afield, three of this command stole from the stockade to dig tubers within sight of its walls. As they bent to their digging, a number of Seneca arose from the bushes and in an instant had converged on the trio, killing one who they forthright scalped, and gave chase to a second who managed to elude them and attain safety. The third, struggling with a stout but brawny Indian, was saved by a detail on the quick-march. The Indian, Wamp, took to his heels. On the 23rd a man named Cottner was shot dead a mile south of the fort; and on the same day a Captain Martel, transferred into the vicinity, was wounded. Martel was part of a new flow of troops encamping close by. However ragged the situation had been until now, it was improving. In this momentous month of August the bayonets promised by the man of the manor house, daily seemingly, were increasing.

If Wallis had intended to bring succor in the form of regular troops to be stationed near his house, he succeeded beyond expectation. In his original plea he had called upon and written influential persons. Since his departure, he was flabbergasted to learn, his valley was gradually being inundated with encamping soldiers. Wallis, from his remote position in Philadelphia, at first thought it might be a minor sally for which these troops were intended. He discounted the size of the force. No doubt the rumor of numbers was magnified. But the rumors continued, prompting Wallis to carry out the duties Cundiff had placed upon him, as ears for the Crown. He made inquiry. The consensus was that next year, not this, there would be a major expedition to settle the frontier. The troops at Muncy were to have been part of the delayed expedition. Lateness of the season, problems getting wagons and securing ample provisions along with the batteaux to transport their supplies, had led to the postponement. Farmers would sooner break their wagon wheels than give them up for worthless Continental notes. The expedition would not start until the spring of 1779, Wallis learned, when many more thousands would link up with those initial troops on the West Branch. Quickly Wallis summoned his man-servant Mr. Africa, and dispatched the woolly-headed Negro to the Old Tun. He was to fetch that charming death's head, Cundiff.

Wallis had underestimated Hartley, senior officer of the troops encamped in Muncy Valley. The Colonel had his own plans, and these were not confined to keeping his force in garrison duty on the West Branch, nor waiting for the coming winter to pass. Drawing provisions from Augusta, the Colonel worked round the clock collecting supplies of food and munitions. He kept a tight lip, but one did not have to be shrewd to guess he was getting ready for a march. Several faces once familiar, long away to war, had arrived with these units. It was a reunion of grim men. The Free Company was on hand, as were the reconstructed remnants of militia that had fought at Forty Fort. It was Sergeant Baldwin who called the Free Company roll in the misty dawn, on the parade of Fort Muncy. Within the great pen of logs were some of the best. Hartley had gained Captains Spalding, Foster, Murrow, Stoddard and Franklin, men who had dreamed of such an expedition, who long contended there would have been no debacle at Forty Fort had an expedition been mounted early in '78.

Included were those who had helped gather and place in a cairn the bones of 86 of their countrymen massacred in July. Every able survivor of that awful event had joined Hartley. The ranks were sprinkled with bitter men. In Hartley's mind was a sally in force, a precursor stab at the rim of Indian villages. To follow them, next Spring, would be the in-depth invasion of the Indian Country.

Wallis observed first hand a portion of the troops which had been authorized for this purpose by the Congress, as these set forth upon the road toward the frontier. While a detachment of the Eleventh Pennsylvania marched from New Jersey to East Town, the remainder of this veteran regiment, being at Philadelphia, marched from that City and took the road toward Muncy. From the Coach and Horses he watched the lines pass through the streets.

Hartley did not want for men. To date, 300 bloodied, seasoned militia from the county of Northumberland, 400 from the county of Lancaster, and 100 from the county of Berks had joined the doughty soldier's command. A small number of horsemen already at East Town, serving under Colonel Kowatz but actually commanded by Captain Lighthorse Carberry, set themselves on the road north. They followed in the dust of the Eleventh or 'Long Legged Line.' Wallis hastily revised his estimates, he by way of Cundiff advising the British a real thrust at the Seneca towns was in the making, but he qualified his statement. He doubted it posed any threat to Fort Niagara, as yet.

Days before Colonel Hartley's arrival at Muncy to assume command, words-meager Colonel Dan Brodhead reached Muncy, bringing the Eighth Pennsylvania Regiment. He encamped and deployed scouting parties in every direction. He would make sure that no red man spied into the beehive valley. Using native clay, this officer improved upon the redoubt near Wallis's home, adding a covered waterway from the redoubt to the stream, and mounted another cannon, a four-pounder. Hartley, upon arrival finding these things done, complimented Brodhead, then asked about the provisions. "Terrible!" responded Brodhead. "Not enough for feeding a thousand on the march."

Hartley made an immediate decision. "I'll not wait. Within this week we'll be skinning Indians!" Unsure as to how far down he must scale his force, in order to survive on the flour available, and how long afield he could commit these men, or what distance he could travel in the allotted time, he penned to the honorable Executive Council of the Commonwealth: 'It will be impossible to tell the troops or people where we are to march to.' Rumor, though, there was aplenty.

This prologue to weaken Indian deviltry was to be conducted with but a fraction of the arms funneled into the West Branch Valley. Some said that Hartley was too cagey a commander to go romping off toward the Seneca, enlisting every last man and leaving denuded and helpless the valley for which the hatchets of the foe were poised. There were those who believed Hartley, to bait the enemy into an attack upon Muncy, was making an appearance of marching forth while in reality he was preserving the bulk of his forces in the valley, these to fall upon the

Indians who might venture to attack the settlers. Others, more close to the truth, noting the lateness of the season, rightfully concluded as to why he was moving out with so few. Hartley would face fatal delay if he waited to provide for a thousand. Winter soon promised, he had to jump off quickly and lightly if at all. He peeled his force to an abrupt minimum before vanishing into the woods. Of the 1,000 he took 200 rank and file, with 12 days flour. Degenerated from a grand plan for invasion of the Indian lands, nevertheless it was necessarily important, small as this force was, to teach the Indians manners. On August 21, 1778 Thomas Hartley marched into the Indian woods.

There was another reason, known to Hartley only, for this Continental Army officer to be on his way. This attack, while to have been on larger scale, was being coordinated with another to be launched from the Northern Department, from New York's Western Frontier outposts Fort Defiance and Schoharie Church, made into a fort, these four miles apart. Colonel William Butler leading the 4th Pennsylvania Regiment, and a detachment of Morgan's Rifles under Major James Parr, had orders to burn the villages of the hostiles on the upper reaches of the Susquehanna. Each expedition, by dividing the Indians attention, was to split and draw off Indians otherwise gathered to attack as one force. Too, he knew that Virginia's Lieutenant Colonel George Rogers Clark, far to the west, by way of Fort Pitt, was in the Ohio Country attempting to reach Fort Vincennes, garrisoned by the French now our allies. This, too, would mitigate effect of reinforcement from the west by hostiles kept busy by Clark. It was Clark's dream with help from the French to mount a future expedition against Fort Detroit. Hartley foresaw his own efforts and that of Colonel Butler as moves to clear the waterways for a major expedition to take Fort Niagara. By doing this, the depredation of the American settlements and all future Indian actions along the Susquehanna and Ohio would collapse, if not the war itself.

March they did. With Hartley went Levi and, for the knowledge they had, the men of the Free Company, woodsmen all. Levi and Tim Murphy, to the joy of each, were reunited. Lieutenant King, Menniger's adjutant, led a representation from Muncy. Then too, Carberry and several other horsemen came along. The cavalry under given conditions could deliver a telling blow. Captains Stoddard and Foster attached themselves as gentlemen without command. Because the bulk of Hartley's force was comprised of Pennsylvania Line men of the New Eleventh Regiment, and the roll call of the accompanying militia read like a list of notables, the Colonel showed no disappointment in his whittled down force. To the contrary, he maintained, "I have the best marksmen and the best powder I ever saw." His men, singing 'Nothing like Grog', departed from Muncy to follow the winding waters of Lycoming Creek northward.

The little army climbed until night. On top of the world they rested, lit their fires, and slept. Dawn in their eyes, they were again on the move, keeping and clinging to the heights where they were protected against attack. Later, compelled to descend, they again encountered the Lycoming, shining in its banks and drawing curses from them all. Twisting as it did, well could they swear. The mountains came down to the stream so that footholds were at a premium and sometimes nonexistent. The hairpin turns of the stream necessitated their crossing and recrossing of it. Twenty times, French computed, he had forded the capricious Lycoming. To add to their misery, by mid-afternoon the rains set in, sheets of water falling upon them. The whole of their travels up the Lycoming was an adventure with rheumatism. They confronted more immediate dangers, the river itself swollen by the rains. It thundered within its banks. It spumed and hissed at their feet as they inched along the thin footpath between the stream and the mountain. During the numerous crossings the troops linked hands where danger was present. A man could be swept from his feet, and swallowed jack-quick by the current. As further precaution, should any man go under, Carberry's horsemen were stationed downstream to scoop the unfortunate one from the boiling waters. Weighed down by 40 rounds of cartridges, the soldier was apt to give out a terrifying yell as he tumbled and flailed about within the torrent.

At last, dropping the Lycoming behind, their enthusiasm dampened by the dousings, the 200 bedraggled soldiers halted in a hollow. The rains by now abated, they lighted fires, stripped off their soaked clothes and let the warmth creep into their bones. As best they could, they had held their powder horns, if not slung about their necks, above their heads. Murphy, with allusion to the Quebec campaign, coyly looked toward Pence, reminiscing how, at the Kennipeck crossings in the Maine woods, Morgan's men smelling from their long march found there was a blessing in those frequent baptisms. "At least the Indians won't sniff us in advance, eh, Pence." 'Dutchy' Pence, the portly Hollander, promptly took a piece of cheese and hurled it at his tormentor.

They encountered days of sunshine. The going became easier. They met the Susquehanna and marched along its banks. They passed over meadowland into a broken series of woods. And with each day's travel their vigilance increased, they detecting ever fresh signs, heel prints and broken twigs.

The day came when down the files from man to man a caution flew, "Easy; pass it along." At a signal from the front a number of men detached themselves from the column, spreading to right and left, fan-shape, so as to flank the path and beat up the woods. Action was imminent. By prearrangement, a new signal being given, the Free Company men as advance scouts, some taking cover behind trees and some sinking to the ground, waited while a party of three, Murphy, Baldwin and Grove wiggled through the underbrush, to disappear ahead swallowed by the forward timber. Behind this line, standing at ready was the New Eleventh. Colonel Hartley, who fully expected a rush from the enemy, scuttled forward, then dropping on his stomach wormed toward the the the threesome. To the frontiersmen flanking the path, the delay in his return seemed overly long. Some men were fixing bayonets to muskets, riflemen each with hand on longknife preparing for close encounter, when the Colonel came back. Whatever the cause of their alarm was a mystery, perhaps a herd of deer, some ground birds rustling, a bear crackling its way.

With a sigh they reassembled, formed up in column and, to a drum beating brashly, this done to deceive the enemy they were the advance of a very large force, they tramped north on the Sheshequin Path as it lay within the forest. The most forward scouts had gone on ahead. Hartley's force emerged from the woods, brushing aside the last branches to see the reason for the long absence of the forward scouts. With a glance at Spalding's column coming into the field, the three were busy watching a clump of Indian houses from which smoke from cook fires still curled overhead. Empty though the town appeared, Hartley after a hurried conference felt the structures harbored diehard Indian braves who, contemptuous of their own fate, might fire a volley into the soldiers. To thwart them Carberry's cavalry, whooping in imitation of Indians, made a racing thrust at the village, discharging their guns as they whirled around the perimeter. The flurry of shots was needless, the place deserted.

It would have been better if Levi, with Sam French at his elbow, had not entered one structure. It yielded information of a nauseous turn. Levi counted nine scalps, all recently mounted. French, his eyes widening in horror, saw one hoop. "Rachael!" he screamed, the world gone bottomless. His rifle clattered from nerveless hands. He swayed before the symbol of death, the long golden chestnut tresses. At Hartley's command soldiers tossed torches through the doorways. As crackling flames ate at the walls, and the fire touched and consumed the fatal trophies, Levi pulled the dazed Frenchman into the open. Led to the riverbank, the Frenchman slumped to the ground, burying his sobs in his hands. "Mon Dieu!" he kept reiterating.

As they formed up, Hartley instructed his officers, "Gentlemen, lest the Seneca detect how few we are, we must move quickly, burn whatever settlements we can, and retreat before we are set against. For sure they think us the vanguard of a large force."

"Will we take Chemung?" asked several captains, knowing this to be a Tory mustering place. Their temper was for it.

"We shall try," responded Hartley. "As far as we dare we shall push our good fortune. There is no return except with the sword. So be brave, and while powder, shot, flour, and fortitude are with us we have nothing to fear. When our supplies are near exhausted, then we shall turn our tails; and that should happen just about when we've poked and smoked the hornets nest enough."

On the morning of the 26th an advance element of 19 men under Levi, a 'forlorn hope', collided with an equal number of Indians on the river path. The Americans had the first fire, this breaking the enemy who fled leaving one man dead. French bent over the fellow who he had shot and, using the Indian's own scalp knife, severed the scalp, then disgusted flung it away. The men clustered around the corpse, examining what appeared to be, by the hieroglyphic on his breast, an important chief. In the sun the dead man's eyes glittered, as did the necklace of blood at the crown of his head. The rest of Hartley's force came on the double, and the expedition resumed its interval. The corpse half onto the path was kicked aside. It was that of the Seneca chief met by Wallis at the Teaoga portage.

They crossed land covered with linden, sugar birch and white pine, this last appearing intermittently; there were also growths of beech and chestnuts. Where the trees had fallen into rot a black soil had formed, watered by numerous springs. From this soil, in perpetual shade and therefore soggy and porous, the wasps and yellow jackets rose and met them by swarms. This was the cause of a series of small retreats and delays. The unhappy soldiers smeared themselves with mud to draw the sting out of their wounds and to ward off further stabs. The deeper into the shade they marched, the more grievous became the insect problem; the men lit dry faggots and carried them to keep the crawling, flying, biting monsters from settling upon their faces and hands. One fellow who stopped to pee exchanged one agony for another. This particular stretch of forest was discovered to be a prodigious hive. The soldiers were reminiscent of Hartley's speech, "We shall turn our tails when we've poked and smoked the hornets' nest enough." Some were of the opinion that this moment had come. Was this an omen their journey should end here?

The blessing of the hornets was not unmixed; there were huckleberries. That night they lay on the cool bosom of the earth, the balsamic pines helping them forget the grueling day, and a clear deep air bathing their bodies. They were lulled into slumber by the clish-clash, and swish of the pine needles.

Levi's patrol, in the first 15 minutes of their next morning's advance, came upon untended Indian campfires. Unbeknownst to either white or red, they had bivouacked side by side, figuratively, in this vast forest, and one could have slit the other's throat had any man fumbled about the woods. Murphy calculated that upward of 50 had slept in this glade. A dog, spitted and roasted as an offering to the Giver of Good Hunting, indicated to Tim that these warriors had been bound southward, and had fled when apprised scouts were approaching. So precipitous was their retreat that they were cut off from the river and their canoes. The canoes abandoned by the Indians were either stove in by the frontiersmen or were impounded for their own use. Eight Forty Fort volunteers took to the water to act as a naval flank for the column of marchers. Hartley wished to catch the fleeing Indians and exploit their panic. He pushed his men, believing the foe would give trouble only if reinforced at Sheshequin or, failing there, at Esther's Flats near Teaoga. Hartley speculated the Seneca might have been from that settlement and were lazily moving down the river, perhaps to join others, some dastardly deed in the making. He had heard tales about the fabled Queen Esther, of French origin, and her sister Catherine, each of whom ruled a Seneca community, and who in their hatred of their own French kind were intensely loyal to the Crown. The distance to Esther's he estimated, would be a day's march if not less.

By canoe and land they rushed northward, meaning to crush the retreating war party before it could organize in resistance. Springing up the path Levi's contingent entered a small hamlet. The canoe element, having maneuvered to a point more northerly, beached their craft, the men tumbling ashore. Hartley's New Eleventh, with a wide detour to the east, in two waves at 250 feet separation swept into the settlement. The valiant exercise was just that, their prize being fifteen sullen squaws. These were interrogated by the Colonel, with Levi translating. The cherry-face women stoically bent their heads, expecting the coupe. "Tell them," said Hartley, "we do not kill women." Their interrogation was interrupted by a shout from the northernmost cabin where a soldier, probing the shadowy interior, had found a naked white woman. He came forth carrying her in his arms. French, with a start, looked unbelievingly at the woman. Though her face was turned in the other direction, the long, golden chestnut locks that cascaded over the soldier's arm were Rachael's! He flung his gun aside and raced to meet the man. It was her! Arms outstretched, tears starting down his dirty, bearded face, he took her gently into his own arms while some one found a blanket to cover her nakedness. Hardy soldiers looked away or fumbled at their flints and powder. "Ma Cher," said French, over and over, setting her upon the grass. "What have they done to you?" He noted her hollow cheeks and the deep misery in her eyes. "Rachael, it is me! Please, Rachael, there is nothing of which you should be afraid."

Menema, the surgeon, waved French away. After some minutes the Doctor beckoned to him. "I'll be blunt. She was pregnant, maybe eight weeks into it when she lost the baby. She either induced its loss, not wanting an Indian child, or was kicked in the stomach. I don't know. Mum about this. Don't tell the troops, or they will believe the worst about this aborted birth. Those squaws might get killed." French tightened his lips and nodded.

Colonel Hartley coming up, bending over the woman asked her, "Young lady, you may help us. Do you believe the Seneca were planning an attack against our towns?"

Haltingly she shaped her words. "There was a deserter from Captain Spalding's Company, Van Alstyne." She paused for breath, and added, "He told me the Indians had been on their way down river for an attack on Muncy, but you came out too quickly."

The Colonel beckoned his officers. "Expect a stiffening ahead. Shall we keep on? Your opinions, sirs." Then he added, "Mine is formed."

"Yes, keep on," contended Captain Spalding. "While by now they are in alarm, it will take them some time to pull together any sizable number of braves, which gives us time to push on a bit further."

"By all means, Colonel, go. Let us plant a flag at Teaoga," Carberry added, using a figurative expression. Captains Foster and Stoddard were of the same opinion.

"If we burn the Indian town at Teaoga, added Foster, "it carries the threat we can do more, at our choice and at any later date. That may make them pull in their horns and give our settlers a respite."

"Exactly my intention," said the Colonel. The matter was settled.

Not so about the 15 squaws, a continuing problem for unhappy Lieutenant Sweeney who had been given duties as guard officer over them. "What shall I do with these charming wenches, Colonel?" asked the perplexed Lieutenant. "Take 'em along?"

"Hell, turn them loose, and fire off a gun to see how much they twitch as they run." Sweeney, a sensitive man, gave his Colonel a disgusted look. Hartley had not intended his words to be interpreted literally.

French, Pence, Sergeant Baldwin and Peter Grove, improvising a litter, loaded Rachael into a canoe. Two men, lamed by the march, were put at the paddles with orders to return to Forty Fort. Hartley believed the country through which they had come was now largely empty of Indians, he having pushed them upstream by his march, the canoe party to be in no great danger returning through those lands. Wading beside the bark, French held her hand until they reached deep water. Standing hip-deep, he watched the canoe disappear down the Susquehanna. He returned to shore as the Captains bawled orders, bringing the troops to their feet. Sergeants ran down the files checking for stragglers, and advising all to have their pieces in battle readiness. A soldier blew three notes on a cow horn. At that moment a red face soldier, pulling at his breeches, rushed from the brush, to be unmercifully bawled out by his unsympathetic sergeant.

They advanced at a half-trot, scouts ahead beating the woods. On their flanks, the little army having pulled inland from the river for easier travel, heard movements and saw signs of the retreating enemy. Tim Murphy, in lead guide position, 'blind man's eye' as it was facetiously called, abruptly halted. He waved Levi and his men to take shelter behind trees. The troops covered their sergeant as he, with a wild unearthly yell, jumped down the lane and landed in a thicket. First a leg kicked up, then a hand; finally a hatchet slithered onto the path and Tim, smirking, dragged forth a crestfallen Seneca, a diminutive fellow, Little Bones, who spouted an abusive mixture of English and native dialect. Hartley questioned the prisoner who answered, "You go Hell."

"Kill the bastard," somebody called. Instead, Murphy, waggling his finger like a school teacher, admonished Little Bones, "You talk like that to my Colonel, you have very short life."

Hartley, scribbling on a leaf of paper, handed the truculent English-speaking Indian his message. "Go," he gestured. "Take this to Tory Major Butler and to your smoky-heads. Let the chiefs know that I have more guns than there are trees in the woods from here to Chemung-town. Tell them how you have counted my scouts, that behind me travels an endless army, like a snake, with cannon, 'thunder trees', which will tear at the Longhouse till no stick stands. Tell them Chemung shall burn by time the next moon sets." Levi translated, to be sure the Indian understood. Then he turned to his commander.

"Let me add something, sir, in his language. I know how these people think."

"Go to it," said Hartley, aware of Levi's talents.

In the Indian's spoken tongue Levi stated, translating for the Colonel's benefit as he went along, "Our Great Chief speaks to you not without pity or reason. If the sachems will propitiate his anger by gifts, and they are sensible men, let them show a white feather of peace, meeting him at Teaoga tomorrow. He will listen and be merciful. If they wish this meeting, then they must agree to this parley before the sun dies on yonder hill. Otherwise, I swear this oath, our Great Chief shall be as Hino, the Thunderer, and shall beat flat your crops and strike fire to your houses. Then shall our hatchets seek those who wear war paint. The fate of your Longhouse people rests upon your chiefs' council." Levi looked toward Hartley. The Colonel nodded, pleased. "Go!" shouted Levi. The dumbfounded Little Bones, limping, fled. As dumbfounded were Hartley's officers by their commander's bluster, and by Levi's added comments. Hartley smiled. He knew Little Bones would spread panic, this at least delaying somewhat the inevitable gathering against him.

"Will they make peace, or will there be a fight at Teaoga?" Carberry raised the question.

"Neither," answered Hartley to everybody's surprise. "My pretended threat, added to by Lieutenant Brady's overture, will convince them we are more than we are, our talk to be puffed up so big, and they perforce to need 300 or 400 warriors to give contest. That number cannot be gathered overnight. They will rendezvous deep, as far away as Unadilla, or conceivably above Chemung, collecting themselves in anticipation of our march toward Chemung. It will take them 48 hours to gather in their forces, and we about the same time in marching to reach beyond Teaoga, to Chemung, where they will be expecting us. There'll be no battle at Teaoga, to answer your question, Captain. Nor will we engage them, as they believe, at Chemung."

Resuming his position close to the front Hartley lifted his hand. "Now men," he called, his strident voice reaching around, "our redskin playmates are nearby, either at Chemung or, if not there, on the mountains. Given more flour, a cannon and iron shot, and were we twice our strength we could and would raze Chemung. It is the den in which every scheme and murderous foray against us has been hatched. Sweet revenge it would be to burn Chemung! I had hoped for that satisfaction. But we must settle for Teaoga. That does not subtract from our accomplishment. We have proven, even as we go northward to Teaoga, that the Indian settlements are as much within our reach as ours are for them. It's a tit for tat. Thus they will pay the price for the molestations they bring to us. We shall prove this, by the scar we leave on their land. So, let's be doing!"

Swallowed by a sea of tall grass covering the upper Sheshequin plains, the raiders, oriented by the soft blue cones of the hills to the north, advanced toward Teaoga. They forded the Susquehanna well below the fabled point where the Teaoga River tributary had its mouth with the Susquehanna. To secure the crossing, the men in the canoes were first to take possession of the opposite shore. The infantry began to file over, wading the Susquehanna. By dark Hartley's force had invested the western flats of the Susquehanna, torching the abandoned Indian town of some 50 homes. One of the cabins, more grand than the others and boasting an ornamental porch, reputedly belonged to the *queen* of this village, Esther the French-Indian woman. With the reflection of the flames dancing in the water, they pushed on, the darkness about them. Tim Murphy had discovered that the Teaoga which they now paralleled, was at low stage and island-clogged, permitting them to leap from mound to mound and thus, virtually dry-shod, gain the 'Point' itself. A thrill of conquest penetrated the core conscience of each man as his feet touched this entry way to the Longhouse country. Reasoning that Ranger Major Butler would have his hands full mustering at Chemung, Colonel Hartley considered his men secure from night surprise and encamped on the portage between the two rivers. These rivers served in the same way that moats filled with water gave protection to castles. In further caution, he posted pickets around his sleeping woodsmen. These pickets he checked personally, once at midnight and twice before morning. He slept little, resolved to be in retreat by dawn.

On a mountain top, directly to the north and overlooking this valley of the two rivers, Esther Montour, surrounded by her displaced people, watched as the flames ate at her abandoned village. She could see the fire reach her home, marked as it was by a porch. For more than 20 years these forlorn fugitives had dwelt on those flats, and before that had been uprooted from their homes downstream. They had lived side by side with friendly white settlers until the French-led Delaware, joined by a few glory hungry Seneca, had made war on the English., any Indian thereafter suspect. In her misery Esther thought of Sam. To see her home burn and those of her closely knit villagers was traumatic. She prayed that he fared better than her in his quest to preserve Muncy.

At dawn Hartley ordered the retreat. More canoes were found at the portage, with 20 of the slowest marchers shifted into these. Several lamed men were put to riding the unloaded packhorses. Swiftly the small army retreated. As much as they could the marchers kept abreast of the fleet. Sometimes they were separated when a long bend of the river would cause the canoes to drop away, or the opposite were to happen were the river to follow a straight course, the canoes to outdistance those on the winding path. Generally water and land groups supported one another, those on shore with wary eye ready to lay a suppressing fire into the woods flanking the river, and the same was true of those on the river, should the marchers come upon trouble. The feeling was shared the enemy would not let them come away without a show.

Murphy, paired with Baldwin, was 20 long strides ahead of the leading frontiersmen under Levi. In like manner, Levi's 15 men were advanced a quarter mile in front of the remainder of the Free Company under Spalding. Murphy had premonitions. His eyes shifted to all parts and corners.

From nowhere a musket ball sliced the wind. Murphy made a wild dive, churning the leaves and rolling toward an uprooted tree. Another ploughed a furrow in the log, flicking chips. Baldwin likewise got behind cover. Whoever had them in his sights was centering down upon them. With a whoop both scrambled for the handiest trees. Levi zigzagged up, stopping within talking range. Murphy advised, "Stay where y' are! They've got this stretch in their sights."

"A fact!" exclaimed Levi, a ball having snipped a twig inches away.

"They be in the pines further up on this hill," cried Murphy, firing at a puff of smoke.

"Trade shots with them," shouted Levi. "Keep 'em busy. I mean to flank the hill, then get above them and rush the devils." He crept off, Murphy and Baldwin observing the rustling of the brush as Levi gathered his men. Levi's 15 rangers, unseen but heard, scuttled by on the left. Firing at whim and fancy, the two peppered the upper slope, blasting at every tremble of the shrubbery, the while jumping from tree to tree, changing their position on the run. Baldwin was worried. Time had elapsed. Brady's force was not in sight, nor had Spalding come up with the rest of the company. The Captain should have fetched his men on the quick-march. The ominous silence perplexed Murphy, he thinking the Indians might have spotted Levi's crawling platoon and could be quietly lying in wait. He joined Murphy behind a large oak. In a whisper he asked, "Where are the bastards?" At that moment they heard Spalding from behind them on the move in their direction.

Murphy's eyes narrowed. Something had stirred on the up slope. He whispered "Just give me room, Baldwin. The heathen have a brave who is anxious for glory. He's working this way. 'T will make a delicate shot." He leveled his gun, finger curled on the trigger. Satisfied, he snapped the flint. The shot went wild and blew a hole in the roof of leaves, Baldwin having jostled the barrel. On the echoes of Murphy's shot there was a wrathful yell, Levi bubbled to the surface of the greenery.

"Damn your eyes, Murphy!"

"Oh, shut up," growled Murphy. "It's the first shot I ever missed. Lucky for you. Why didn't you challenge? I thought you to be an Injun."

"You'd never see an Indian shake the bushes. You'd see only his gun barrel, if that," testily said Levi, stalking down to meet his two scouts. Murphy was muttering there were Indians dumb enough to do just that, shake bushes, and lieutenants dumb enough to pass for dumb Indians.

"Where's our hellion play friends?" asked Baldwin as Levi's men popped into sight.

"All run off," the Lieutenant responded. "You two grow roots and stay here. I think it best my men and I go back up the slope and occupy the crest until Colonel Hartley's by. It'll be safer up there, anyway, away from you."

Levi's small command disappeared up the slope scarcely ahead of Spalding's company filing into view. "What sport, boys?" he addressed his sergeants.

The Lieutenant told us to set up a covering fire while he flanked whoever was up there."

"Flanked them?" dubiously said Spalding. "With a platoon?"

"Yes, sir. And he's done did it. The Lieutenant's holding the heights from being retaken." Without further parley, Captain Spalding detached half his company to go up the hill, in reinforcement, and to hold there until their small army had passed safely by. He'd berate Lieutenant Brady later, if by then his temper hadn't cooled.

Hartley's column double-timed toward the firing. The Colonel, learning Indians were in the vicinity, halted his column, redeployed his men into three compact units, each capable of independent action, yet also capable of giving support to the others if required. He placed his own Pennsylvanians foremost, with the Light Horse situated between the Pennsylvanians and a contingent serving as the rear guard. A few cavalry, likewise, four to be precise, were disposed on the west flank of the advancing battle line. Here the trees were spaced. And they were able to reconnoitre without risk of entrapment. Carberry took charge of this reconnoitering unit. Having gone by the critical hill, the main command was rejoined by Levi Brady and that portion of Spalding's company sent up to reinforce him. These men and the Lieutenant in particular received an ovation. So far, so good.

The first exchange of shots had occurred at noon; then, about 40 minutes later, there was another burst of fire. Again the muskets of the enemy fell silent, the foe disengaging as soon as a front was presented. It became apparent that an undetermined number, sufficiently large to be bold, were being driven before them. This did not disconcert Hartley. "Bloodletting will purge out their fever," said he, not in the least showing anxiety.

At two o'clock a heavy fire threatened the rear. The Light Horse under Carberry made a vain attempt to draw the Indians away from the imperiled guard. The woods proved too thick for a saber charge. One horseman was dragged from his saddle while others were hard put to escape. Indians were rising from every bush and springing at them from behind trees. As Carberry withdrew, the unfortunate platoon of guards, completely isolated, volleyed into the foe. The army sought refuge on a piece of high ground to the left. Hartley, his rear guard cut off and his cavalry scarcely able to rejoin him, gave orders on the mountaintop for his troops to form a square, setting a reserve at the center to bolster any weakening of his line.

Within the quadrangle of troops the cavalrymen heard Carberry cry out to Colonel Hartley. "Good God, Colonel, our lads with Lieutenant Sweeney are fighting for life! Must they perish? Let me employ my dragoons as infantry. The Indians have Sweeney in a net. A brave countercharge could save him."

"Fat chance you'd have of extricating them. On ground of the enemy's choosing, more likely you would be in their net, too. The guard will sell their lives as they must, to preserve the Army."

"Colonel, you have not been down there. You did not see their eyes when we came so close to a junction, yet were forced back."

"How then would you snatch them to safety this time?"

"I say, sir, our horses encumbered us. We'll charge horseback almost to them as before, but this time slip from saddle and storm to a junction. I know the terrain - I was just on it. I can get them out!"

Hartley deliberated a fraction of a second. The majority of the Colonel's command, moved by the Captain's plea, was for forsaking the strategic high point to go to their rescue. Every reverberation from the woods augmented this resolve. Sensing his men would desert him, they choosing folly over caution, should he not acquiesce to Carberry's request, and he also was aware that sometimes the wildest, most impossible scheme succeeds when there is passion among the men, he snapped, "Go to it, Captain!"

Attacking on their horses, dismounting quickly, at command of 'fix bayonets', Carberry's men skewered those Seneca who rushed to meet them. The Indians busy with the cornered rear guard, upon hearing the death halloos of their own people, and seeing the unnerving cold steel in the hands of Carberry's men with a purpose to use it, lost their zeal for pressing the encircled guard. They saw themselves about to be put in a box. Sweeney, picking up his wounded, upon making juncture with Carberry, nodded his thanks. Carberry returned that compliment with a ceremonious salute to the brave guard. But this gesture was a brief luxury.

On Sweeney's heels came multitudes of newly arrived dusky warriors, by their appearance these about to rescue their retreating brothers. Earlier these new arrivals had encountered Levi's patrol. Fortunately for Levi, they had overestimated the advanced element of scouts as badly as Levi had undervalued their numbers. In the interim between Levi's and Sweeney's actions the red men had shifted from harassing the army's van, testing it with small sniping action, to mounting the present full fledged attack on the rear of Hartley's men. This latest encounter placed the expeditionary force in a perilous position. For Hartley to engage the foe at the foot of the hill, by so doing to abandon the heights, would be foolhardy, perhaps fatal. Yet the Colonel could see that the enemy were too many for Sweeney and Carberry combined, the weight flung against that part of his command outnumbering his entire force. It was a choice of damned if you will, damned if you don't.

Smoke saturated the woods. Carberry's men, kneeling, were firing into seemingly endless hordes. Sweeney's men, who for the first time realized how many had been the enemy they had faced, to their credit left off toiling up the hill toward safety when they saw Carberry's predicament. With exception of their wounded they reentered the hand to hand conflict in support of Carberry. At this precarious moment Hartley decided against his own wisdom to stay on the mountain top. If there had been merit to it, it was diluted by the unfolding drama below.

He plunged down the hill, sword drawn, at the head of his men. Nothing else, and perhaps not even this made sense. Fate, God, honor, loyalty, duty if you will, guided him, and not any thoughtful wisdom.

The forces now in direct opposition, a heated exchange by bullet and yell ensued. With a whoop the war party threw themselves, muskets, knives and tomahawks, at Hartley. For an eternal moment the two sides grappled, victory and death touching this or that one. Momentarily worsted, the Indians dropped back a few paces where, shielded by the trees, they resumed the battle, putting up a galling fire. Again they advanced, screeching, their cries chilling. Behind them were green-clad whites, Tory officers flitting about, encouraging, urging them on. The tide of warriors streamed over their own dead. The right wing of the militia, buckling under the weight and shock of the frenzied onslaught, was reinforced by 20 Muncy men. At the center a similar disruption had all but broken the Continental line. Sensing victory the Seneca surged forward, indifferent to appalling losses. Two New Eleventh sergeants, their officers down, their platoons dispersed, and their powder exhausted, clubbed at the foremost wave. Everywhere was single-handed encounter. Levi was to save Captain Stoddard. This officer, flattened by a blow from a tomahawk, nevertheless on hands and knees was dazedly crawling along the lines of combat when a Pine Tree ornamented chief in black and red war mask, hatchet scintillating in the sun, leaped to finish him. Levi likewise leaped, catching at the upraised arm. Thereupon the Indian locked his heel behind Levi's knee, and both men went down hard, rolling. In the maneuver the red man's hatchet flew from his grasp. As they struggled and thrashed about, a momentary cease-fire occurred pending the result. Levi perceived his opponent was a chief of repute, and liable to give him a bad time. He did, kicking him in the groin, and bouncing Levi's head against every rock over which they tumbled. His head ringing, Levi clamped his teeth on the ear of the fellow who with a grunt relaxed his grip. In that instant Levi had his man. He shifted his hold, wrapped one arm around the leg of the squirming chieftain and seizing him around his waist, lifted him bodily above his head, hurling him much as a spear, head first against a tree, splitting the man's skull.

The death of their leader led the Indians in this quarter to desert the field, carrying with them the corpse. Catching his wind, the initiative having passed from the Seneca, Levi directed a counterattack. "Take them by the flank!" he shouted, and seizing a musket from the ground, waved for the troops to follow behind him. Perhaps a battle is won by the effort of many men. Yet, sometimes in the see-saw of events, a special act decides the issue. Levi had set in motion such a result by killing the Seneca chieftain. Thrown back, flanked, the foe retreated toward the river, trading space for the time they would need to regroup. The chance was not to be.

Paddling down the river, the invalids and slow marchers had drawn their canoes abreast of the battleground. Climbing the steep embankment, then in a charge up the slope of the hill this force of 70 men hurled itself at the backs of the Tories and Indians. It was a blind assault that depended upon audacity. War-whooping in imitation of their foe, this little party's intention was to reinforce the beleaguered line, not confront the Indians by themselves. In an unexpected way they won the battle. The Indians, with startled glances over their shoulders, misreading the size of the party, construed their abrupt arival to be a maneuver to catch them in a crescent of guns. Everywhere Indians wavered. Those who could not see the oncoming soldiers, heard them. The Continental yells sounded like a thousand. Abruptly the Seneca broke. They disengaged in good order. Where there had been struggling figures, now was emptiness. The foe had evaporated, had melted behind the trees, escaping the jaws of the supposed trap. By the silence it was as if they had never existed.

Hartley's men had no inkling as to how well they had been matched until, viewing the retreat, when they truly saw the character of the fellows they had bested. As the foe disengaged, they were methodical, posting a protective fire, falling back with shouts of encouragement from group to group. "Sanondi Gwawandi! Do not be daunted. We shall try them another day. Oonah! Oonah! Shondoweko! Death to the honio!" The absence of panic indicated picked warriors were under capable leadership. Tory Butler himself conceivably, might have been directing the retreat.

"At least," said Spalding, wiping the sweat from his forehead and sitting down in the grass to favor a spent leg, "we gave them one hell of a fight they'll not forget."

"How we did it," Hartley added, puffing from exhaustion, "I'll never know. Had we known their quality beforehand we would have been palsied by our fears." The two grizzled veterans understood better than their brash junior officers the miraculous nature of their preservation. Thirty four soldiers, of which fourteen were dead, lay on the ground, some in extremes, and some in hopeful circumstances, these last tended by Dr. Menema. Casualties inflicted upon the Indians could only be estimated, they having made off with their own wounded and the dead that had not fallen in American lines. A dozen of these unrecovered corpses were found, some to be scalped by the frontiersmen.

Footsore and wayworn by their 300 mile trek, on the 5th of September Hartley's companies reached and were disassembled at Forty Fort. The Colonel had proven the Indian Country could be invaded, that given bullets and bayonets and a sufficient force, and cannon, the Continentals could bring permanent peace to the frontier. Momentarily he had stabilized the border. On the porch of the Longhouse he had turned the war against those who had painted themselves and raised their tomahawks. Here, at Forty Fort, in a public ceremony he promoted the two heroic sergeants to the rank of ensign. Next, as the flag of the new nation rippled in the breeze, he accepted the salute of the Eleventh Pennsylvania, Valley men, as it passed in review. He, for their part, was a colonel due their admiration.

Hartley himself would report to Philadelphia, his accomplishment going before him, he to be honored by Congress cognizant of his daring raid and the settling effect, though impermanent, this would have on the Frontier. Upon the streets of Philadelphia he received the handclasp of that most important landholder, the respected Quaker Samuel Wallis. Wallis could not help but admire the man, it being not inconsistent with his character to recognize himself in others who, too, were driven by resoluteness. For the Colonel this was meaningful. Wallis was the land king of the State, his Muncy plantation itself being 7,500 contiguous acres located along the Susquehanna waterway. So vast was his business and speculation that his name was recognized afar, even to his being agent for the Holland Land Company, comprised of Netherlands capitalists, in its acquisitions of western lands.

Accepting Congress's platitudes, the Colonel had warned, "Unless reinforcements are sent quickly, you may have your Frontier much lower down than you expect." It brought home Philadelphia's danger.

Chapter XVI

HOMECOMINGS

A scribble of roofs cut the skyline. October crisped the leaves and coiled the chimney smokes. But for the presence of officers and military patrols the City would have reverted to normal. It did not seem that a few months earlier the British Army under Sir Henry Clinton had been in full occupation and the British caissons had rattled over the cobblestones. True, normalcy could not be restored entirely; the economy was somewhat jolted by events at sea, by the British blockade of the ports. Optimists however, flourished. The French ships, they said, would break the chain of cruisers, which heretofore disappointed the efforts of European friends to supply the beleaguered. That the helm of the privateer again was pointed out to sea could be seen on the docks. British warships were not in the River. Except for presence in the Bay, they were absent. There was hope. The cargo from the prize schooner HANNAH, captured by the armed sloop COMET, was at public venue at Mays Landing on Great Egg Harbour River. Otherwise, except for such booty, traffic was yet at standstill. Sea trade to and from the Indies was curtailed; Canadian journeys were of the past. Wharves and brick warehouses were untended, boarded, and empty. By the same breath, Freedom had come with great noise into the City. From the State House steeple Pass and Stow's Great Bell of liberty, brought from the safety of Allentown, along with the many bells of the churches rang the hour, presiding with its deep, oddly melodious notes which hung suspended in the air, intoning the message cast on its surface, a passage taken from Leviticus XV, 10 - 'Proclaim Liberty throughout the land.' Philadelphia by its people alone was distinguished from all new world towns. Queerly dressed Quakers and full-blooded Oneida lent it a fantastic atmosphere. Officers of high Continental Army rank, bewigged with great clusters of temple curls, shouldered their way through equally bewigged, pigtailed, and powdered naval personnel. These last were captains of private craft, equipped for preying on British commerce. Lawyers, with their hair high-tied, scuttled in and out of the State House. If doctors, merchants, journeymen, farmers, each by hair-do, 'clothe' and conduct were identifiable, where then, and who were the Tories? What badge distinguished these? Some were known, having sheltered and dined the recently withdrawn British; others were suspected; and a few whose sentiments were not fully understood were wrongfully calumniated as lovers of the King. Partisans of strong central government like Freneau the poet were accused of Toryism. These last would set the States towards a new monarchy with their "His Excellency Washington" attitude. And many members of the wealthy merchant class, for their aristocratic mannerisms alone, were viewed with suspicion. Even signers of the Declaration of Independence, some of whom were given to the same aloofness, were not exempt. In every age there being jealousy toward the rich, smear was upon steady-on patriots Morris, Wilson, Nicholson, and Mifflin. Such is the ferment within a revolution. Of all the people within the City, one class alone worried not a whit about reputation or politics. These were the whores of Philadelphia.

Changes of armies and allegiances had no effect upon their trade. Tory-come rebel, the essenced, stiff-laced paramours lavished their allures, none their enemy, they friendly to all. A man's purse, or rather the money in it was as a fuel, and by it were the Rights of Man governed, as ladies of pleasure saw it, in this aptly called City of Brotherly Love. From Fourth to Sixth, from Market to the State House Square was the heart of the City, and whores' hunting ground. It was also the preserve of Commerce.

At noon Samuel Wallis closed his high top desk, nodded to his associates Henry Drinker and Abel James, and passed into the street. It was from this unpretentious office on Sixth above Market that he conducted his affairs, that of frontier land jobbing, of coastwise shipping, and general merchandise speculation. He walked the few squares to the Indian Queen Inn on Fourth near Chestnut. In '76 the framers of the Declaration here repaired to toast the Free and Independent States of America. The Queen offered finely furnished upper rooms. In one of these Thomas Jefferson had been deep in his studies prior to composing that document. From the yard of this establishment arose shouts. Stable boys vying for a rich carriage, by their cries had fetched the angry innkeeper who, cuffing one lad, sparking the buttocks of the other, dispensed civility to these nobodies, all to the merriment of two fashionable dames within the carriage. Wallis was reminded of French, found under such circumstance. To the Queen came merchants, captains, drovers and wagoners for the company accorded, for its food and lodging. Here, in advance of the Coffee House, news could be had. To the Queen came scribes of the Pennsylvania Gazette, the Journal and Weekly Advertiser. Here to sup, to place ready money, to talk and listen came the Msrs. Andrew Hodges of Water between Arch and Race Streets, John Stokes the Marshall at auctions, and Levins of Market Street and Strawberry Alley, all shrewd merchants. Within this magazine of information, amid the hubbub of a hundred voices, protected by this background of noise the most intimate of conversations could freely occur. Too, a man could sell or buy the indenture of an Irish-Scotch wench if he so much as fancied her to make his bed and she to be amenable.

Scarcely had Wallis seated himself when that image of a death's head, Cundiff, appeared from nowhere and skated a chair into position. Cundiff had arranged this meeting, even to the reservation of this table. His spidery fingers stole around the glass of brandy meant for Wallis. "Faugh!" said the merchant as Cundiff drained the contents at one swallow.

"Curse me. Go on, curse," Cundiff replied, wiping his lips on the sleeve of his coat. Fraternally he leaned toward Wallis who involuntarily drew back. The fellow was intolerable.

"No nearer!"

Cundiff rocked on two legs of his chair. "As you say." A Negro waiter in ruffled shirt, hair powdered, hovered at his elbow. "Nothing," he said, "save a bowl of blood with your black heart swimming in it." He smacked his lips, and the black man, anger repressed, retreated. In this white world 'all men are created equal' was hyperbole, meaningless to a person of color as were all the phrases of that celebrated document, the Declaration. Cundiff cackled, pleasured by his crude dramatics.

"You manage your own amusement," observed Wallis in contempt.

"More than that. I put the fear of Hell into him. I showed him the Devil. Am I not the Devil, Mr. Wallis?" Wallis stared with scorn at the play actor. Cundiff tilted his head in the direction of two gentlemen nearby seated, engrossed in their glasses, yet glancing toward them. "There," said Cundiff, "you see a colonel who is most eye-compelling in his blue and white uniform and with him the other man in nondescript brown, as dull in appearance as a warty toad. That is Stevens." Wallis watched the man spreading butter on a slice of bread with his thumb. "He is this very instant arranging a pass through the lines for you, your horses and diligence, to go and come without challenge from the sentries on the road north from here."

"Worthless effort. I do that already. And where do I go, and why, prophet of my future?"

"Sir," said Cundiff, affecting civility, *"that* you shall learn in proper time."

"Confound you with your rattle-tattle secrets!"

"The Colonel, you can see, is leaving. As soon as he is gone, go yourself. From here, Fourth Street, walk to the prison. There, wait for Stevens. Put your questions to him. All I can say is that your meeting has something to do with the frontier." Cundiff leaned back and grinned at Wallis's unease.

Wallis rose, locking eyes with Stevens, then passed his table muttering, "Wipe your thumb before I shake your hand."

At the intersection of Chestnut, looking east and west he realized he should have asked which prison, the one on Third and High, or on Sixth and Walnut, both within a few minutes walk. It was too late to turn back, so he continued east the short distance from Fourth to Third and High. Gazing about, not seeing Stevens, he decided this must be the wrong meeting place. He walked the one square to Walnut, then the three west to Sixth. Walnut Street Prison stood on the northeast corner of dismal Potter's Field. In pits and trenches 2,000 soldiers, victims of camp fever and prison starvation, were buried here. As he approached the front of the debtor's prison, at call of "Mr. Wallis!" he looked up and down the street. At a second call he discerned high in the prison wall at a window directly overhead the face of a man he had seen before. "A fine afternoon to you, Master Wallis," said the fellow. Wallis raised his eyes, better to view him. From the speaker flew spittle. "There, sir, on my indebtedness a payment!"

Wiping his cheek, Wallis verbally spat back, "Rot before I cancel your debt!"

"Rot I may; and rot you shall, too, you of smug countenance, my incarcerator. May the flesh that girds your bones and the fat on your body, you Quaker bastard, dissolve. May your carcass be without identity, shoveled upon and trod over by every lowly foot. A plague upon you! A joyless departure from this life, Samuel Wallis!"

Wallis contrived not to hear the ribald laughter of the spectators in the prison. He removed himself to the end of the square where the man in brown impatiently waited, he witness to the despicable spittle incident. "Stevens?" Wallis proffered his hand. Though wiped clean of spittle, Stevens, of buttery thumb, refused to take it.

Stevens was peremptory. "Let us be done with formality, and done with our business as speedily as consistent with perfect understanding. You have an office?"

"Yes."

"Hereafter we shall recognize one another only in the privacy of that office. Agreed?"

"Agreed. A question, why am I to cross the lines?"

"Cundiff is indiscreet. Your carriage goes, not you."

"For what purpose?"

"There may come a need to smuggle in more agents. But, as my time piece reminds me, the day escapes; I came here on other matters. What do you know of the McIntosh expedition?"

"McIntosh who commands Fort Pitt?"

"The same."

"I've heard nothing."
Stevens was disappointed. "Wallis, you are, I am informed, familiar with the paths to Niagara and Detroit?"

"I have some knowledge chiefly about those toward Niagara."

"Good. We may make use of your knowledge in a way which you shall soon learn, but which I cannot presently divulge. You may be of great service to the Crown."

"You flatter me," said Wallis, unenthusiastically. "You acquit yourself with honors in the department of saying nothing." With sarcasm he added, "Thank you for your confidence."

Stevens ignored the barb. "Keep at what you have been about. Discover what you can as to the Susquehanna expedition. Find out who is to lead it, Gates for his seniority? Or will it be Sullivan? Is it true, yes or no, next spring's proposed expedition is pointed at Niagara, as seems obvious? And what are we to make of Hand's leaving his command at Fort Pitt, with McIntosh succeeding him? As happened with George Rogers Clark, Hand too for want of supplies was defeated in his attempt to hold Vincennes after taking it."

Stevens, grasping a button on Wallis's coat, pulled him closer, as if in deep confidentiality. Wallis resented his familiarity. Stated Stevens, "Hand was unable to carry the war to Detroit. Why, then was Hand rewarded for his failure, he to be Colonel-come-General? Is his replacement by McIntosh a signal of renewed activity against the Shawnee-Delaware? It looks like another American try for Detroit. Together with plans for the Susquehanna expedition, it seems General Washington intends to invade Canada in 1779. He is free to devote troops to that, Burgoyne's army in the north having surrendered at Saratoga. And the French are into the war. More and more this frontier presents itself as the theater of action. Therefore our work by appearance becomes of first importance." Here Stevens pulled from his pocket a paper with a list of names. He thrust the list into Wallis's hand. "Burn this once you have read it. These persons will interact with you. Some will report directly. Some will be couriers. Others will be at distance, helpful to you if you require, or to be helped by you if demanded. All information goes to Governor General Haldimand in Canada via Captain John Andre, with whom you dined when the British were here. Cundiff is your bridge to Andre, if not myself. To give you an understanding of our group, we are as a handle to a larger body known as the Associated Loyalists, though we ourselves are unknown to them. They are busy recruiting members to be armed as a loyalist militia. A fellow Rankin is their leader. Also, you will receive funds, through me, to reward our network. Disguise your outlays as purchases of merchandise by these individual. In your ledger show the name of the party, the amount paid, and some fictitious transaction, these entries to a casual eye harmless. It keeps us healthy were your office searched. Remember that Drinker, your partner, along with other Quakers are in the eye of the Council of Safety." Stevens passed him a package. He turned and walked off. It contained 500 guineas, a sum to outfit and arm a privateer, one to so wish.

Wallis scanned the list. Other than the identities previously mentioned by Cundiff it included Tench Coxe. Tory to the bone, Coxe had remained in the City during the change of armies to care for his dying wife, taking the oath of allegiance as had Wallis. Coxe by marriage was related to the extremely wealthy Thomas Willing whose mother was a Shippen. Young Coxe had become president of the City Library Association, many of its members also in the Associated Loyalists, Coxe second in its leadership. One name Wallis did not know, the Episcopal Reverend Dr. Jonathan Odell. He pocketed the list. As of this instant, de facto, he was paymaster for the British spy ring in Philadelphia. Two military officers were walking in his direction, one a major, the other a colonel. They saluted the well known Philadelphian and he nodded. In tardy recognition he realized the Colonel was William Rankin of the Northumberland Militia, the same who was conspiring to raise a Tory regiment!

Suddenly, in his mind, he had an answer for another matter which disturbed him. Since his return from Muncy a troubling letter had arrived from Menniger. Colonel Bolton had failed to suppress the Indians. The fragile arrangement was fracturing because of the infusion of troops into Muncy. There was a solution at hand, Rankin! He'd have Rankin's secret Tory force seize his own fort! A foggy morning assault would reduce casualties. There would be no more Indian raids. Muncy could then serve the British as a forward area for Butler's Rangers, from where they could march against the Susquehanna's bastion Fort Augusta, perhaps even to Carlisle, storage place of weapons and gunpowder for Western Pennsylvania's defense. But then Wallis had second thought, his enthusiasm waning. There was no reality to his plan. 'T was a pipe dream, no more. It would be impossible for Colonel Rankin to contend against those same troops. He could not in any manner muster the needed number of Tories. This scheme died aborning.

Homecoming & Departure

The very next evening of their homecoming, Captain Spalding's Free Company, standing amid the ruins of Forty Fort valley, was provoked to extraordinary session. Choosing an open field under the stars, a bonfire their light, the soldiers surveyed their task. This valley was dead. Forty Fort had died in a rush of Seneca feet. In this cool night air the men were touched by a vast loneliness, no dog barked, no roster crowed, no human voice other than their own filled the night. Homes and forts were charred heaps, and human bones still lay in the burnt fields. Faced by this desolation, Captain Spalding's volunteers confronted the sad duty of gathering up remains. But, prior to this, they must build some sort of fort to secure themselves, and to serve those survivors who would return.

As Spalding laid out the tasks before them, Tim Murphy was narrowly watching Levi. Tim perceived Levi was wrapped in the sorrow of the place, utterly despondent. Unquestionably, it would be best others seek Abby's remains, not he, and if to be found bury her. By degrees Tim kept engaging his friend, talking about the McIntosh Expedition to leave from Fort Pitt. Tim knew his friend, usually with unbounded enthusiasm, must become involved elsewhere than this melancholy vale, with action the best cure. The more they spoke together, the more Levi responded until, driven by Tim's new purpose, and urged on by several others, he rejected fort-building and bone gathering.

Captain Spalding was sensitive, he himself wondering how to alleviate Levi's despair. While the priorities of the Captain were the Captain's, Captain Spalding would brush these aside when Levi confessed his newly preferred course of action. "Sir," he stated, "some of the men have asked me to speak for them. The story is around that General McIntosh is leading an expedition toward Detroit. For sure our old friends like Bald Eagle will be heading there to do him in. The General will need frontiersmen like ourselves, seasoned scouts to uncover those who would ambush his force. I do not feel the few of us who wish to join McIntosh would be missed. During our absence you've men enough to cut and lay up logs, and as for the Indians on the Susquehanna, after our recent foray they will have little stomach for battle once you've built your walls. I'm no man for garrison tour. With your permission, sir, I'll bring the boys back by time the ice cracks on the river. At the latest, we'll be with you, come thaw."

Spalding thought a moment, reaching for justification to agree to Levi's argument, then stated, "If McIntosh is blind for want of scouts, there's merit to what you say. He'll be grateful for your eyes. But you'll be wanted sorely here come spring when all hell will break loose. Name your men." At muster their names were called.

"Peter Grove." He stepped forward.

"Peter Pence."

"Yay!" said the Dutchman.

"Sergeant Tim Murphy."

"Present!"

"Bradford *Hotkiss,*" Brady mispronounced the name. Murphy blew a kiss.

"Sir!" shouted Hotchkiss, glaring at Murphy.

"Corporal Samuel French."

"Ici!"

"Hugh Swords."

"That's me," said a six and a half foot Welshman lately transferred to the Free Company. He towered over all.

"Sergeant Thomas Baldwin."

"Available, sir!"

"Henry Weaver - Daniel McKinney - Peter Nottey."

Spalding was brief. "You are now detached. Lieutenant, see you in the spring, God be willing."

At first light the eleven rode, sharing eight horses, strays that had fled the desolate valley, returned from the woods neighing for the companionship of man. They reached Muncy that afternoon. From Captain Stoddard Levi acquired two horses. "If you don't take 'em," wryly remarked Stoddard, "the thieving Indians will." The Captain was mending from the glancing blow he had taken. A third horse, a beauty from Levi's father's farm, Levi reserved for himself. Captain Brady, troubled by an earlier injury, knew his campaigning days were done. The trio, the two Bradys and Stoddard, met in the Wallis house. Menniger, of courtesy, plied these respected officers with both drink and food, and offered Levi flour and other supplies, as well as a pack animal.

"Your friend Carberry is ahead of you," mentioned Menniger. "I assume you, too, will follow the West Branch toward Pitt."

Levi nodded, then asked of his peers, "What are McIntosh's chances for taking Detroit?" He knew his father had been west.

Captain Brady hesitated, then responded. "McIntosh is a newly appointed general sent west for no reason but to get him out of sight of vindictive friends of Button Gwinnett. Congress had created but one new appointment in rank of Brigadier. Both men wanted the 'star'. McIntosh's Carolina friends in Congress got the better of Gwinnett's. Blood at boil, it came to a duel, with McIntosh to mortally wound the signer of the Declaration. He lingered abed, dying hard. His friends lined up ten yards long, to kill the new general. McIntosh was sent west to get him out of their reach. In straight language, I say this campaign seems of poor promise, 'specially if McIntosh who knows nothing of his task ahead, thinks he can take Detroit. It's a Jonah."

"Why?"

"When Hand commanded Pitt he too thought it would be a frolic. It looked simple. Go down the Ohio and over toward the Cuyahoga where the fort's located, and destroy it. Five hundred horsemen with colors and drums set out vowing to seize the magazine. There being a thaw the snow became watery, the plains like unto lakes, canoes wanted more than horses. Never was there a dry bivouac the whole journey. We cried for a Moses to lead us to dry land. The magazine which we intended to blow? Tempers went up, not it. The Indians we set out to capture? We met and fetched back as captives two bedraggled squaws. Because of this, the campaign appropriately is known as the 'Squaw Campaign', and there's laughter over it. Hand asked to be removed from command of Pitt."

"And," interjected Stoddard, "Congress obliged Hand, a colonel, by promoting him to general. Mind, I don't belittle Beanpole Hand. Ten years ago he came to the colonies with the Kings 18th Royal Irish Regiment, then resigned his commission, to raise the First Regiment of Pennsylvania's Continental Line. He's got smartness in that long skull of his, and McIntosh could learn from him. McIntosh ought to know, starting this late, he can't take, much less reach Fort Detroit afore the snow flies. And once it snows he'll be marooned in camp, afterwards to face the waters of the thaw as happened to Hand. More'n likely McIntosh'll settle for taking the small fort at Sandusky on the bay of Lake Erie."

"Then why the expedition?" asked Levi, disillusioned.

Both Captains looked at each other, Levi's father choosing to answer. "Go back apiece. You are just off the Hartley Expedition up the Susquehanna to the door of the Seneca Country. Originally it was to have been a major expedition with Hand leading it. At the 11th hour only a raiding party proceeded, Hartley's, with a limited objective, to dampen the ardor of the Indians coming against our settlers. In this Hartley succeeded, we hope. Like Hartley, McIntosh, too, seeks to put the fear of holy hell into the natives, if but to quiet them down in their raids. I think he only seeks to make a feint at Detroit. It justifies doing what he can, for the now. But it will take a full blown expedition of many legs going from Pitt, and from here and Schuyler, all marching in the summer, if we are to win in the Western Department. So I figure it."

The officers at the table simultaneously nodded. Schuyler in western New York could boast having some damn good men.

The veteran Captain reminded his son, "For us to throw the British from their forts, while the troops required are not yet available, wouldn't make sense. But the effort must have a beginning and this is it."

As the meeting was about to break up, the militia captains, inclusive of Levi who had served in Morgan's Rifles recruited in Virginia, discussed former Royal Governor John Murray, fourth Earl of

Dunmore. In '74 he sent troops to the forks of the Ohio, which then was claimed as Virginia territory. Captain Brady stated. "I was there. The troops were to garrison Pitt and protect the settlers. In reality Dunmore wanted those malcontents as far away from home as he could get them. With the fever for getting rid of Colonial governors he didn't need these dissident colonials spoiling his gardens. He couldn't disband the infected rebels, so he sent them west. But, anyway, it terminated in their ouster of him. 'T is a story." The ailing captain, leaning upon his cane, wished his son, "Godspeed," and a better time of it than all who went before, giving his chip of the old block son a hug.

On the morrow, before the light was in the sky, Levi had risen from his bed and said his farewells. Once more Levi was to depart Muncy Valley, to leave at the head of a small band of armed and intrepid adventurers. In '75 he had gone to join Morgan; in '78 he had gone to help recruit and train the Free Company at Forty Fort; and now he was about to join McIntosh in the far west. For Samuel French, while his return to Muncy was momentary, it stirred up memories, his thoughts of Wallis the best. For those in this small band able to have brief reunions with their families the event was one of pure joy. In their departure this time there was no singing of patriotic airs, war a dirty business, soldiering filled with hardship, their resolve knitted by companionship and by obligation to each other. They were veterans.

As for Mrs. Baldwin, upon the reappearance of her sometimes tavern keeper spouse, she debated putting the frying pan to the bald head of her sergeant 'liar' husband, remembering his departure words last June, 'a 60-day enlistment.' Ha! And then that madness of Hartley's. She had a right to clobber her errant husband. But she thought better and went to bed with him. Maybe he'd forgotten there were better ways to enjoy life, such as, in bed. "Come, my hero," she ordered him.

Chapter XVII

FRONTIER WINTER 1778-79

General McIntosh was a canny man, despite Captain Stoddard's assessment. He understood and did not underrate the dangers of a winter campaign. The odds against him were the wilderness that lay between Fort Pitt and his objective, the taking of Fort Detroit. He would need guides. The Scotch brigadier of this furthermost American bastion, as a preliminary to his march had summoned into council a delegation of friendly Delaware. Who better knew the country? The Delaware having lost a war with the Seneca had been uprooted from their Nation's eastern haunts and were scattered by resettlement at several locations, one being toward the Ohio Country under the eyes of their victors. Here the Minsi were indistinguishable from the Shawnee, sometimes called southern Minsi. Confusion existed in differentiating a friendly Delaware Minsi from an unfriendly Shawnee red man. The Seneca perimeter lands were lined with Delaware settlements. By the Seneca they were called 'women.' They festered under this imposed humility. They angrily resented the watchful eyes of their conquerors living nearby. Were they not a proud people? Were they not, in rank, the grandfathers of the once lowly Seneca? Of mind to recall their past grandeur, of necessity they came to parley with McIntosh, the Great Chief Warrior who commanded Fort Pitt. "In a heart beat," eloquently said the Delaware spokesmen, "we would embrace the American cause, had we arms for our young braves to help you war against our common enemy." This McIntosh knew was true in part, but it carried the suggestion he arm them.

He patiently explained he did not expect from them that which they could not give. Nor had he spare weapons and ammunition, so he told them, to arm their braves. He was no fool; far be it for him to give muskets to warriors who might use these against him! Blandly he turned their request aside. "But there is something you could give me, to show your friendship," he stated. "I need scouts. And above all I want your friendship, as I must skirt your villages." In exchange for peaceful trespass, with the same instructions that once had been given to Levi to woo Seneca Chief Cornplanter, the General dangled before Sachem White Eyes, Medicine Man, War Chief Killbuck, and Chief Warrior Captain Pipe two most desirable gifts. The first was the gift of creating an Indian State in the Union. They, the Delaware, would have representation in Congress! And secondly, in the interim, he would guarantee them security against retaliation from their enemy. He said, "Are not the British forts which sustain the Seneca, at a distance, while I am here near you? Who can receive more comfort, your enemy from an ally at a distance, or you from a friend who is an enemy of your enemy, and close to your lodgments?" In their paints and feathers, these delighted chiefs accepted McIntosh's offer, agreeing he could pass over their lands that he might wage war. A neutral country before him, McIntosh marched from Fort Pitt on the first of October. He took with him the 8th Pennsylvania, and Gibson's 9th Virginia, this latter an unbloodied body, in all a force of 1300 men. Carberry's detachment of Light Horse was included in that number.

Levi's small detachment reached Fort Pitt scarcely three hours behind the Army's departure. The militiamen rested, drew a ration of rum from the Commissary, and then continued in the wake of the army as it paralleled the Ohio. They overtook the expedition at the mouth of the Beaver, coming abreast of a group of marchers, some 300, all dressed in deerskin and wearing fur caps, to whom Murphy called out, "Hey, stumblefeet! Do you shoot as well as you march?"

A burly marcher called back, "Pull down your britches and hold straight your pecker so when I shoot I can cure you of your venereals!"

Murphy ignored the retort. "What outfit be you?"

"You talk too much!" came back the response, in a Virginia drawl.

"Up you-know-what," stated Murphy, affecting the same pronunciation of his words.

"Pipe the man!" cried one. "Listen to him talk. He's from Virginia like us!"

Murphy corrected him. "From Forty Fort up-river the Susquehanna, above Philadelphia."

"Ha!" another commented. "A Quaker with a gun. Youngster, say 'sir' when you talk to the likes as us. Your eye is looking at Virginians commanded by the best officer ever, Colonel John Gibson."

"Bully for you," Murphy responded, in pretense of a yawn. He recalled Gibson when a company captain.

"Dunderhead! Ever heard of 'Captain Longknife?' " the miffed Virginian asked. "That's our Colonel's name, gotten three years ago when he was here as a captain in Lord Dunmore's War. Got it 'cause of his reputation with a sword. He slices the enemy lengthwise."

"Dunmore's War? Skirmish, wasn't it?" This elicited curses from the Virginians, roars from the Pennsylvanians.

"Let's break a few heads," yelled their irate spokesman. He broke rank.

Hearing the disturbance, the Colonel himself rode back. His angry commands restored order. Glaring at the small contingent of militiamen, source of this rumpus, he demanded, "Why are you men marching alongside and causing trouble? Fall in behind us if you can't find your place where you belong. Who's your officer? Say now," he added, studying both Murphy and Levi, "I've seen you before. Why, you be from Dan Morgan's 10th Regiment!" This discovery by the Colonel was electrifying to the Virginians. There was never a fighting man better than a Morgan rifleman.

"Colonel Morgan's men formerly, Sir," volunteered Levi. "Sergeant Murphy and I are now serving in a Connecticut Company since break up of the Corps. I'm Lieutenant Levi Brady out of Forty Fort on the Suquehanna. The men I command are volunteers detached to join you as scouts, by orders of my captain."

"Welcome, then. Fall your rifles in behind us. We can use your talents, Lieutenant, and yours, Sergeant 'Sureshot'. I know what your shooting did at Stillwater. I have been out here, at Pitt, celebrating too many birthdays with me. I have an untested garrison command needing steadying up from veterans like you."

"Sir," stated Levi, "my company commander expects us home by next thaw."

"I'll have you on any condition," stated the Colonel, pleased. The riflemen and those under Gibson indulged in no more banter.

As soon as the column encamped Levi learned yet of another reason behind Gibson's enthusiasm. The Colonel had brought out a command of one-year men whose enlistments were about expired. How many would re-enlist he didn't know. He needed to bolster his ranks, these soon to be depleted. It seemed madness, but a man could quit in the middle of a pitched battle if it coincided with the date he was to be discharged. Too, Gibson sorely wanted these frontiersmen as scouts to protect the army against its very own Indian guides, the Delaware. Gibson confided in Levi, though the Delaware Chief White Eyes had sworn allegiance to the Americans, and was trustworthy, the inscrutable Delaware guides were not. Two had deserted. It would not surprise him that the deserters by now were in touch with the British and conspiring to bring about the expedition's downfall. "Ambush, Lieutenant. I half expect it. Be watchful of our guides. The troops are on edge."

This apprehension was furthered the next night when a drunken Virginian shot and killed a most important Delaware, a dreadful happening, the victim being Chief White Eyes. The Delaware abruptly departed the cantonment. Except for the loyal Hanyerry, an Oneida tribesman, McIntosh's Expedition was without native guides. After the Delaware had vanished Hanyerry discovered their tracks, as the Colonel had surmised, leading toward Detroit!

The enemy to be informed or not, McIntosh persevered in his resolution. He built two forts in his march, one named for himself, Fort McIntosh, while the most western was called Fort Laurens to honor the President of Congress. Leaving Colonel Gibson with his Virginians and the attached frontiersmen as a garrison at Laurens to face the winter, the General withdrew the army, returning to Pitt. He would make a fresh beginning at the enemy in the spring.

At Laurens the air of foreboding deepened when the Virginians, their enlistment up, despite Colonel Gibson's plea voted to return home.

221

No urging would keep them to their responsibility of manning the Laurens outpost through the dark and bitter months ahead. Gibson had his regimental adjutant post orders affecting the retreat. Without fighting an enemy, they had been defeated from within.

"The shame of it," growled Murphy, his voice tinged with melancholy, and loud enough for the Virginians to hear. He waved his hand at the posted order for retreat, and at the Virginians. "Were these Morgan's men and not Sunday soldiers, Lieutenant, this wouldn't have happened."

"They're Sunday Soldiers, for sure!" exclaimed Levi, suspecting that Murphy was up to a trick.

"For sure," echoed Murphy, shaking his head in shame for the Virginians. "Dan Morgan's men wouldn't quit a fight, even were they rushing into the throats of a battery of cannon, which we aren't. I suppose, though, there's a difference between Morgan's riflemen who are mostly Pennsylvanians, and these fellows living off the credit of a Virginian such as Dan Morgan. Lieutenant, it looks like we, you and I and a few others are going to be left here by ourselves, to protect Virginia and cover the asses of these heroes about to march off home." Muttering among themselves, the nearest soldiers of Gibson's regiment shuffled away from the loud-spoken Murphy.

"Now you've done it," groaned Levi. "How are we to go back on your promise?"

"What promise?"

"Why, you dumb blow mouth, you just publicly stated we'd stay on and man the fort by our lonesome."

"Did I say that?"

As incredulous as was Murphy's expression, more so was Levi's reaction to Murphy. "You sure did, you idiot!"

"So what if I said it. What's wrong? We'll stay a couple hours after them, and then strike for home.

"No!" said Levi. "If we stay, we stay; if we go, we go now. If we retreat, the place has to be destroyed first, it not to fall into enemy hands. But, if we fire it, the smoke will attract far more Indians than we few can lick. To chop it down would take a month of Sundays. Either we march with Gibson, and burn the fort as we leave, or we stay until relief comes, praying it will happen before the Indians discover how few we be. And, you've put Morgan's reputation on the line by your smart-ass talk. We can't leave."

Colonel Gibson crossed the ground. "Lieutenant Brady, may I shake your hand?"

"Why, yes; yes, sir. I mean, why, sir?"

"A very strange thing is happening. My men have been coming to me, one by one. A story has gotten around that you will stay with your volunteers. They've reflected on their own decision and, by Holy Jumping Jehovah, they're re-enlisting! You shamed them! I've 60 so far. I may have most of the rest when they're done talking." He waved toward knots of soldiers in discussion.

That evening, at roll call, Gibson had 150 Virginians stiffly drawn up before him. A sergeant hissed at Murphy, "See. We're heroes, too." Then he winked at Murphy who smiled back. The hold outs, seeing themselves dangerously too few, fell into formation.

At Laurens there could be no boredom with Gibson commanding. His ramparts incomplete, he had his men fell more trees to brace the walls. They built blockhouses, improved the firing steps and platforms, dug a pit for a privy and, done with that, chopped firewood for the cold days ahead. With snug barracks, a tight fort, and men in good spirits he faced the long vigil. He had one worry only, the diminished supply of flour and meat; spoilage had been found. And though General McIntosh had promised to send up supplies with Carberry, because of the severity of their loss, in the interval it would be difficult to sustain themselves. Levi's scouts hunted ceaselessly in forests bare of wild life. On the other hand the scouts reported the woods deserted of enemy signs. This was incomprehensible, by now the Delaware who had fled would have spread news of the Americans perched in the woods. There were ears aplenty close at hand. They were on the doorstep of hostile Wyandot, Miami, and Mingo tribes. Gibson prayed for an early and harsh winter: the Indians were noted for hibernating when the wind turned bitter. Gibson must have been a religious man. The men may have wished him less so. The winter came howling out of the forest, its snows piling high against Laurens walls. Gibson sighed, relieved. This weather, though, posed a new problem. Short on clothing, the men shared garments when standing the frigid watches. Sentries, their beards encrusted, eyebrows white arches, looked sightlessly into the whirling snowfall, stamping their feet and holding their blue-red noses down deep in their jacket collars. The winter raged at them like a mighty sea, surging against the sides of their wooden vessel. Hunger became their enemy.

This was on Gibson's mind when, through the flakes, one sentry spotted several heavily furred persons moving toward their fort and among the trees. Colonel Gibson, upon receipt of this intelligence, hurried into his great coat and, fixing the chin strap of his three-cornered-hat, rushed to the firing step, calling to Levi on the way, "Food, Lieutenant! Happy Day!" From the parapet he shouted across the field, "Captain Carberry, is that you?" His answer was a shot. Incredibility upon his face, Gibson crouched, staring at his gaunt Lieutenant.

"Mingo," spat Levi. `They've come out. A fine welcome."

The shot had roused the garrison; the return fire of the sentries sent the entire command swarming to the walls. "Down!" yelled Gibson. "Don't let them count you. Off the walls!"

From that day forward, the enemy prowled the neighboring woods. Gibson tripled his sentries; it was imperative to convey that the garrison was at full strength, the numbers to suggest it. Weakened by hunger, some were not fit for duty. At last, miraculously, floundering through heavy rifts, Captain Carberry led his pack horses into the fort, these laden with meat and flour and some powder and shot. His detail of 15 men trod into the fort as if they were on a Sunday-go-to-meeting trip, unworried and unstressed, except for the problems of deep snow drifts. Half the Virginians rushed out, escorting him inside with his precious supplies. Carberry noted their pinched faces, then stamped his snow-caked boots. He thrust back his hood, letting it drop on his shoulders. His smile was as a sunbeam. "Hello Fat Man!" he cried, spying his leaner than ever friend, Levi.

"Oh, how I love thee!" exclaimed Levi, as they pounded and hugged. "How did you get through?" Carberry looked at him quizzically.

"Saw no Indians?"

"Indians about! I thought only Tartars, Siberians, and imbecile subordinate officers like myself travel in this weather." Carberry paled upon learning he had passed through enemy infested woods. With him he had brought letters, newspapers and dispatches. He also had news of another massacre, this one at Cherry Valley in the Mohawk region.

To Gibson he reported, "The General entrains from Pitt when the weather breaks. Colonel Brodhead is with the 8th Pennsylvania at Fort McIntosh and advises these supplies must suffice until the army arrives. Then, we move for Detroit, our blow coinciding with a push up the Susquehanna and a strike west within New York across the top of the Mohawk lands, and toward Niagara. At least that was the talk at Fort McIntosh." Then he added, consternation in his voice, "We miscalculated. I brought too much gunpowder at expense of supplies of salt meat and flour. I'll waste no time coming back again. Besides your critical shortage, what may I report as to your situation?"

Gibson assessed the news, and the speculation advanced by Carberry. It was an ambitious scheme, he thought. "You are staying here with us?" he asked.

"No, sir. My orders call for my reporting how I found you."

"Tell General McIntosh I have Depeyster's rangers from Detroit dispersed in my woods, as well as a force of Mingoes under The Turtle. I also believe we have Seneca. Our foes are men of great patience. But so are we, since there is no place to go. Then, with an attempt at some humor, he added, "Our spirit is excellent, if we are to measure it by the number of our desertions, none." A sharpshooter's bullet, which spattered against the gate, illustrated his remark.

"I see what you mean," said Carberry. "I'd best leave tonight under darkness."

"There you're mistaken. In the evening they slip over the field, and crouch by the walls, waiting for a quick shot at any sentry who peers from the palisade. You'll go in the morning. But you would be bettering your chance of keeping your health were you able to stay with us."

Carberry and his 15 took an early leave, at dawn bidding the garrison good luck. "Good luck yourselves!" stated Gibson, who watched them wade across the field.

An hour and a quarter later firing was heard from the direction which they had taken. Gibson feared the worst. The Indians had discovered Carberry. Gibson gripped the edge of the palisade, his knuckles white. Levi, too, roused by the noise, bolted from the barracks half dressed and climbed the firing steps. The faces of Levi, Gibson and the sentries were etched with consternation. The men they had seen go out were now off in the woods, dying. More soldiers came from the barracks as the firing quickened. They shouldered their weapons and formed to march, anticipating their commander. The Colonel fought from looking down into the upturned eyes, he himself vacillating between reason and emotion.

"My God, Colonel," whispered Levi, "aren't we going?"

"I can't order my men out. 'T is death to go."

"What if I take my own men?"

"That's your decision. I'll not object."

Baldwin who overheard the conversation, lifted his rifle and started for the gate. "Aim to be going anyplace?" asked Murphy.

"Might, at that." Dutchy Pence joined Baldwin. Pence's prodigious strength, his shoulder jerking upward against the gate bar, snapped the stout timber from its icy moorings. Thereafter the gate yielded. Pence trusted he could support his mountainous weight on the heavy crust of frozen snow which had drifted and piled in front of the fort. He sank to his hips. "And I thought I had lost weight," he joked. Joined by the others, after him wallowed the frontiersmen, their steps to be guided by Carberry's tracks.

Having gone a mile, again they heard firing. "A sign they're alive," said Baldwin.

"One volley, men," cried Levi. "One into the air, as courage for Carberry!"

"No!" argued Baldwin. "It's a fool thing to do. If the Indians are any size at all, they'll be straight at us, and we'll never take them by surprise."

Murphy broke silence. "The Lieutenant's in command, Sergeant. And his plan's good. Try it and see. The Mingo may think the whole fort is on the march."

"Right!" snapped Levi. "And it'll give Captain Carberry a chance to draw off."

Eleven guns blazed at the gray sky. As the echoes subsided, they listened. Then Pence shouted. "Hurrah! It works. The Mingoes have stopped shooting!"

"Or Carberry's wiped out," responded Baldwin. "Get ready for a fight, and watch your rear."

Black figures appeared up front in the thin woods. Rifles went up, stocks were nuzzled to cheeks, and then were grounded. A swelling yell of triumph broke from the scouts. Retreating toward them, breathing hard, came Captain Carberry and eleven men, of which four were being supported or carried. "Obliged," panted Carberry.

"Anybody yet out there?" asked Levi.

"Only those who'll never be back. They caught Johnson alive; killed Williams and Turner; and Prescott shot himself rather than be taken. It was Blacksnake who picked up our tracks over the mountains, then set up the ambush. I should have gone another way out. I murdered my own men." His voice was choked with emotion.

Several days later Carberry led out his reduced detail, two of his most injured remaining. The beleaguered waited and listened. No firing was heard.

From that day through the ensuing weary weeks the trapped garrison maintained constant vigil. By the arrival of January they had consumed Carberry's supplies. Survival was impossible, with so few barrels remaining. Again details combed the fringes of the adjacent woods, hunting for game. The perilous task proved fruitless. During this period an escort of 18 soldiers was dispatched with a wagon for collecting firewood. In passing an Indian burial mound, a half mile from the fort, they were overwhelmed from behind by Indians concealed on the western slope of the grave. A platoon of Virginians later located the frozen bodies of 16 of their comrades. Unaccounted for were two who, presumed to be prisoners, were considered worse than dead. The corpses were brought to the fort where, 100 feet out from the main gate, along with seven others killed on the walls, they were interred. At the sight of the mangled dead, with their heads knocked in and brains protruding, gloom encompassed Laurens. Digging in the frozen earth was a hell of a job, like scratching at body lice, a pure futility almost.

They had three enemies, the Indian, his winter and the food supply. They studied their fate in the dwindled rations. In the woods the flitting figures had multiplied. With the vigil of wolves, comprehending the plight within, the Indians waited, their taunts carried clear on the crystal air to the soldiers on the walls. Guns cocked, the sentries chafed and often hurled abusive retorts. But the Indian was wily. He would not be lured or goaded from his sanctuary of the nearby woods, being content to duel with words. By night the Mingo made good his threats.

After sunset he and his brethren, in small parties, would steal to the fort and bring death to those on the parapet. Never was such a sortie completely successful, the momentary unmanned breach quickly mended, with return fire bringing casualties to the raiders. These bitter encounters were consequently infrequent. Nevertheless, those within the fort on the walls would be joined by men off duty, to stand on the parapet sometimes until dawn dispelled the uncertainty of the night.

For Gibson survival rested on two propositions: if the food would last, and if nerves could withstand this indefinite hell. He foresaw succor in the spring, but Spring was a lifetime away; and the Indian, tiring of this cat and mouse game, might decide to storm his walls and overwhelm the weakened garrison. Soon they were down to firecakes, burnt dough. At every muster Gibson counted his effectives, less at each roll call, and debated rushing the Indians while there yet remained strength for attack. He would trade starvation for glory, slow death for a quick one on the chance of breaking the siege. But the opportunity slipped; the moment passed by. They were far too decimated by famine, with a fifth of his surviving troops unfit for parade.

"Hello!" cried Gibson, one morning gazing at the crest of a nearby hill. He cupped his hand, shielding his eyes from the glare of the snow. "What's there?" The Colonel's exclamation was echoed by shouts from posts one and four. The men on the walls and at the loopholes stared. It was a fantasy, a dream, a horrid nightmare. The Turtle, or Girty, or Blacksnake, or whoever commanded the Indians had arranged a living proof of superior numbers. The red men in continuous file topped the rise, each in his turn gesturing with his musket or tomahawk before being displaced by those crowding after. The endless display infected the riflemen with despondency. Where before they had estimated 200 maybe 300 were out there, by count were 850, signifying that some 500 reinforcements had arrived, an overwhelming warrior force. "Capitulation or death," Gibson remarked.

Hanyerry, the Oneida, studied the spectacle, then grunted an expletive. "Brothers, we may die, but I do not believe the Great Spirit has meant we be taken by a ruse. The Mingo walk in a big hoop. You see the edge of a circle. You see a few Mingo walking in the circle. My eyes have counted one, named Shawneee Dog, five times. Deceit is a Mingo weapon. Soon they will send a messenger to offer a pow-wow. You tell the brave 'Go to Hell', for he will promise peace while in his heart he thinks, once our weapons are laid aside, how quickly we shall go into a kettle. They are hungry, too, and will eat human flesh. I do not want my eye from inside the kettle looking at Mingo."

As Hanyerry predicted, an envoy, a British Ranger officer waving a white cloth attached to a twig, struggled over the snowfield. "Flag of truce!" he shouted. Twenty rifles were trained at his breast. At command from the fort, he halted.

"With your permission, Sir," Levi asked of Gibson, repressing his excitement, "I should like to treat with the man."

"Don't turn aside his overtures too quickly. There may be an advantage in his propositions. They, too, may be weary of this prolonged siege."

"Sir," Levi informed him, "if there is any consequence to this meeting, be assured it will be to our advantage." With these words Levi stepped through the unbarred gate and advanced to the officer waiting about 80 feet from the wall.

Levi's greeting was flippant. "Know the devil by his step! Frey!" Levi confronted the man who once, in the see-saw of frontier fortunes, had held him as a prisoner.

"The squirrel hunter, zounds! Again my prisoner."

"Not so by grace of these stout walls, Lieutenant Frey."

"Mr. Brady, a matter of time will correct your circumstance to favor my statement. We have you surrounded and outnumbered. To spare life we would prefer foregoing an inevitable successful assault. I bear for your commander Captain Girty's compliments. Colonel Gibson has defended himself and this fort with dignity, and having acquitted his conscience, if he will accept Captain Girty's terms, that he march peacefully there from and stack arms, he with his men will be received and their personal integrity respected."

"Lieutenant, you speak with scant foreknowledge of Girty. 'Spare life! Personal integrity respected!' Words-prattle, flapdoodle. Has Girty acquitted his own conscience? When he deserted Fort Pitt before joining you, he lighted trains of gunpowder to two powder kegs in the fort and, but for discovery would have blown his own friends to kingdom come. Since then, the Frontier stands shocked by his atrocities. He's a butcherly dog."

Frey flushed. "Sir! You are impertinent and you assume a dim view of our hospitality."

"The last time I tasted the hospitality you offered, if I can ever forget it, your friends served us both with poisoned food. As for Girty, what hospitality did he give those captured recently?" This was a shot in the dark. It scored.

Frey responded, "Calumny!"

"Are the prisoners alive?"

"Come, Brady, we are not talking about two men, but about the lives of a garrison. Would you throw away their chance, their lives because of a wild suspicion? Go into council. Consider his offer at value, not at discount."

"If the purpose of your flag is to discuss surrender, the suggestion is preposterous, for we have but to sit tight and see you driven off by our reinforcements. Perhaps Girty wishes to discuss his surrender?"

"Reinforcements? Are you mad? Your General McIntosh has abandoned this western campaign. Washington is in enormous trouble. Since you marched west the rebellion has been fair crushed."

"You lie in your throat, my friend. How gullible do you believe us? Is it that you tire of the siege to put on such a front, to strive to trick us into surrender? Sir, if you are not prepared to discuss the surrender of Girty and his men, we shall not only hold this fort on the Ohio, but when our reinforcements come we shall break out and pursue you to your death."

"Brady, you rant like a fool. Does your Colonel Gibson command an army, or a rag-tail garrison? We know you are so depleted that to maintain appearances you have put your whole force on sentry duty."

"Then storm us, if you are an outnumbering party. See if you can get past our squirrel guns."

"Pshaw. Fools you are to spurn a warrant of safety. And fools you are to pretend at superiority. Fools, too, you would be to seek the glory of dying for a flag that has been hardly sewn and, like your United States, about to unravel at its seams. As for your dying in action, we shall deprive you of that dubious glory. Brady, we're not in a hurry. We have patience and we have food. Sir, you are starving, for this indication is in your face. We shall wait upon that."

"Wait in vain. True, we do not feast; yet we are not as depleted as you think. My dear Frey, you guess wrongly, concluding so from my pleurisy, and its mark on my face." He affected a cough to dramatize his lie. "Our barrels of food are ample."

"Prove it! Furnish two casks of meat if your supplies are so plentiful! Ah, you can not?"

"Sir, detail eight men to this gate at four o'clock. You shall have them."

"It will be my pleasure." Frey retired, walking as stiffly as the snow would allow.

"It would suit my temper," said Gibson when the proposition was known, "to fill the barrels with excrement. Shit, in plain words. We cannot afford the loss of provision. There are but four barrels in the storehouse. But, in our giving them these two, if it serves to break the siege, at least we shall be able to forage the woods for game. Give that sucker what he has requested. His men are as hungry. Maybe this will bluff the bastards into departing."

Precisely at the appointed hour across the crust of snow floundered eight British dragoons, not too healthy looking themselves, Frey at their head. From the fort Murphy, Grove, Pence and French, and four 'hearty-looking' Virginians trundled the casks. "Your barrels, with Colonel Gibson's compliments. May you choke on them," said Levi. Frey blankly gazed at the kegs, pivoted on heel, and barked orders to his soldiers. They hoisted the booty and began their return journey. Levi flung a warning. "Tell Girty, this April we burn the Ohio towns if he hasn't vacated these woods by morning!"

Frey did the unexpected, turning toward Levi, and shouting back. "You're a damned good man, for a rebel!" Astonished, Levi just gazed, then gave him a salute.

That night, as the main guard was being changed, there was an infernal commotion within the woods. Blood curdling screams and ferocious shouts wafted from the forest. A case of jitters possessed the listeners who imagined an attack enforce. Then, at midnight, the frenzy diminished.

By dawn all was quiet, deathly. Not a figure flitted in the woods, not a shot struck the palisades. Cautiously, from the fort scouts slipped over the snow-field, prepared for precipitous retreat should the woods erupt. The woods remained quiet. Having come to the scarf of the forest, emboldened, the scouts - some going one way and some another - entered the timber and plunged from sight. On the wall Gibson, in ramrod posture, watched and waited, indifferent to the flakes of snow which pelted against his cheek. Forty minutes went by.

First to return were Murphy and Pence who had observed nothing, not a sound or sign. The woods were empty. Minutes later Levi,

Grove and French were spotted working out of the woods. They, too, contributed little, save that they had found Johnson's remains. Wolves or Indians perhaps, the latter as famished as was the garrison, had eaten portions of his body.

Concern for the third group, delayed in returning, was dissipated by Hanyerry's whoop. He, with his scouts, had located the two barrels, broken and empty, and prints leading off toward the Sandusky Country. The enemy had decamped; the ruse of the barrels and the bluster leading up to their delivery had cracked the siege. They were free men!

Free men they were, with a barren storehouse, and a wilderness to travel. The woods, which had not supported Indians, would be as unfriendly to whites. Gibson debated staking all on a wintry march. Not a fourth of his men being fit for an extended trek, there would be prodigious death. There was scant comfort in the alternative, which he saw on all sides, of men dying slowly, clawing for frozen grass that they might stew it in their kettles, peeling white oak for palatable bark, digging for roots, or boiling strips of leather taken from their own garments. Through two indecisive days he watched his men, at last to beckon Levi. "Lieutenant, I have not forty men able to march out of this hell hole. Were I to take them away from here, their weaker comrades would lose spirit. Even the search for bark would cease. Yet, to march with all the regiment is impossible. Your men appear to have survived the rigors of winter better than we. Take your independents. Try for Fort McIntosh. Try. We shall live in that hope. Tell Colonel Brodhead we've beaten off every disaster but starvation. Maybe we can nurse the sparks in our bodies another fortnight, the hardiest of us. Go, bring us food, food!" And he wept. As had been those at Valley Forge the men were living skeletons. The emaciated scouts filed through the gate, the sunken stares from the men on the walls following them. The Virginians weighed their own fate, theirs to be death by starvation within the fort while these Pennsylvanians sought a private death, a death high in the mountains where the shafts of winter were quicker than those of hunger.

Levi had elected to climb the mountains rather than risk ambush in the passes. The enemy, having withdrawn from siege of the fort, would be expecting couriers to travel from the garrison through those valleys. By frequent halts he and his handful ascended the heights. A cold sun at their shoulder, in the late afternoon they paused on the mountain top. They had calculated they would be onto plateau-land once they had climbed the great hill. By now their mistake was apparent.

Levi's men looked from the summit at the obstacles ahead. Moodily they contemplated a ponderous picture of unending snow peaks. They looked, and they gauged the warmth within their bodies. It was inadequate. In an oppressive, united silence they leaned upon their guns. In every practical sense, they were finished. To retrace their steps to the fort would be purposeless; death was inevitable in that quarter. To descend, then search for a new way through the mountains, made no sense either. Time would be lost, dooming those in the garrison, and more than likely they would gain nothing, freezing to death while searching for a passage that might not exist. Mulling over their predicament, they built a fire to warm themselves, and by tearing at parts of their garments, threw strips of leather into a pot filled with melted snow. They were of the notion that the tannic juices of the leather might shrink their stomachs. Hunger was so acute as to prohibit clear thinking.

To go forward, down into the valley, and march along the foot of each succeeding mountain come what may, was their decision. They'd chance ambush. Rising, abruptly Murphy threw down his gun and ran to the edge of the mountain where he dropped to his knees, and seemingly was about to cast himself off the heights. Levi and Baldwin, in the same instant, sure that hunger and cold had made inroad upon his mind, seized Murphy by his legs, he meanwhile babbling and flailing at them with his fists and elbows. "Behold, the Lord delivers!" he shrieked.

"Tim's gone mad," sobbed Levi, trying to wrestle his friend to the ground.

This produced frenzy in Murphy, who tore loose from their grip and bounded erect. "Jehovah has heard!" Warily his two friends sought to grab him, but he danced away. "You damned fools!" he yelled. "Look! Look down!"

They observed where he pointed and then, where had been one lunatic there were 11 capering on the hilltop, praising the Lord, shooting off firearms. Below, in the valley, on its shadowy floor wended the van of a mile-long packhorse train! With the wagons marched a half thousand soldiers. McIntosh had come!

For Levi Brady the General carried special orders.

Chapter XVIII

A MYSTERIOUS SPY BY CARRIAGE ACROSS THE LINES

Winter had embraced the first city of the land, fondling the capes of the dignified, nipping their ears and noses. General Benedict Arnold, worshipping Philadelphia his footstool, rode down Chestnut Street, his carriage pulled by a brace of geldings. He nodded at Lawyer Wilson, and likewise acknowledged General Mifflin of Stamp Act fame. Close to the State House, and but two squares removed from Fourth Street where Judge Edward Shippen resided, his carriage halted before a pretentious mansion on the south side of Market just 60 feet east of Sixth, earlier Howe's headquarters, now his. Philadelphia was not yet ready to compare Arnold with Howe who they had burned in effigy. Yet, as easily as Howe, Arnold exploited his position, he requiring the best in everything, in viands, in creature comfort. A patriot was to be excused these liberties. More, this famous General, now Military Governor of the City, had inherited from his forefathers a taste for opulence. His grandfather ten times had been elected Governor of Rhode Island, the elder Arnold dying wealthy only to have his son, Arnold's father, fall into bankruptcy and poverty. This state of insolvency the General had surmounted, he wealthy in his own right through shrewd sea voyages, he procuring and selling lucrative cargoes, a way to riches as others had found. Robert Morris whose home was on the corner watched behind drawn curtains as Arnold alighted, he registering an unguarded dismay. Morris, in some respects a greater patriot, had more power to influence the Revolution than any who wielded the sword in military combat. He, as financier of the new government, could inspect the character of this general and, as would some in Congress and the Pennsylvania Council, find him wanting in the manner of his friends, these largely avowed Tories. Arnold enjoyed a style pretentious by any standard, equal to that of General William Howe's when in occupation. Morris's distaste for the military governor was to be softened by practicality. Arnold's style befitted his role, that of a person of affluence and power. From his pocket he entertained Philadelphia's wealthy and members of the Congress. And for a time he provided quarters within his mansion for the newly arrived Minister from France, Conrad Alexandre Gerard. Too, from his own resources Arnold had advanced the moneys to feed the troops he commanded during the Canadian invasion. Fully expecting reimbursement, three years now the Board of Treasury had failed him, quarreling over pennyworth details in the accounting. Morris grudgingly knew these gala affairs at the mansion provided a relaxed setting in which influential people could meet, these events taking on such importance that Martha Washington herself acted as hostess on one occasion.

There was another observer who viewed the wounded hero with great dislike, this amounting to personal hatred. One should not cross JOSEPH REED, soon to be president of the powerful Pennsylvania Executive Council. This radical Whig held Arnold to a higher standard than most generals, many who replenished their fortunes by mercantile transactions, no law preventing this. The Commonwealth of Pennsylvania, as host to the new nation, shared the State House with the Congress. Pennsylvania was foremost in financial support, and was major provider of troops to the Army, 18 regiments to be exact. Reed, his civil power in conflict with the City's new military governor, had vowed to bring Arnold down. Designer of laws to wrest property from Tories, this former bankrupt enjoyed a fine home and a matched brace of horses and carriage confiscated from a loyalist owner. In a different vein two boys, awed motionless, their sleds at the side of the street, gawked as the immortal General descended, assisted by a sergeant. He hobbled indoors, his leg crippled and foreshortened.

A few squares away a less conspicuous man, Wallis, brushed snow from his collar and entered the Indian Queen. Francis Lee, keeper of the Indian Queen, deferential to the wealthy Wallis, saluted him by name. In the farthest corner of the wide-windowed hostelry Wallis greeted his friend Hooper seated at a table dominated by his girth. "My dear Hooper," said Wallis, clapping the Colonel on the shoulder.

Hooper labored under a burden. Because of ears too close to their table, until these people had left, he refrained from speaking freely, instead making light talk, dwelling on a lesser matter. "I am kept too busy by General Washington. As Deputy Quartermaster I am rounding up stray horses which from weakness or because of injury the Army has left behind. In Northampton and Bucks Counties, and in Suffolk, New Jersey I've asked my deputies to place newspaper advertising and to post notices on trees, these to advise the public such branded animals are to be surrendered to my deputies at their locations, and if not, then the holders of these animals, when discovered, will be prosecuted."

"How goes your collection?" asked Wallis, dragging out the subject.

"'T would go better were I to collect fillies of a different nature, these aplenty within the several squares about us, and far more pleasurable to ride. These ladies of convenience pant for companions, the British troops now gone. They, in their extremes, have no objection to accepting money of any sort. Even the Continental dollar, for whatever it will buy, from some poor soldier if needs be. By the same measure, were the troops to afford that luxury look how Army morale would pick up in that pox infested camp." He suddenly interrupted himself, the table next over vacated and all nearby tables emptied. Of precaution, he dropped his voice, the discussion to be couched in low-pitched tones. "Let us come to business."

"What have you learned?"

His voice a whisper, Hooper related, "There is a rumor about ridding the City of spies. I thought, with the hangings of Roberts and Carlisle, though their only crime was their Tory sentiment publicly expressed, that the witch-hunt would be over. Despite your plea to Reed, despite Roberts having 10 children, and despite 1,000 Quakers, yourself among them, walking in protest behind the condemned men, nooses at their necks as they followed the wagon with their coffins, Reed had no mercy then, and now. He's behind the present fever." Wallis shook his head in half disbelief, fascinated as Hooper fished in his pocket and extracted evidence of resumption of the killings, he plunking a misshapen lead ball upon the table. "This pellet I pried from a wall. Yesterday, secretly and to avoid clamor as happened during the execution of Roberts and Carlisle, thanks to Reed and the Committee on Safety a man was lined up against a brick warehouse wall and this went through his flesh. He still breathed, so an officer blew out the poor bastard's brains. The firing squad, outside of being both nervous and rather bad at the business, in its duty was methodical. And so is the suppression of news. Within twenty-four hours, unless there is an outcry, I swear others will be executed. In this instance the charges were apostasy, treason. These secret executions may be designed to produce terror."

"Who was the man? One of ours?"

"There's the joke. He was an innocent; his one fatal fault was his blatancy, his public love for the King his one condemning virtue. Reed is out to purge the City. The hunt is on. His is a fearful dedication. This latest execution whets the appetite for more. Murder, to some in authority, is a greater stimulant than lying abed properly attended."

Wallis thought on it. "In consequence of this passion for blood we had best take notice by special caution. For the immediate we must avoid one another, only meeting under urgency." Clearly Wallis was alarmed.

"Agreed," responded Hooper.

Wallis tapped the table with the back of a spoon, thinking, then confided, "I must share with you a suspicion. We may all be pawns. Something's happening I don't understand." He bent nearer to Hooper, his voice reduced to a whisper.

"There comes among us, shortly, an agent clothed with such mystery that I am fearful of his powers. To bring him over the lines my carriage has been requisitioned. As goes the expression, a new broom sweeps clean. Were I he, what better way is there to create your own web of operations than to dispense with a structure which does not fit your plan? That person may tolerate Stevens of necessity. But beyond Stevens, he may wish to be rid of us."

"I do not follow you. To begin with, from whom came your information about this newcomer? Stevens?"

"Not really, though early on, when we originally met, he casually hinted at his someday use of my coach and horses. But first to have at your question, I heard this news from Cundiff, and it was said by Cundiff in a manner most foreboding."

"And do you believe or take faith in Cundiff or his remarks? He is but a courier, a hack, one who enjoys being the presentment of evil. Why, the fellow's an ex-slaver who fancies himself a master of hell and likes to make people squirm. He's got to you. You overreach in your conclusion. So what if someone comes. If there is evil being fabricated against us, as you fancy, it springs from your imagination."

Wallis was taken up with his own reasoning. "All this may be as you say, but 't is fact Cundiff has a nose for calamity. Expect the worst. Courier that he is, he carries the cast of events in his pocket. And he always knows the contents of a message sealed or unsealed, whether in cipher or openly written. So to speak, his clock is set ahead of ours."

"Sam, what brings you to conclude this unknown person is of such importance, so high on the ladder as to be a threat?"

"The luxury accorded in bringing him to Philadelphia. The person must be of some stature as to warrant a stylish passage across military lines. Think, my conveyance is being dispatched to usher the fellow into the City. What comfort! Cheek! Arrogance!"

"You worry too much. Maybe there's comfort this news came to us from Cundiff rather than Stevens. Stevens may no longer be in the loop. Good riddance I would say. By the way, I just found out the bastard's first name is Thomas, he formerly a King's tax collector in New Jersey where he also served British Intelligence. He's a presumptuous son of a bitch. I liked him not from the start. Now I dislike him even more. Stevens was and is a nothing. Forget him."

"Perhaps you're right. But does that save you and I? We may be in the sack to be drowned like unwanted cats. I distrust this change. Even though I could be overwrought about the stranger, I'll hazard Stevens, to increase his indispensability with the newcomer, now or later will set a trap to bring upon us swift calamity. Many ways it could be done, by accident or by killings in the night"

"That may be," agreed Hooper, "but we can take measures of our own to prevent any of that. There's a process by which we can silence Stevens and so by doing totally allay your fears. Make him believe we have the goods on him. That'll seal his mouth. Tell him we know he has cultivated a man of high public position. Stevens wouldn't dare contrive our deaths were he to think you've deposited in a sealed envelope an affidavit, sworn to me in my capacity as judge, and filed with a trustworthy citizen. With unblinking eye, state to him it declares him to be a traitor attempting to bribe an important figure. Elaborate to him that it charges he has connived with the British Conciliation Commissioners to secure support for their peace proposal from persons able to influence members of Congress. We know they seek support for their proposal. We know Stevens has been ingratiating himself with unknown persons of influence. His purpose may well be as we believe."

"And just who is that person of importance we can claim he is wooing?

"Joseph Reed himself."

Wallis shook with silent laughter, choking on its absurdity. "Impossible. He is the paragon of virtue, the model for all rabid patriots. He is, in all but title, judge of the black court. Men have been hung in the commons by this sometimes *General* Reed, his victims George Spangler for one this last August, followed by Frederick Vernor. At a snap of his fingers men literally 'dance.' Has he not threatened to make a public hanging of 500 Tories? He is above reproach."

"Not in the opinion of Lord North's peace commissioners Carlisle, Eden and Johnstone. The former governor of West Florida, Johnstone, attempted to bribe Reed, the sum substantial, it contingent upon his giving his services toward a settlement of this war. It is a fact. You saw the printed article in which Reed disavowed the 10,000 guineas and the best office in the colonies, which was offered him."

"That's just my point," said Wallis. "Plainly there's no case against Reed. He's lifted himself above all suspicion by his public disclosure of the offer. And he's no fool as to allow himself to be approached again, either by Crown representatives and certainly not by Stevens who holds no credentials and would be hung sooner than tomorrow comes, were he to try."

"Hold your thought there," said Hooper. "Perhaps Reed made public the Commissioners' bribe out of duress. He may have had to.

Among the three so approached Reed was the last to make the offer public. His hesitation shows us something."

"Not true. Reed was in camp at Valley Forge visiting General, Washington when the others repudiated Johnstone's offer. He reacted as quickly as he could, promptly upon his return."

Hooper shook his head. "I'm stubborn in my thought. For all of what you say, I cannot but believe Reed has found some kind of advantage in the offer."

"Hooper, my dear friend, we have never quarreled, but in this matter there is nothing to be gained by trying to tar Reed, stating he is the person with whom Stevens is involved. No, Reed is not that public figure."

Hooper belabored the issue. "Just a moment. This does lead us to another, an equally large fish, Follow my logic. For one, we know Reed spurned the British bribe. In my opinion he was less prompted by patriotic righteousness than by fear, there being rumor about the offer. I think he, by the reasoning of his convoluted mind, through a back channel has suggested another person be honored with the bribe, that man a mainstay in our Army, valued by many in Congress, though with enemies enough among the hotspurs of our Revolution."

Wallis gave Hooper a queer look, surmising the name. "Who?"

"Benedict Arnold."

Wallis spattered the hot drink in his mouth, bursting with contained laughter. "What! Reed to suggest Arnold be the beneficiary of the British largess of 10,000 guineas? Ridiculous! No two men hate each other more. Only civility prevents their carrying into practice their reciprocal thoughts of murdering each other. Reed would have Arnold court-martialed and hung, and Arnold in turn would like to de-gizzard Reed with his sword. Arnold is no fool, nor would he be traitor. My friend Colonel Hooper, you, too, have a convoluted mind to think such. How do you come to your conclusion?"

"Reed is not above setting a trap for Arnold. He will have a spy in Arnold's camp, watching especially those who are newcomers to his circle. It's that simple. If Stevens serves as the intermediary, Reed will catch 'em both, Arnold to dangle and Stevens to keep him company. Reed has hated Arnold from the moment he arrived in the City as its military ruler like a Roman Emperor, in a coach-and-four preceded by Philadelphia's Light Troop and a regiment of Massachusetts Continentals. While Congress was yet in Lancaster Reed upon return from Valley Forge could have sent word to Johnstone in New York to sound out Arnold, and this in turn brought our esteemed Stevens into the middle of this nonsense. Say what you will, Arnold's the man."

"Perhaps it was the other way around, Stevens to have recommended the name of Reed to the British and then, that offer repudiated, in a second try Stevens to have advanced the name of Arnold."

"Which changes nothing. We come out the same way. Arnold's the man. And we have Stevens as candidate for a noose." Having made his point, Hooper momentarily excused himself to relieve his bladder.

Wallis was in a quandary. Hooper was aware of his congenial sociability with Arnold. But he was unaware that, arising out of a common experience, that Wallis and Arnold, both having owned shops plying the Caribbean trading among the sugar islands, had a partnership to accumulate the fortunes which were to made. Affluent men like Robert Morris and Thomas Willing had achieved their wealth from pooling their money to operate as sea merchants. Morris and Willing each had created a series of interlocking partnerships, Wallis included. But Hooper was without knowledge Wallis and the General had gravitated into a confidential partnership, one to produce handsome rewards. It made sense now that the French Navy guarded against British sail, and enabled merchant-owned ships to enter American ports with much wanted goods from Holland and France. By this protection the risk of losses at sea was minimized. Too, were a ship to founder in a storm, the loss would be offset by the four-to-one mark up on all goods safely landed. The secrecy suited Arnold well. This arrangement would not be in the public eye, more importantly not in the eye of envious Reed. Wallis furnished the drivers and carts, sparing Arnold further complaint as happened in a venture prior to their partnership. Reed wrathfully accused Arnold of using 'public wagons' supplied to the Army by contract, diverting the military drovers for a work of personal profit, the transport of cargo to Stansbury's warehouse. The goods had been off loaded from a privateer in whom the General had a half share. Wallis's arrangement with Arnold, too, had a different twist that could raise Reed's ire. There was the patriotic practice of selling certain goods at a cheaper price to the Army. Clothier General James Mease would have first say on any goods brought into port, namely shoes and clothing, he thereafter to declare portions of these purchases as surplus to be resold at a fraction of cost. The catch was Wallis by design, repurchased his own goods. Not only was a profit made in the difference between original sale and the fractional repurchase, but the goods now could be brought to market for additional profit. It was not beyond reason in gratitude Mease would be remembered in a befitting manner.

Wallis had become intimate with the General at dinners in his grand residence; these planned by Edward Shippen's daughter Peggy. Shippen, Philadelphia's richest citizen, was a commanding figure, he biggest in body, owner of the largest mansion and possessor of the most sizable carriage. He always shook hands and chatted a bit with his Quaker friend Wallis. These functions, patronized by 'closet Tories', angered Reed as much as his exclusion, neither he nor Mrs. Reed were invited to sit in the sumptuous dining room. As neighbors they viewed the comings and goings, gall in their hearts. The dining room furniture had been provided by Stansbury, the items crafted by one of the City's great cabinetmakers. Howe and his blonde mistress Mrs. Loring, before their departure, had stripped the house. Hooper, retuning to the table, studied Wallis, lost in thought. "What say you?"

Wallis refocused his thoughts, reviewing the matter at hand. In bottom soundings he was convinced Stevens was involved with the British Commissioner. To what degree was Arnold, that would be pure speculation. While Arnold fitted the plan, in another sense he had his detractors among those in Congress, and it seemed unlikely the British Commissioner, through Stevens, would approach the General to influence Congress toward reconciliation. Again, it was possible the General through his many friends could be of some help, indirectly. Perhaps the General wished to secure his future, this war to go awry. Yes, Arnold as he, for security reasons, for the benefits involved, could be looking beyond the moment. He, Wallis was now fully convinced Stevens should be confronted. There was much to be gained.

Wallis decided. "I think you have it right," he said. "Mentioning to Stevens Arnold's name should insure everybody's hide, ours and unfortunately detestable Stevens. I'll talk with him."

"Good," commented Hooper, "Fuck that arrogant, pompous son of a bitch. We've unfastened the hemp from our necks." He looked about. "Wish for the Devil, Stevens! Don't twist in your chair. He attaches to those at the bar. Once I leave go to that horse's ass. You've reason to draw him aside. You told me you've advanced the payroll for our helpers in absence of money the British were forwarding which the bastard diverted to feed his gambling habit. Ask that piece of manure, this 'gentleman' why the sums have been delayed. Inform him your people grow restless. Then play the role of fool, somehow slide onto Arnold. State you've heard he and Arnold have met. Say it casually. Stevens will surmise we are into the bowels of his secrecy and that you have been able to convince Arnold, for Arnold's good, he's a loose cannon to be spiked. That'll get Stevens worrying for his own hide. He'll begin to sweat inside. If he has a brain, he'll drop any evil scheme against us, and drop Arnold likewise. Be sure the jackass comprehends that he can read his own fatality either way, to be shared with ours were we to be betrayed; or he to come to mean end from parties wishing riddance of him. Scare the piss out of him." Hooper lumbered to his feet, still whispering, "I have just learned of another matter, I think of importance, but for now it can keep." Then he added, unable to contain himself, "Another time I shall tell you about some barrels of gunpowder and a mad plan of Stevens." He laced between the tables and exited from the Inn.

Wallis, his tongue having been blistered on coffee which he had no remembrance ordering, paid his bill, and wandered toward the exit. As he was about to pass Stevens' table he hesitated, bent close to the ear of the spy, none to hear, saying, " Mr. Stevens, there is some pressing business which cannot wait. At my office, sir, within the hour."

"Damn it, man, at your office," said Stevens, exhibiting annoyance, a bawdy tale interrupted. As Wallis turned away, purposely for the merchant to hear him, Stevens to his companions complained, "A money-worshipping Quaker who would as soon skin a man out of his inheritance as not."

At the jobbing office Wallis, while waiting, sorted several folders of papers. He smiled over a bill of lading dated 1761 at Quebec. It refreshed memories of salty captains, nautical voyages and humorous incidents connected with his transportation business. These were meaningless to keep. He ransacked a cupboard looking for papers to discard. In the depth of one closet his fingers touched an unfamiliar leather packet. Inside, apart from letters, was a sheaf of paper which he spread upon his desk. "Abel, Abel, come this instant!" Wallis's associate, Abel James, looked in. "See, Abel, see what I've got!"

"Oh, yes, Galloway's papers. When Galloway was suspect as a turncoat, a noose was sent him in warning. Before he fled, he gathered all his papers, knowing his house would be combed for treasonable correspondence. From among them he entrusted these with me. You'll pardon their appearance in your office, but my safe was full and my desk overflowing and I saw this corner--"

"Did you examine the contents?"

"No. It's not my property."

"This is the property of every man. These are the writings of Benjamin Franklin. They describe his parental history and upbringing. Twenty three pages, and notes for continuation."

"The good Doctor must have given Galloway these before sailing on his embassy to France. I believe Galloway has quite forgotten about them, as I have, and as Franklin must have." Page by page Wallis and James scanned the manuscript. "My," murmured Abel, "a learned treatise. And in a rare vein. A companionable instruction for the young if it were increased."

"You must write Franklin."

"By next sail." Abel James took possession of the Autobiography. "A treasure," he said, retiring.

Papers in order, and door shut, Wallis kept pacing his cubicle. An hour had elapsed. Where was Stevens? The delay was insufferable. The bells of the City tolled high noon when the dilatory Stevens, twirling a walking stick, sauntered into the jobbing house. His suave expression vanished, once in privacy with Wallis. He thrust his cane at Wallis's waistcoat, pinning the astonished merchant against the narrow desk. "Fool! You acknowledged me. You addressed me in a public house. Is not our profession a risk without doubling the hazard? Other than in this office we were not to be in conversation. A nod would have sufficed, not an intimate whisper in my ear, and before a number of persons. Sir, you have defied my order!" Wrathfully, Stevens jabbed Wallis.

The merchant, equally choleric, wrested the cane from him and snapped it in two pieces. "I am not a dog to be ranted at, nor to be prodded with a stick, nor do I need reprimands from the likes of you. Your betters respect Samuel Wallis. Shall we get along, or shall I blood your nose, sir?"

Flabbergast, Stevens was at loss for words, "Of all the impertinences."

"Impertinence! Perhaps I should have written you a letter and sent it by way of the antipodes to tell you we are a hair's breadth from ruin."

"What's this?"

"If it matters to you, our network dissolves for want of money. Without money I buy nothing, not a fact, not a man. There are eight pockets, which must be filled. While you consort with whisky swilling gents, promising them their fortunes if they but abet the British in their design, left to me are the meaner duties, to wit, making payments to our 'sergeants' and 'lieutenants' for the services they render, the use of their ears, their cleverness at ferreting out the doings and plans of this new government. To my embarrassment you have not been punctual with these sums. From my own pocket I have advanced their payment. Where, sir, are the funds sent by Burling the banker in New York? My patience is exhausted. I will draw no more from my account. I must meet my own extensive business expenses. I am being made into a banker without recompense."

"You know, Wallis, I've never questioned the sums you requested. If Burling is slow, then I am slow. Come to think of it, this may be the time for your providing to me an accounting your expenses. Over a period considerable funds have been advanced to you."

"Correction, not advanced to me, but in reimbursement for my fronting agents because of your untimely distributions. And these distributions have become wider spaced in coming back into my pocket. Why the delays? Look, here are the latest receipts bearing the signatures of those to whom I have opened my purse. As you once suggested, these receipts are disguised in the form of fictitious merchandise transactions, firkins of lard 'popular stuff', and on and on. These represent information received and secret services rendered. Here are 600 pounds spent, advanced by me. Sir, I am not the Exchequer to indefinitely front such."

Stevens adopted a conciliatory tone. "You shall be reimbursed from the resources in my name on deposit with Burling. When Cundiff goes to New York, you'll have your 600, in gold if you wish."

"Well and good, and I thank you for the promise. And yet it does not supply the funds I need today. Funds, and I'll buy you a general, a real, live American general." Wallis said this casually, but it had the effect of a bomb blast.

Stevens blanched. He regained his composure. "Who?"

"That is my secret."

"Mind, Wallis, your services are appreciated. Yet, you may have overstepped in your ardor. Should you be duplicating my effort, your general may become suspicious of all. Too many cooks spoil the broth, as the expression goes."

"Ah, Stevens, you are so right. I shall desist. I should have perceived, by the company you cultivate, where your aims were. I trust I have not infringed upon your progress with - with General Arnold."

He shot Stevens through the heart in naming Arnold. If Stevens had expected Wallis to name any among the many generals, last would have been Arnold. Wallis was on the mark. The comment left him stammering, unable to form words. "You - you - you." That's all he could say.

"Conceal your emotions, Mr. Stevens. Let the name of Arnold never crop up again. If you go near him, expect the worst. As you go, do put on a face for the benefit of those in the outer office. Smile, my friend, as though we have just concluded a most satisfying business, and have an understanding, which I'm sure is the case." Wallis did not think it necessary to be bring up the subject of a sealed disposition deposited with a judge. Stevens was scared.

Wordless, Stevens opened the door and walked the short hall leading to the outer room with its windows facing the busy street. A gentleman in fur coat, impatient to see Wallis, stood up from a bench. Stevens accorded him a wan nod, as each stepped aside to allow the other to pass. Wallis had followed Stevens down the hall, knowing persons with appointments were in this waiting area. Heeding Wallis's instructions, Stevens invented a parting adieu. "As you say, Mr. Wallis, I shall expect the land patents from you. I will abide your advice. Good day again."

Wallis could not resist responding, "'A very, very good day, Sir." Stevens jammed his hat down over his ears.

There were three clients in succession, and finally General Mifflin to see Wallis on an inconsequential matter. General Mifflin having gone, and with him the afternoon, Wallis cleared his desk of maps. On the street a lamplighter, lifting his rod of office, splashed a pool of white-glow upon the icy cobblestones. "Well?" asked Drinker, who shared with Abel James another office. Their enterprise was devoted to financing passage of immigrants by finding employers to pay the sum, then the immigrant to redeem his or her obligation through work. Muncy farm had come into being through this source of labor. "Abel has put up his quill," Drinker stated, "and I, too. Are you for home or burning a tallow"

"Papers above my head, Henry. You go on. Throw the latch." Alone, he gazed at the snow drops filtering from on high. Little by little his head bent forward and the murmurs of his breath were the only sounds in the building.

He dreamed of a woman in a swirling mist, like unto the wrappings of gravescloth, or as would appear a person standing by a river overcast with fog. As she was at a distance her features were indistinct. Yet, with familiarity, she stretched out her arms and called his name; and lo, the voice was Esther's, she with whom in his youth, and now more recently he had lain abed.

He had not dreamed of Esther in the long months since their briefly rekindled passionate evening at Chemung. It was as if she was reaching out to tell him something. Beckoning, she receded into the mist. He, spellbound, ventured onto the nebulous carpet and, as his did so, from behind he heard Cundiff's choked laughter, it following as he advanced, ringing with scorn and deriding his uncertain steps. Wallis angrily turned. He could see nothing. Again he attempted to proceed and the convulsed but invisible Cundiff, this time in his ear, shrieked. Enraged, Wallis jerked about, and then shuddered, for Cundiff's devilish features, his face drifting above him, glowed in a ruddy light and his eyes leered down into his. Next, he vanished, to reappear squatting astride his shoulders. And there was the sound of a drum, a dry rattling drum, the source of which was nothing other than Cundiff's skeletal arms rising and falling, beating upon his pate. Cundiff was mounted on his back! Heave his shoulders as he did, Wallis could not cast off the misshapen gargoyle. Louder grew the sound, his head nodding and jerking from the agony it produced. His eyes fluttered open. Awakened, still not realizing it had been a dream, he glanced wildly around the room, fearful Cundiff would be with him. The noise, the drum sounds actually originated from a door latch being rattled by someone seeking entrance. Taking up a candle, walking to the window by the street door, Wallis rubbed a clear patch in the heat steamed windowpane. He recoiled. Separated by the thickness of glass, his eyes peered into a pair of huge eyeballs protruding from a black face. "By Holy Scriptures, Mr. Africa! You shocked me," he said as he unlatched door.

"Master!" blurted the Negro, trembling from fear more than cold. Try as he did, he could say no more. All he did was groan.

"Possess yourself!"

With visible effort the loyal fellow managed to say, "The Debbil, Master, with a cloak whipping like it was a bat's wing, the Debbil is in your house. First, there was a heavy stamping and in walks four men, like undertaker bearers, between them a coffin, and behind them the Debbil. I run from there, Master, I run. I scared."

"Come along!" said Wallis, hustling into his coat, covering his head with a beaver hat. Emboldened by his master's presence, Mr. Africa followed.

Wallis, convinced robbers had entered his home, seized a pistol from his desk and crammed it into his pocket. He ran, snow squirting underneath his heels, from Market to Arch. On Arch he lost his expensive beaver. Mr. Africa scrambled and retrieved it. As Wallis approached the house, he saw that it was ablaze with lights. In crossing the street he slipped on the ice, and sprawled. As he lifted on elbows, horrified, he saw a horseman moving with the speed of a bullet bearing down upon him. Wallis and Mr. Africa, both, screamed. Heavy hooves flew over the merchant's lowered head, missing him by a fraction, and the rider, Cundiff, was past, his startled curses trailing in the air. "Th-that-that's him, the Debbil!" stammered Mr. Africa, who perceived his master unharmed. Wallis's face was pasty. Mr. Africa's ebony features, too, had a sickly cast. The blackamoor, in the tongue of his forefathers, uttered an incantation to ward off further evil.

Entering his home, a pleasant structure of brick as were so many in the City, he plucked the pistol from his pocket, then took another from the drawer of a small beautifully designed, inlaid wood stand, beckoning Mr. Africa to take a second weapon kept here. He placed the firearm in the shaking hand of his servant then, perceiving this more a menace than an aid, took it from him. The house was large. Searching the ground floor from room to room, he found all to be empty. Lights burned in the hall on the landing above. Alone, he crept up the flight, wondering what or who might await him beyond his view, further down the hall. Fortunately, by examining the reflection in a silver ball, hung by a chain over the landing, he could sweep the hall just before reaching the top step. In doing this he shuddered. There, at the entrance to his bedroom, mirrored, lay a long rectangular box, the 'casket' as described by Mr. Africa. A man of milder temperament would have fled. Steadfastly, he walked toward his bedroom, guns leveled, prepared to shoot down whoever or whatever might fly out of the box, human or devil. Then he saw at close hand this was no coffin but a trunk, aye, of size and weight to conceal a corpse, aye, two by its height. Upon the wings of this discovery came another thought. Its owner would be he who had just arrived over the lines, the master spy! If so, it was a pleasant turn of events. To himself he reasoned, 'This man if to be lodged with me, my fears of a scheme against me are over, my day of worry needless. Damn the fellow, though. He is bold to quarter himself so nicely and quickly. But who placed him here? Not Stevens certainly, his star to be eclipsed forever by this shift of responsibility to this new person. Stevens' absence of knowledge about this selection of residence further demonstrates his diminishing importance. The man's gambling habits, no doubt, and his irascible nature, perhaps detected in dealings with the next man up the ladder, Samuel Burling, may have led to this.'

On tiptoe Wallis stepped by the trunk. At his bedroom door he paused, debating whether to knock of politeness, or burst through the doorway, pistols drawn. What if robbers were at his valuables, the trunk their means to carry these away. It was a foolish thought. His dream, Mr. Africa's alarm, his nearly being killed under a horse's hooves, and the worries of the day connected with Stevens, and now this mystery of the trunk, all had strained his powers of reason. He compromised with himself by putting away his pistols, then opening the bedroom door and entering without warning. He could always pull his pistols if needs be, apologize if required.

Immediately he spluttered. He viewed fineries, womanly things draped and strewn about. "A female!" he ejaculated.

"No, a woman," was the unexpected response, as the woman herself, materializing from bathing, snatched at a garment to cover her breasts. He, too, was as unprepared as she was, with indrawn breath viewing her. He could not contain the surge of desire, the primitive lust that swept him. She was a beautiful creature, nay, ravishing. She had black tresses that cascaded to her hips and brows which arched above dark lashes, and her black eyes, if they flashed anger, nevertheless had a quality of smoldering lust, enough to rivet him. He turned his head away, she dressing. Indeed, he was surprised at himself, that he stayed, and that she did not of modesty order him to leave. Eyes averted, a flush on his face, chancing the wrath of this woman of picturesque body and feature, he remained. In him she promoted the sweetest pain and wildest folly. "You may look," she said, then added, "Mr. Samuel Wallis." Even her voice, contralto, was erogenous, consuming. She knew this and inwardly reveled at the effect she had, enjoying being mentally stripped, though her pretense was otherwise.

"You know my name," he said.

"You were described by Mr. Burling of New York who arranged my living here, and explained what little he knew about the Philadelphia operations, but deferred to you to further my 'education' once settled. There is one thing Mr. Burling misinformed me about. I had expected a gentleman."

"My dear, I am all of that. Only by the accident of events have I viewed the wondrous body which Nature has bestowed upon you. It is magnificent and I should be forgiven for my constraint. Think what advantage a younger man might take under the same circumstance."

She changed the subject. "I have a name. It is Margaret."

"By coincidence I have a niece by that name."

"That is why it was chosen as mine. And I know, too, it is very unlikely she and I will meet, your brother at odds with you for many years. Also, I have been given a surname, yours. The assumed kinship will disarm the curious. Now, my dear 'Uncle' Samuel, will you leave my bedroom that I may finish my toilet and do my unpacking. And I am famished."

He backed from the room, leaving her to continue arranging her clothing while he consulted with Mr. Africa as to what might be had for a late supper. Mr. Africa was much relieved their visitor was not the devil, but a niece of the master. Calmed by this, the black retainer proved his wizardry at improvisation.

There was a slice of fat turkey that needed only warming, and green turtle soup intended for tomorrow's menu. For the lady, in her honor the black man had fruit, cheese, a sweet potato pudding, preserved pippens, brandy, rose water and coffee. Miss Margaret, informed of dinner, behaved elegantly, with dignity, grace and suppressed fire, which gave an added quality to the candlelight. By his lavish attention the old servant demonstrated acceptance of her. He heaped her plate, filled her glass, and jumped at her elbow. She won him completely when she said, "Please, you may call me Margy."

Wallis knew not what he put on his knife nor into his mouth, engrossed as he was with the charming visitor at his table. Too, he felt a heavy burden of responsibility for her safety. He must properly school her in many details of family, of politics and the purpose of this Philadelphia ring, her life and perhaps his at forfeit should she commit an unforgiving error, make a slip of the tongue, set persons at suspicion. But again, she was so disarming, so bewitching. These were weapons to defeat the most skeptical. He decided, since his group's primary function was to divine the plans for the 'long bruited' frontier invasion, and if these were to embrace parallel campaigns against the British forts at Niagara and Detroit. It seemed logical. He first must familiarize her with the geography of the intervening countryside. He asked, "After dinner, would you be up to looking at maps? Or are you too tired?"

"Why not," she said. Then to his great surprise she teased him with a seductive wink, stating, "That will be exciting, eh! Better than retiring on a full stomach, wouldn't you agree?"

Wallis did not know what to make of it. Was she saying as he thought, or did his lecherous heart pump too hard for his brain to properly function? 'Damn testicles,' he said to himself, 'they'll be my undoing.'

With dinner over, he steered her to a long mahogany table on which were maps overlapped to show Forts Pitt and Detroit. One was Nicholas Scull's map of 1737, another Lewis Evans' Middle British Colonies map of 1743 which identified the Teaoga branch as Cayuga, and showed the river nearly as large as the Schuylkill. "Margy, if I may, " he said, "knowledge of these frontier lands may seem of remote value to you, yet you must become acquainted with this country, better to shape meaningful though innocent sounding questions as you go among the American officers, acting womanly ignorant. The officers by your flattery of them will puff up with their importance, divulging to a beautiful woman as you are, information under any other torture they would tell no one. Those of my gender are fools. In all candor, I would not be exempt were I in uniform, and would be in a fever to know you better."

"Why, thank you, 'Uncle', for the compliment. How nice. Now that I have your 'confession', shall you explain me your maps?"

His finger pointing he explained, "Here the war will focus. From here, here, and here will arise the American forces that will strike at the King's two most formidable forts that guard the great lakes. Below, in the country of smaller lakes are the chief villages of the Seneca, Onondaga, Mohawk, Delaware and the supposedly neutral Cayuga, these Indians loyal to the Crown. Their villages are to be attacked and burned to the ground. Some already have been destroyed by two raids, one up the Susquehanna by a Colonel Hartley who went as far north as Teaoga, and a New York regiment that came south out of Albany which burned the villages lying northerly from Teaoga."

This introductory comment was scarcely out of his mouth when Wallis, amazed, saw himself being tested, not she. "'McIntosh has failed," she stated, with this casual remark plunging Wallis into turbulent water.

"I'd not say that. He's built two redoubts toward Detroit, McIntosh and Laurens from which he can launch a spring campaign.

"Do you imply Detroit's the rebel goal?"

"You mistake me. Niagara ranks foremost as their objective. Other than Fort Augusta, Philadelphia would be within reach of forces dispatched southward. Sentiment dictates reduction of Indian attacks directed from Fort Niagara. It arms the Indians and coordinates Tory strikes against the settlements, and can deploy supporting troops. In reprisal the Indian villages are to be torched and crops destroyed, the raids on the Frontier to be lessened. I think Detroit's secondary.

Margy looked at him, questioning, "Do the rebels have the ability to conduct two major campaigns, both forts attacked?"

"I'd say no. The rebels haven't that strength. The troops for these endeavors would have to come largely from the same pot, the Continental Line and militia units already on the frontier. Were I General Washington, I would let the present Detroit effort support itself, win or die. If McIntosh's army but ties down British troops and Indians in the Ohio Country, this itself would be a service. Those Indians, otherwise, would go to the aid of the Fort Niagara garrison and would be unavailable to reinforce the Seneca whose villages the Americans would attack."

Margy thought on this. "I see your logic. The question is how to prove what you say, that Niagara is the principal objective. Were there evidence such as a slip of a tongue by a senior officer, or a letter, order or document which speaks to that conclusion of yours, then I would treat this as fact, stating so in my report to Governor General Haldimand. He has listened to the alarms of Colonel Bolton at Niagara, and Colonel DePeyster at Detroit, each asking for reinforcements. To settle this squabble among the colonels, to discover the objectives of the 1779 plan is why I am here. As you already have guessed, the Governor General wishes me to enter Philadelphia's social circles, to meet and mix. This is not to say you have wasted on me your compelling presentation. To the contrary. I am impressed. You should have been a general."

He laughed, saying, "On which side?"

She shocked him by her unexpected answer, "The Continental Army." Then she added, "You have a perception how they think. You are an invaluable man for that alone. Again I say, Samuel, you have it right. The Susquehanna will serve as the way into the Indian lands." She indicated Hartley's path where that Colonel had gone from Muncy northward to Teaoga, following the river, and then she traced a line northwesterly through the lake country to Niagara. "The conclusions we make, if to be correct, offer the British-Indian forces the ability to concentrate around Niagara, knowing this is the place threatened, and to then take the offensive, taking the frontier war toward Lancaster and Philadelphia. Ours is a heavy responsibility. By our conclusions we may alter this war. This task cannot be trusted to likes of Stevens. That was a mistake and General Haldimand knows it. I am instructed to place in your hands overall responsibility. For security reasons this decision was not placed in writing, instead I was sent to you to personally relate it. Effective as of now Stevens reports to you."

"Where, then, do you fit in this new arrangement?"

"Well, bluntly, in anybody's bed, especially military officers who can confirm our suspicions, if seduction will achieve our purpose. If I must bed with them to do it, I shall!"

Wallis was taken aback. "To what extreme does one go?"

Testily she replied, "Does the Quaker reproach me for immorality? Are we apart? If you risk all, knowing it will entrap men, sending them to their death, and your soul must answer for the consequence of your clandestine action, while I but surrender my girdle, who then is more immoral? Pray then, which of us surrenders the most, you or I? Do not talk of immorality. Oh, Uncle Samuel," she added, amused, a twinkle in her eye, and with an intimate tone to her words, "I do believe I could bind you despite your pious protestations, despite your pretense at shock, and despite your strong will and intent, for these are pretenses to disguise your lust. You have coveted my 'wonderful body', as you called it, from the moment you first put eyes on me. And I also do not find you unattractive, you in your dignity and with a perceptive mind, and a balding head which makes you the more want-full. So, let us not quibble." She suppressed a yawn.

His cheeks red, he stepped back. "You are more than perceptive." He snuffed the candles in the library and, offering her his arm, ascended the staircase. Next, pulling together his willpower, overcoming his passion, at the portal of her chamber instead of entering, he patted her shoulder and said goodnight.

"You lack perseverance, Samuel," she said, chiding him.

"On the contrary, I groan from it. Please, to bed, and be quick before my resolve dissipates."

"Alas, you practice a monstrous morality, in which you deceive yourself. Sam, you cannot dampen the flame as you did with the downstairs candles." Unbidden her lips came to his. It was an offer he could no longer reject.

Chapter XIX

SPIES, MAPS, AND AMOURS

The cold sun slanted through the window, crept across the floor, and painted the foot of the bed. Someone had renewed the fire in the hearth; the room was tight and warm. Away, the great bell was pealing the hour, nine o'clock. At twenty minutes past, Margy, the sun washing into her half-opened eyes, wiggled her toes, and then dangled one leg from the bed. With abrupt decision, stepping barefoot onto the heavy rug and viewing herself in the looking glass, she arched her body, and being content with appearances, found her slippers. Powdered, rouged and dressed, she was marvelously quick at this, and with a final look at her reflected image, she swept downstairs. Mr. Africa was ready with coffee, buttery hotcakes and sweet buns.

For Margy to sit at home on her first day in this unexplored City of cities, would have been as novel as for Wallis by habit at his office at stroke of seven, to have deviated from his schedule. In this City, frequented by men who had come a long distance to buy, sell, do business, and be as early on their journey home as possible, the merchant community kept early hours. For Margy, still savoring the special quality of the night just done, lingering abed was as an afterglow experience. Now, she must see the City and perhaps let the City see her. Declining Mr. Africa's aid, bundled in furs that accented her beauty, she walked unattended the two squares to the commercial center. In Philadelphia as in Quebec she attracted instant attention. On the State House Square men of circumstance, the affairs of the Nation gloomily weighing upon their features, nevertheless saluted this winter vision and, once she had passed, swiveled their heads, affairs of another kind in mind.

Margy, aware of the pleasant ripple she created, was piqued when one tall fellow, a pinch-face frontiersman whose garments hung in folds, failed to notice her. He was striding from the State House, his eyes focused beyond, when his foot, he more used to the springy sod of the forest than iced cobblestones, suddenly slid from under him. He flung his arms wide, spun, and crashed to the frozen walk. Levi looked up at the most twinkling eyes he had ever seen. He was captivated. "Miss," he said, making no effort to rise, "I have no children, no wife; and I detest snuff. I do not contract debts, and am honestly come by this coat, rag that it is.

"I own land disputed by the Indians it is true, and one day may set a log house on it. When shall we be married?"

"Lord," she exclaimed, "has your tumble rattled your wits?"

"Not my wits, Miss, but my bones. Pray, I beg you assist me up." Since she didn't respond, he added, "That is the direction from which I came." Not waiting her answer, he lifted on one knee, then grasped her bodily and arose dragging a leg. "What have I here," he asked, holding onto her, "a leg or a broomstick? Be so kind; this limb is either fractured or sorry for itself. With your help I can reach the Coach and Horses, just over the road." He grimaced as if in pain.

"A favor for a favor," he asked, as he hobbled into the renowned inn. With care he placed himself on a bench, foot stiffly extended. "I've heard there is to be a military reception in this city. My leg would improve considerably, given a few days rest and the inspiration of knowing I would have on my arm the most beautiful woman in Philadelphia. Give me license to escort you thereto. I am Levi, Levi Brady, Miss, an officer in the Connecticut Militia, a fortnight removed from the freedom of Hell and the privileges of the damned, in short a survivor of Fort Laurens, a place toward the Ohio. Surely you will accept my invitation, Miss, Miss--"

Levi's wooing exploded in disaster. Into the Coach and Horses strode General Washington! "Lieutenant Brady, follow me!" Levi jerked to his feet and then, too late, remembering his feigned lameness, swore.

Margy tittered. "Go, go!" she cried to him. Her hand to her mouth she continued to giggle. Distressed, Levi hastened after his commander in chief. There was something about that gaunt, starved looking lieutenant. More, he was on staff of General Washington. Certainly a man to cultivate.

Wallis, behind in his office routine, had intended to be home early that he might pursue his relationships with Margy. This pleasure went by the board as visitor upon visitor paraded through his room, with his desk accumulating more and more paper work. At last alone, he adjusted his spectacles and resumed his research into a dossier of lands to be deeded in the morning to Mr. Nicholson. It was dark before he was done with this. Next he addressed the task of preparing a patent for Thomas Clarke. Outside and in, hung an oppressive silence broken now and then by the scratch of his pen. He put the quill into the fount, sanded the paper, drummed his knuckle-ring on the wooden desk, descended from his stool, consulted a ledger, closed it, shuffled a stack of land diagrams, and with his chores attended, picked up the candleholder. Done, he walked toward the front entrance preparatory to leaving, when the frost covered glass pane by the door shivered to the rap-rap of someone outside. "Samuel Wallis?" called the person.

Wallis, blinded by his own taper, could not make out who might be the fellow peering at him through the glass. Irritated, he called out, anxious to blow the candle and leave for home, "Come at a less improvident hour. See me in the morning. I am shut."

"In the name of the Congress, open Patriot, open."

"My urgent fellow, be you from the court of Rome, I will not open. Only to Jehovah would I open at this hour. Do you not perceive I am locked, tight, and done with the day?"

"Sir, for the sake of your duty, and mine, I beg your hospitality. 'T is I, Levi Brady, sir."

The merchant lifted the latch. "Ah!" he exclaimed, eyes upon Levi. "Inside with you, young Brady. I am indeed surprised to see you here in Philadelphia, but I suppose your fame on the frontier has reached to the House of Congress, you to be greeting me as you do. Except for your name, I would not have opened, fearful a pretense was being practiced to gain entry and rob me. What is wanted of me?"

"If you will, sir," Levi responded, tendering Wallis a wafer-sealed paper.

Wallis lit a candle in the bracket next to the desk of Abel James. He scanned the page and its signature. "Lieutenant Brady, have you knowledge of the contents, here?"

"Not precisely, not as to the words. But I have been given verbal instruction. General Mifflin who was in discussion with General Washington recommends your inclusion in a secret matter, in which I too am involved. As you have just read, we are to draw a map."

"To collaborate, yes." Wallis touched the candle to the letter and dropped the confidential message into a copper pan, "Witness that I have reduced to ash the letter, the subject of it known to you and I. General Washington puts great trust in you. General Mifflin, too, believes that by combining our talents we can provide an in-depth broad scale map of the Indian lands. I quite agree. I am told you have been north to Niagara, as a prisoner, and are fresh from Fort Laurens. Your singular travels are such that I almost believe these qualify you to stand alone without me in this matter."

"You flatter me, sir. By your reputation you are an encyclopedic source on the waterways and paths within the Seneca Country, and have knowledge of the lands of the Mohawk and Cayuga nations, as General Mifflin says. It is common coin a major military invasion against the Longhouse is in view. As forerunners, we both know, were the two smaller ventures in which I participated, the thrusts of Colonel Hartley up the Susquehanna and General McIntosh's preparatory effort to take Detroit, each laying important groundwork.

These were tests for more ambitious movements to follow."

"I agree," stated Wallis.

"Thus our work is cut out for us. We shall require a map of Indian villages, estimates of their populations, distances between locations. From your personal travels among the Indians over a lifetime longer by far than mine, you must have passed over lands beyond the reach of most men."

"Lieutenant, we will make a good pair. Before this war you were a surveyor. Together we shall do fine. But the task cannot be compressed in a night. Do not unbutton your coat. Tomorrow we shall commence."

"In the morning, then."

"Too soon. And for other reasons, no."

"But--"

"No protest. Would you have me disrupt my office routine and so invite questions from my partners? We shall labor at my home in the unaccountable hours. Within my study I keep maps, draughts, treaties, old land deeds and folios of sketches of these frontier lands. These last were produced from notes made during my travels into the depth of the Longhouse. It has been my habit to save every scrap that might be of pertinence, in event any portion those far reaches, by treaty or otherwise, were to be opened up for purchase. I am a land jobber, you know. My notes shall serve us well. From these we can construct General Washington's map! Patience, Lieutenant, have patience with me. Yes, tomorrow night, Lieutenant, see me after supper. You need some plumping by the looks of you. I am on Arch; anyone points my place out. Now, consult your lodging. And, caution! Avoid me by daylight; the town is full of spies."

With their appointment fixed at six o'clock, the Lieutenant departed into the night. Wallis, shocked by the turn of his fortune, with glee hustled into his snug coat, slipped on his gloves, twice twisted the key in the lock and walked toward home whistling 'Old Hundred', an air brought into the City by the troops. His jubilation stood in contrast to his recent gloom. 'My, how my precarious perch has improved,' he thought. 'Collaborating on a map! A position whereby I am rid of that leech Stevens! Moreover,' he meditated, 'if Stevens were to denounce me I shall have no less than General Mifflin on my side.' He recalled that Mifflin, when Howe was marching to take Philadelphia, had asked him, among some 80 others, to be eyes and ears as to the doings of the British. That in itself would be justification for his present association with any Tory scheme. Wallis's worth to Mifflin, thanks to Howe's adjutant, Captain John Andre who fed him innocuous stuff, was well proven. 'Tis why,' Wallis reasoned, referring to Mifflin, 'the General trusts me today and involves me in the present planning. I am above reproach!' Wallis, become adept at the game of being a double agent, once more with the change of armies in the City found himself in this very best of positions. In this spirit he reached his home, bursting with news of Brady's visit and the purpose of it.

"Good tidings!" he shouted, broadcasting his presence. "Margy! Margy, where are you?" There being no reply, he called out, "Mr. Africa!" Once again he called with no response. Perplexed, he stepped into the kitchen. The back door was unlatched. He saw a lantern moving from the barn toward the house. "Mr. Africa?"

"Sir! I was bedding the mare. Did you want me?"

"Where is Miss Margy?"

The faithful retainer, first blowing out the lantern and then hanging it on a peg, scratched his head. "Why, she should be inside."

"She does not answer. Perhaps she is in her room." He said this as much to himself as to Mr. Africa. Shucking coat and gloves, he bounded upstairs.

Margy's bedroom was empty! Troubled, gripping the balustrade, he descended to all but the four last steps where, having a view into his library, he discovered the beautiful temptress of last night tucked into his favorite chair, a leather journal on her lap. Instantly his disposition altered from pleasantness to rage. Entering the library he exclaimed, "For shame! By whose authority are you reading my personal diary, Miss Pry?" He snatched it from her hands. Then, seeing the page, his face became livid. He stormed, "You have trespassed! The key to my house may be yours, but it does not entitle you to snoop and ferret through my confidential writings. Why?"

Gazing at her lap where the book had been, in a small voice toneless in expression, she said, "I wish I had not."

"The wish is antecedent to the fact. Be aware, Margy, there is no redress for the injury you do me. This journal, written when as a young man I traveled the frontier was meant for my own review. It happens to detail a love of which you have no concept. I must tell you that the woman Esther Montour whose amours are described as candidly as my pen permitted, is a person irreplaceable in my heart. Do not think for a moment that you have seized upon a cheap scandal. Written in this journal are descriptive passages detailing my passion. They are not bawdy tales. You have bared me to my depth. Were you a man, I would have killed you for exposing them. To you, a woman, I say be envious. It is one thing for you to have enjoyed a man's body as last night, quiet another to posses his soul. Do not equate an evening's hunger, a passing appetite, a momentary physical possession as being a conscript of my person. Ours was merely an engenderment of lust. This book is not your affair." He abruptly stopped. The woman in the chair was laughing convulsively. She seemed on the verge of hysteria. Wallis misinterpreted it as ridicule. Infuriated, he grasped her by the throat. Then, horrified, his hands fell. He recoiled, pointing at her. "You -- you --"

"Yes," she affirmed.

"Her eyes, her chin, her cheeks! Can such duplication be?" Quailing before the hideous thought, in retreat from his infamy of last night he cried, "My bone and flesh! No!" With his next breath, thinking only of himself, he beseeched, "Why, Lord, have you cursed me? Why did you plant lust between father and child? In his grief he crushed a drinking glass, letting the pieces fall from his hand to the floor, the blood from his palm trickling onto the carpet. Oblivious to his injury he reached with that hand toward the mute woman. Margy at that juncture half rose from her chair, screamed and toppled to the floor, having fainted. Swaying above her, he wept in dry sobs.

Levi Brady, coat off, sleeves rolled, his sword hung on a chair, had flopped onto the bed in his room at the Coach and Horses. He meditated on the rush of events. In less than a month he had come by the special hand of Providence from Fort Laurens to Philadelphia. Twenty five days ago he had stood on a wind-swept mountain, despairing of life. Five days and six nights later he had stood at attention before the tough old Indian killer, Colonel Dan Brodhead, at Fort McIntosh, who negligently had said, "Oh, yes, those orders. Lieutenant I don't know who the hell wants you in a hurry. I've been instructed to let you feed your face, allow you time to piss, give you a fast horse, push you out the door and point you in the direction of Headquarters at Middlebrook. So get the hell out of here. Somebody of importance wants to pick your brains."

Reporting at Middlebrook, Levi was directed to Captain Alexander Hamilton, Washington's aide. Levi and the auburn hair Hamilton, both in their early twenties, had instant empathy. "It seems, Lieutenant, whenever the General thinks about the Seneca Country he somehow thinks about you. I don't know if that's a compliment or curse, recalling the problems you had after he sent you to find Cornplanter. Your instructions are to meet the General in Philadelphia." Hamilton, with a smile, handed him his orders. "Posthaste, Lieutenant."

At Philadelphia, from the Commander in Chief's questions Levi saw he contemplated a frontier campaign of magnitude. Washington sought opinions beyond Levi's knowledge, these embracing warrior strengths of the Mohawk, Cayuga, Seneca, Minqwa, Shawnee and the

Onondaga. This session finished, one of the secretaries drafted a letter to, of all persons, Samuel Wallis! It was this letter which Levi, prior to retiring to the inn, had delivered Wallis. Unable to sleep, needing to unwind from the ordeal with the General, Levi pulled from his pocket a seldom-smoked pipe, then put it back into his pocket. He paced the room. Bored, he put on his tattered coat, set his tricorn at a rake and with afterthought slipped a loaded pistol into his belt. "By my long-skull ancestors I know where I can have a time, the Old Tun Tavern!"

Old Tun, on the Delaware, was a roof for bold and desperate blades. A score of Morgan's men had once visited the rowdy, boisterous hall, and had come off second best in a pitched battle. They had been ganged upon by the crews of several ships anchored at the wharves of funnel-shaped Dock Street. It was a friendly fight, with all carried out limp, or thrown into the street. The hell had been whaled out of Morgan's invincibles. Such was the 'Tun', never dull. Here, beneath the rafters, the military lodge of the Masonic society had made momentous decisions. Largely, the Continental Army's officers belonged to the Masonic Order. Here, in another spectacular session a hundred swords had been unsheathed as their owners were sworn in as sea-musketeers. Marines, they styled themselves. Levi, in quest of diversion, walked the five squares to the waterfront, unmindful of the biting cold. Offshore, in the dark harbor, he saw a light blink twice, a signal to the land batteries scattered up and down the Delaware. His inquiry of one of the battery gunners, a volunteer who was drinking hot flip to keep warm, was as to the whereabouts of the Old Tun. This elicited, "That way, sir, and you'll hear it afore you see it, and you'll smell it afore you enter." Rapid strides took him over the unlit cobblestones. A rising chorus of sodden voices in song, and the thumping of feet, spoons, and mugs told him he was upon Old Tun.

He paused in the doorway. The place was impossibly jammed with soldiers, unwashed seamen and scented young fops. The din as well as the sour stench was overwhelming. Levi inched his way in. "Way, if you please!" he called, elbowing toward a vacated seat at a bench. A hand plucked at his coat. Angered that a pickpocket might have fingers in his purse, he looked sharply about. A strikingly ugly person, with tightened skin over the bones of his face, Cundiff, gazed up, saying nothing. "By God, if you are not death itself, I will dispatch you to him. Let go!"

"No offense...a word."

"Loosen your dirty fingers and talk fast. You have lost me my table. Whatever your message, spit!"

"Come with me where it is private. A Captain Sunfish would speak with you."

"Captain Sunfish? 'T is a name only." He shrugged. "Very well, but no tricks. If this is a design, though you have six friends, I'll break their heads. 'T is death for all, I swear!"

"You are a delightful fellow," responded the death's head image, unruffled. "See the balcony and the green curtains, and where these are parted do you see the eye looking at us? That is Captain Sunfish. I was sent to the floor to fetch you." He guided the Lieutenant up the steps to the balcony, partitioned into stalls masked by green curtains hung from the ceiling. If any occupant in these cubicles cared for a sight of the floor he had merely to separate the panels. At a gambling table in the first of these enclosures sat a big black man who Levi would have recognized anywhere.

"Peter!" exclaimed Levi, and clapped the Negro on the shoulder. Black Peter returned the blow, staggering Levi. How and where Peter had been educated, this having happened long before Levi came to know him, Levi had no inkling, only that he was of exceptional mind, and to shame most men. By firelight, Levi recalled, the black man read whatever was at hand.

"You are out of the past, boy, ten years out of the past," the Negro said, and he hugged Levi who, for a moment, was in fear of crushed ribs. "Levi, time is short, and a sloop lies in the harbor waiting for me. Providence sent you to this place. Providence guided my hand to part the drapes and espy you entering the door. I must speak, lad, quickly, and warn you that upon your next move your life depends."

"Depends?"

"You will be a corpse, should you stay in Philadelphia and complete a map which would be helpful to the American Army in invading the frontier. You will never leave the City alive. Go, work out your own destiny while you may."

Levi was in shock, this matter of supposed secrecy commonly about. "What are you saying? How do you come by what you say?"

"Ah, that takes too long to answer. I know you left Middlebrook to prepare a map of the Indian lands which the Americans will use this coming spring. You will be killed perhaps on your return journey to Middlebrook in bringing it to General Washington." Obviously both Sunfish and Levi were ignorant of Wallis's treacherous intent to distort the map, thus to mislead the Americans.

Levi inquired, "Who, Peter, are you? Why this forewarning?"

"I forewarn you from respect for your family. Listen to me, young Brady. The King's purpose is met, and your life saved if by pretext of illness you don't finish this map. If you do, you die. And, Levi, my name is not Peter anymore. I am Sunfish, Captain Sunfish. These fineries, lad, this splendid lace and blue coat, they represent my power. The captaincy is not affected pomp. I am commissioned by the British. I am briefly here, on other business, because I am a Black man who nobody suspects. Tonight I return to Canada, and then again into the woods. Goodbye and take to heart my advice."

"Stay!" exclaimed Levi. "Peter, what makes you owe me this?"

"Because God sent you here and your father befriended me." Sunfish alluded to an event five years past. "Levi," he continued, rolling his large eyes, fastening them on Cundiff who shrank from him, "I have climbed to power since this seller of flesh, hater of my kind, Cundiff, sold me to the Quaker Man." He tweaked Cundiff's nose. "Now circumstance has put wretched Cundiff into my company, a distasteful experience I must tolerate. As for you, Levi, I shall always be grateful for the bread put in my mouth and corner in the woods where your father hid me after a fight in which I killed one of the Quaker Man's servants, who tormented me. I fled to your father, he a goodly man who I knew would help me, and did. Lad, when they stopped searching, I vanished into the deeper forest of the Seneca who adopted me and gave me a new name, Sunfish. Let that suffice you. Now my debt is repaid." He rose, and though Levi tried to detain him, strode down the steps and pushed through the crowd, Cundiff in his wake. Levi hastened after them. Reaching the street, he glanced both ways. Sunfish and the imp had flown.

At once Levi realized he must put forth an effort to find and stop them. He let out a blood-curdling yell borrowed from the savages, which instantly halted the merriment within the Old Tun. Half its occupants, mostly soldiers, came spilling out believing murder had been done.

"What's up!" cried a burly sergeant, all for a bit of action. Levi was about to explain that he wished to form the men into a search party when, as if in answer, he heard the heavy sound of a booted patrol double-timing toward the tavern. The patrol came to a quick halt, bayonets ready.

A major, obviously the Provost Marshall, seeing a man in deerskin at the center of the crowd, forced a passage to him. "What's your trouble, fellow?" he asked bluntly of Levi.

"Spies are loose ... a blackamoor in fine lace; and a death's head of a man, dressed in black. Catch them, or Liberty suffers!"

"Pray, what wild and drunken prattle is this?"

"No prattle!" Levi produced from his pocket evidence of his own rank and responsibility. "I know those bold fellows, and they are self-confessed spies."

Enlisting the aid of volunteers, with rapid orders the Major put these and his platoon to combing the dark alleys. After a half-hour of feverish search, every barrel on the dock examined and swords thrust into more than one black buttock and after a top to bottom inspection of two small vessels anchored at port, the fruitless hunt was called off. With a nasty look at the Lieutenant, the Major marched his men away. The muttering crowd, thinking Levi had set up a hoax, as much as told him to begone, or they would break his head and spill out his imaginative brains. Obviously the pair had paddled out to a sea rendezvous.

His brow furrowed, Levi retraced his way home to the Coach and Horses where he quaffed three tumblers of local whisky and woozy retired, to sleep and dream. In the morning he awoke confused as to where the line of unreality lay and finally half-dismissed the threat to his life, though he vowed he would cultivate peripheral vision during his stay in this dangerous City of Brotherly Love.

Levi was preoccupied with the more immediate. His tattered deerskin warranted discard. He employed the forenoon being measured by the tailor at Hand & Shears who, responding to Levi's urgings for haste, found a uniform meant for another which, with small alterations, fitted the Lieutenant. While waiting, Levi wandered the street, selecting from a leathergoods house a pair of boots, and then purchased a military hat which, to trust the shopkeeper, duplicated the quality of the tricorn worn by General Arnold. His purchases under his arm, Levi returned to the inn where he shaved, bathed, and dressed. When he appeared in the dining room he had every eye. The tall, thin-face Lieutenant to the inch looked a soldier and a gentleman. Ladies throbbed to know him. This evening he would have preferred to dally over his coffee, but knew he had an appointment at the home of Samuel Wallis. He surrendered his table to a colonel. Levi recognized Polish born Tadeusz Kosciusko who had selected Bemis Heights near Albany as the place to confront Burgoyne's army, it to surrender at Saratoga. Murphy had earned his sobriquet 'Sure Shot' taking down General Fraser, the General's loss irreparable.

Early at Wallis's, Levi detected something wrong. Wallis, his mind astray, asked, "Did we have an appointment?"

"Sir! You are a master of forgetfulness, so lightly to treat an appointment that could affect posterity. The fate of an army, the success of a campaign, the triumph of Liberty depends upon our efforts together. Hang my rhetoric. Let us make a beginning. To work, sir."

Wallis, laboring under the strain of his unhappy affair, error though it was, attempted to put on a better face for Levi. "You are early," he commented, eye on the clock, smiling.

"An incurable habit."

"To your credit. Saves on candles. Your hat and coat, sir."

"Thank you," said Levi noting Wallis's bandaged hand.

"A puncture caused by glass." Wallis waved him toward the thick carpeted library. From a wall length bookshelf he gathered up land warrants, atlases and sketches. "This," he said, tapping the cover of a voluminous manuscript inscribed Jesuit Relations, "provides us with the discoveries of these early explorers of the Indian lands. The deeds and warrants are of more recent date. They define land purchases from William Penn's Manor, settled upon and passed under the settler's plow, and the doings of the Connecticut-formed Susquehanna Land Company in conflicting rivalry. They shall be the least productive for us. But here, this is the treasure!" He handed Levi a worn leather bound journal. "My own notes made when, with Joseph Brant as my companion, I explored the northern and western sectors of the Seneca Country. Moreover, I have a second journal filled with intimate personal data, but from which I shall read you portions pertinent to our purpose." Filling a glass of canary for the Lieutenant he inquired, "May I ask as to the breadth of Washington's plan? The letter you brought me simply stated we are to map the lands north and west of the frontier. We could shorten our labor were we to know which British fort, Niagara or Detroit, if not both, Washington intends to attack. 'T would be needless to plot a course of march through country removed from the immediate objective. You said when you visited me at my office, 'Perhaps 't is to strike at Fort Niagara, perhaps Detroit', or does my memory trick me, this being an unexpressed thought that crossed my mind? Lieutenant, do you know? We should confine our task accordingly."

Blandly Levi answered, "My instructions were specific, Mr. Wallis: A map of the entire region. No limitations. This map should include mountains, lakes, rivers, and paths leading to both forts, also the notable Indian villages along the way."

"If the extent of the map indicates the ambition of the military, 't is gigantic!"

"Infer what you may. You are presuming, sir, presuming a move will be made against both forts. Who is to say? Not I, certainly. Nor you. We must prepare our map with the thought that this campaign, whether bound toward Niagara, or Detroit, or to both places, will involve staggering weights of armaments, commissary supplies, and sundries. In consequence we should focus on the water routes to oblige a flotilla. Supplies were a problem in mounting the Hartley Expedition, and supplies and weather brought to an end the McIntosh Campaign. Large amounts must be gathered and transported. We'll have to consider the distance of navigability and presuppose bateaux, for their low draft, will be used."

Wallis reopened the Jesuit Relations. "These pages may supplement our knowledge about the principal rivers which the French, in the person of LaSalle, and before him Etienne Brule, agent of Champlain, were first to explore."

An hour later Wallis wiped his spectacles. Levi, dourly, leaned back from the table. "Damnation!" swore the scout. "We are in a morass of obsolete data, a century old. And it will take another century of scholars to untwist these names, and for what? The Jesuits speak of the 'Andaste' people at a place called Carantouan near the confluence of the Susquehanna with the Teaoga, and I very well know, if such a village was found by the French explorers, today the houses and the people are dust. I've been to that spot. Nearby, though just below the point at Teaoga, as we both know, was the Seneca Village Hartley burned. We are too far back in time. Let us go forward."

Wallis frowned. "In this instance you are correct, but if you wish to know the paths of best travel, of centuries of wear, the Jesuits writings are the source for these. And I will say this, while the Andaste have vanished, the very sites they selected for their towns no doubt today are Iroquois encampments, because of their adjacency to water, the contours of the land, and so on."

"Aye, I cannot dispute your logic. Yet I tire from the effort. It's scarcely productive, its time-wasting."

Wallis, who wished to protract the session in hopes of fatiguing the Lieutenant, he to drop his guard and confirm the extent of the 1779 expedition, responded, "My dear Lieutenant, is there another way? If we seek knowledge of the lands westerly of Teaoga and toward Pitt we are forced to examine the Jesuit Relations. Only a handful of Englishmen, mostly trappers, have ever penetrated the great Indian forest."

"Very well," surrendered Levi, with a sigh.

"Now, continued Wallis, to further drown the Lieutenant in detail, "let us look for a moment at the West Branch of the Susquehanna. To this the Jesuits give the Indian name, Quenischachchgekhanne, a tongue-tripping name translated 'the river which has long reaches and straight courses'. This aptly describes the West Branch. Knowing both are the same, we can record on the map the French information concerning the towns along its shores."

"Go to the Devil!" shouted Levi, jumping to his feet, glaring at Wallis. "I will be old and you will be dead long before we are done, at this pace. Burn the damn Jesuits Relations! Feed it to your fireplace!"

Wallis calmly replied, "Brady, you demanded a map, a broad map. The one precise method lies in comparing every scrap of writing, French, English, Dutch. I will be first to declare the task is prodigious."

"Monstrous is the word, too monstrous," snapped Levi.

"Then, without courting error," compromised Wallis, "I see only one other way to foreshorten our work. Since we don't know to where the Army will march, we could narrow our task were we to know from where our troops will depart, whether Fort Pitt to follow the Allegheny and Ohio rivers, or to assemble near Albany and follow the Mohawk River westerly, or gather at Fort Augusta to go up the Susquehanna."

If Wallis sought to draw Levi out, he failed again. "Am I in command of the Army, to say where it will march from, and what walls its cannon will knock in? And would I say, if I knew? It's not for us to know." His tone was suspicious.

Wallis took offense. "That, sir, is an inference upon my honor!" He was rankled. "It is not curiosity that prompts the question. You forget I am vitally concerned with the success of Continental arms. I am not a dispassionate player in this high stakes game. My property, and you know my investment to be substantial, are within easy reach of the Indian marauders. Do you wish this task of ours to be properly accomplished?"

"Yes. I apologize to you."

"Accepted." Wallis perceived he had been stonewalled in his attempt to ascertain the scope of Washington's plans, whether to be a major attack aimed solely at Fort Niagara, or to include Fort Detroit.

"All I ask," Levi begged, "is for you to exclude this Jesuit cock-a-doodle. Plague take the Jesuits. I will agree to anything, but no Jesuits!" Levi paused, disturbed. From the upper floor of the house came a sound as of ... of.... "Sir!" exclaimed Levi, with perplexed glance. "Is someone weeping?"

With a muffled oath Wallis shut the library door. "Drat! It is Margy, my niece, sobbing for no reason. I restricted her to the upstairs that we might be at our business in secret and uninterrupted." Wallis jerked his spectacles from his face. "She bawls and I cannot concentrate. Enough for tonight, Brady. We'll resume tomorrow, time and place unchanged."

Levi buttoned his jacket. He traversed the library and, standing on the Scottish carpet in the vestibule, retrieved his tricorn and coat, and affixed his sword belt.

"Your entrances and departures," Wallis cautioned, "should be unobtrusive. Tories live on this street, and there are patriots of doubtful warmth among my callers, some to arrive unannounced at my door. Be on guard, always."

To himself Levi thought, 'So said Captain Sunfish. Twice warned is to be forewarned amply! Like rats in a cellar, this City must be full of spies.' Aloud, to Wallis he stated, "We had best have a signal, should you have company."

"I'll light a candle in the library window, should I have a visitor."

As Levi prepared to leave, hearing a fresh outburst from above, he suggested, "Mr. Wallis, I do not think there would be any harm in letting the child come down when next we meet. She will certainly cry if you again lock her in her room. And there might be danger in our over-secrecy."

"What you deem best," concluded Wallis. "But she is no 'child'. Goodnight, sir."

Softly Wallis closed the door, the smile on his face exchanged for a harassed expression. He resumed his position in the chair, and sat twenty minutes deliberating, the index fingers of his hands pressed into the pits of his cheeks.

Outside, Levi momentarily forgot the melancholy mystery as he swore at the dead French priests. 'Dong!' went the big clock, sounding the hour to the night-wrapped city. He lapped his collar; it was a bitter evening. 'Dong!' the giant bell spoke again. He plodded along the dark street, counting the ten strokes. Snow stung his face. It sifted from a starless heaven onto his hat and shoulders. He stepped into the road, treading in the depression of a recent vehicle. Again his thoughts reverted to the woman upstairs.

Arrived at his public quarters, he stopped before the main hearth, toasting his numb fingers, vowing to buy a pair of gloves in the morning. The place was deserted except for the sprightly barmaid to whom he gave his order. "Toddy! Toddy hot, sweet girl; and I'll thank you to be quick." Quick she was, soon to set the toddy on a bench by the fire. In so doing, by chance or deliberately, she placed herself in a bent manner between him and the bench. This seemed to be a suggestion, invitational in nature, as she held herself, perhaps overly long, in this posture. Levi, to his ruin, could not resist a mischievous tweak. Had she not encouraged it, as she did, she might have been angry. She tittered, which further set the design and architecture of his folly.

"Ah, sir," she bantered, "you did deceive me. All you handsome lads have the same thing at heart."

"Aye, then you have an understanding as deep as Dame Nature. Away with prudence."

The last was beyond the scope of her intelligence. "'T is compliments, sir? Off with you! Me standing here, and you smirking the while, thinking a simple girl as I will coo, if you but feed me sweet nothings. If it's chatter only you offer I've a mind to get on with my chores. I've a new broom which my master will examine, to see if I've used it; I've glasses to wash; I've work to do."

Levi switched to plain expression. "Work you say? Why, your hi ... kind was made for pleasure. Come, is there a price on your favor?"

"Oh, sir, to hear you say! You make me blush. Shall we say my generosity in exchange for your generosity."

"Aye. Pretty Betty, I shall be hospitable with my pocket book. Tonight is the night. All I ask is you show me the skills of a woman in every and any position."

"Lah! I can show you."

"You know my door," he said.

"Be sure it's open," she whispered, as a late traveler, stamping snow from his boots, ended the conversation. Levi downed his toddy, paid the charge, and added a Spanish dollar, this bonus with a wink.

Upstairs were the guest chambers. The darkened hallway caused him some perplexity. He dubiously inspected one door and then another. The third, he decided, was his. In the pitch black he undressed, smiling with anticipation, then slipped into bed. With a yowl akin to a stifled war whoop he bounded to the floor, fumbling for sword, candle and flint. The other creature in the bed, equally vociferous, footed out and - by the subsequent thud and curse - met with mishap, slamming his head against the opposite wall. Levi, too, had banged his head, reviving the pain from the tomahawk swipe when captive. With candle and flint come to hand, he flashed the flint, but the wick on the candle did not catch. Simultaneously he heard a pistol's click at his ear, a fortunate misfire. In the brief flash from the flint he saw a man in a long night dress, verily a prophet by appearance, who blinked at him, clutching a faulty pistol. "By Jumping Jehovah!" ejaculated Levi, trying to cover his own nudity. "I paid for privacy."

In the darkness, the other responded, "Oblige me with no excuse. You are a would-be sodomite and this is my room."

Levi, at this juncture, managed to light the candle, his eye catching the glint of gold bullion on a captain's jacket draped over a chair back. He held the candle close to the man's face and guffawed. "Ha-ha-he! Ah, sir, we are met before! Lighthorse Carberry! Ho! Scarce would I recognize you, swaddled and swathed as you are, like a Daniel come to judgment. He-he!"

"Ha-Ha you," growled Carberry, "you bare-bottomed monkey. You know me, eh? He squinted at Levi. "Original Adam, if we have met, by Christ I was not introduced to so much of you! Put the candle nearer your face. Ha! The madcap Brady! Ho-ho, this is comical! He-he!" Carberry in merriment flopped on the bed. Levi, who had lowered the candle, had unwittingly set it on the table nearby his discarded breeches which, touched by the flame, were on fire. He snatched at the garment, dismayed, beating out the flame.

"Damn, I'm undone. My only breeches with a hole as big as made by an eight pound shot."

"Punishment for invading my room. All's well, though. Straightway in the morning I'll send up my tailor, John Fullerton, who will make the cloth as new."

Levi extended the candle to arm's length, lighting the corners. "Lighthorse, I confess; I perceive you are right about this room. Mine should be next. Lock your door hereafter. Someone might slide a knife across your throat in the night. Goodnight. And send for your tailor, Fuller.. Fullerton as you promise. My indebtedness to you, sir."

"Not so fast. Stay!" Carberry remonstrated. "Why so determined to part company? Gratify my curiosity provoked by the rare circumstance of this meeting, and tell me the how and why of your visit to Philadelphia,"

"Another time. I must find my room."

"There's a friend. I save you from rot in Niagara, and off you will go, with no time for friendship. Who is the woman, you rogue? Not the wench at the bar who they say has six different kinds of clap and venereals? 'S fact, it must be! The British were here before us." He wrung his hands mockingly. "Venery, venery. Woman chases man under the sheets and thus new life. Nine months from now don't name the bastard after me; don't cry if she blesses you with a freak as well as with a foul disorder."

Levi, whose face was burning like a candle, swore softly. He started for the door. Half through it, he jumped back.

"Ah," said Carberry, "you have reconsidered?"

"Yes!" He had glimpsed a candle moving in the hall, the bearer drawing near. The footsteps paused before the partially opened door. In a panic Levi dropped to hands and knees, and wiggled underneath the bed. The candle in the hallway being snuffed, whoever stood at the threshold made bold to enter, and pushed on the door. At once the draft from the corridor gutted the candle on the table. The room was as black as any chamber of the forest at midnight.

"Honey?" whispered a familiar voice, the barmaid's.

"Aye," responded Carberry, his reply muffled in the blanket. "Mum, or no tailor," hissed Carberry to Levi crouched on the cold floor.

In this unfavorable posture Levi heard the series of sounds and rustlings of garments being divested and dropped to the floor. Then the bed creaked. Soon there was a rhythm to it. 'T was ludicrous to be defrauded by Carberry. "To hell with this!" he exclaimed, not in the least entertained by the sighs and coos of his would-to-have-been mistress, from whom he was separated by the thickness of a mattress. Disgustedly he humped the bed underneath them. At once the girl emitted a startled cry and fled the room in terror, as naked as the convulsed man under the bed.

"Damn you!" said Carberry, and began to laugh.

In the morning Levi wakened with a headache. The reality of last night seemed as an unreality, or was it the other way around? His britches were in perfect order, appearing as new. Had he dreamt the ludicrous incident? For sure his headache was real.

Chapter XX

PREPARING THE TRAP

Samuel Wallis, pondering in his chair, an ear to the muted sobs above, counted his blessings as few. "Oh, Lord!" he groaned, procuring a bible from a table drawer. His eye fastened upon the First Chapter of Proverbs. 'I will laugh at your calamity; I will mock you when your fear cometh; when your fear cometh as desolation, and your destruction cometh as a whirlwind; when distress and anguish cometh upon you. Then shall they call upon me, but I will not answer; they shall seek me early, but they shall not find me --' "Faugh!" exclaimed Wallis, speaking to his reflection in a mirror, "Absent comfort! Empty writings! I am my own reliance. Aye, 't is Samuel Wallis who will do for Samuel Wallis, and none in Heaven. The girl weeps, eh? Then it is I who will correct her."

He marched upstairs. The door open, he entered her chamber. She, her face blanched, her eyes inflamed, redoubled her sobbing at sight of him. "Enough!" He spoke sternly. "Enough of this!" He seized a pocket glass and forced her to look at her reflection. "Ugly is as ugly thinks. What do you see, here? Oh, you are a dreary portrait, your eyes screwed, your mouth twisted! And for why?"

"I am damned," she choked, and commenced to sob anew.

"Ha! Damned is it? As God judges the daughters of Lot, begot with child by their father, He judges you, and by comparison you are innocent. 'T was done in innocence, a mutual premeditated gratification, no more. It was not conscious sin. We knew not other than that I was a man and you a woman, and our act was in natural consequence. Our intimacy was witless! Listen, girl, if there is punishment on this earth it comes from within. And you punish yourself unjustifiably. Away with tears. Put on your earrings and bracelets, and again be your beautiful self. You have important work to do. Smile!" She smiled wanly. He knew she now was at a turning point. It was time to retreat. "If you wish, be down in a half hour. Join me in the library. I have important news to share."

She was down in twenty minutes, wearing her smile like a mask, her face otherwise drained of color and expression, her eyes blank until she saw the toast and tea which he had prepared. He made a pretense at browsing in his books, muttering over Mitchell On Agriculture, while she nibbled on a slice of buttered bread. Then, noting the return of her vitality, and giving her no moment to fall again into self pity, he spoke pointedly. "My dear, there is a young officer who has been in this house tonight, and who will be a visitor tomorrow. Under our roof we shall have the very person who can, if we be clever, give us the rebel intention, whether they march upon Niagara or Detroit. Ironically, and as unexpected as lightning, the officer selected to prepare a map for the Continental Army expedition was sent to me.

"Viewed as I am, the patriot, the holder of western lands, and once an adventurer among the Seneca, as you well know, I am considered an authority able to help him. While I am not in the bosom of rebel planners, in this instance our visitor, Lieutenant Brady, enjoys that privilege."

Her interest quickened at the name. "Did you say Brady?"

"You know of him?"

"Not really. I briefly saw a man at the Coach and Horses who introduced himself to me by that name, and was called away by General Washington."

"A double coincidence. Fate favors us. It will be our challenge to probe his mind while presumably assisting his task. To date I have been foiled in ferreting out General Washington's intentions. You may well succeed where I have not. Providence has delivered to our doorstep the very person who possesses information we seek, and for which you were sent here. What luck! You, my dear, tomorrow evening must disarm him with your charms."

"He is not without attractiveness," she said.

As Wallis continued to speak about Levi, her color revived. "You must understand," he said, "why this fellow was picked, he a mere lieutenant when there are a dozen brevet colonels who have had posts along the Indian lands. Many know the frontier in part, and have transacted business with the red men, yet only a handful, Brady foremost, have gone through a goodly part of the Longhouse, he as a prisoner on one journey, and into the Ohio Country --"

"With the McIntosh Expedition?" she supplied. "Am I right?"

"I marvel at your knowledge. As I was about to say, don't underestimate Lieutenant Brady. His honest eyes, affectionate smile and boyish familiarities are armors, not immaturities or weaknesses. If you will inspect his history as a Morgan's rifleman, as a Free Company lieutenant, and as a prisoner who flew the dungeon of Fort Niagara and also as the man who tricked Captain Girty into raising the siege of doomed Fort Laurens, you'll have his makeup. He's granite inside. His reputation has reached Philadelphia. The sword at his side, the pistol in his belt are not ornaments or pretensions. He's quick to perceive danger, even to distrust me although Washington's order sent him to me. On your guard; he'll know you before you know him."

"Yet he is a man," she said, warming to the challenge, "and passion can unbind his strength and his secret."

"Careful with this one, my dear. 'T is a simple trick to give catnip to a kitten, another, to a cougar."

True to promise, Lighthorse Carberry had obliged Levi with a tailor. His dignity restored, Levi sallied from his room and from the inn. He bestowed his scowl upon the faithless barmaid. The morning was frosty, yet the sun peeping up over the houses gave prospect of pleasant weather. The genial pursuits of the City beckoned. As he walked the streets, Levi in his gallant uniform presented an appealing picture to feminine eyes, such as were about. But first he had his breakfast at the popular Coffee House, read the Philadelphia paper thoroughly, he now a man at leisure with the day to kill. Later, as he toured the outworks of the business area, on the corner of one street was a small shop with a modest sign advertising that the occupant, Betsy Ross, was a seamstress. A widow, her late husband killed while in the Continental Army, she took patriotic pleasure sewing regimental colors. As a Quaker she would be read out of meeting for this. Levi took note of the location, should he again need repairs. It was exhilarating to be in a city where there was hustle and bustle, yet this way of living, one house close upon another, wasn't to his liking. He began to be conscious that not only was he enjoying the sight of so many women but that he was attracting their attention with sometimes a bold look up and down as if measuring him without clothing. The day wore on in this meaningless pleasantry. What a contrast to the terrible struggle to stay alive as at Laurens! Perhaps that's why he wandered, to refill his life with life, with the pervasive motion of the city.

As the light of day waned, after taking supper, by roundabout walk he arrived before the house on Arch Street. Wallis welcomed him. "Lieutenant, you preserve your reputation for punctuality."

"I would not keep the Jesuits waiting," he replied.

"Your affection for them is apparent. Very well, let us retire them into their musty graves."

"Good!" exhaled Levi. "Good riddance."

"Now," explained Wallis, receiving Levi's surcoat, tricorn and gloves, "I have taken your advice to heart. My niece Margy is to join us in about an hour, as I have pledged her a few moments of sociability. We all need to unwind. Then, perhaps after a bit of relaxation, if you wish we can return to our task." Wallis thought it prudent not to mention the two had already met.

It was a wondrously successful session. In manifest congeniality they furthered their project, drafting the map, sketching in details, estimating distances from the documents on hand. Streams, swamps, mountain ranges were denoted. Portages between lakes and rivers were recorded. Their map defined the Susquehanna to its headwaters. It was a mighty river, as a tree with great branches, one of which was the Chenango which led down into the Susquehanna. With some difficulty on their part they attempted to define its counterpart, the more westerly river system which led northward and past Fort Pitt and wandered about, namely the Allegheny River. Brady was uncertain as to the distance between the two rivers, the Allegheny and the Susquehanna's branch, the Teaoga, This played to Wallis's hand. Wallis deliberately sought to show the Teaoga extended westerly at some distance, making it appear as a more inviting way for an army to travel against Fort Niagara. It served his purpose to add difficulty by placing the army on a longer march and in deeply wooded terrain. But Wallis's inward concern was, would Levi have second thought about this route, the length of the Teaoga and navigability? Did he really believe the Teaoga was as depicted? How far had he ventured up the Teaoga until taken prisoner? Would he favor another way? Aside from his private thought, to their mutual satisfaction, they had devised a map, true with empty spaces and with work yet to be done, but a map withal. The merchant stretched his arms. "We have but one sticking point, as I see it, our discussion on the length of the Teaogo westerly. We shall revisit this during our next session. Aside from this, if I may express a sentiment, we have carpentered well. We have yet to calculate the distance between Fort Niagara and Albany - Stanwix, were troops to be sent westerly across the foot of Lake Ontario in like purpose. Our studies all but convince me it is not Detroit which would be the objective, and surely not Niagara and Detroit together. Perhaps the intent is only to level the Indian villages thereabouts, by itself a large enough ambition."

Stonily Levi stared at him, more in statement than question. "You presume, first, the expedition marches upon Niagara, to exclusion of Detroit; and now without your asking me, you seek my confirmation if it is to be neither fort. And then again, it seems you want confirmation from this lowly lieutenant, mind you my rank, that Fort Niagara is the goal." Levi emphasized each word by striking the palm of one hand with the fist of the other.

"Well, there is merit in an argument for Niagara. The Mohawk River with its due west direction from Albany and the Susquehanna's westerly branch, the Teaoga, both are paths toward Niagara. It takes no genius to realize these water systems can serve as collaborative approaches for troops bound toward the jewel of British forts, Fort Niagara."

Levi gave no further answer. He kept close counsel, seemingly bored.

To dispel suspicion, Wallis chuckled heartily. "I am too opinionated. Time for refreshments and a sort of celebration." He uncorked a brandy bottle. "Full glass?"

"Enough for opening the eye," responded Levi, crooking his middle finger. The drink was never poured. At that moment the melodious grandfather clock struck the hour of eight and precisely

Margy descended the staircase. In her long lavender grown she was ravishing to behold.

Disbelieving his good fortune, to find within this house the beauteous, creature met in the State House Square, he could only blurt out, "You!"

Margy broke into laughter, "Hello, Mr. Limp-leg."

His sensibilities recovered, he responded, "Now you know; my bones heal rapidly. But I did pronounce the truth in every word of what I said when sprawled at your feet, Miss Margy."

She teased him, "So you found me out, and came a-chasing?"

"In honesty, I had no inkling who you were, knew nothing about you except that you were a vision beyond compare."

Wallis coughed. "May I interrupt? Lieutenant Brady, I present to you my niece, Miss Margaret Wallis. Margy, this is Lieutenant Leviticus Brady, a friend and visitor on business. With this, I ask your indulgence. Please excuse me while I take a short nap upstairs. Help yourself to the sideboard. Mr. Africa has prepared a few delicacies, and you know where to find the liquor cabinet. Enjoy your visit together." With this he bowed and retired.

Shrewdly, Wallis had briefed Margy for the tête-à-tête to come, having instructed her about his family tree. He anticipated Levi's curiosity and questions he would ask. The Lieutenant would be quick to sense, in an inept response, that something was not right about her. Had not the frontiersman, previously, to a question probing the purpose to which the map would be put, although the question was a natural one, almost jumped down his throat.

"Tell me about yourself," stated Levi, to start the conversation.

"There's not too much to say," she said modestly.

"It's obvious you've had a good education. Do I detect a British accent in the way you speak?"

"My secret is out!" she laughed. You are observant. My father Joseph, a younger brother to Uncle Samuel, sent me to England for part of my schooling. There I fell in love with a Naval officer who, to my sorrow, was swept overboard during a violent storm off Jamaica. By time the news reached me I was at my home in Head of Elk, Maryland. For a while I have been withdrawn and depressed, with this visit to lively Philadelphia designed to put color in my cheeks. You, sir, did something about that, Mr. Limp-Leg."

They both laughed at this. "So this explains last night's tears," he said, becoming serious. "The sorrow still lingers."

"You embarrass me."

"I am embarrassed, too, by the passion you generate in me. I don't understand it, and I don't want to be too forward, so let's talk of other things. Let's get acquainted. You said home is Head of Elk, the place that Howe landed to march overland to Philadelphia. Your style of life makes this Susquehanna River boy's life, by comparison, dull and beggarly."

"Don't demean yourself. You are an exciting man. I am as much a resident of the Susquehanna, being but 12 miles removed from where its broad mouth forms its junction with the Elk River, creating a cape, Turkey Point where Howe disembarked."

"I sometimes believe, had Howe taken his transports up-river and not ensnared himself in the comforts of Philadelphia, he could have made juncture with Loyalist and Indian forces coming downstream. From the Capes to the headwater in New York, all the States would have have been cut apart, North from the South, and our War lost."

"A sharp view. You should be wearing colonel's epaulets."

"Ha! Flattery. I shall tuck it into my thin purse. If there's to be flattery, let me rightfully direct it to the beautiful woman that you are."

"You impress me, Lieutenant, with your understanding of women. It is the value of herself being appreciated which compels her to seek company, especially of a handsome man. So speak on, Lieutenant. You charm me out of my senses."

Levi changed focus. "Have you been to the City before? No? Perhaps I should show it to you and to myself for that matter."

"I gather we're both newcomers here."

"How is it you've not visited Philadelphia until now?"

"For years my Father and Uncle had a strained relationship. In a hunting accident my Father killed my Uncle's friend John Beaver who was mistakenly shot when thought to be a bear.

This happened soon after they separated during the hunt and were circling back. My Father, until of late, never forgave Uncle Samuel. I am the peace offering."

"Enough of this," he said, lifting her hand and planting a kiss, thinking of her words in a different sense. "I wonder," he stated aloud, gauging his opportunity.

She fled around the chair in mock terror and seized a pair of fire-tongs. "Wonder though you may, I trust you value your skull, sir"

"Would you do that to me?"

"No," she admitted. They were into each other's arms. It was more passion than either expected.

Wallis finally heard Margy mount the stairs. "Well, girl?"

"He claims Howe has lost the war by not advancing up the Susquehanna. This tells me the Americans, by a thrust upstream on the Susquehanna, intend to nip any downstream plans from the British at Fort Niagara, as was the attack on Forty Fort. The Lieutenant believes the Indian attacks are prologue to a major thrust, by a combined force of British and Indians, aimed to cut the rebel states apart. Fort Augusta alone stands in their way."

Wallis, more so than before, fully realized why Colonel Bolton valued his services. "What more is to be said? Anything else?"

"He made to ruin me. I collected passion, not strategy. I learned of rebel arms, of candlelight endeavors, not campaigns. I was running out of information about the family when he, preferring other sport, turned up his passion."

Wallis chuckled. "So, be patient. Every man brags his trade. Unto a comely woman a soldier above all. Indulge him."

Indulge him!" she disclosed a bruised shoulder.

"So Brady is ardent. Good. You will be into his confidence."

"And where will he be with me? While I proceed to unlatch his secret, he contrives to undo my bodice drawstring. He gives me no time."

"Have you arranged his leisure, to slow his advances?"

"I have, for self preservation, been thinking on that.

"Tomorrow, with exception of his time with you, he has attached himself to me from wake to sleep. And I believe he would like to interfere there!

Wallis clapped his hands "A healthy sign of your convalescence, my dear. I, too, found him close-mouthed. We were sketching several routes, all following rivers, one from Fort Pitt up the Allegheny, and another from Pitt along the Ohio, with thought that Pitt could serve as assembly point to attack Detroit, or to send troops up the Allegheny, these troops then to turn east overland to join other forces coming up the Susquehanna from Fort Augusta to attack Niagara. As for a simultaneous attack on Detroit and Niagara, I doubt such an ambitious plan can be matured, looking at distances and supply problems. I think Niagara is the prize they seek. I made this point to Brady. He resented my speculation. This strengthens my belief."

"Then," she said, "you must distort the map, somehow confuse them in their march, they to find themselves on a battlefield of our own choosing."

"That thought has been in the back of my mind. Your suggestion is good. Let me think aloud. 'T will take some doing. Braddock was defeated by an ambush. Forty Fort was lost by catching its garrison in the open between a river and a swamp where a sizable Indian force was hidden. Maybe we can repeat that tactic somehow. If I could only be certain their army will follow the Teaoga and not depart from it to go northward along the shoreline of one of the Seneca lakes, then westerly overland. Brady's knowledge, as a captive brought to

Niagara, is of the lake country route. I will have to persuade him the best bet is the Teaoga. For our purpose it borders on marshy land suitable to setting up an ambush."

"And meanwhile I'll vex his heart and soften his mind, if I can only do so by stages." As she uttered this a strange duality in thinking divided her. The trap she would lay for the Lieutenant's heart and mind, she half sensed, already had been sprung upon her own. His amusement with her had set in motion a compassion which, like an itch, would only inflame, were he to touch her again. Her sentiments lay with the Crown, but she already was beginning to sense her own vulnerability. She was endangering this handsome man, maybe abetting his death, he surely to serve as a scout in the campaign planned for the summer.

"You're a pushing lad," said Margy on the following morning when Levi, true to his program, stood at the foot of the staircase, he whistling as she descended. He attempted a kiss, but was repulsed.

Nonplused, in Quaker mimicry he observed, "Thee be incredibly confusing. Thee tempts, and then thee spurns."

"You construe advantage where there is none," she replied haughtily.

"A wise general does not hesitate."

"A pretty speech, better said on the field of battle than in the court of Romance where more is won by Modesty, Forbearance, and Retreat."

"Quarter!" he cried. "I am in capitulation. I yield to Love's rule, so Love may then yield to me!"

Their second morning, much like the first, was a repetition with one exception. Their verbal joust was tempered by sudden and impulsive smiles and hand holding. It was obvious to all that passed them this couple was lost in each other's eyes. Margy knew she was losing the battle and could not, nor would not alter the rush of warmth that came to her.

Their third day, unlike those previous, was one almost of silence, as if they had come to an unexpressed understanding, each content to walk in quiet contemplation that something beautiful was maturing. The weather had changed from blustery to fair, the sun melting the ice on the walks. On the ledge of one shop window a robin was so brave as to make a premature appearance. As they strolled the street, taking in the warming afternoon, they were the conspicuous ones; she especially. Old men cracked their spines while young fops, bowing to the ground, saluted this vision. Military officers, Philadelphia's streets filled with uniforms, passed the couple, envious.

At the corner of Strawberry and Market she admired and he bought an ivory comb in a store which advertised on its placard, 'harbines, camlets, calimancoes, durants, tammies, laces and buckles ... sold as low as any in the city for ready money.' Promenading down Second Street they lingered at the windows of H. Taylor, upholsterer, who had decorated his front, in taste, with neat saddle-type traveling chests and window curtains. 'This trunk,' proclaimed the accompanying card, 'features a device affixed within that will amputate pilfering fingers.' Also for sale was an ingenious lock, 'a lever tumbler by Robert Barron of England that will foil any thief.' Levi's and Margy's eyes met in the window reflection. He winked, she squeezing his arm for reply. Sauntering on, they crossed Arch and ambulated toward Race. Short of Race they were attracted into Coat's Alley by the famed Derberger display of flutes, regimental fifes, pistols, gongs and bells, spurs and chains. They entered the cluttered store. The proprietor was preoccupied with a customer. "Fair warning," whispered Levi, as he pretended to study a brace of pistols, his lips near hers. Deftly with her elbow she struck a gong from the Orient which emitted a wake-the-dead sound throughout the shop. Derberger, seeing Brady with puckered lips and surmising the by-play, tried to conceal his smile. Levi scowled back, grabbed Margy's hand, and fled. Safely past the door, and to the corner on Second Street, he stopped. "Margy! You wench!" Then, with a chuckle of his own, he asked her, "Have you ever had a more interesting afternoon?"

"No," she admitted, linking her arm into his, and looking up at this marvelous man. She titillated inside for him.

That evening Levi and Wallis undertook reviewing the Teaoga River from its mouth on the Susquehanna westerly into the Seneca Country. If he could overcome Brady's hesitancy, here Wallis meant to spoil the map. With an easy show of knowledge with a pen he pricked his pen a location on the Teaoga. "Here, sir, is the first village, the notorious hive of the Tories, Chemung Town."

"But," expostulated Levi, putting a rule to the paper, and measuring, "by scale you have Chemung Town fifteen to twenty miles upstream. 'T is nearer the mouth, from my own experience. I have reconnoitered it."

Wallis, answering Brady, commented, "You didn't spy Chemung Town. You presume that you did."

"I saw a large town, the first town above the mouth of the Teaoga River. It was about eight miles upstream."

"You saw Old Chemung."

"Eh?"

"Yes, there are two Chemung towns, Old and New Chemung, or Newtown, the former being familiar to you. It is now used mainly as a military base, most of its inhabitants having migrated away from the battle threatened community. I understand you were made captive somewhere between the two towns. You had no opportunity to examine the course of the river beyond that place."

"That is correct," admitted Levi. Wallis, inaudibly breathed a sigh of relief. He was free to distort the map, extend the Teaoga far beyond its truthful length, invent Indian village sites, in effect baffle any expeditionary force. First, though, he must cover his own tracks, if later called to answer for this twisted-awry drawing.

"You know, Lieutenant, I too must admit I did not know the course of the Teaoga much beyond that point. But I have been spending the day researching some of the writings in the Journals of Robert de la Salle, and of the Jesuit Dablon who made mention of the river in his Relations covering the year 1672. These seem to suggest the Teaoga extends westerly at some distance, as I propose to draw it, and feel confident the Allegheny therefore may be reached by an overland passage of short duration. I've gone so far as to identify the locations of those river-connected villages which Dablon mentions but, in truth, I'm uncertain if these sites exist today as Seneca settlements."

Levi made a snap judgment. "Let's draw it. It's better than leaving the space blank."

Wallis explained further, as he outlined the meandering extension of the river, mixing much truth with purposeful deception. "The town next after Newton is Goughpeekin; then Sinsing." If Levi was to be befuddled it would be here and now. "Mark you well," said Wallis, "just before Sinsing the river divides. Sinsing is on the branch you should avoid or you will blunder into the Great Swamp." Here Wallis, while truthful about the geography, reversed the location of the Swamp, placing it on the wrong leg of the fork, thus positioning the Army to fall into this marshy stretch.

As Wallis rapidly sketched the course of the river, Levi watched him enter the name of the village Little Poosica. "I see you've placed a mileage figure."

"It's a best guess. Within 25 miles of Little Poosica is or was Great Poosica. As its name implies, it had a sizable population. The importance of this last location is that it is on a plateau, with the Allegheny River flowing from here to Fort Pitt. It places the two streams closer than we estimated."

"If this is correct," said Levi, repressing his excitement, "troops from Fort Pitt could navigate almost to Poosica, beach their boats and trek overland, joining those coming up the Teaoga!" He clapped Wallis on the shoulder. "Can we be sure?"

"Can we be sure of anything in life?" Wallis responded, hunching his shoulders, beaming inside, thinking, 'Oh, the fool!'

Margy, who had reappeared to say goodnight to Levi, after the Lieutenant had left the house, overheard Wallis repeat, this time aloud, "Oh, the fool!"

"What are you saying?" asked Margy.

"As you suggested, I chanced a deception. What a deception! For one, I created a length for the Teaoga which it does not have; nor does he realize the river's draught makes navigation an impossibility. Heavily laden batteaux, never! Secondly, the river leads by a large swamp, an ideal location for ambushing the Americans. Tonight, my dear, we have saved Niagara, for it is Niagara they intend to attack!" Then he added, "I shall be with little sleep tonight, staying up late to make a copy of the map, which I shall further update after tomorrow morning's session with the Lieutenant. The copy goes to General Haldimand."

They were done! The map entire lay on their working table, the Great Map, as Levi would call it, a map of the lands beyond the mountainous Pennsylvania frontier and of the lake country westerly of Albany. Done at last! Wallis put aside the 1753 Journal of John Martin Mack, and Scull's map of 1759, which defined paths that radiated from Muncy. Viewing the completed map at far range, Levi remarked, "Truly Muncy appears as a spider in a web." East from Muncy ran the Forty Fort path; south, the Shamokin path; northerly, the Sheshequin path. Numerous smaller paths advanced westward.

It was magnificent to behold, spread out as it was to their view. Levi folded the bulky map into thirds, then rolled it into a scroll. "Shall we seal it?" questioned Wallis.

"At your will, Mr. Wallis."

Wallis set the edge with melted wax. He wrapped the scroll in oil-skin, tying this with leather thongs. He then inserted this in a wooden tubular case, with a strap for affixing it to a saddle. This he presented to Levi. "And now, as a farewell gesture, I have instructed Mr. Africa to prepare a mid-afternoon repast, and shall leave you two alone. I am out of sorts. There is one question I must ask. I presume you will saddle up and be on your way in the morning to deliver this personally to General Washington at his Middlebrook Headquarters."

"Correct, sir."

"For safekeeping, would you want to leave the map here, and come back in the morning for it?"

"No, sir! It stays on my person."

"Then, at least, though you are within walking distance to your room, I will have you delivered by carriage when ready."

"My thanks for this precaution. I must make this as short an afternoon as is my trip long, therefore early to bed, so say my travels."

"Now, excuse me while I go find Margy." He ascended the stairs and in a whisper stated to her, "We are done. He is downstairs waiting you. He will carry it to Middlebrook in the morning. I must inform Stevens that I have a duplicate of the map, this second map having no error in it, that I wish delivered to the Governor General. There will be a separate note with it, describing where best the trap should be laid. The British have a picket ship offshore in the Bay nearby the widening waters of the river at Cantwell's Bridge on the Delaware shore below Wilmington. All ships' captains have alike instructions to send a longboat ashore, provided in advance a signal is flashed to the ship's lookout. The captain has standing instructions to break off his patrol, and to approach the port, to await a passenger. By the number of flashes he knows which of the nights he is to come from the Bay into the river. I must make arrangements with Stevens, so that the nearest ship will know by tomorrow night that on the following night a passenger will be waiting. I will be there to hand Stevens the map, he to go aboard."

Wallis instructed Margy, "Keep Lieutenant Brady entertained. I shall be gone an hour. Tell him I truly need a nap and have retired."

Wallis made a stealthy back-door exit, tip-toeing out and shutting the door with care, not to create any sound. Once on the deserted street he began to walk at a brisk pace. The Indian Queen was his objective. This public house was witness to scenes of all types of comings and goings, a place of oddly timed meetings. Wallis knew Stevens room. The fellow, surprised from his bed, let him in. "Matter of importance!" hissed Wallis.

"Shut the door, and speak low." He put his finger to his lips."

"I have discovered General Washington's intention."

"Really," sardonically said Stevens who, since the arrival of Margy, considered himself passed by.

"You must convey a map to New York, personally. It warrants enormous precaution; no soul is to view it other than the Governor General. The honor will be yours to bring it to our friend in New York, the banker Burling. It goes by sail. You will rendezvous with the ship two nights from now."

"Mr. Wallis, I thank you for the privilege of a sea trip in the worst of seasons, and a long ride from which I may die of frosted lungs."

"Remember, two flashes of the lantern repeated until acknowledged. The one problem is, if the rendezvous is to be timed to happen, the signal must be given by tomorrow night. This means you have a choice. Either you make the trip, starting by dawn this coming morning so as to signal the ship by nightfall, and then stay over at the nearest tavern for the next night's pick up, or in lieu of sending the signal yourself to find a substitute tonight. He would have to leave early this coming morning to do the signaling.

"Understood. I have the fellow. Now, for the map."

"It passes to you from my hand at first dark at Cantwell's Bridge, no earlier. I shall meet you there. Be there. I will lead your horse back and keep it stabled until your return. Now I must get back not to be missed. Lieutenant Brady is at my home. As for you, Mr. Stevens, as I leave, you must be on your way to find your man. In this weather, to cover the distance to the signal point at Cantwell's Bridge he will need to be in his saddle as early as Lieutenant Brady who travels to Middlebrook. Tell your man to be on the road no later than dawn."

As the door closed, Stevens hurriedly dressed, the while smirking. He had plans of his own, orders given him by Captain Sunfish. The map was not to fall into Washington's hands. He would do as instructed by Wallis as far as arranging for a signalman, and would be there to go aboard ship as planned. But this night he must also alert Cundiff about Brady. There would be little or no sleep, Cundiff and the new man would need to be on the road ahead of Brady, to set an ambush. No map must reach General Washington. Such were Stevens' thoughts. He was unaware Brady's version was designed to bring harm to the rebels, not give help to the Continentals. Stevens wondered if he should participate in the intercepting party. If he did it would mean he would have a long evening ahead, and soon thereafter a longer one with a sea voyage to cap all. Actually he was rising from a sick bed, fatigued by a cold, depressed by his descending fortune. He was reduced to being a mere courier. He began to think, were the lieutenant killed, 't would be easy enough to dispose of Wallis in the darks of the waterfront, good riddance to him in the deep running water. His fortunes might ascend.

As the hour approached for departure of Levi from Margy, he sensed their briefly brought together lives here might separate. For Levi this was an intolerable thought. He wondered if Margy's emotions matched his. He realized he wanted this woman for life! For wife!

Forever. In like vein Margy was troubled, her feelings more complex because her whole posture was a lie fabricated to conceal her real purpose as a spy. By her actions she endangered the man she loved. Hers was a terrible dilemma, loyalty to the Crown versus her feelings about this most wonderful man, unlike any she had known. The question she asked herself was, were she to confess her role, would he still want her. Her thoughts were not on her own endangerment. She knew there could be no foundation for a marriage, this secret to be kept from him, and were it to be found out, as ultimately it would, would he continue to love her? That uncertainty only could be answered by her confession, and she knew it.

Levi embraced her. "Margy, if you knew, from the very first instant that we met how deep my love is for you, then you will understand why I ask for your hand, poor man that I am. My only craft is my gun, although I have tried my hand at surveying and perhaps can earn a living from that when this war is done. It would not support you in the style of your upbringing, and that is the truth."

She pulled back from him, continuing to hold both his hands in hers. "Levi, I do love you, passionately. I do yearn to be your wife without any preconditions on my part. I think of you as I lie abed; I dream of you asleep and awake; and I would sooner die than be parted. And yet, if this marriage is to be, first I must confess who I really am, and what my real purpose is in Philadelphia. If you still love me after that, then I shall love you forever. Levi, I am in terror, driven only by love as I go about making this disclosure to you."

He kissed her. "Whatever you say, I love you too much to let anything destroy our future. Let us sit before the fireplace."

She hesitated, then began, "It is true my name is Margy. It is not true, however, that Samuel Wallis is my uncle. He is my father. My mother is Esther Montour whose home and town you burned nearly five months past. I did not know who my father was, and certainly never expected it would be him, until after I arrived here under orders from Governor General Haldimand. This house was selected as my temporary residence because Samuel Wallis, like myself, serves the British cause. I know you are shocked. I know what I say now is unbelievable. But it's truth, truth which strains one's credulity. It may be said a strange providence led me here to discover my unknown parent. This I learned from reading his personal diary in which he tells of his affair with my mother. He never knew a child was conceived. And as to the reason I

293

was sent here, I am not an unattractive woman. Using the weakness of men, I am capable of serving British desires to learn more about American plans. More unimaginable is the fact my father, Tory spy that he is, was trusted by the Americans to assist you in designing a map the Continental Army will use to strike at the British forts. Levi, in my telling you this I expose myself to being hung, but I am driven to risk all, so passionately do I love you, so wantonly do I wish forever to be yours. I also do not wish, were my vain hope to come true, harm to befall you, as it would, I to become your widow. I fear for your life above my own." Her voice was beginning to tremble. "My love rises above loyalty to any flag, how be it striped, horizontally or diagonally."

Levi did not wait for her to finish. He lifted her from her chair, swept her tightly to his body and, looking deeply into her eyes, and softly said, "Will you marry me?"

"I will! I will!" She broke into tears, daubing at her eyes, then continued. "There is more to tell. The map, it is flawed. If you but look at the mouth of the Teaoga, by the size of its discharge into the Susquehanna you will see it is far less in volume, therefore length, than presupposed. Beyond Chemung it cannot support anything more than canoes, much less batteaux laden with supplies. And, in our casual conversation while shopping, you mentioned a Captain Sunfish's warning of an attempt to be made upon your life, the map to be taken from you. For one, I would conceal it on your person, not carry it in open sight. And ride with much caution. I have seen at times when we parted at the door that there was a watcher of this house. How Sunfish and his people knew about the map I do not know, but it does not surprise me they intend mortal harm. Who they are I know not, but I swear their conspiracy is theirs, not my father's. He would want Washington to receive the map, it meant to deceive. Having bared my soul, were you to have a change of heart, I'd understand."

"Don't talk foolishly. Instead speak of marriage. When? When?" Happiness flooded her.

"When the trees are in bud, when the grass brightens to life, when the song birds come to our ears."

"Capital! Hold no fear for your father. I'll plead his case to the General, no harm's done and his usefulness has ended to the British." Alluding to himself, he added, "As for the man who burnt the home of the mother who bore you, he needs to be forgiven, too, by a wondrously loving woman named Margy, soon to be Brady."

Levi was gone prior to Wallis's return, telling his betrothed he would pass by the house just before sunup in his early morning departure for camp. The ferry he would take was at the end of Arch, a few blocks removed from the Wallis home. The weather promised to be worse, not better, for his trip. The snow kept coming. He told Margy, depending on military orders, as soon as he could return to Philadelphia from Middlebrook, he would then place on her finger the symbol that they were pledged. For the time, she would have to settle for a kiss, it to be remembered and to remind her of his adoration.

Wallis, after meeting with Stevens, retired to his bedroom, the sky full of flakes. Cold always sapped his energy. Tomorrow he faced a day of appointments at the office, with a noon meal to be shared with his friend Colonel Hooper. He wished to know more about the man Roxbury recently recruited by Cundiff. What were his talents or skills, and for what purpose was he brought into the circle? Too, now that the map was done, and perhaps Brady's life as a soldier put at greater risk because of it, he was bothered by that fact. He had warmed to the young Lieutenant. And he sensed Margy's attachment was far deeper than she intended. Thinking of Margy, Wallis also thought of Esther, homeless, her village destroyed by Colonel Hartley's men. How sad! He speculated she and her people in abandoning their homes may have fled to her sister Catherine's village at the foot of the lengthy Seneca Lake north of Teaoga. Or had she gone to Newtown above old Chemung? Wishfully he thought, had things to have been otherwise, they would have married. In this manner he drifted off to sleep, dreaming of a man who had two faces to his head, to the rear the face of Cundiff, while up front it was his own face.

Suddenly there was a fuselage of bullets from a firing squad; he was falling and the face of Cundiff was contorted in delight, the imp screaming as Wallis fell face forward, his eyes focused on the bricks of a walkway that led into a warehouse. Abruptly Wallis awoke.

Chapter XXI

THE AMBUSH

As planned, at 4 A.M. Levi dressed. He heeded Margy's advice, removing the map from the case, refolding it to fit beneath his jacket. His horse, saddled, was brought from the stable of the public house. Colonel Hooper, Quarter Master, by orders had secured for Brady a mount of proven stamina for the daunting winter trip, a chestnut gelding of thirteen hands. Once owned by Caesar Rodney of Delaware it had carried him 58 miles in a day, timely for him to sign the Declaration. Levi's journey would be of equal length. The horse was in its prime, equal to the daunting task more so made by the weather. Traveling along Arch Street, illuminated by the street lanterns, he found Margy at her bedroom window, a candle casting light upon her face. She lifted the candleholder up and down. Removing his glove, putting fingers to his lips, he gestured a kiss, she responding. Then he was gone, the sound from his horse's hooves lost in the blanket of snow, he disappearing into the darks of this wintry night. She worried. He would cross the Delaware on the Arch Street ferry. He would have the sometimes moon.

A raw wind coupled with intense cold purpled Levi's nose and put a blue-gray chill into his fingers. At first light, about 6 A.M., the wintry sky was leaden, promising worse. The cold sucked at his breath so much that he stopped to fix a make-shift mask over the nostrils of his gasping horse, then to dig his own nose and mouth beneath the lapels of his coat. The countryside was deserted, totally featureless save for the evergreens bowed by white burdens, sentinels which flanked the lonesome mostly obliterated road. On the road not far from the Delaware River he passed a stranded coach, traces empty, horses, passengers and driver nowhere to be seen. Only the urgency with which

General Washington awaited the map forced him onward. Levi touched his breast with gloved hand, reassuring himself the document lay snug in the fold of his jacket. In the distance he saw two travelers, dismounted, near a small shed or break-wind. The wayfarers had built a merry fire. At sight of him one of their horses champed and neighed. "Hello!" Levi called as he rode toward them. Too late, he recognized one of the pair, the death's head Cundiff. In reply Cundiff leveled a pistol.

"You are easier taken than I thought."

"Well, now," Levi answered, affecting a friendliness, "what malice do you bear me, my friend?" His mind was at hammer. He knew they wanted the map. He considered the chance of spurring his horse, or of standing to fight, and the odds of extricating his sword from its scabbard. His gloved hand slid to its guard.

Cundiff met his maneuver with a sharp command. "Desist!" At once Cundiff's companion, a tall gangling fellow with a pockmarked face hardly beautiful except by comparison to Cundiff's, produced a musket and edged around Levi.

The fellow ordered, "Come down; for life, do as you're told." Levi freed one leg from the stirrup and dismounted. The musket-armed person patted the Lieutenant's garments. With the tip of a finger he tested the bulge where Levi had placed the map.

" 'T is nothing," said Levi. "My tobacco."

With a twisted grin the fellow remarked, "We shall soon see." He unbuttoned the coat. "Eh!" he exclaimed, "Your tobacco turned into a map!"

Levi nodded. "Yes, a map. Worth a fortune, too, if you lads know its value. At least your masters do. I trust they have paid you well for the trouble of getting it. If you be smart, you'll double your money. I'll pay twice the sum if you let me go! All you've to say is that you missed me in the storm."

Cundiff sniggered, "Ha! Since when are rebel lieutenants paid so handsomely that they can talk as high as you do? You waste our time. Besides, if you have a purse, I'll take it anyway." Cundiff pilfered Levi's pocketbook. "Fie!' said Cundiff, its contents counted. "Seven

Continental dollars! You couldn't buy kindling wood. With this thin gruel you bribe us? Brady, take a long look, and then pray."

"You will answer to Captain Sunfish."

"That's neither here nor there. He gave you your chance to live, but you didn't take it. Now you're going to have an irreversible health problem. Die you must."

"Like hell I will!" Levi hurled himself sideways, the gun exploding in his ear. The shot by providence struck the horn of his saddle, at which his horse kicked its hind legs, lurching and knocking 'pock-face' off his feet. Dropping his musket, he crawled away from the caracoling horse. Cundiff, pistol empty, threw it into the snow, lunging at the Lieutenant with a knife. Levi jerked out his own, hidden beneath his wrappings. As the pair grappled, wallowing about, the other man staggered to his feet, grabbed the pistol from the snow, and smashed the butt down on Levi's head. But not before Levi had plunged his knife into Cundiff's throat. The blow to Levi's head was glancing and was cushioned by hat and scarf. As Levi looked into Cundiff's glassy eyes, these an inch away, the second blow descended, blotting out the world.

When his eyes opened he saw two American officers silhouetted against the sky. Hand to his head, Levi noted one held his runaway horse. Horse and man were fuzzy. The second was wrapped against the cold like a Chinese mandarin, little save nose and eyes visible. "Foul play Brady?" spoke the first man, his voice familiar. Levi confused him to be Carberry.

"Carberry! For God's sake, get them!" Levi's vision still was fuzzy. The man retrieved Levi's knife from the throat of Cundiff, wiped the blade clean in the snow, and presented it to Levi.

"It's me, Tom Boyd." The Captain who spoke was a Morgan's company commander.

The second officer scanned the tracks. "Whoever the other is, he can't be far in this snow. We must have scared off your play friend when we fired a gun to reign in your horse. Can you ride, Lieutenant?"

"Yes, sir. Hoist me into my saddle. My head's on the swim but I'll be all right."

Boyd obliged. "After the blasted scum," the Captain growled. "'T is time for a hanging if the fellow's a deserter."

"He's a bird of another plumage," stated Levi, head a-throb, working his eyes, blinking them. "Those men were spies."

"Spies!" Snow crusted eyebrows were elevated. At once the trio induced their horses to a sharp trot. Steam from the nostrils of their mounts rose in the air.

"We'll see him soon," said the mandarin figure. "He can't hide. The country's level. Spare your mounts 'til he's sighted."

His analysis was verified in due moment by Boyd's shout,"There he is!" The pursuit took flavor. "Hup-hup" called Boyd in his booming baritone, and his merry-legged roan shot forward, its mane a flag for Levi's horse. The wind was at their backs,favoring them. Behind Levi and Boyd pressed the mandarin, who pumped saddle and invectives to the alarm of the fugitive. Being nigh on his heels, the hunted man was inspired to flail his animal.

"One for the mark!" barked Boyd with impatience. His rifle cracked and missed. He rammed the weapon into its leather holder, scowled, flicked the buttons of his coat, and jerked forth his pistol. It was a futile gesture. At Boyd's rifle shot the tall man, who Levi last remembered having the map, clapped spurs, roweling his horse till blood flowed. Levi, led by his Morgan's Rifles friend, forged after the fellow.

Fields gave way to timberland. The man bee-lined toward a copse of evergreen. Levi ventured a shot. Untouched, the scoundrel thundered into the pines, yelling a taunt, "You bastards!" Within this thick and gloomy arbor the path intersected others. Yet he could not conceal his prints which unerringly led them into a clearing. Levi and Boyd drew rein in the clearing. It was more of a meadow, a strip between grove and unbroken forest. Disappearing into the depths of the forest was the man's riderless horse. Levi bit his lips. "Old trick! The fellow grabbed an overhead limb, then somehow managed to throw his body sideways off the path, while yet concealed in the grove, leaving no track. He covered himself with snow. As we went by, we never saw him. Smart man! By now he's burrowed where we can't find him in this snowfall, or we will get a fatal surprise for our pains." Foiled, they reloaded their rifles.

In affirmation, Captain Boyd waved an arm at the snowflakes, by this time descending in such quantity as to cancel all clues. "We'll do well to rejoin the Colonel." So! The mandarin was a colonel. "This storm thickens by the minute," added Boyd. They groped through the copse, midway colliding with a finely dressed rider who had debouched from a secondary path.

"Sirs!" the rider shouted, "Were you after a deserter? I saw a man vault off his horse, and while it went on one compass he set himself on another."

"Which way?" chorused the officers.

The stranger pointed. "Twenty rods down the path to the right, and then to where it splits. Follow the left fork."

"Away from the woods?" Boyd asked incredulously.

"Yes," replied the stranger. "And a tall rascal he is, with a powerful set of legs. Haste, if you would claim him."

"Thanks. You've done a service!" They wheeled their horses. As they turned away, their charitable informant, with a change of face, lifted a pistol and aimed at the receding back of Levi. Mastering the impulse, he lowered the weapon. Stevens, for Stevens it was, was satisfied. The map was in his pocket and to be proof of his indispensable service to the Crown. He had denied Washington the map. He would carry two maps on his voyage to meet Haldimand, these being the one his subordinate Roxbury had just handed him, and Wallis's copy when to be received two nights hence. As the Continental officers forked away in pursuit of Roxbury, Stevens hoped Roxbury or Brady, if not both, would perish in the skirmish. That to be. What matters it? He would be on the high seas. He toyed with doing in Wallis, when they met this coming evening at the docks, then dumping him into the Delaware.

Their benefactor had been correct. In the snow the fugitive Roxbury's imprints, freshly made, were yet distinct. At the western edge of the copse the rogue's strategy became obvious. At home with the terrain, he had gambled that his pursuers would chase the tracks of his free running horse into the heavy woods, or search along the western perimeter of the copse while he, taking opposite direction, made an ingenious escape by climbing up and over a long running but narrow ridge of land, the far side of which could conceal him as he made his passage away from the search area. As the storm increased Roxbury must have congratulated himself. The fresh fall of snow would obliterate all traces. Somehow during the chase the Colonel had fallen behind.

Levi and Brady, their horses all but foundered, tethered their mounts to a tree, then scampered up the embankment and quickly down its counter slope. Here they dimly discerned a dark object shuttling over the snow. "We have him," exulted Levi. "Take him alive, if we can." Boyd struck off on a tangent while Levi doubled his stride. "Halt!" Levi yelled. The fellow spun around facing his pursuer. There was no surrender in him. Levi and the man fired simultaneously.

"A hit!" shouted Boyd. The wounded man knelt in the snow, fetched out a pistol and proceeded to level it. The Captain terminated this with a point-blank blast. Slowly the twice wounded man straightened up. Eyes glazing, in defiance he hurled the unfired pistol at Boyd, then with a spasmodic shudder pitched backward. The dead man's pockets yielded nothing. "A nameless grave for this one," remarked Boyd, "if the buzzards and beasts don't get him first."

"I was certain he would have it," swore Levi."

"Of good cheer, my dear Levi. Whatever you prize, it must be of importance, two men to die for it."

Light began to dawn on Levi about the third person met on the road. The man was so timely in being met in the copse, and why to be there; then in hindsight the reason appeared obvious. He was there to conduct business with those two who had just been killed. "And we let him get away!" he muttered in disgust.

They regained their horses to hear a large explosion close at hand. Meeting the Colonel, by now no longer a fuzzy image, nor as wrapped in his garments as he had been, Levi exclaimed inwardly. He knew this Colonel.

The Colonel stated, "Let me explain what happened, leading up to the explosion you heard. When I saw a third man come out of nowhere, I at once connected him to the others. My suspicion was confirmed when he bolted after I hailed him. It was a short chase with an unbelievable ending.

"Knowing he would be overtaken, our quarry did a damnably stupid thing. He went for a tobacco shed. Its wreckage you see burning in that field. It didn't hold tobacco. It held a cache of gunpowder. God knows who put the barrel there, but I'll wager it was for no good purpose and was there by his placement. Anyway, rather than surrender, the fool set off the powder, blowing himself to hell. What's left is a booted foot and charred scraps of cloth. Crazy. Crazy."

Levi, by now realizing the snow-covered Colonel was no less than the commander of Fort Augusta, made his apology. "Colonel Hunter, my senses clearing, I am embarrassed for not recognizing you. I have no excuse, having been to Fort Augusta."

"No apology needed, Lieutenant. You've had a bad knock on the head and a mean fight in the woods. It's a wonder you've done as well as you have. May I take a guess at what's behind all of the foul play? Were you bound for Middlebrook?"

"Yes, sir. Headquarters."

With a wink at Boyd, Hunter further inquired, "What business brings you to General Washington?"

"Sir, did I say I was commanded to the General's marquee?"

"You did not. 'T is inferred your business must be of importance, it to have excited the interest of those poor devils strewed back there in the snow."

"I was bearer of an article they wanted."

"Was it a map?" pursued the Colonel.

"Eh!" The deduction startled Levi. The canny Colonel smiled. He and Boyd extracted maps from pouch and saddlebag.

Boyd, raising his snow-covered tricorn, rumbled in his deep voice, "Welcome, Brady, welcome into the society of frontier cartographers."

"You, too! Maps!"

The Colonel nodded. "General Washington is thorough. While he honors each of us for our knowledge, you alone have had the dubious distinction of being valued by the enemy. It would appear our 'Mr. Bits and Pieces' back there had the two other rascals do his dirty work while he waited aside, they to bring him your map. Mr. Almost Corpus Delecti, celebrate your life! Waste not a moment mourning over a lost map. Memory will serve you." Lapsing into silence the three trotted along the sunken road gouged in the frozen meadow.

Levi quizzed Boyd, "What happened after the Rifles were broken up, following Saratoga, and our nick-of-time saving of Fort Stanwix from the forces of St. Leger's and Brant with his Indians?"

"This past year I got my captaincy and stayed with the Northern Army, serving under Colonel Bill Butler who, with four companies of Rifles was attached to the 4th Pennsylvania Line. When Hartley started up the Susquehanna from Muncy, we set out from Fort Defiance in Schoharie Valley toward you to cover your asses. We scattered Indians south down the Delaware, then turned west to the Susquehanna, then southerly burning 16 settlements. One, Unadilla, a Tory gathering place northeast of Teaoga, was a pity to burn. The houses had polished floors and glass windows with pleasant views of nature, and stone chimneys. Too, we torched Onaquaga where Brant puts together his Seneca and Mohawk war parties. Everybody fled before us. We were posting advanced notice by our black smoke. We burnt villages of the Mohawk, Seneca, Tuscarora, and Delaware. It wasn't my cup of tea, burning those Unadilla homes."

"How many Seneca did you kill?"

"None."

"How many Mohawk?"

"None. Nor did we go after the neutral Onondaga."

"Neutral! They got hair bags like the rest. What else did you do to brag about?"

"We climbed mountains until our tongues hung out. Three times we forded rivers. I guess I'm here in this company because of the wisdom gained. I'm skilled in burning houses, skilled in climbing mountains, skilled in fording rivers."

"Speaking of your improved skills, as to the fairer sex how less than rotten are you in this department? Don't answer."

The Colonel who at first pretended not to hear two of Morgan's best, tossing insults, finally gave the pair a nasty look. They fell silent, sheepishly grinning at each other. For some time silence prevailed. It was a bitter cold and tiresome trip. The hours were trying. Briefly they stopped at a tavern. Hours later, they finally reached a lonely crossroads where a sentry presented arms and indicated the road to follow. They knew the way. It was their old encampment beyond Morristown, Levi and Boyd there in '77. Here, as at Valley Forge, they had known hunger. Further along this valley, itself protected by high ridges, were the shelters, square-hewn log huts. Everywhere was the bleakness of winter bivouac.

"Pass on," said a second sentry, blowing on his hands.

In front of Headquarters was a wooden pole supporting a 13-star flag, limp under a weight of falling snow. The trio surrendered their horses to a young private of the New Hampshire line. With bayonet affixed, another soldier of exceptional height, nearly six feet, one of Washington's life Guards, presented arms. Stamping snow from their boots they acknowledged the salute. Entering the dwelling, they were met by a brigadier, a tall beanpole of a man who could fit no ordinary bed, General Edward Hand, Washington's planning officer. "Ah, Hunter!" the General exclaimed, accepting their simultaneous salutes, nodding to each. His cordial greeting compensated for the dreary trip.

"General Hand," said Hunter, "With me are Captain Boyd and Lieutenant Brady on business with the General."

Hand stated, "Gentlemen I am happy you are here. You are expected. Stand at ease. Opening a door, he consulted within, then reappeared beckoning them. "General Washington, I present your frontiersmen!" Anew, crisp salutes were given.

Washington had been gazing at the continuing snow, a cup of Holland tea in his firm hand. He drained the cup, then waved them toward empty chairs positioned around a table, this cluttered with correspondence and drawings. These Hand pushed aside as the officers removed their snow-covered coats. The awe inspiring Virginian, known for his dignity and integrity, was without benefit of a wig, his cropped red hair exposed, giving him a more youthful and approachable look. He resembled as he appeared when a provincial colonel during the French and Indian War, except that the brightness of youth was gone from his eyes, this replaced by a steady on certainty. That certainty gave purpose to their military lives. The visitors stood until the Commander in Chief took a seat. "Well, gentlemen, by your arrival in a group, you show like crows in a corn field come at one swoop. As each of you now knows, more than one person was put to the same task. You are here because of your collective wisdom about the Indian lands which the Western Department confronts, these being the lands drained by the Susquehanna, Delaware, Allegheny and Ohio Rivers. It is a large area, never fully mapped. Each of you has visited part of the region. An expedition is to be sent to the frontier this summer. Its purpose is to end hostilities against our villages by destroying the nests of those who bring war to us. The towns of the Six nations, except so much of which is inhabited by the Oneida who have always lived in amity with us, are to be visited by our torches. There is some thought of capturing Fort Niagara from which come down the Indians and Tories. This is a decision yet to be made. It would require another 100 miles of travel through forests. The risk has to be weighed. Aside from this, gentlemen, since your arrival here was to be in secrecy, each without knowledge about the other, I am baffled. Was the secret no secret? Are our endeavors not as guarded as I had thought?"

"General, 't is not deniable we show together," stated Colonel Hunter. "Of this there was a moderate chance. Our appointments coincided, and the principal road to Middlebrook from Philadelphia was the one we traveled. By our backgrounds, we surmised we were posts in the same fence. However, you are right. More to the mark, the enemy does know our business, and this gives us pause as it does you."

Washington's eyes had come alive. At this point Colonel Hunter deferred to Brady.

"General, I was traveling alone when waylaid, my map forcibly removed and my murder intended. By the providence of these gentlemen's appearance, the would-be assassins in turnabout were surprised, one to be fatally stabbed, another shot dead, and the third when cornered in a shed where a keg of gunpowder was stored, blew himself to smithereens, map included. The man who was stabbed went by the name of Cundiff, he known to me as a spy."

Hand interjected, "You imply earlier acquaintance?"

305

"Yes, sir, and no, sir. I knew enough about him to root him in evil. He was a slaver a few years back. Spydom is not beneath his character. I know beyond question he was, until his demise, the tool of a network of Tories.

"Say on, Lieutenant," responded Washington, interest heightened.

"While in Philadelphia closeted with Samuel Wallis preparing the map, one evening I decided to visit the Old Tun Tavern by the docks. At the Old Tun a curious adventure befell me. There I renewed a connection with a black giant who some years before had been befriended by my father. At that earlier time he was a fugitive from bondage, having been employed on the Wallis farm at Muncy, where he killed a man, for which he was being hunted. He had been goaded into it, we so believed, and my family gave him shelter. When I again accidentally met the black man he freely admitted he was in the pay of the British and held a captain's commission, and that he had been posting information to his superiors. Further, in the presence of Cundiff, evil little man, he forewarned me I would forfeit my life were I to complete this map. Out of gratitude he told me this, stating he owed me my life because I helped him escape a fate either of death or worse, slavery, years earlier"

Washington showed surprise. "Captain Sunfish! So the elusive Captain Sunfish is a black man! Lieutenant, he has caused us much grief and embarrassment. He is a clever fellow whose identity we never could establish. Would that your father had left Sunfish to perish, or that you, in the Old Tun, could have detained and seized him."

"I tried, sir. Before I could grasp him by his coat, he flung himself through the crowd in the tavern and was out the door. When I reached the street, it was dark and deserted. The Provost Marshall, responding to my outcry, put forth a search, but naught was found of Sunfish. Anyway, his duties are done, and his authority transferred to another. He said he was leaving for Canada. If we are to trouble ourselves, it would be his successor that we must locate. I believe Sunfish had finished his work, otherwise he would not have disclosed himself, even to saving my life."

"Let us dispatch the business on hand. Then, after this meeting, Lieutenant, we shall speak again. Gentlemen, as you see on the wall, General Hand has posted a large sketch of the Indian Country west of

New York, and on it is shown the Susquehanna River as it drains the lands of the Seneca southerly into Pennsylvania. You will note our sketch includes a slice of the Ohio Country west and north of Fort Pitt. Far to the north we have placed the Ontario. This rectangle represents Fort Niagara.

"As you look, sirs, you see we have empty spaces. And that is I why you are here, to debate and decide what should be included. Our plan, as said, is to penetrate to the heart of the Indian settlements and, the venture to be favorable, to capture Fort Niagara. Some urge, as does Lafayette, that with Burgoyne defeated, we should invade Canada." The General continued, alluding to Arnold's failure in '75-'76 to take Quebec, "You, Captain Boyd, too well know the importance attached to settling the frontier. It had to wait until it was within our ability. Before I excuse myself, there's venison stew coming. And brandy. We live a bit better here, eat more generously than the style to which we have had to accommodate ourselves." Smiles appeared. "Never have we had a healthier army, auguring well for our ambitions. We are at a turning point upward in our fortunes. Gentlemen, I leave you with General Hand to hold the chair. I have duties. Brady, we will converse further when this meeting ends. I want to talk spies." All stood as he left.

Following the meal Hand consulted a list of subjects. The meeting gathered momentum. Boyd presented his facts on the Owegy or Shenango, a north branch of the Susquehanna in New York which leads down from Lake Otsego. "This is a way for our troops to come down from the north against the principal settlements of the Seneca," he explained. "Likewise the Seneca warriors go up it to raid the New York towns whenever they are mindful to assist their Mohawk cousins. They would gather at Onaquaga, now in ruins."

After some debate between Hunter and Hand, the two agreed only a Glouchester type boat carrying two or three tons, of low draught, could be used going north from East Town to Teaoga. Hand had transported horses and cattle between those two locations in peacetime, but only in the high tide season, between the breaking of the ice and to the middle of May when the Susquehanna began to drop.

They discussed roads. Where supplies could not be moved by water, roads would have to be built or widened. At places these were hardly more than a hunter's trace or a path marked by a tree blazed by an axe. "Will the country admit our transportation of artillery?" That question touched off debate. Cannon in the wilderness? Cannon would be an encumbrance going overland and their weight, if placed aboard boats, would make these difficult to handle. Hand settled the argument. "Washington is adamant. He states, 'A recruit thinks his musket heavy, but he carries it. A general cannot think, because of their weight, to throw away his cannon.' There will be cannon, gentlemen. The savage will be in mortal sweat, unnerved by the noise." It was settled. Colonel Proctor would carry a mix of artillery, light cohorns to six-pounders.

The final topic was the staging of supplies, Colonel Hunter being asked to comment. "Where would there be a proper place, or places for magazines, Colonel?"

"Why not have Fort Augusta as a grand magazine until you place a depot upstream, say at Teaoga? We could use Forty Fort and Wyalusing as interval supply centers as the troops move past these locations. I would say use Fort Augusta for collecting supplies from farms in Cumberland, Berks, and Lancaster counties, and retain Forty Fort for cargoes brought from the Jerseys by way of East Town."

Hand reviewed the total distance from Augusta to Teaoga, one hundred and sixty miles. "And you would stage your supplies from Augusta to Forty Fort, then to Wyalusing, and finally these to reach Teaoga? How far apart are these intermediate places?"

Brady responded, "Approximately sixty-mile jumps, sir. Only forty from Wyalusing to Teaoga."

Hand liked the distances. "Convenient!"

A drummer just beyond the window began beating a long roll. The General's Life Guard, all tall, brawny men, was assembling. Washington reentered the room, the meeting concluded. Casual conversation stopped. He studied the figures representing distances. "Such is our hope, gentlemen. I congratulate you and am grateful. An aide will escort you to your quarters. As for you and I, Lieutenant Brady, let's have our chat about spies."

The General ordered tea for the Lieutenant and himself, then asked for the door to be closed. "To think," he said, "tea is blamed for this war. If it had the effect on Bostonians to move them toward Independence, then - by convoluted reasoning - for the cause of Liberty I shall drink it till my bladder has its own rebellion, and in that moment of relief I shall think of England's Prime Minister, with the greatest of compliments saying, 'To Lord North!' Now, as to the web of spies in Philadelphia, your map, though destroyed, has been of great service to us. Because of it we have learned Sunfish, a spy we have long sought, is a blackamoor. This narrows our search. We have people among the French in Canada who may find him before he does further damage. As for Cundiff, by your dispatching him to his Maker, you have restrained whatever disagreeable business that Tory ring was set upon doing. There remains the question about Wallis to whom we entrusted so much. What part has he in this murder plot?"

"None as far as attempt on my life. He is not of that style."

"Have you other reason to be suspicious of him?"

"I can answer that in three parts. I do not believe him to be a traitor in the truest sense of that word. Nor could I, during our time together, think of him as such when by your order it was an endorsement of his character. Too, in preparing the map, he was most helpful. Thus, were there fault in the map put there by design, I was not of mind to search for it. It was not until later, and I will get to it, that I was warned the map contained an error. In retrospect, were I to assay the man, I would say were he anything, he is a closet Tory as are so many others. The difference is he has been pressed into a task not of his choosing, not therefore a spy by intent, but a non sympathizer. His tilt is Tory and he saw an advantage to be had."

"Well stated," said the General.

Then Levi touched on something with which the General was familiar, Washington having been involved in land companies. "Secondly, I think we have put Wallis into a most uncomfortable box, he a land holder with properties facing the Indian people who live at Muncy. Unlike those living in the Wyoming Valley where deep hatred exists between the Connecticut settlers and the original Indian inhabitants, and who had no bridges of friendship by which to reconcile differences, Wallis has such bridges in his Seneca connections. In the past he had a romance with Queen Esther Montour, a French and Indian woman by whom he had a child. He has deep ties that motivate him. He does not seek harm, but rather seeks to protect those those who give him no harm, as suggested in this campaign. He is an avowed Quaker. Mainly they oppose war. Call them Tories if you will."

The General and Levi sipped tea in silence. "Are you saying he is without sin?"

"No, sir. He is. I do suspect he may have some part in acquiring information for the British since he rubs up against just about every general and official in Philadelphia. But so do others who fall in and out of suspicion. We cannot hang a man on suspicion. But, in all candor, I believe there will be no more harm, if there has been any, either from him or his associates."

"Why?"

"Because last night I became engaged to his daughter whose mother is the Seneca-French woman Esther Montour. Margy warned me Wallis had introduced error into the map. He doesn't know about our engagement yet. But surely once he learns we are pledged, it will be to her he will answer in his every move, if I know Margy."

"Lieutenant Brady, for two reasons I find merit your response. For one, a member of the Montour family and I enjoy a friendship dated back to the Forbes War. Andrew Montour, uncle to your betrothed, was my companion and translator when I was a colonial colonel. We were sent west in a less than successful effort to build a fort where today stands Fort Pitt. My second reason for sparing Wallis arises out of your being a student of nature. Weddings do much to change men from their ways. as this certainly shall with respect to our Quaker. Congratulations to you and to your bride to be. I am giving you your wedding present beforehand, exactly what a lieutenant in your circumstance would best appreciate. "He dipped a quill into the ink stand, then quickly wrote and handed the Lieutenant a thirty day furlough. Levi was shocked. "For two purposes, this," the General explained. "One is for your personal comfort. Marry her before the month of April is half done as I may need you thereafter elsewhere. You are this moment appointed Chief Guide to the expedition. The second purpose is my wish Philadelphia know you are betrothed, that you have visibility. It will give your future father-in-law a case of leprosy insofar as any Tory friends visiting him. Be on your way, now, Brady. Let only love be in your heart. Draw from the camp paymaster what little he can spare. Take quarters here tonight; and tomorrow, the roads permitting, try to travel with less excitement than you had coming here. Stay wary." Then the General did what few generals do, he rose from his chair and warmly shook Levi's hand. 'T was the quality that endeared the General to all.

A more dazed lieutenant there was not. Chief Guide! Thirty day furlough! Marry her! Marry her! Let it snow all night, he would be on that road to Philadelphia!

After Levi had gone, the man with the three silver stars lifted and drank the remainder of his now cold tea. The General was troubled, more so than he admitted to his lieutenant. He knew this about Wallis. Wallis had befriended the Continental Army, yes. When in the Great Valley, at Valley Forge, at the lowest moment in the fortunes of the Revolution, Wallis had saved the Army from dissolution through starvation. The man had used his personal credit to provide beef cattle for those emaciated scarecrows. There lingered yet in the ears of the Commander in Chief the repetitive chant, "No, meat. No meat. No meat." Too, Wallis when recruited by his fellow Quaker General Mifflin, had proven himself an able spy upon Howe, helpful in small matters. The General mused, 'How can one provide death by the cord to such a man, even were his appearances of guilt proven?' The General now knew Howe all the while was using Wallis for his own purposes. Howe, like himself, had been at this game of supplying his agents with inconsequential information to enable them to be above suspicion and to get on with matters of importance. Wallis was a double spy. "Deucedly clever," said Washington, aloud. "Samuel Wallis is for Samuel Wallis, this is for sure." Without the falsified map, Washington thought, no case could be made, in any event. And there were other reasons. Wallis was so well regarded by Philadelphia's wealthy society of which he was a member, and was held in equally high esteem among the Society of Friends that his arrest would inflame a wide band of citizens, with this to further fracture a badly divided Philadelphia. This city needed healing, being the capital of a fragile new government. He asked himself, 'Should I bury this incident in silence?' With these thoughts taking shape in his mind the General reviewed the possibility of further subversion. 'Perhaps I had best take another quiet look at him, provided he has not already flown.' The General summoned his Chief of Intelligence, Major John Clark.

Chapter XXII

A QUICKENING SEA

It was the day Samuel Wallis wished to be abed early, his trip to be long tomorrow. At Cantwell's Bridge, a place where privateers hid within the coves of a nearby twisting Indian stream, this known by an equally tongue twisting name of Appoquinimimink Creek, he would pass Stevens the duplicate map. It would be carried by sea-transportation to New York, and from there conveyed to no less a person than Governor General Haldimand. It was a conciliatory gesture toward this conceited fellow whose pride had been wounded by his being displaced as foremost in the nest of spies. Stevens' bitterness, Wallis realized, needed assuaging. This ranked as an important assignment, and as one of trust. The intolerable nature of Stevens which signaled an inability to deal with shortcomings of any kind, be these his own, might be softened, so thought Wallis. At 6 A.M. as Wallis walked to his office he did not know that Stevens by now had in spectacular manner confronted his own failure, having cornered himself in a tobacco storage building. There he kept gunpowder for some fancied thought of blowing up the rebel Congress when in session in the State House. Unknown to Wallis, Stevens was at that moment turning himself into motes of nothing, leaving behind only a leg in a boot.

Hooper's noon appointment to meet Wallis was to be Wallis's last. Hooper had information Wallis wished.

"Sam," said the always affable Hooper, "I have a few small facts about the man Cundiff enlisted without your authorization; but perhaps Stevens had beforehand knowledge. His name is Roxbury. My source of information, himself a drunken seaman, chooses to call this man Roxbury as he himself can best be described, a half-crocked bastard.

312

'T was stated that Roxbury, and here I use the language of my informant, 'should have a broom stuck up his ass and his fucking tool cut off and stuffed in his ear.' I take it Roxbury is rotten from his teeth to his genitals, and is in want for swilling and fornicating money, in that order perpetually. He, as I am told, knows how to shoot, and when one of his intoxicated friends, in an obscene gesture dropped his britches, and pulled his cheeks apart to show his contempt for Roxbury, Roxbury plucked out his pistol and shot him through his brown spot. I take it that the man was recruited because the dwarf has special doings, private business which he seeks to keep from you, for which this fellow is needed."

"That being true, Cundiff then has come to the end of his usefulness."

"He may have already. The public houses buzz, at least at the Coach and Horses, with a happening on the road toward Middlebrook, a few miles beyond the Delaware. Two bodies were found in the snow, buzzards in the air marking their separate locations. A party of military was seen riding from the scene. One riderless horse was discovered nearby, a black-as-midnight stallion, like Cundiff's, though there must be many riders with similar animals."

Wallis retained his own thoughts about this event, that it somehow tied into Brady's departure. He let the matter rest there, too tired to think.

Hooper, sensing his friend was not in the mood for small talk, confined himself to this brief exchange, then left. Once home, Wallis timed the distance he must travel. He set his time piece to waken at 4 A.M., and prior to retiring carefully arranged his outer garments. This gave him time for tea and toast, and ablutions. With morning's arrival, he donned his Greenfield boots, bundled himself into his greatcoat, fitted his snug beaver hat to head, and placed a scarf over his hat and ears, its ends knotted beneath his chin. He reassured himself that the map was properly seated in his greatcoat. Then he put on his riding gloves. Accoutered for blustery weather, in the John Elliot looking glass he was impressed by his own appearance, somewhat formidable with all the wrappings. He patted the pistol in his pocket. Let no man trifle with him. He would break his trip home, staying overnight at a tavern in vicinity of the convoluted stream with the Indian name. He would pass over the Schuylkill at its lower ford. So were his plans.

Not permitting another moment's delay, leaving by the kitchen door he took the path to the stable. He lifted the bar, hearing the whinny of his sorrel mare. It had been saddled by his orders. She was a four-beat gait animal of steady stamina, capable of maintaining a four to eight mile per hour average, though this pace - in the present circumstance - was wishful thought. Wallis calculated five miles per hour. The weather was bitter and the cold attacked his fingers despite the gloves, as he rode through the streets, these glazed and treacherous and all but deserted. It was a terrible time to be traveling, but the saber of necessity, more sharp than the inclement weather, led him on. He would have the last of the moon, though at times the snowfall all but blotted his vision. He weighed loss of time, but decided to break the journey to rest his horse and refresh himself. The long hours were wearing. As daylight faded into darkness he began to realize that at Cantwell's Bridge finding Stevens might be a problem. Where along this darkened, deserted shoreline? Somewhere tied to the wharf pilings he might discover the ship's gig or cutter waiting. Darkness and inclement weather slowed his search. By this time, he reasoned, Stevens would be impatient, cursing Wallis's tardiness.

His thoughts turned to his suspicion about the despicable Cundiff that, if truly he was one of the dead men in the snow, and Brady the other, might this argue for caution? Was this map a death ticket? In the least it was as an omen that in this dark and lonely stretch of the shore there could be another intended victim. He himself by Stevens' hand? Who else knew Brady's departure plan and might find advantage in his own demise?

He took stock of his surroundings. In the darkness barrels became waiting assassins. All was not tidy. This nasty night and Hooper's news produced growing distaste for the present business. Oh, so gladly would he be rid of this monstrous fold of paper in his pocket. Yes, the very soul within him cried out, "Be done!" As with Stevens, the uncertainties of this game which could be deadly made it no longer a challenge, but an unpleasantness. He looked about but could see no tethered horse, either the horse wandered or Stevens yet on the road.

Half-frozen, Wallis tied his horse to a post on the waterfront, spread a blanket over the animal's back and floundered through a snow bank onto the white-crusted boards of the wharf. He scanned the black pit of the harbor, seeking a telltale light, or a bulking shadow. Nary a gleam, nary a change in the night's texture encouraged him. Heavy droplets clung to his eyelashes. He brushed them away, also spanking the collar of flakes seeping down his neck. He waded through drifted snow and walked to the end of a second wharf. Below he heard the splash of an oar! A small boat edged from its hiding under the dock. He leaned over the water, waving his hand, exclaiming so that those who may not have seen him, nor heard his footfalls, would not pass him in the dark. "Pox!" said someone from the shadows. "We are numb, waiting you." To others, obviously inferiors, the same voice spat, "Give him a hand, bully boys. Jump down, sir, we'll catch you. Quickly now, or we'll all hang high, if not from rebel's gallows, from our own Captain's yardarm." Obeying the voice, Wallis sat down on the wharf and slid from the boards into nothingness. He was caught by horny hands which guided him onto a slat seat.

"Am I expected on ship?" asked Wallis, puzzled, not seeing who he addressed.

The same voice chuckled. "Who else? You have a mad humor."

Wallis fell silent. Apparently Stevens preferred warm quarters aboard ship and sent back a navy crew to fetch him aboard with the map, rather than stand the discomfort of the piers. Breaking from the pier, with utmost stealth the crew plied their oars, the gig bobbing with each swelling wave. The sea was quickening, and with it the snow. It was a night of sheeting droplets and blackness. Wallis dimly discerned the nearest sailor hard-tugging to best the tide. For ten, maybe fifteen minutes, they crept forward. "Now! Ship your oars!" said the boat lieutenant, and uncovered a lantern, shielding its light with a tarpaulin, not to attract eyes of observers on shore. "There she lies, more off port than I calculated." In response to the wink of his lantern there came a flash at sea. They pulled on the new bearing until, towering dead ahead, looming toward them at a perilous rate, hoving in the seas was a big black hull. The officer cursed, then in a calm voice had his men back oars and, when it appeared collision would be inevitable, had them fend these against the ship. Oars and oarlocks were snapped by the impact. The boat yawed, took water, then skittered half the length of the frigate. A coiled line cascaded upon them, followed by a second and third. They fastened tight. From the same invisible heights a Jacob's ladder drifted down, its rungs lit by a dull red lantern held topside. Up this swaying, hempen stairway scrambled Wallis.

"Welcome aboard," said a man in what appeared to be a commodore's hat. The man's silhouette and the timber of his voice suggested the rank. In the gloom Wallis saw the officer's arm stiffen in salute. "There's light and whiskey in my cabin; come below, sir." The same ship's lantern lit them down.

The efficiently furnished compartment, to his surprise, held no Stevens. "Where is he?" Wallis asked, bewildered.

"Who, pray?"

"Stevens. The one for whom I have the map."

The ship's captain seemed bewildered. "Are you not Stevens? Who, then, have I lifted aboard?"

"Plague on Stevens. He's late. I am Samuel Wallis. Here is the map to have been delivered to his hand. Just put me ashore and take him aboard. By now he must be on the pier."

At that instant an excited junior officer hurled himself into the cabin. "Captain! Running lights one point off port bow!"

Rapidly the Captain gave his orders, and as an afterthought to Wallis said, "If they spike us in Delaware River, God in his mercy alone will put you safe ashore." With that the Captain dashed topside and Wallis, beginning to view the unfolding events as preposterous and unreal, followed up the ladder. In the whirling flakes he could see little. The periphery of his vision was blocked by the frigate's out-billowing sails. The men in the rigging responded to their officers who shouted orders through cupped hands. Wallis felt the ship gather strength and labor with the waves. The wind, ramming from behind, harped in the shrouds. He braced himself, clinging to a halyard as a comber slashed over the deck. As they picked up momentum, the darkness of the night was halved by the suggestion of dawn. Through the night Wallis was not the only one who prayed that the weather, foul as it was, might turn worse, hiding them from pursuit.

It would be ironic, he thought, if his own bottom, the CHANCE, requisitioned and commissioned as a privateer by the Committee on Safety, was the vessel forcing him out to sea. Wallis's sloop CHANCE, among others, had been fitted with cannon and sent to prowl the seas. It would be no match against this formidable warship.

The intruder was not to be shaken. Twenty minutes passing, then another twenty, the mysterious intruder raised to port. She was gone again, reappearing abeam. "Hard starboard," growled the Captain, striving for sail to windward, and signaling his gunnery officer. His words were almost lost in the gale. The ship yawed as the steersman complied. "Rot you! As she goes! Steady!" Matches lit, pieces trained, the gunners waited for the wheel-master, the wind, the angle of the deck, and luck to coincide. The snow -drenched ships were closing.

Wallis's dinner flooded in his throat; he heaved unnoticed, to have the wind fling his own vomit back into his face. Weakly, he braced himself, expecting a salvo, only to find the Captain's grimaces changed to smiles! Instead of decks splintered and men smashed, instead of torn halyards, and limbs bedabbled with gore, the crews of both ships were huzzaing, the sea-lantern at each masthead disclosing the Royal Jack. His Majesty's Ships sailed briefly side by side, then separated.

Chapter XXIII

SPY WITH NO SHADOW

If Samuel Wallis fretted as he rode toward Cantwell's Bridge, once aboard ship and past the Delaware capes, with the safety of the ocean passing beneath the bow of the frigate, he regained a sense of his importance in having served the Crown. The Union Jack overhead whipping in the breeze held assurance he could not find in the flag of a new nation struggling to survive. And the might of Britain, represented by this ship-o'-war ruling the waves, visibly confirmed to him that, in its opulence, this world-powerful Empire could and would reward men like himself. Caught up in the deception of his own importance to the outcome of the war, in his obstinate belief of the might of the Crown he could not bring himself to see that England's war was unraveling, France upon the seas. If ever he had felt doubt, gazing seaward into the wash of the tiller, he could laugh at the runnels of indecision which had disturbed his self-confidence. He almost wished he could mount to the crow's nest from where a man could command, at least with his eye, the expanding horizons. This ship beating north had been summoned for his handiwork, the map. Wallis, nurturing manorial ambitions, conceived for himself the award of lands west of the Sinnemahoney, north of Pine Creek and east of the West Branch, granted to him by the grateful Crown. With these idle thoughts he threw off his depression. 'Aye,' thought Wallis, 'needlessly I have reproached myself about the deaths at Forty Fort. 'T was their fated course as is mine equally preordained.'

A naval craft being what it is, and a rough sea shaping up, Wallis retreated to the cabin. The tossing of the ship quickened, with crests of foam splashing against the closed porthole. He tried to read from a book on the Captain's desk but found the jiggle of the lamp impossible. Morning's breakfast he forewent, his stomach out of sorts from the heavy

318

roll of the vessel, though toward break of day the seas quieted. If he thought he could clear his head by a stroll about deck, this was denied. The biting air of morning drove him back to the warm cabin. Wallis made no further appearance topside until well after sun-up. Even then he found a frosty reception. The Lieutenant charged with the morning's watch twice passed him without speaking. On the third occasion, being stopped by Wallis and asked how many knots they were making, the officer frigidly replied, "Eight, sir!" Wallis tried to expand the conversation, and with patronizing familiarity inquired as to the number of men aboard. With equal brevity the officer assured him the ship was in full complement. He thereafter excused himself.

'Evidently,' thought Wallis, 'the man's afraid of me. He senses that I am a person of some substance. 'T is respect which stiffens him.' Thinking and viewing himself as such, he walked the deck in aloof seclusion. Likewise, the crew gave him privacy. Sailors mending a rope became motionless as he passed. A crew member humming a dreary chantey, stopped. Another, the wheelsman, when Wallis passed him, stared sightlessly ahead. Rather abruptly a group of seamen ceased conversation as he came near. Upon his retirement from their station, their discussion resumed in more subdued tones. There was a convulsion of laughter as he drew further off. At once he realized there was an additional peculiarity to his position, one which he did not appreciate. Since he was a guest or visitor aboard, he could not take part in the exercises and duties of the ship, nor refuge in its society. He found himself alone. This solitude began to bore him. Aye, he would be received with congenial deference, in the company of better men.

In the late afternoon of the second day at sea Wallis, being bundled against the cold, was taking a turn on deck. He stood for several minutes, clasping the rail, seeing the waves part before the bow, appearing like so many white cuirasses of a host of knights, as they fell to an aside. The captain, a man in his fifties who might have been an admiral but for a blunt and outspoken manner, came stamping across the deck. Hungering for conversation, Wallis gestured toward him. "Good day to you," said Wallis, to be surprised by the officer's response.

"I would not make capital of your misfortune, sir,"

"What misfortune?" replied mystified Wallis.

"Well, sir, in error we have you aboard. Yesterday you said your absence could lead to your condemnation, the rebels to know you gone, the fabric of your efforts against their beliefs, your 'plot', if you will, to stand in exposure. Further, I understand you to believe your very life shall be involved in danger should you return. For a fact we have taken you off into exile."

"'T will not be for long, then," easily responded Wallis. "This war will soon be over. Until the full tide of British victory, I shall ride out my time either in Canada or England, my name not unknown."

"You are indeed a man of hope and conviction, both as to this war, and as to England's welcome."

"And you, sir, how do you stand?"

"As to this war, oh, we will make a solution of it. England always does. But, as to yourself, sir, with our country divided, some for, some against the pursuit of this war, you will not find the enthusiasm you expect, or the heart in many to continue this struggle with you colonials. There is no clear course to lead to a quick victory. In more ways than one you are at sea, your journey longer than you think. What, therefore, is there of good fortune to come of this, for a man in your position?"

Wallis would not be dragged down by the man's pessimism. "Perhaps financial gain, perhaps a title, perhaps who knows."

With repugnance the Captain looked away. 'Sir, you have an ambitious regard for your services. You seek honor and money. That is why I call it a misfortune. You have been a prosperous man from all appearances, and now you depend upon the nebulous recompense of Parliament. To play with words, your course is set on a current which will sooner strand you than put you in an easy channel. You will be in low tide and mean rocks, Mr. Wallis. You shall be lucky to come off with a whole skin. M'lords will not float you. As for my opinion, the business of yours has no honor in it; honor cannot be compounded where there is none. There is clamour against this war, and not reward. A whole skin is all you have, and that's more than the many who have been taken under."

"You talk like a Whig," disgustedly responded Wallis, half turning his back. He could not silence the Captain and regretted engaging him in conversation.

"Whig sentiment it may be. Those in the Service, be they admirals or generals, are as divided as to the carrying on a fratricidal argument as is our Parliamentary leaders."

"Then it is those who voice opposition, who show no vigor, who protract this war, who are responsible for the delay in winning it! Like yourself!"

"God pity you, sorry rascal that you are, reducing yourself to slanderous accusation. In the extremes of your affairs you shift your own dishonor upon others. I will not brook it, sir!"

"Captain," said Wallis, angrily, "I shall report you."

"Speak as you wish of me. You are an informer, a spy. Aye, you have privilege aboard this ship, sir, but not my respect. I shall wash the deck where you stood, once done with you." The Captain turned on heel. Wallis remained topside looking westerly toward the coast from the port rail. Pivoting, the declining sun now at his back, it painted images of the frigate's masts and rail onto the deck boards, but there was no silhouette of him, a phenomenon of which he was unaware, he deep in reflection. Had be noticed, he would have recalled an Indian superstition that a warrior with no semblance of an image was a man destined for oblivion, a dead man without comfort and without prospect of a marked grave.

Chapter XXIV

INTERLUDE

For two months the Free Company had toasted their feet in front of a fire within the barracks of the fort they had constructed in the white wastes of Wyoming Valley. Spalding's veterans stood watch over a trackless valley. Lately returned from Fort Laurens, Murphy, French and Baldwin had exhausted the credulity of their companions with their preposterous tales of bravery.

In their frayed deerskin the trio of stubble chinned non-commissioned officers swore the Continental Army was coming onto the Frontier! They had proof of it at Fort Pitt, which they had visited while returning from Fort Laurens. "Aye," said Murphy, "we shall not fight alone, come spring. Pitt bustles with troops. They talk of resuming where we left off."

"And," added Baldwin, "by the size of things at Pitt, it's to be more than just another march. 'T is a plan in which we will be hitting the Indian lands and British forts in a tied-together effort. Our two main forts, Pitt and Augusta will be our assembling places, the Pitt people to go up the Allegheny and the Ohio and our people to be the largest division, we to repeat our Hartley march, this time to really go at 'em!"

Captain Spalding was skeptical. A double prong assault on two forts? At the moment he was more concerned by the precariousness of his position, the reality of his fragile hold of this valley. He had considered withdrawing by spring from the valley, fearing the Indians might overwhelm him by successive and increasingly heavy attacks. Yet, were an expedition coming, an advance fort such as this would be an eye on the Indians, a holding position against deeper incursions until arrival of the army. "'Why do you believe all this is to happen?" Spalding asked his returned sergeants.

"'T isn't simple to put in words, Captain," answered Tim. "You're conscious we came home without our Lieutenant. We're here and he isn't, and that tells a lot."

"Come to your point?"

"Well, sir, when we got back to Fort McIntosh, first off Lieutenant Brady was brought before Colonel Dan Brodhead who told him to make tracks for Headquarters of the Continental Army. We asked ourselves why, and we come up with but one answer, there's nobody other than him who has been all the way through the Longhouse and lived to tell of it, except maybe those who are Tories. Inside his head is a picture of the paths that lead through their country and of the defenses of Fort Niagara. It's plain to see, the Susquehanna which leads up to the southern door of the Seneca lands, and Fort Niagara which guards both these lands and the lands to the west, are all connected. We're to see action up the Susquehanna, lots of it!"

"The blow for Libertie!" exclaimed French. "Voila! From these moment I despise death!" In his loose fitting clothing and gaunt face French did not cut a figure supportive of his bravado.

It was a hope to buoy Spalding's men through the long watches and endless days, and enough to decide Spalding to hold out, despite present conditions. An expedition against the Seneca! A march up the river and then westerly following the Forbidden Path! 'Pray this comes to pass,' thought Captain Spalding, looking at the northern woods. Sooner this hope than envisioning the Indians to pass again down this bone-scattered valley. He wondered if he would live to see those troops. There would be bloody blows and teeth spitting, come spring. The Indians would come by the hundreds against this fort, to pay him for having sat through the winter thumbing his nose at them. Pray for the expedition! Pray it came first, although this was unlikely. Spalding put on an appearance of carefree ease. It was not so. He went about the fort, slapping the backs of his men, catching their grins in their assumption an expedition would be marching through the valley. Behind such a barricade of hope Captain Spalding's company waited. Spring was yet a long way off. For the while the winter was their ally.

Imprisoned within the triple walls of boredom, wooden palisades, and snow, the Free Company men stood on their ramparts thinking and talking of the expedition until, as a topic, it was stale. With little else to talk about and nothing to do, their close quarters brought them into low spirits and made them irritable. At first Spalding invented duties for them to perform, gathering firewood of which they soon had a mound, strengthening the walls, with this amply done; and, despite never a moccasin print to be found, constant forays until the purpose was perceived for what it was, no more than a busy movement. By degrees the soldiers grew restive, even to sentry duty. Spalding's authority over them, an elected authority, virtually was at end. His militia commission carried scant powers. Wisely Captain Spalding waited. Spring would correct matters. Spring would uncover the bones of the dead; and by spring his men would be damned good soldiers again.

As the snows turned to slush and the forest wakened to the warming air, magical changes occurred. Correctly Spalding had predicted the men would bestir themselves knowing the coming season would summon the Indian. They welcomed any encounter, fatal though it could be, as an exciting relief. They talked nonsense, of going out and provoking a 'complication'. After the dull winter, in contrast sweet would be the courting of violence, musical the cry of the savage. Unexpectedly it happened and almost too suddenly.

With the thaw the Seneca exploded against Spalding's walls, two hundred and fifty of them, their enfilading fire making untenable the firing steps of the structure, save along the parapet side which flanked the river. The overwhelming numbers, the paralyzing suddenness of the attack nearly smothered their resistance. Wrapped in smoke, dinned at by voracious Seneca, at first the soldiers cowered, panic stricken, than sprang to life. Men answered the fire, and fell. Men tried to climb the steps, and died. Sergeant Baldwin tumbled to the ground, falling from the steps that led to the firing platform when the man climbing the steps ahead of him was hit and toppled, knocking Baldwin down. A warrior ascended the wall and Pence cleaved off the man's wrist, then died himself, he shot in the temples. Pence's gigantic body hung over the wall. Struck again and again by bullets, it crashed to the ground outside. Despite losses, the soldiers rallied. They began to return a brisk fire. Murphy, ignoring the patter of lead sweeping over the palisade, climbed to a perch atop the wall. With deliberate aim, he shot down eight Seneca, two with his double gun, and with guns fed up to him. It broke the momentum of the attack. As the Indian fire fell off, those in the fort sensed the enemy was regrouping, again to storm the walls. Spalding gave his orders. Every man would be at his loophole. They were not to be surprised this time. Whooping, the Indians launched their rush for the outer palisade.

The action was quick and bitter; the foremost warriors were impaled upon the planted stakes, and that many again were laid to the ground by bullets from the wall. The remainder scattered, some to flee, some to attempt recovery of the bodies of fallen friends. In a maneuver completely unorthodox the Free Company jumped from the wall and killed those Indians who were bringing off the dead. Then treading over the dead and dying they pursued the flying foe who, met by reinforcements at the woods, suddenly rallied. With a return of prudence the Connecticut soldiers retreated. Sam French, last man into the fort, slammed the gate virtually in the faces of the enemy's swiftest, Dry Elk and Little Bones. This pair of braves, finding themselves shut out and rifles being inserted in the loopholes, before the deadly weapons could be brought to bear, zigzagged for the river, it being nearer than the woods, and dove into the icy stream, bullets chopping the water. Whether by hugging the bank they effected their escape downstream, or riddled and waterlogged went under, a howl of dismay came from the woods. For the moment, the battle rested. Night was approaching. The Indians encamped and built cook fires beyond reach of the fort's rifles.

If ever Murphy felt himself hemmed in by trouble, it was this instant. He but wished his good nature companion Levi Brady was with him now. In tight spots Levi could always make them seem tighter, then miraculously blunder out of them. Intuition told the sharpshooter the Indians would make their all-out effort at dawn; he knew the fort would be lost, were it not reinforced during the small hours of night. He asked his companions to put up a distracting fire.

Tim slipped over the wall, made his stealthy way to the Susquehanna, and swam to the far shore. His teeth chattered from the cold water, but it did not stop him from his swift endurance run. By his reasoning a detachment which sat at Wilkes-Barre would be willing to enter the fort, provided they were shown how to come in. Murphy, who knew the disposition of the enemy's surrounding force, and knew that the Indians kept no watch on the river, under cover of the last of darkness led the Wilkes-Barre garrison upstream. In utter silence, abreast of the fort, they swam over. Captain Franklin's twenty seven, by Spalding's calculation, rectified the odds. Franklin's Company, too, was armed with Kentucky rifles. News that Franklin brought also bolstered their spirit. The Wilkes-Barre Captain had received a dispatch from Fort Augusta, confirming Murphy's story, that an expedition would come up the Susquehanna! Franklin displayed to Spalding the marching orders for both their companies, they to join the Army at Middlebrook Encampment. The two Susquehanna companies were to act as guides, scouts, and instructors for the troops to be engaged in the frontier warfare! The militia was to march at once.

Sarcastically, Spalding reacted to the 'at once' portion of the message. "We'll do that. 'T is a very excellent suggestion, that we leave. The thought charms my ears and my sensibilities. All we must do is discover our fortunes with those fellows outside. Now, sir, let me propose how we shall get ourselves from here into Middlebrook, or into Heaven or Hell, whichever!"

The newcomers, having wiped their firelocks dry, were told of the next move. At dawn the gate was unbarred and the reinforced command sallied forth. Two minutes later the advance was converted into a precipitous retreat; the entire Seneca Nation seemed to rise from concealment. Only because the Indians were unprepared for this bold sally did the soldiers escape the converging foe. For dear life the Connecticut command sprinted homeward, slammed the gate, and at the loopholes stood panting, each man holding onto his sides from pain. "Well, that didn't work," said Spalding.

Tiring of this grotesque comedy of 'now you chase me' the garrison squatted inside resigned to siege. Providently it was of short duration. Their display of numbers had affected the Indians. "Ata! The whites have mysteriously multiplied!" Rounding up the cattle, with surly gestures and truculent remarks the Seneca faded into the woods, shooing the lowing herd before them. If they could not barbecue the garrison, they would their cattle.

On the next day, their dead buried, and litters improvised for the wounded, the two companies of militia abandoned their forts on the frontier, and set out for Middlebrook. Pence would be missed. It was a glorious day for marching. With springy step the contingent of riflemen set forth to join the invincible expedition. They marched from the valley knowing they would return, widening the frontier and the prospects for ultimate peace in this land.

Chapter XXV

WITH FLAGS, DRUMS, AND FIFES

The advent of warm weather had brushed the snows from the streets of Philadelphia. General Benedict Arnold, having resigned his command of the City but continuing in residence, on April 8th was married to Margaret, daughter of influential Edward Shippen. 'Peggy' had been the toast of British officers during General Howe's occupancy. Of far less notice to the City was the marriage of another Margaret, 'Margy' Wallis, daughter of the absent Samuel Wallis, to Lieutenant Leviticus 'Levi' Brady, the newly designated Chief Guide to the Continental forces gathering for the expedition to come. The marriage of Levi to Margy, while the announcement was lost under the shuffle of events, namely the springtime preparations for war against the Longhouse, as an event was to be celebrated in a modest and befitting way. Under a canopy of drawn sabers provided by Carberry's former unit, the First City Cavalry Troop, in attendance witnessing the nuptials there being Sergeant Murphy, Sergeant Baldwin and Corporal French; and also present were a host of officers from the Encampment. In this manner the handsome couple were properly married and thereafter driven the short distance to the seclusion of the Wallis home where they would spend their brief honeymoon. Mr. Africa, who handled the reigns of the carriage, by his smile and by his motions, his elbows jumping, reflected his happiness about the occasion. One of the bridesmaids was the beautiful widow Rachael Greenacre, betrothed to Corporal French. She attracted many eyes.

In this period, when hope was rising, when the counties of central Pennsylvania were being made aware of the multifold needs of an expedition, with dark humor it could be said all boded well. In a pig's eye. On the frontier, spurs jangling a column of horsemen swept from the woods, aiming to relieve a beleaguered outpost. A half-hour later thirty-three scalps lay on a blanket. To lesser degree individuals alone in the field, and families fell to the tomahawk. Aye, sweet conjecture of victory, brave promise of succor, these thoughts were coming too late. Men continued to fall in ambush, Captain Menniger of Fort Muncy by hidden guns. The bloody, God-be-damned war on the frontier was going forward, the settlers neither reinforced nor the Indians contained.

For Levi one piece of news reduced him to tears. Lighthorse Carberry, that marvelous companion, his counterpart in many adventures, the immortal Carberry was dead. After their chance Philadelphia meeting, he had been sent to Fort Pitt with dispatches. Upon his return trip while accompanied by a sergeant, a few miles from that western bastion he had been fatally wounded by Indians in ambush, these led by Simon Girty. His sergeant managed to bring the Captain away, he soon to expire. Carberry was interred in a forest grave, with a detachment from the fort participating in the burial. The rush of events was to keep Levi too busy to mourn, yet his perils were the same as had been Carberry's, he now more conscious of his own vulnerability. He felt his mortality.

In New Jersey the State militia would take over the guard post held by the New Jersey Continental Line who were to move from their encampment by regiments and march directly to East Town. Elsewhere at Fort Pitt these was parallel activity. The ponderous enterprise had fewer delays than expected.

While ponderously the Army assembled, Levi as courier for the Commander in Chief clattered over distant roads, conscious of the wider path of blood, the ribbon of scarlet that lay across the frontier. Pistols in his holsters and knife tucked in the belt of his fringed hunting shirt, Levi rode through the vast stretches of forest, carrying confidential orders to General Clinton in New York and Colonel Van Schaick poised on the Mohawk border. But his first message was delivered to John Sullivan in Rhode Island, lawyer, first in rebellion, now Major General. He was to command the Expedition. The General instantly left Providence for the Middlebrook encampment. The forces were moving into position.

Among the busiest in preparation was Colonel Hooper, charged with purchasing and assembling more than 1,500 packhorses and sundry mounts. A fleet of riverboats were a building, an inland navy to carry the necessaries of the several thousand men going up-river, who would be joined by General Clinton's force coming south. In all a significant portion of Washington's Army would assault the Indian lodges. A detachment of pioneers already had been sent ahead, and had suffered casualties from Indians lying in wait as they with their axes went about the business of carving roads through the woods and bridging otherwise impassable swamps. Slowly, painfully the corduroy road extended itself.

Orders were issued to the Fourth and Eleventh Pennsylvania, the German Regiment, Morgan's Rifles, Schotts Rifle Corps, and the Light Horse, these to be in readiness. At Fort Schuyler eight rifle companies under Van Schaick were more than ready. Their ordnance was in firing order, knives honed thin, bullets poured and canteens filled. The 600 decried delay! They had been ready a year! And at Otsego Lake, which discharged its waters southerly to help create the Susquehanna, General Clinton assembled his troops. Clinton confided that 770 rangers were expected to join his battalion of 1,500 regulars; thereafter he would come downstream to meet Sullivan. At Fort Pitt, meanwhile, boats were being constructed to go up the Allegheny, these to be laden with supplies and a complement of 650 soldiers. In total some 6,000 men would fall in with the Expedition. Fully half, the very best of the Continental forces were to participate. Except for a guard on the Hudson and scattered forces to the South, the Army was forming for western action. The fate that awaited the Indian was as self evident as truth, and was as prophetical as the Bible.

To Sullivan who was absolutely faithful to Washington, yet inwardly seeing no glory and much chance for disaster during the conduct of this wilderness march, Washington gave assurances. "General, you will command one of the largest offensive forces in this war. Troops from five states will be marching under your banner. And, John, your staff shall not want for experienced officers." He ticked off their names. "Hand, Poor, Clinton and Maxwell, brigadier generals of known capability. You shall have twenty senior colonels, each deserving of a generalship. Congress has appropriated, as you know, a million dollars for your supplies and equipment. This should reveal the significance attached by that body to your enterprise. Moreover, your expedition captures the imagination of all Americans; it has awakened even the most torpid mind. In my view, John, we are a nation inhabiting a narrow coastal strip of a vast unexplored continent. We need to claim these lands which are yours to win. If this nation survives this war it may again in some future time face renewed hostilities. Pinned to the Atlantic coast, we could readily be pushed into the sea. But, with lands won to our west, these settled, we may become the great nation promised. Go win that future war for us, General."

General Sullivan knew by this that it was not the capture of Niagara but the claim to territory which was the prevailing thought in Washington's verbal directive. The storming of Niagara was left to his discretion. A weight was lifted from General Sullivan's shoulders. Doing the near impossible, the taking of Fort Niagara, was a decision for the commander in the field to make.

The Continental Army was to enter the Indian Country in three divisions. The first and principal division consisting of 3,000 men plus 1,000 allied service troops, boatmen, wagoners, drovers, cooks, scouts, road builders, would follow the Susquehanna northward. The second division, some 1,500 infantry, would proceed through the country of the Mohawk. It would come downstream from Otego Lake on rafts to the waters of the Susquehanna where, at the mouth of Teaoga, branch of the river, the two forces would be joined. The third unit of 650 men would leave from Fort Pitt, to act as a diversionary force, going up the Allegheny River under Colonel Brodhead, uniting if they could with the main force, by overland march and use of navigable waters. To do this was the question. Chief Guide Brady had reservations about the distance they must overcome in leaving the Allegheny to cross miles of forest in search of the Teaoga. That distance well could be vastly underestimated.

Daily grew the urgency for mounting this campaign to destroy the Indian towns. Dispatch riders came over the mountains; scouts from far settlements conferred with General Washington, bringing reports on the latest destructions and dispositions of the enemy. Road parties moved toward the Pocono Mountains, improving the roads for passage of the artillery. In the Middlebrook encampment all was hustle and bustle. Gun crews, boatsmen, pioneers, riflemen, guides, surveyors, bakers had been melded into a coherent force. Bayonets and knives sharpened, rifles rebored, powder allotted, buttons sewed, shoes mended, at last they were ready. Marching was a drumbeat away. Levi could see the wisdom in the timing, there was no call elsewhere for troops, the fighting in the east at a standstill. British inaction probably stemmed from their troops being shifted in expectation of an assault upon their lakeside forts, and possibly the taking of Montreal, a likely and long held rebel objective.

General Washington had one final meeting with his senior officers. At the General's request this conference was to be attended by his chief guide, Lieutenant Brady. Levi would write, years afterward, his best remembrance of Washington's comments, he admitting he was inexact in capturing the phraseology.

"Gentlemen, you go from here upon perhaps the greatest march in history, to be compared with the invasion of Persia by the Greeks. The rights of man to be governed by principles of justice rest in the Declaration which you, by this march, affirm. At stake is the expansion of this Nation beyond its present narrow borders, a vulnerability that would affect the permanence of our liberty. We cannot be pinned to the narrow coast, in any future settlement More, we clearly see the tide in this war is at a turning point to our favor, of itself forecasting a triumph for the American cause. With Burgoyne's army surrendered, with France become our active ally, with other European nations, foremost Spain, friendly to us, peace is predictable. Peace is openly proposed in the British Parliament." Here, Levi noted, Washington pointed to a table map, and with optimism stated, "There is much in favor of this expedition. The British are divided in their sentiment to continue fighting, their generals confused as to where we may next strike. Yes, they believe we imperil their upper forts, but which? We threaten Niagara, Oswego, Montreal, and Detroit. By this the enemy's troops on the St. Lawrence are prevented from moving southward, standing instead in readiness as reinforcements. Likewise the British may be weakening their garrisons on the Hudson against which, by capitalizing on your diversion, we shall renew our attacks. Your expedition will move the peace talk toward reality. General Sullivan, while I have directed you to destroy the Indian towns from which they make war, should they show a disposition for peace I would have you encourage it on condition they give you evidence of their sincerity by delivering up some of the principal instigators of their past such as Butler, Brant. This negotiation may have to be addressed by secrecy. Take caution, guard against the snares which their treachery may hold. They must be explicit in their promises and give substantial pledges for their performance. Hostages are the only kind of security to be depended upon." If Levi's remembrance about that meeting was accurate, so had spoken Washington, the old Indian fighter. Levi also knew the General wanted to live in peace with the Indian Nations.

As the regiments prepared to leave Middlebrook a slight delay occurred when there was a last minute shooing of public mounts, the horseshoes just arrived. The personal arms and accouterments which each scout and rifleman carried included a knife, shot pouch, powder horn, cartouch box, sufficient quantity of flints for his rifle, haversack, canteen, and axe, scythe, or fascine hatchet 'ground fit for use.' Weapons in perfect order, confidence was running high. One less than admirable soldier, by his language that of a braggart, boasted he would 'make wolves' meat' of the enemy. It stemmed from the nature of the frontier war.

In Sullivan's General Orders to the Army, a declaration which reflected both caution and optimism, he said: "The army will soon be called upon to march against an enemy whose barbarity to our fellow citizens, has rendered them proper subjects to our resentment. The General is of firm opinion they cannot withstand the bravery and discipline of the troops he has the honor to command. Nevertheless it ought to be remembered that they are a secret, desultory, and rapid foe, seizing every advantage and availing themselves of every defeat on our part. Should we be so inattentive to our own safety as to give way before them, they become the most dangerous and most destructive enemy that can possibly be conceived. They follow the unhappy fugitives with all the cruel and unrelenting hate of prevailing cowards, and are not satisfied with slaughter until they have totally destroyed their opponents. It therefore becomes every officer and soldier to resolve never to fly before such an enemy, but to determine either to conquer or perish, which will ever insure success. Should we thus determine and thus act, nothing but an uncommon frown of Providence can prevent us from obtaining that which will insure peace and security to our frontiers, and afford lasting honor to all concerned."

Of necessity a traveling forge was to go with the army. Wagons loaded, arms inspected, the riflemen stood at ease, waiting. The artillerymen were in pell-mell activity. Bombardiers, gunners and matrossers swarmed about their howitzers. These ugly pieces would scatter canister among the enemy and perhaps batter Fort Niagara. Under a warm sun Colonel Thomas Proctor's Pennsylvania "Regiment of Artillerymen" loaded solid shot into wagons and tied canvas over the muzzles of their guns. Thirty pieces ranging from a tiny hand trundled cohern to ponderous six pounders and terrifying eight inch howitzers were to be carried into the wilderness. Drag ropes were issued, horses brought forward. The cannoneers wheeled their weapons into the column of march. The quartermasters of each regiment and battery had drawn four days hard-head and salted meat. Tents struck, baggage loaded, everything and everyone was in place.

A mood of seriousness settled over those waiting the signal to march. This march would lead them through smoky swamps and along paths between unnamed hills. Some prayed; others inquired as to who was their Chief Guide. The name of Lieutenant Levi Brady went around. Those who knew him, and a number did, spoke well. Even so, men who knew the formidable foe realized brave lads would lay down their bones before this march was done.

Orderly drummers began signaling up and down the line. The cry went forth, 'Slope arms!'

There was an unreality about this grand scene, it seeming to be a contrivance of imagination, so picturesque and unique this assembly. They were no longer barefoot and hungry; they were uniformed, professional in manner and appearance. To carry that image forward, Levi envisioned the positive effect upon Congress were but a portion of these troops, bound for East Town, at a cost of two days additional march to be first paraded through the capital City. This scene in Levi's thoughts was father to that happening. The representative regiments would be ferried from the Jersey side of the Delaware to the foot of Arch Street where they would reassemble.

At first there was a faint ripple of sound, these murmurings on the warm May air resembling that of a multitude of bees-humming over a new-mown field. In the street and in the State House all routine duties went unattended, men of commerce and men of Congress at curb or window, looking and listening. 'T was true! The troops had broken their winter encampment and were marching toward Philadelphia. Carriages were being routed away from Arch Street along which the Army would march. The sidewalks overflowed with spectators, fair ladies, peddlers, teamsters, disengaged officers, and persons of every craft or station. Curious onlookers stared at the French officer and his cavalrymen waiting at an intersecting street, there to join the line of march. Colonel Charles Armand-Tuffin, the Marquis de la Rouerie, head of Armand's Legion, a ruffian body composed mainly of Hessian deserters, gazed at the approaching flags.

As the vanguard of the marchers moved upon the City an undertone took form, becoming the pitapat of many drums struck on their rims. Now the drums broke into voice. The sound grew, rumbled, reverberated down the streets; it seethed into buildings, soaked the very air with its mounting crescendo, dragged men to look in fascination, smashed into membranes of ears, put flush on cheeks, and set blood at frenzy. To the whir and roll of the grumbling, snarling drums, to the shrill piping of fifes the lead platoon of the New Eleventh Regiment broke into view. Girls and women darted into the street, blew kisses at the oncoming troops. Behind the flag, line after line, the companies marched into sight, passing between the crowds. In passage was the famed 'Long-Legged Line.' Unique among the troops was Morgan's Rifles, a regiment which had survived countless gambles. The sure-shot marksmen marched with nonchalance, their specialty fighting, not parades. They had been four weary years putting the great business of the nation upon a more respectable and happy establishment. Of note, for the first time to be observed were the iron gray bayonets affixed to the muskets of the infantry soldiers. While snow lay upon the hills, Steuben their drillmaster had given them a newly acquired skill, the mastery of the bayonet, with its silent, deadly thrust in battle.

Suddenly Colonel Armand stared in disbelief. He had caught sight of, and recognized the Frenchman, once Wallis's coachman, now corporal in the Free Company. The Colonel, shocked, amazed, excited, momentarily deserted his post, edging his horse forward, forging abreast of the Free Company. "René!" he shouted. "Do you not know me? It is I, Armand, your friend. I thought you dead. Your father, Monsieur le Baron, has made a stone in your memory. I will see you later. We will talk some more." With that he wheeled his horse about. Like a bursting dam, memories flooded French's mind. He knew his name, his rank in the French army, and recalled everything leading up to the blow to the head received while a passenger on a small French vessel when it was overtaken off the Barbary Coast, and sunk by an armed Portuguese schooner. Dazed, without memory, he had been taken into bondage.

Murphy, who had overheard the conversation, asked, "What do we do now? Salute you, kiss you on both cheeks, your Highness?"

"Do nothing," stated Sam French. "I am a corporal, you are the sergeant. We go to fight for Freedom."

"A hurrah for Sam French," called someone, and a hurrah they gave him, several dozen voices in unison. It was going to be a damned good campaign.

A captain of cavalry pranced his horse toward the van of the line of marchers. Seeking Levi was Captain Lighthorse Carberry. "My God!" exclaimed Levi, reigning in his horse, "I thought you dead and buried in the wilderness." Carberry's features broke into a broad infectious grin. At that moment Levi briefly turned his head, acknowledging the shout of Mr. Africa from the crowd on the sidewalk, he thereafter to ask, "Who, then, is in that western grave?" As he posed his question, something was happening to his vision, the sunlight playing tricks on his eyes. What best might be described as a halo of light surrounded Carberry, and seemingly the Captain's image was more in outline, his figure evanescent, the sun striking through both rider and horse until the likeness of the mounted officer had entirely disappeared with nothing of substance remaining.

Levi Brady, caught up in the forward motion of all about him, being pushed onward by the tide of humanity, gazed back, thinking to see him again, bewildered, the while moving off in the stream of rifles. Had he seen Carberry, or was this caused by the heat and excitement, an illusion? As to this last, some might think otherwise, the unquenchable spirit of Carberry ever with his friend Levi, and even with us to this day, and on occasion in later time to have been so observed. It can be said, on authority of this chronicler, Captain Lighthorse Carberry and Lieutenant Levi Brady both were and are, and ever will be in that stream of rifles, in perpetuity to be remembered. It is in our salute to the Flag. On a Philadelphia parade day, when there is a gap in the line of march, and the sun is just right, one feels almost sees the presence of the two riders and the Free Company, Sergeants Baldwin, Pence, Grove, Murphy and yes, now proud Sergeant French, and every man of that company, rifle to shoulder, marching in this Nation's Independence Day Celebration. So let us believe.

It is said, should you see a flag bearer in Continental blue, behind him invisible are these imperishable men. There are some who swear that those today in the Philadelphia Light Horse, which Carberry once commanded, too, have had similar presentiments.

THE END

ADDENDUM

It was not from the yellow fever which swept Philadelphia in 1798 that Samuel Wallis fell victim, but from small pox, the practice of inoculation opposed by the Quakers. When his hand was most needed, his fortune in disarray from the land panic that ruined many investors in frontier lands, Samuel Wallis died, none to mourn him. His corpse along with numerous yellow fever victims was carted to potter's field, there the piles of bodies interred in pits and trenches. This location today is the pleasant park Washington Square in central Philadelphia. Here, during the American Revolution, were buried soldiers and sailors who died of wounds or starvation in British prison ships anchored offshore, or of 'camp fever' at Valley Forge. Wallis's life as a spy remained sequestered from view because Major John Clark, Washington's Chief of Intelligence, refrained from uncovering him. Wallis, a double agent, had possible future value. That he did not dance on air suggests Clark knew he was friendly to Captain Andre, British Intelligence officer, and could, as in the past, be helpful. This he was, but not to Clark, he encouraging Arnold in his defection. In the trunks containing Wallis's papers, included are notes from Peggy Shippen Arnold. Appearances indicate Wallis was a man in whom Arnold could confide.

Esther Montour, after the 1778 destruction of her village, fled to her sister Catherine's community, today Montour Falls. It appears she participated in the 1779 gathering of chiefs at Fort Niagara. Their towns and crops having been burned by General Sullivan's army, the Indians were searching for a way to survive the coming winter. The Swiss born Governor General of Canada, Sir Fredrick Haldimand, who cared for the thousands of Loyalists seeking refuge in Canada during the war, equally welcomed his Indian allies. Because her village was among the first to be destroyed, and her people to be resettled under the British flag, at that gathering Esther urged others to follow her example, to accept Haldimand's generosity, Canadian relocation. It offered the speediest recourse. Many would stay with their land, the year to follow seeing violence anew on the frontier. Sadly she is forgotten for the person she was. Instead she has been maligned and depicted as a fiend involved in the slaughter at Forty Fort. Succeeding writers have assigned her a role out of character with the admiration and respect given this French-Indian woman during her life. In the journals of those who marched under Hartley, never is there any statement the expedition's purpose was designed for revenge upon an individual. That sentiment would have been reflected in the reports and journals of those who participated, were it so. No such personal animosity existed toward her. She is not named as a witch or monster, nor suggested in context with bloody rock at Forty Fort. She was incapable of the barbaric deed of wielding an axe on hapless captives as suggested by an irresponsible poet. Of late scholars recognize that her soft and womanly nature stands in evidence, refuting that untruthful portraiture. She was not at Forty Fort, nor was Brant. May she rest in peace.

Esther is a tragic figure. She lost everything, family, home and reputation. A roadside marker denotes her village site. Her remains, likely in Canada, would be identified by a necklace of pure white beads with a cross of stone or silver polished to brilliance by long use. These contrasted with her soft and fine black hair. Beneath the soil along the Susquehanna River flats, where her town was located are the charrings which identify the settlement. Her home, unique because it had a porch, may one day be found by archeologists. It will be known by objects excavated at the site of this cultured leader's residence.

Differing from history's view of Esther, her sister the equally stately Catherine, who also fled her Seneca Lake home as Sullivan approached, would return and rebuild her life after the troops had passed. She enjoyed a long life and the respect of her white neighbors. Catherine rests in a small cemetery within the woods nearby the site of her community and close by the southern shore of Seneca Lake. Her burial plot is claimed by shadows. A monument celebrates her life.

Margy or Margaret, while an invented character, is a name which existed in the Montour family. Also, Wallis's brother Joseph had a daughter who was so called. There is no connection of the character Margy to either of the others. She is a generic representation of beautiful spies throughout time.

Levi Brady is a composite figure of three militia lieutenants, all of whom survived the war and are honored for their part in the American Revolution. They were Sam Brady, John Jenkins and Moses Van Campen. Their adventures are remembered in actions of the fictitious Levi. An historic marker at Muncy recalls the Revolutionary War Captain John Brady who, with his valorous sons, participated in that struggle. He was killed April 1779 near Fort Muncy.

Colonel Marion Bolton, after long and honorable service at Fort Niagara, in ill health took leave of his command to seek medical treatment in Quebec. Enroute, aboard ship, overtaken by a lake storm all perished, inclusive of a company of young soldiers. His importance may be measured by the importance of Fort Niagara, paramount fortification.

Captain, later Colonel John Franklin, at war's end sought to form the 14th state of New Connecticut. He failed in this, and in his final years was reduced to poverty, being supported by local charity. He is buried on a knoll south of Athens, this community to have been the New Connecticut State Capital. The grave's enclosure until restored was used as a pigsty. In coincidental effort, in 1778 Delaware Chief White Eyes signed a treaty designed to admit that nation into the Continental union, with the Delaware western lands intended as the 14th state. He met an untimely death by 'friendly fire' while on the McIntosh Expedition.

Colonel Thomas Hartley, as a member of the Pennsylvania Legislature, led an effort to establish the Nation's Capital and a palace for George Washington on the beautiful lands within the great curve of the Susquehanna southerly of Wysox. At that time it was central to the Nation. The location is near the mountain known as Indian Hill where in 1778, his force outnumbered, he successfully withstood possibly 400-500 Seneca. His dream, alike Colonel Franklin's, remained unrealized. An unexpected consequence was that the French nobility, in fleeing their country's upheaval, while searching for a capital in exile, were led to this picturesque location. French officers accompanying Sullivan had been impressed by the beauty of this Pennsylvania-Connecticut claimed valley. Prominent French nobility, political figures, planters and military officers resided at Azilum (1793-1803). In part, the amnesties offered by Napoleon and the loss of their hopes for a New France in Louisiana, they disheartened by Jefferson's purchase of that territory, led to abandonment of the settlement. In process of constructing this settlement a French dug road was connected to the Wallis Packhorse Trail, as later this supply route would be called.

Mrs. Hartley herself deserves a footnote, several persons including President Washington remarking, after dining at Hartley's home in Pennsylvania, about her extraordinary beauty and grace.

New Hampshire lawyer Major General John Sullivan was to die a pauper, his business neglected during the war, his health ruined. His subordinate officers, when gathering for the funeral, were confronted by an undertaker who refused to bury their General until paid. The demanding undertaker changed his mind with alacrity when persuaded by a loaded pistol in the hand of Colonel Joseph Cilley (1st New Hampshire Regiment) and the possibility of needing an immediate burial himself. Many leaders of the Revolution, inclusive of those who signed the Declaration, found poverty and ill health were their rewards, and not Jefferson's lofty pronouncement 'Life, Liberty, and the pursuit of Happiness.'

Antagonists Tim Murphy and Blacksnake, each, lived to a ripe old age, Murphy reaching 90, Blacksnake (Twynesh) dying in his hundredth year. Both men had undimmed memories of the Revolutionary War. Blacksnake would later fight on the side of the Americans in the War of 1812. He was the nephew of the great religious orator Handsome Lake, and would encourage, when he became chief of the Seneca, the education of his people and preservation of their culture. Great Shot and the Panther did not survive the war, killed in a forest fight with Brady and Peter Grove. In his diary Grove recorded the event. As evinced in Blacksnake, an Indian who could be ruthless in barbaric times, could rise above himself, with all honors given him, in after years. He devoted himself to perpetuating the culture of his people. Tim Murphy remained in unremitting hatred of the Indian. He is remembered primarily for the three in a row shots fired, depriving Burgoyne of his best general and turning the course of history in favor of establishing a new nation. His fame was known throughout the Continental Army.

338

Joseph Brant (Theandeaga) lived to be 65, dying in 1807. He gave his people a written language, translating the Bible, thus furthering Christianity among the Indians. Many books cite his history. He remains a controversial figure. One cannot envy his role, he caught between two cultures. In seeking to preserve the best of each this great Pine Tree chief succeeded beyond the credit given him. In 1796, upon occasion of Washington's Farewell to the Nation, among those to do the General honor were Brant and Cornplanter. Brant had just returned from an audience with King George. It is speculated he bore Washington a message of appreciation for American neutrality in matters between England and France. It is on record Brant had Negro slaves, a mark of affluence. Through times he remains a fascinating figure, in part because he defies the stereotype characterization undeservingly given Indians. As to impugning his reputation by claims of barbarity, Brant would write a note to the commander of an American fort in 1777, returning a child taken during an attack on that fort, "I do not make war on women and children." Referring to the Tory rangers in that action, he added, "I am sorry to say that I have those engaged with me in the service who are more savage than the savages themselves."

Hiakatoo died at the age of 103. His wife, the noted white captive Mary Jemison, described him as most gentle to his friends and extremely cruel otherwise. Emulating the practice of the Americans, he rented out portions of his land holdings to white settlers. It is to be presumed they were prompt in their obligation.

The incident which describes Carberry's capture while bearing a message intended for Cornplanter is based on a misadventure which befell Peter Sitz, a dispatch carrier, and death and scalping of Lieutenant Frederick Wormwood, his companion.

Cornplanter was half brother to Chief Handsome Lake who designed a Code of Conduct (1800) or New Religion effective in preserving the National character of an Indian society facing extinction as a culture. Cornplanter's father was a Dutch trader named John Abeel. While Cornplanter fought for the British, he was a conciliatory leader. In recognition Pennsylvania accorded him the Cornplanter Grant, refuge of the Seneca until 1961 when the U.S. Corps of Engineers drowned the land in constructing the Kinzua Dam. This author, while attending a gathering of notable Seneca held on the shores of the Susquehanna, had proposed for ceremonial adoption several important Pennsylvania officials. Not to exclude a colonel of the Engineers who at that time was in the vicinity, inappropriately his name was suggested. This was rebuffed by a lightning response of the chiefs, "Kinzua! Kinsua!" repeated from mouth to mouth with vehemence, their eyes hatchets.

Shickellamy, born of French and Cayuga parents, as it is claimed, was kidnapped by the Oneidas at the age of two. He rose to be Vice Regent or Ambassador representing the Confederacy in keeping peace among the Indians of various tribes settled along the Susquehanna. These included the Confederacy-defeated and relocated Eastern Delaware. Seeking lasting peace with the Proprietors he negotiated away lands occupied by the Delaware Minsi tribe, this to produce an opposite effect upon his death in 1748. It is important to remember the long peace that existed along the Susquehanna shores during his representation. The last half of the 18th Century saw the rise of war leaders.

Tisot is a character created to represent a throwback Seneca culture. He ever carries a *'red belt.'* He chooses the metaphors of speech of a generation earlier than Brant's, and reflects the extreme views held in 1763 by Pontiac and his followers. That remarkable Ottawa Chief viewed the French capitulation to the British, which ended the French and Indian War, as an opportunity to rally Indians of many nations against the English and drive them from the continent. He succeeded in enlisting tribes as far south as the Gulf. This gifted leader then led his multi-national force in a prearranged simultaneous assault on the principal British forts. The uprising failed when instant victory was not achieved and the attackers had to resort to siege warfare. His forces weakening in the face of winter, they needing to provide for their families by hunting, he made peace with his foe. The treaty angered those like Tisot who were reluctant to give up the dream of a great confederation, all whites driven from Indian lands. Pontiac was murdered in 1769. The Indian who killed him believed a rumor Pontiac was receiving British pay to prevent further eruptions. The death of the great Shickellamy ten years earlier had opened the way for war leaders like Pontiac. The untimely death in 1774 of Sir William Johnson, Crown superintendent who wished all Indians to remain aloof from the coming white man's war, opened the way for ascendancy of Hiakatoo. The Confederacy, fashioned for the preservation of peace, was powerless in matters of war. Nor was a war leader, in his tenure, ever firmly seated, divisive forces at work, particularly among the Seneca.

General Daniel Morgan was, by his troops, called 'the Old Waggoner', he having driven a team during the Braddock Expedition. He received unjustly 99 lashes for which a British officer later apologized. Morgan would repay in bullets the king's men. In 1775 Morgan was among the first to raise a company of Virginia and Pennsylvania riflemen, these marching to Boston where they participated in the battle known as Bunker Hill. Captain Morgan's riflemen were to be augmented by other rifle companies from Pennsylvania, Rhode Island and Connecticut, these under his command participating in Colonel Benedict Arnold's Canadian expedition. Some of Morgan's officers later achieved high rank. An enlisted man, Sergeant Thomas Boyd (later captain) was considered 'the strongest and stoutest man of the party', yet he nearly died from starvation and exhaustion of spirit as he struggled to cross a moss bog during their terrible march north. In the summer of 1777 Morgan's 7th Virginia Rifle Regiment was reconstituted as a corps, and ordered to join the northern army. Five hundred riflemen from the Continental Army, led by Colonel Morgan, turned the tide during the two bitter contests in September 1777 just above Albany, New York, known as the Battle of Saratoga. Here General 'Gentleman Johnny' Burgoyne capitulated to the American Northern Army. Untrained in frontier fighting, Burgoyne failed in his attempt to cut the rebelling colonies into disconnected and ineffective sections. Sergeant Tim Murphy's sharpshooting deprived Burgoyne of his two senior officers and wounded a third in the first engagement at Stillwater. General Simon Fraser was Burgoyne's best general, a key factor in the respective fortunes of the contending armies. At Valley Forge in the winter of 1777-78 Morgan's corps was broken up. Four of the companies would serve under its brilliant former second in command, Lieutenant Colonel William Butler, in the destruction of Indian and Tory settlements along the northern reaches of the Susquehanna. This raid was timed to coincide with Hartley's raid more southerly. Both operations removed obstacles otherwise to impede the Sullivan-Clinton Expedition during its 1779 invasion of the Indian Country.

The Continental Army was at the verge of dissolution during the wintry encampment at Valley Forge. As late as March 31, 1778 Washington had written Connecticut Governor Jonathan Trumball pleading for more troops which were "wanted to enable us to act merely on the defense" so desperate was the situation. Washington could not, although fully aware of the frontier problem with the Indians, do more than encourage self defense; to facilitate the raising of frontier militia, he furloughed officers from the Army for that purpose; and then, seemingly counter productively, Washington would press the States for new levies, more troops to replenish the dwindled Continental Line. This was to the detriment of the frontier fort commanders hard-placed by increasing hostilities. By receiving the additional state regiments and by instituting the requirement those newly enlisted were to be inoculated against smallpox and serve for longer terms of enlistment, gradually the depletion rate was reduced, with a healthier, stronger army to resume the field from there on. Valley Forge was the watershed where the fortunes of war began to change. Entry of French forces assured liberty for the indomitable Americans. The expression 'Lafayette we are here' uttered in WWI when American doughboys (infantrymen) landed in France, expresses that debt.

In 1787 the Tory-come-patriot Tench Coxe and Thomas Mifflin entered into a partnership foreseeing manufacturing to be "the means of our Political Salvation." They reserved 700 acres along the Passaic River where the drop was 70 feet, with intent to foster manufacture of products such as straw hats and iron wire.

Sergeant Thomas Baldwin, who took part in the Hartley hilltop battle, returned four years later leading a small party to nearby Lime Hill in an attempt to rescue Mrs. Roswell Franklin and her three children abducted by the Seneca. In Baldwin's four hour battle with the abductors, some being whites painted as Indians, the mother was accidentally killed, but the children were saved. One of the raiding party escaped. This was the last encounter with the Indians and the last act of the Revolutionary War.

341

Robert Morris, whose genius enabled the young nation to find credit, in management of his own affairs became a bankrupt. He spent lavishly constructing a pretentious home in Philadelphia, monumental in size and furnished beyond compare. It would undo him. In November 1798 Washington returned to Philadelphia and visited Morris in his jail apartment where, with his family, he had languished since February and would until August 1801. Morris owed too much to too many to be released sooner. Washington left the City on December 14th, 1798 after having discussed the progress of the new Federal City being readied on the banks of the Potomac. Exactly one year to the day following his departure from Philadelphia America's 'first in war' and 'first in peace' president would be dead. Morris died a pauper.

Captain Carberry, after raising a cavalry troop of light horse out of the Eleventh Pennsylvania Regiment in 1778, was mortally wounded on the snowy frontier in January 1779. Liberty has been taken by the author to add several months to his life span. His association with the Philadelphia 'Silk Stocking' troop is fictional. In every respect he was a courageous leader..

In a final twist, his double life never to surface, after the War Wallis employed a man who had been Washington's foremost spy, Gershom Hicks. Each was unaware of the other's oppositional role as a spy. In friendly relationship they lived out their lives in that ignorance. Hicks was the scout Washington secretly sent in 1778-79 into the Seneca Country to independently map the route. Washington believed in redundancy, and in using double agents.

Lieutenant General, Sir William Howe's dalliance with Mrs. Elizabeth Loring was not the reason for his losing the war, this affair more of a diversion. He didn't wish to win that fratricidal conflict by bloody encounters as occurred in the taking of Bunker Hill. By conciliation he chose to woo the majority of Americans away from the radicals. His speeches in Parliament show him, as was his brother Admiral Richard 'Black Dick' Howe, to be an ardent Whig. In 1774 Benjamin Franklin visited England seeking a way to head off war. While attending a meeting of the Royal Society he was invited to play chess, at which he was a master, with a certain lady, the sister of the Howe brothers. The Admiral was to use the several chess meetings as an innocuous way to approach Franklin, the purpose shared by Franklin and himself, being to effect a reconciliation. At Admiral Howe's request Franklin prepared a proposal for delivery to Parliament. Instead of receiving Franklin with courtesy, he was to hear with disgust "base Reflections on American Courage, Religion, Understanding, & in which we were treated as the lowest of Mankind." By such tirades he was to be abused before the House of Lords and in the House of Commons. It convinced Franklin, while the Americans did have friends in high places like the Howes who were cousins to King George III, reconciliation could not happen, severance of ties now inevitable. General Sir William Howe, a courageous and brilliant general in battle, before and following the Revolution, was an invincible leader. It was not in his heart to crush the feeble army arrayed against him. For this reason some called him - after Washington - America's greatest Revolutionary War general. As cousin to the King, he was immune from whatever anger lay in the breast of Lord North toward the Howe brothers, General and Admiral. Franklin, most certainly, had endeared himself to the Howes.

Lord Dunmore's War. John Murray, 4th Earl of Dunmore, colonial Governor of Virginia, in 1774 sought to repress the Shawnees located at the fork of the Ohio, considered part of Virginia's domain. Bitter fighting had broken out following the murder of noted Chief Logan's family. Dunmore was accused of sending his militia troops to fight on the western frontier for reason of their questionable loyalty to him and to prevent their participation in the approaching war with England. In further steps to offset the dissident militia, in 1775 he raised a hodgepodge army consisting of Tories, Indians and 900 slaves, the latter promised their freedom. With these he was unsuccessful in waging war against the Virginia militia, though he did send a ship up the Potomac, threatening to burn the plantations of those owners behind the revolution, including Washington's Mount Vernon. Additional companies of American militia hastily were raised to protect the properties. Retreating to an offshore British warship, he fled the colony and arranged for passage of himself to the Bahamas, taking with him the remnants of his beaten force, his soldier-slaves. There, his liberation promise forgotten, by cash tempted, before embarking for England in 1776 he sold the surviving 300 blacks for his own enhancement.

Major General Richard Montgomery, who had been a British officer during the French and Indian War, was killed in 1775 leading American forces storming the walls of Quebec. He had foreseen the value of the bayonet, proposing that American muskets, wherever manufactured, should have their barrels extended two inches to give the Americans an advantage in reach during bayonet thrusts.

Thomas Boyd, leading a forlorn hope during the Sullivan Expedition, would be captured and experience a most excruciating death. On September 25, 1779 Sullivan's Army, as it prepared to leave off its march through the Indian Country, paused to celebrate by a running fire of muskets, and with discharge of cannon their successful campaign, saluting the news received of Spain's declaration of war against Great Britain. Of the thirteen toasts made, number 10 spoke to the loss of Captain Boyd two weeks earlier. This memorial toast saluted the brave 'Boyd and the soldiers under his command who were horridly massacred by the inhuman savages and by their more barbarous and detestable Allies, the British and Tories the 13th Instant, - he ever dear to his country.' As was the function of an advance element, that of detecting the presence of the enemy, it was near Canandaigua his scouts stumbled upon the flank of a well-concealed foe, only Hanyerry the Oneida managing to evade capture. Boyd was subject to every aspect of agony typical of Hiakatoo's doing, from slow torture by fire, unwrapping his intestines, limbs being cut off and finally his head severed. These mangled remnants of a brave man, nauseating to behold, were buried by the advancing troops who, had it not been for detection of the foe, might well have incurred many casualties. In 1791 Hiakatoo was involved in a similar cruel slow death by fire of another fine officer.

General Lachlan McIntosh, born in Scotland, at beginning of the Revolution as a colonel commanded the First Georgia Regiment. Elevated to General he was selected by General Washington to lead an expedition against the Western Indians. In 1779 he took part in the siege of Savannah, later was taken prisoner at the capture of Charleston in 1780. Never did the vengeance of those ready to challenge him to a duel, death by sword poisoning, catch up with him. He died in 1806 at the age of 81.

Colonel John Gibson was a Pennsylvanian by birth and upbringing, being born in Lancaster (1740). At the age of 18 he participated in General Forbes's expedition to capture Fort Duquesne (Pittsburgh). Later he became an Indian trader. With others he was captured by Indians, and was to have been burnt at the stake, but managed to escape, perhaps because of friendships formed. He spent the remainder of his life interacting with the several tribes, and was fluent in their language and knowledgeable in their customs. He died at the age of 82, having witnessed the War of 1812 which Washington foresaw.

The defeated Delaware, a nation scattered and resettled by their enemy the Iroquois, in this story is represented by their great leader Bald Eagle. He has earned his place in history. This nation, which came to be known by many names, is viewed today as a composite of nations. In seeking to convey the undefeated characteristic of these people, we have introduced Bald Eagle's name and his presence into scenes appropriate to his behavior. The great Indian chief, while hunting near Fort Pitt, was ambushed and slain by Virginians in 1774. His corpse, propped upright in his canoe, was set adrift downstream toward his village. He is forever memorialized in the endless mountains of Pennsylvania.

The Montour family

Fascinating in its history, foremost in shaping the future of America as to the opening of the west, replete with Indian chieftains the Montour name rises to view in the history of early Canada.

In 1667 the Frenchman Pierre Couc (Peter Cook) arrived in Canada. He would lengthen his name, he to be known as Pierre Couc La Fleur. He would marry an Algonquin woman Marie Mite8ameg8k8e. One of her children, Louis, would discard the name LaFleur, choosing Montour as his surname. Serving as a lieutenant, in 1694 he was wounded in the stomach in a fight with the Mohawks near Lake Champlain. Nursed back to health in an Indian home, he became friendly with the natives, and took up trapping, to find himself shut out from selling his furs to the French government. Joncaire, likewise a lieutenant in the French Army, and the Marquis de Vaudreuil, Governor of Canada, had a cozy business arrangement by which the former had a monopoly on selling furs to the government, with a percentage of the price going to Vaudreuil. Prevented from selling furs secured from nearby Indians, Montour persuaded 'the far Indians', Miami's and Wyandots, to travel with him to Albany where he marketed their product. For trading with the enemy he was shot dead by orders of the Governor. Joncaire would carry out the execution. Montour's family, vowing revenge, would leave Canada, to side with the British.

As was the Indian custom, the name Montour continued through the female side. Montour's sister, born about 1684, became known as Madam Montour, perhaps in an invented yarn to raise her stature. She was widely believed to be a daughter of Frontenac, Conte de Palluau, governor of New France. More likely, by her mannerisms and upbringing, she was brought into his household in her early youth and raised in his residence. She had reached maturity at the time of his death, being 15 years old in 1698. She was fluent in French, versatile in the native tongues, statuesque, eye compelling. She would become a translator representing the British at important events. Her son Andrew, following her footsteps, did much to nullify the French in their efforts to woe the Five Nations, thus were prevented from dominating North America. Madam Montour's daughter French Margaret would marry Peter Quebec (Katariontecha).

French Margaret's two daughters were Catherine and Esther, each a queen of a Seneca village during the American Revolution. Both these daughters come down through time as women of great charm and attractiveness.

The Ambush at Chemung

There is justification for the belief that Wallis's map, which has not survived, was examined by the British and served as the basis for engaging the Continental Army at Chemung. It finds support in the configuration of that location and the strategy of the British-Indian force. The River, which has changed its course, was near a ridge of land overlooking its flats. Easterly of the line of ambush, was marshy land. The location was well chosen, suiting the purpose of the force of 800 lying concealed on the ridge. The ridge offered a commanding view of the approach along the meadowland as the Army passed between the river and their location. Though much inferior in numbers the Seneca and rangers were protected on one flank by the marsh which would impede the Continentals should they seek to get around and attack their wing or obtain their rear. Too, a small force of Indians was held in reserve at a higher elevation, ready to swoop down as needed. All this was in conformity with the map drawn by Wallis, and his intention of an entrapment. Chemung exactly responded to his concept. The Army led by its chief scout was alert to the possibility of entrapment. The Army's plan of battle was solid. In a flanking move coupled with the noise of the cannon, which terrified the hidden Indians who abandoned their position, the Army scattered the warriors. Sullivan's forces were able to overcome the marshland and with fixed bayonets in a steadily advancing front take the battleground away from the enemy. To the credit of the Seneca, they had lain for two days under a blistering August sun determined to defend their homeland. The Battle of Chemung (Newtown Battlefield) weakened their ability to make war and ended any downstream British-Indian move toward taking Fort Augusta and threatening Philadelphia. Philadelphia, in effect, was twice saved. It was preserved by arrival of a French fleet, with the occupying British troops evacuated by sea just ahead of being bottlenecked, and was again preserved from future harm by the defeat of Indian forces, these to be smashed at far off Chemung.

THE YELLOW FEVER PLAGUE

It is difficult to grasp, from the perspective of today, the effect that the outbreak of yellow fever had upon the population during the last quarter of the 18th Century. Its major appearance in August 1793, and reoccurrence documented from that date through to the end of the Century, had catastrophic consequence. The scythe of death was hardest at work in the seacoast and river port cities, particularly Philadelphia. In 1791 the name 'yellow fever' was coined in description of the morbid skin color of its victims. Initially the source of the fatal affliction, at least so believed learned Philadelphians, was the air they breathed, it tainted by an odor of putrefying coffee. A ship out of Santo Domingo had dumped its spoiled cargo onto a Delaware River city wharf. Within three weeks 600 persons perished from the plague. The prevailing treatment generally consisted of massive purging of the blood, a treatment itself life threatening, causing the claim more blood was lost to this practice than on the battlefields of the Revolution. The malady widespread, treatment ineffective, exodus became the best response. The City was emptied of half its population. By time the fever had run its course one of every ten residents was dead.

From that year forward the fever reoccurred each summer. In great virulence it came back to Philadelphia. In 1798 and 1799 the City, for fear of it, was all but deserted. Those too poor to flee were left but one choice if not to stay within their homes, to live in tents along the Schuylkill River. In the late 90s, instead of blaming the air, the water was suspect. Were good water to be piped into the City to replace waters from wells contaminated by the runoff from streets, cesspools and outhouses, the plague might be alleviated. The piping system was not built. It remained a thought.

As people began to abandon the cities, typical was the announcement of one David Durham who 'has removed his goods from his store No. 26 Moore Street, New York to Springfield, New Jersey where he expects to remain during the warm season, or until the health of the city be restored.' New Jersey passed laws against persons 'subject to the Health Laws and Port Regulations of either ... New York or Pennsylvania, (who) are hereby strictly prohibited from landing on any part of the State of New Jersey ... especially those ... (who by their states are) enjoined to perform quarantine.' Ships with sickness were prohibited from discharging passengers.

In mid-September 1798 the plague was in Philadelphia, Wilmington, New York, New London, Newport, Providence, Portland, Portsmouth, Newburyport and Boston. Reported one gazette, 'The daily deaths at Philadelphia for a week, has been from 80 to 100, at New York 40 and upward.' A newspaper column with a heavy black border reported the deaths of two important editors, one in Philadelphia, the other in New York. They were eulogized as zealous supporters of the Rights of Humanity,' men with virtue and honor. 'Who mourns them? NOT the Tories.' Even in death the position for which they stood, as to the kind of government best suited our nation, was emphasized. There was an unreality about the City. Philadelphia's streets were described as so empty as to make the creaking of the dead carts the only sound heard. Much as Martha Washington had liked to visit Philadelphia, this was not one of those times. The numbers of the dead would grow as the heats progressed. Superimposed upon this calamity was the continuing flow of corpses of those not vaccinated against the smallpox. Among these were the Quakers whose beliefs forbade vaccination. In one passing cart was the body of the Quaker Samuel Wallis. The Century would close with the death of George Washington on December 14th, his pneumonia treated by excessive bleedings, the same treatment as prescribed for those with the plague.

The effect of the plague or of battle casualties suffered, in ratio to the population was enormous. Best to be understood, today's population is a hundred-fold larger. By that number multiply those mortality figures to place those losses in perspective, to perceive the impact such events would have today. The cairn which demarks the 86 slain at Wyoming becomes a horrendous figure.

The Council of Conciliation - 1790

While March into the Endless Mountains purports to cover the beginnings of hostility between the Indians and American settlers on the western reaches of the United States during the American Revolution, it was not until 1790 that a Council of Conciliation with the Indians was to meet. It set the tone for preventing the eruption of further violence. In the East there was an uneasy peace, at the point of crumbling over the murder of two Seneca. Because of these killings President Washington was aware the Seneca were about to resume the warpath. With the United States still at war with the tribes to the west, Washington sought to head off the Seneca from joining these western Indians, the tribes of the Delaware, Shawnee and Wyandot. He sought to placate the anger of the Seneca, authorizing Colonel Timothy Pickering, a man of most able qualifications to meet with the aggrieved and offer reparations for the injury done their tribe. Pickering was imposing in stature and possessed those qualities the Indians respected in their own chiefs. An Indian Council was convened in November, this held at the 'Southern Door' to the Indian domain, today known as Athens, Pennsylvania. The location of this meeting has been described as 'Teaoga', later as Tioga Point. The name also described the river. Today it is named the Chemung. Just before it pours into the Susquehanna, near the neck of land above that juncture, is the place of ceremonial importance, where a guard of sachems kept watch. No marker exists.

Anticipating a small meeting with several Seneca chiefs, Colonel Pickering was surprised to find not only were the Seneca present but representatives from other nations, more than 500 Indians in all. Seneca runners had circulated to a number of tribes that there would be a big fire at Tioga Point. Aided by Colonel Simon Spalding, once a foe of the Indians, now viewed by them as a worthy and respected neighbor, and with others in this delegation including Thomas Morris, son of Revolutionary War financier Robert Morris, Colonel Pickering met with the Chiefs. These included Red Jacket, Farmer's Brother, Little Brother, Big Tree, Aupaumont and Fish Carrier. Some had traveled great distances bringing their families to witness this historic meeting with the Commissioner that Washington had sent. Represented were the Seneca, Onondaga, Cayuga, Oneida and Stockbridge Nations. At conclusion of this ten day Council, one marked by picturesque speeches and libations, and the giving of black belts of remorse to the kin of the slain, and many presents distributed, the Seneca decided to adopt Morris. He had been sent a month in advance to Canandaigua to make the arrangements for the meeting, the results exceeding his own expectations. During his stay he had become popular among the Indians, their decision being to adopt him at this time. Red Jacket presided during the adoption ceremony. Five hundred Indians were in attendance. This ritual included offering up homage to the moon, with the novitiate then placed at the center of a large circle of Indians. On one side a large fire had been built and a post planted, this last symbolic of the torture stake. Supposedly this colorful ceremony was to conclude with a war dance. It was all of that, during which the forest rang with their wild yells and boasts of valor. One dancer was an Oneida whose nation had sided with the Americans while his audience had lifted their hatchets with the British. His boasts about the number of scalps taken instantly changed the mood. The Seneca in turn boasted of the scalps they had taken from the Oneida, and called them cowards. Weapons began to glitter in the moonlight and it seemed as though a death struggle was imminent; but the aged Cayuga Chief Fish Carrier rushed forward and ordered them to cease. He struck the torture post a blow, and his words carried a sting, "You are all a parcel of boys; when you have attained my age and performed the warlike deeds that I have performed, you may boast of what you have done; but not till then." Saying this, he threw down the post, ordered them to disperse and to retire.

Thus concluded the conference leading to peace between the Indians and Americans. It also demarked a new relationship among the Native Nations, one of rancor toward each other, never the instruments of Confederacy again to unite them, the tribes each standing alone. The frontier war decisively ended their union, their confederation badly fractured by the raising of tomahawks in separated actions. Thereafter war chiefs such as Joseph Brant would be replaced with conciliators. All, including Brant, had the double challenge of adjusting to a changed society while attempting to preserve the best traditions of their culture. To a degree future generations were to know the greatness that was theirs, though in a changing world much tradition was lost. Shattered was a social order attuned to the natural beauty of the region in which it thrived.

Sidelight: The Western Indians were not subdued until 1784 when at the Battle of Fallen Timbers in Northwestern Ohio, on the Maumee River, General Mad Anthony Wayne's force of some 4,000 soldiers met and defeated a near equal number of Indians. As had been in Pontiac's uprising, the assembled force consisted of Indians from many tribes. They had expected but did not receive the British troops promised them. Disheartened, they abandoned the war. There was among these western Indians a striking counterpart to the Seneca woman Esther Montour. Her name was Mary Ward. Born of a white father and Cherokee mother, given the name 'Beautiful Woman' she was tall, and as her name described her, a handsome woman. She too realized the Indians would be defeated in their war with the Americans. She vainly sought peace. In 1781 she addressed the American commissioners, "You know that women are always looked upon as nothing; yet we are your mothers; you are our sons. Our cry is all for peace ... Let your women's sons be ours; our sons be yours. Let your women hear our words." In 1795, two years after the end of the American Revolution, General 'Mad Anthony' Wayne concluded the Treaty of Greenville which formally ended the western war. The Indian War for Independence here, too, ended. The Council Fire of the Indians had been extinguished.

In the dreams of some a new fire should be lit, honoring all gone before, and so is the purpose of the Susquehanna River Archeological Center of Native Indian Studies.

FRONTIER FORTS AND COMMANDERS

FORT NIAGARA

Located at the mouth of the Niagara River, originally constructed in 1725-26 and garrisoned by the French, Fort Niagara served as the most important military post on the Western frontier. At conclusion of the French and Indian Wars the fort became a British bastion from which, during the American Revolution, numerous war parties of British allied Indians and Tory militia conducted war against the American settlements. This Western Department fortification was commanded by Colonel Marion Bolton.

FORT DETROIT

Constructed in 1701, named Fort Pontchartrain by the French, this fort was seized by Major Robert Rogers of "Rogers Rangers" in 1760. Thereafter it would be known as Fort Detroit. Besieged by Indians under Pontiac in 1763, it was saved by a heroic British defense, and as well by the besieging Indians becoming dispirited by news of the treaty of peace between their French allies and the English. At time of the American Revolution this bastion, like Fort Niagara, served as a base for Indian attacks against American frontier communities. Senior ranking officers at the fort were 8th King's Regiment Captains Richard B. Lernoult and Arent S. DePeyster, the latter American born.

FORT PITT

At the confluence of the Monongahela and Allegheny Rivers an English fort in 1754 was beng built when it was seized by the French and named Fort Duquesne. In 1755 General Edward Braddock's expedition of 1200 men attempted to retake the fort only to meet with ambush in the woods.

Two years later the French blew up the fort one day ahead of the arrival of a second expedition consisting of 6,000 men under General John Forbes who then rebuilt the fort and named it in honor of British Prime Minister William Pitt (the Elder). In 1772 Fort Pitt was evacuated by the British, and later would be occupied by Virginia Militia and Continental troops under Colonel Edward Hand. He, upon his promotion to General, was recalled to assist in planning the expedition of 1779. He was succeeded by General Lachlan McIntosh who, like Hand, would fail in attempts to march upon Fort Detroit.

FORT AUGUSTA

In 1756 the Provincial Government of Pennsylvania issued instructions leading to erection of a fort at Shamokin at the forks of the Susquehanna River, the fort overviewing the east and west branches. 400 men were involved in its building.

This blunted French ambitions, the French in process of striking overland with a similar plan to control the river by constructing a fortification at that location. Twenty years later during the American Revolution Fort Augusta under Colonel Samuel Hunter helped stabilize the lesser frontier forts lying along the river, these otherwise to have been overwhelmed by Tory Rangers and Indian forces. This important river fort would prevent the Susquehanna, which curved southeasterly toward the Chesapeake from becoming a liquid highway which, were it to be controlled by the British, would cut apart the rebelling American States. Augusta in 1779 would serve the Americans as a staging point for mounting the Sullivan-Clinton invasion of the Indian Country, this expedition to threaten Fort Niagara. The taking of Fort Niagara was never seriously contemplated by Sullivan, the lateness of the season and the problems of supply working against him. The storming of the Ontario bastion, if to be accomplished, would require the forces sent upriver from East Town, and those under American General Clinton sent downriver to join together at Teaoga, with this juncture to be further complicated by receiving at Teaoga a third body of troops dispatched from more westerly Fort Pitt. The latter third force would be traveling easterly following the Allegheny, then along the Teaoga River to its mouth, as per course described in Wallis's secret map. Logistically it was unworkable. Sullivan's health, too, was not the best, he being transported by bateau as he came upstream. Fort Augusta would become the main arsenal of supply, supported by a magazine of gunpowder at Carlisle. Augusta, too, offered shelter to frightened settlers and potential shelter to an army in retreat, although for that same purpose Sullivan would build an immense fort straddling the carrying path between the Teaoga and Susquehanna Rivers, garrisoning it with 200 men prior to his moving westerly.

THE SPANISH HILL FORT

This fort was located north of the junction of the Teaoga and Susquehanna rivers. By the thousands of artifacts recovered on its slopes and top, this hill has been the scene of battles unrecorded in time. Speculatively the Spanish were the first Europeans to arrive here. They were exploring both coasts during the last half of the 16th Century, suggesting the name has some substance. The formidable fort, which encompassed eleven acres on the crown of the hill, attests to engineering skills which the Spaniards had. This major work marks the northernmost fortification of the powerful Susquehannocks. It is significant that here, at Spanish Hill, the ice age experienced melt back. This formation is a terminal moraine left by the gouging of glacial ice. Erosion flattened its top.

In 1915 Pennsylvania recognized that the explorer Samuel de Champlain (Father of New France) had sent his emissary Etienne Brule here in 1615 to recruit the Susquehannocks.The plan was for them to join the French and Hurons in battle against the English and Iroquois. Brule's hosts preferred feasting rather than fighting. Winter at hand, amorous Brule availed himself of their hospitality. In the spring, curious about the river, he took off downstream to become the first known European to explore its great length.

About the Author

The credentials of Ray Ward have well prepared him for writing this reconstructed history of the Revolutionary War during the year 1778. Colonel Ward, who lives in the region he describes, ably calls upon his knowledge and writing skills to sketch the effects of intrigue and warfare, and the terror produced as these apply to the settlements along the Susquehanna River. Ward graphically demonstrates this as he delineates the clash of cultures during those turbulent times. He demonstrates how one man almost changed history.

Ray is a member of the Cornell University "War Class of '43" where he trained in infantry tactics, later to serve in the USAAF, subject of his five-star rated book Those Brave Crews. He is a member of the prestigious Authors Guild. Ray was editor of the University's Literary Quarterly and was a founder of the Cornell Radio Guild, student radio network, writing radio documentaries broadcast coast-to-coast on NBC and CBS. After WW II Ray continued his studies, graduating from the United States Chamber of Commerce Institute for Organization Management conducted at the University of Delaware. He is a life member of the Association of Graduates United States Air Force Academy. Ward is listed as a pioneer helicopter pilot, prior to the end of hostilities having flown the first model Army helicopter, the R-4, displayed at the USAF Museum, Wright-Patterson AFB.

He first cut his teeth in journalism as a reporter of a country weekly that won first prize for its class among New York papers. He moved on to be acting bureau chief, employed by Gannett's oldest daily.

Ward served under three governors of the Commonwealth of Pennsylvania during the Centennial of the Civil War. He interacted with the executive director of the State Museum in developing programs of interpretation, which involved multi-state cooperation. He received New York's Bronze Medallion, conferred by Bruce Catton, noted author and historian, then chairman of New York's Civil War Centennial Commission. United States Interior Secretary Conrad L. Wirth issued Ward a letter of commendation for management of major public events at National Battlefields and Cemeteries. Ray's relationship with the American Indian has earned him formal adoption.